Praise for *Fall...*

'I envy Daisy Rockwell, who has lived w... least two decades . . . Beguiling . . . Daisy ... because it is so unobtrusive. The flavour ... ...omes through behind the form of the English words, sett..., ...is classic free to reach an even larger audience than before'—Nilanjana Roy, *Business Standard*

'*Falling Walls* is a terrific, deeply engrossing read . . . [It] is also a multi-layered portrait of intersecting worlds, with Chetan as the fulcrum. It is about relationships in a lower-middle-class family, about young people trying to find their way, about missteps and successes, sexual awakening and minor transgressions. It is a ground-level view of three cities at a very particular time in a nation's history. And it is an enquiry into what it takes to be an artist, and whether the effort is worth it . . . One of this narrative's achievements is that it is wonderfully fluid even though the structure is really very intricate'—Jai Arjun Singh, *Open*

'Riveting reading . . . Ashk is fortunate to have found Daisy Rockwell as his translator for not only does she have the stamina and tenacity to take on this mammoth cycle of novels but also seems to have a rare devotion for Ashk himself . . . *Falling Walls* becomes compelling reading simply because it transcends the personal and particular. In its slow unfurling of a mind looking to expand its horizon, in its insistent exploration of the darkest recesses of the human heart it no longer remains just the story of one young man. Also, given its richly textured narrative, its setting in provincial Punjab and its depiction of a Punjabi youth struggling to find his feet in a literary world dominated by Urdu writers, it chronicles a world located at the cusp of change . . . Ashk is nothing if not brutally honest in his portrayal of all that afflicts a young man raised by a devout mother and depraved father in an atmosphere of utter suppression of the most natural of human impulses. What emerges, then, from a reading of *Falling Walls* . . . is the arresting portrait of a young man wanting to become an artist'—Rakhshanda Jalil, Wire.in

'[*Falling Walls* is] a 1947 novel by one of Hindi literature's best-known names, Upendranath Ashk, [and] offers an intimate portrait of lower-middle-class life in the 1930s. From the back lanes of Lahore and Jalandhar to Shimla's Scandal Point, *Falling Walls* is also about the hurdles an aspiring writer has to overcome to fulfil his ambitions. The six-volume novel cycle [*Falling Walls*] earned the author comparisons to French novelist and critic

Marcel Proust. Ashk was the recipient of numerous prizes and awards during his lifetime for his masterful portrayal, by turns humorous and remarkably profound, of the everyday lives of ordinary people'—*Economic Times*

'[A] superbly crafted and meticulously detailed, larger-than-life novel . . . Magnificent . . . *Falling Walls* will not fail to impress. It is as if an entire microcosm of old town lanes, teeming with people of all kinds suddenly comes alive . . . Ashk writes with a clear hand and is served well by Daisy Rockwell as she recreates a compelling narrative'—*Dawn*

'*Falling Walls* is a keenly modern novel . . . Rockwell's immense research shows in her deft translation, where nothing jars as she effortlessly conveys the local colour . . . She moves the Hindi text towards the English reader but knows how far it can be pushed from its terrain . . . This novel must be read, not least for its description of our forgotten literary cultures and a subaltern history of pre-Independence times'—*The Hindu Business Line*

'In the world of Hindi literature, Upendranath Ashk was a towering figure . . . best known for his six-volume novel cycle [*Falling Walls*]'— *The Hindu*

Praise for *Hats and Doctors*

'*Hats and Doctors* offers the English reader the first proper glimpse of Ashk's very particular sensibility: profound yet light-hearted, satirical yet deeply engaged. He unravels the ironies of his protagonists' lives with a wry humour: sharp as a scalpel, yet somehow understated'—*Mint*

'*Hats and Doctors* offers readers in English a taste of Ashk's short fiction, in which complex themes like marriage, mortality and the colonial legacy are rendered with a lightness of touch'—*The Hindu*

PENGUIN MODERN CLASSICS

In the City a Mirror Wandering

UPENDRANATH ASHK, 1910–1996, was one of Hindi literature's best known and most controversial authors. Ashk was born in Jalandhar and spent the early part of his writing career as an Urdu author in Lahore. Encouraged by Premchand, he switched to Hindi, and a few years before Partition, moved to Bombay, Delhi and finally Allahabad in 1948, where he spent the rest of his life. By the time of his death, Ashk's phenomenally large oeuvre spanned over a hundred volumes of fiction, poetry, memoir, criticism and translation. Ashk is perhaps best known for his six-volume novel cycle, *Girti Divarein*, or *Falling Walls*—an intensely detailed chronicle of the travails of a young Punjabi man attempting to become a writer—which has earned the author comparisons to Marcel Proust. Ashk was the recipient of numerous prizes and awards during his lifetime for his masterful portrayal, by turns humorous and remarkably profound, of the everyday lives of ordinary people.

DAISY ROCKWELL is an artist and writer living in northern New England. She paints under the takhallus, or alias, Lapata (Urdu for 'missing'), and has shown her artwork widely. Rockwell holds a PhD in Hindi literature and has taught Hindi–Urdu and South Asian literature at a number of US universities. Apart from her essays on literature and art, she has written *Upendranath Ashk: A Critical Biography*, *The Little Book of Terror*, a book of paintings and essays on the global war on terror, and the novel *Taste*. She has translated a collection of Ashk's short stories, *Hats and Doctors* (published in Penguin Classics), and a widely acclaimed translation of *Girti Divarein* (published in Penguin Classics as *Falling Walls*), the first volume of Ashk's epic novel cycle. Her translation of Bhisham Sahni's iconic Partition novel *Tamas* (also published in Penguin Classics) is regarded as the definitive English rendition of that work. Most recently, she has translated Khadija Mastur's *Aangan* (published in Penguin Classics as *The Women's Courtyard*).

UPENDRANATH ASHK

In the City a Mirror Wandering

Translated from the Hindi
with an Introduction by Daisy Rockwell

PENGUIN BOOKS

An imprint of Penguin Random House

PENGUIN BOOKS

USA | Canada | UK | Ireland | Australia
New Zealand | India | South Africa | China | Singapore

Penguin Books is part of the Penguin Random House group of companies
whose addresses can be found at global.penguinrandomhouse.com

Published by Penguin Random House India Pvt. Ltd
7th Floor, Infinity Tower C, DLF Cyber City,
Gurgaon 122 002, Haryana, India

First published in Hindi as *Sheher mein Ghoomta Aina* by Neelabh Prakashan 1951
First published by Penguin Random House India 2019

ISBN 9780143425991

Typeset in Adobe Garamond Pro by Manipal Digital Systems, Manipal
Printed at Repro India Limited

My novel is a mirror of life and it reflects, while it journeys down the highway, the blue skies and the mire in the road below.

—Stendhal

My footprints are still restless here
I've wandered these same paths for years

To Life's intricate paths

Translator's Introduction

But the question is, in this age of struggle, for whom does the storyteller write? Does he write for the wealthy and aristocratic writers or critics of today, who now take the place of Kalidas's maharajas, or does he write for the thousands of people engaged in struggles just like himself? Kalidas and his contemporaries lived under the patronage of rajas and maharajas, they created literature solely for the enjoyment of their masters, and what would be the use of sickness, sorrow, poverty, the tiny, aggravating details of life that leave a bitter taste in one's mouth—those utterly ordinary, negligible events—to a raja? Some of our critics even see themselves as the rajas and hold similar expectations of the writer. But if the writer doesn't write for them, if he writes for the thousands of other mud-smeared souls, like himself, then clearly he won't show them the beauty of the lotus but all the other items in the lotus tank: the spreading roots, the mud, the slime, the weeds and all the other matter the writer wishes to clean from the tank—all of it—all such items are responsible for the spread of countless germs of illness and filth, whether five lotuses happen to bloom there or ten.

—Upendranath Ashk, from his Introduction to *Falling Walls*

I. The Muck in the Lotus Pond

In *Falling Walls,* the first volume of a planned series of novels covering five years in the life of his autobiographical protagonist, Chetan, Upendranath Ashk made clear his intent of writing about the not-so-pretty aspects of lower-middle-class life in Punjab. He was recording not the lovely lotus as it floats in the tank, but all the other muck and slime that can be found beneath. He was writing about real life and for ordinary readers. In this second volume of his epic tale of a young man climbing out of the metaphorical pond-scum of his existence towards the light of aesthetic expression and worldly success, he embraces this goal with renewed vigour. *In the City a Mirror Wandering,* first published in 1963—sixteen years after *Falling Walls*—takes the modernist 'pattern', as Ashk called it, of the epic novel contained within a single day made famous by Virginia Woolf in *Mrs Dalloway*, and James Joyce in *Ulysses*, and drags it through the literal muck of the Jalandhar streets one grimy monsoon day, stinting nothing in airing every bit of dirty laundry that caught its writer's eye.

In these provincial city streets, we meet goondas, halfwits, bullies, frauds, drunks and misogynists of every stripe. Chetan leaves his family home, and his sleepy wife, Chanda, early in the morning, still smarting from the recent marriage of the woman he loved, his wife's first cousin Neela, to a middle-aged accountant from Rangoon. He sets out on an aimless tour of the city streets in search of some sort of emotional and spiritual comfort. He wants friendly companionship, or sympathy, or at least a sense that he has done something with his life of which he can be proud. Instead, he is greeted at every turn not only by crude humour and bullying, but also by neighbourhood gossip about the fresh accomplishment of his former classmate Amichand, who has just qualified to become a deputy commissioner. This rankles especially because Chetan had recently encountered Amichand in Shimla, and been greeted superciliously, as though Amichand had already reached such a high level that Chetan was now far beneath him. In Chetan's mind, Amichand is nothing but a crammer—he had possessed no extraordinary talents or intelligence that would have suggested his rise to such heights. And yet 'Amichand'—not 'Chetan'—is the name on everyone's lips.

This epic journey of revulsion and despair ends where it began, by the side of the sleeping Chanda, in a small rooftop room in his family home. He had gone on a manly quest beyond the hearth, and walked among his fellowmen, yet found everyone and everything profoundly wanting. It is only deep in the night, when he raises the flame of the low-burning lamp by the bedside to gaze at his wife that he realizes that all the love, compassion and respect he seeks is here, in the woman he had dismissively abandoned early that morning. This realization is touchingly poignant, but it may also seem absurd to the contemporary reader. Is this what it takes for a man to recognize the humanity in his wife?

In the City a Mirror Wandering is hardly a feminist tale, despite the careful portraits of the callous abuse of women that Ashk documents. But it can be read as a finely wrought portrayal of the inhumanity of men, not just towards women, but also towards one another, in a cultural context plagued by generations of poverty, illiteracy and superstition. The walls that Ashk hoped to see falling are the barriers to progress posed by an entrenched culture of urban want, and one such barrier is that which divides men and women, rendering loving and respectful communication nearly impossible (as well as creating an epidemic of sexually transmitted diseases). Chetan's realization that he can open up emotionally to his wife is a revelation in an environment where woman are seen entirely from a sexual and reproductive standpoint and their worth is measured in terms of ownership by their husbands and symbolic ownership by their caste-communities.

This is nowhere more apparent than in the final conflagration of the novel, a mini-epic battle between the neighbourhood's Khatris and Brahmins over the beating of Bhago, a Khatri woman who had run off with a Brahmin. As Bhago lies bleeding on a charpoy in the middle of the mohalla, there is less concern for her comfort and well-being than for exacting justice against the assailant, her caste-mate and Amichand's brother Amirchand, newly emboldened by his brother's triumph. Indeed, it is decided that she should be carried on the charpoy to the local police station to be presented as evidence, and only after that should her grievous head wounds be tended by the local hakim, who is present throughout. The history of male literature is littered with women desperately needing medical attention while men do important things (think of Fantine, delirious with fever, and abandoned for many pages, while Jean Valjean embarks on a quest relating to his identity in *Les Misérables*), but it is always hard to bear.

In Hindi, the verb for 'hit' or 'beat' is the same as the one for 'kill'—*mārnā*. This ambiguity is borne out throughout the scene, with reports coming in that Amirchand has beaten Bhago, but it is unclear until the end if he has beaten her to death (*jān se*). Indeed, her condition is still unclear when the conflagration devolves into a round of virile wrestling between Chetan's brother Parasuram and his friend Debu under the referee-ship of Chetan's father. What was really at stake was the relative masculinity and power of the two communities, and Chetan's father is only reminded of Bhago's plight when he's about to take the two wrestlers for their reward of fresh milk at the sweet shop.

Throughout the novel, Chetan is disgusted by the callousness, bullying and hollow posturing he sees around him; at the same time, he clearly derives a measure of voyeuristic pleasure from witnessing it. He is generally the most educated person in each interchange, and the most sensitive, yet from time to time he steps in as an enabler. When his goonda friends land themselves in hot water for pranking passers-by by knocking off their hats, Chetan intervenes by speaking in English and introducing himself as a writer for a respected newspaper in Lahore. He does the same at the police station and at other junctures as well. This device serves the narrative well—how could we believe that our protagonist would spend an entire day hanging around with frauds and miscreants if he did not take some pleasure in it? Chetan wishes to rise above the pond—he aspires to the lilies—but as of now, he still belongs to the muck.

II. Part Two, Sixteen Years Later

In the City a Mirror Wandering was published sixteen years after *Falling Walls*, in 1963—a much longer gap than Ashk had originally intended. In the interim, he'd recovered from tuberculosis, moved to Allahabad, started his own publishing house with his wife, Kaushalya, and made a name for himself in the world of Hindi letters. As he explains in his unusually short introduction to this work, the writing of this volume was effortful and impeded by many bouts of ill health (a favourite topic of discussion for him). The temporal distance from the era described in the series had ballooned to thirty years, and his anxieties about the lateness of the work and the increasingly unrecognizable landscape it described are apparent in small ways throughout the novel.

In a style reminiscent of 'what you missed in last week's episode' segments in TV programmes, Ashk devotes a substantial chunk of the opening chapters to a recap of the main plot points in *Falling Walls*. He was both anxious that readers may have forgotten, and keen to make the text accessible to new readers who hadn't come across the first volume at all; it was always his intention that any of the volumes could be read independent of the others. Readers for whom that volume is still fresh in the mind are not advised to skip ahead however, as interspersed between these recaps, presented as Chetan's early morning reveries, are a literal trail of clues leading to his brother Parasuram's calisthenics routine, an aspect of the story which will eventually become integral to the novel as a whole.

Despite the long interval between the publication of the first and second volumes, Ashk adhered very strictly to his plan of writing an uninterrupted narrative. Chetan goes to sleep at the end of *Falling Walls*, and at the beginning of *In the City a Mirror Wandering*, he wakes up the very next morning, fretting about the events of the previous evening. The same holds true for the third volume, *Ek Nanhi Qindil* (A Tiny Candle), 1969, which opens the morning after the present volume. Fans of Chetan's elder brother, Bhai Sahib, will be disappointed to learn that since Chetan quarrelled with him late in *Falling Walls*, and he is not in Jalandhar during the one-day period of this volume, he will not reappear until the third volume, at which time the brothers will finally have a chance to hash out their disagreement, some five hundred pages later.

Though Ashk's writing style is more or less consistent between the volumes, *In the City a Mirror Wandering* has a tighter structure and a brisker pace. Readers may also observe an increasing number of side notes supplied by the author (all footnotes are his, unless otherwise specified), as well as asides for present-day readers, for example, explaining how Chetan's friend's new bride could have been robbed of her dowry while waiting between the signal and the station. Ashk's descriptions of places are extremely precise and he was always keen that his readers know exactly what he was talking about. As he explains in Chapter 30:

Jalandhar station was probably about a mile or so from the gate. Nowadays, there's not even a full yard of free space from there to the station, but in those days, the line passed through a complete wasteland between the two. There was a pool of standing water near the line that was thick with reeds.

Ashk always revisited the places he was writing about, to verify his memories of specific street names, crossroads and other aspects of the urban landscape. Unlike authors who prefer to rely on nostalgic memories of places from their childhood and youth, Ashk not only wanted to get it right, but also make sure that contemporary readers understood what he was talking about.

III. Quotation and Misquotation

Part of the richness of *In the City a Mirror Wandering* lies in the sheer number of poems, folk sayings and songs quoted throughout the text. Some of these quotations are from famous texts and will be readily recognized even by readers of the English version, and some are not. Among the famous quotations, several contain errors. Where I and other readers have identified these, I've added translator's footnotes, giving the correct version of the text, especially if it was from another language (Sanskrit) or from a famous line of Urdu poetry that we retained in the translation.

But why did Ashk include so many errors in his text? Was it because he had no internet, or relied on faulty recollections of famous poems? Was he sloppy and did he not check his work? Having researched his files years ago, I am inclined towards a different explanation. What I found then was that Ashk was a compulsive editor. If an article was written about him in a newspaper or journal, he'd clip it out and mark it up, as though he were the author himself. This was not so much to make something appear more favourable or flattering, but rather to correct what he perceived as flaws in style or grammar. He would then have these documents retyped and placed in the file alongside the originals, drawing upon them for the purpose of blurbs or further quotation in writing about critical responses to his own work.

Take for example the passage from Stendhal's *The Red and the Black*, at the very beginning of the novel, which Ashk quoted in English in the original text:

> My novel is a mirror of life and it reflects, while it journeys down the highway, the blue skies and the mire in the road below.

This passage must have been taken from an English translation of Stendhal's French text, and a cursory glance at the original shows that it is incorrect:

> *Eh, monsieur, un roman est un miroir qui se promène sur une grande route. Tantôt il reflète à vos yeux l'azur des cieux, tantôt la fange des bourbiers de la route.*

A correct translation would have been more like this:

> Ah, Sir, a novel is a mirror strolling along a highway. At times it reflects the azure of the skies, and at others, the muddy potholes in the road.

At first, we might be tempted to give Ashk the benefit of the doubt. Perhaps he had a poor translation of the novel, or had memorized it imperfectly. After all, he hardly had the access to the internet that makes it so easy nowadays to find the precise wording of a quotation heard long ago. I would argue, however, that though he might indeed have had a poor translation, or an imperfect memory of the quotation he wanted, he most likely changed the quote to suit his needs.

I can easily imagine Ashk taking his red pen to the Stendhal quote and making it his own. This is about *my* novel, not any novel—a bit solipsistic, perhaps, but very Ashkian, nonetheless. In researching the Stendhal quote, I too faced my own dilemma. Should I 'restore' the original quotation? Should I add the rest of the quote, which is really rather fine and ties in so well with what Ashk wished to express in the novel? In the end, I left it as he had published it, but leave here, in my Introduction, the full quotation from *The Red and the Black*:

> Ah, Sir, a novel is a mirror strolling along a highway. At times it reflects the azure of the skies, and at others, the muddy potholes in the road. And the man who carries this mirror in his pack will be accused by you of being immoral! His mirror shews the mire, and you blame the mirror! Rather blame that high road upon which the puddle lies, still more the inspector of roads who allows the water to gather and the puddle to form.

How greatly Ashk must have identified with this sentiment, of the blaming of the novelist for the social ills he presents, when they are mere reflections of the ugliness of reality. And how very like Ashk's own quotation at the beginning of this introduction, using instead of the metaphor of the mirror and the highway, the lotus and the pond-scum in which it thrives. And so I end with an exhortation to you, readers and critics, not to blame the author (or the translator!) for the ugly side of life portrayed in this work, but instead, following Stendhal, blame civic inspectors who should be cleaning out the pond and allowing more lotuses to grow.

Acknowledgements and Dedication

Translating a novel set in 1930s' Jalandhar involves quite a bit of historical excavation and linguistic research. As a non-native speaker of Hindi living in a rural part of the United States, I would have had no chance of completing this work without the internet and the many kind people therein who have offered me their wisdom and insights. My debts of gratitude extend all around the world to many people and organizations. First and foremost, many thanks go to the members of the Ashk family who have supported this work and granted me permission to translate: Adamya, Sukant, Shwetabh and Anurag Ashk, thank you all for granting me the honour of bringing your grandfather's work into the English language. I am also greatly indebted to the United States National Endowment for the Humanities for a generous grant in support of this translation. I would like to thank my wonderful editor at Penguin Random House India, Ambar Sahil Chatterjee, and my meticulous copy-editor, Arpita Basu, for all their help and support.

An extra special thank you goes to Urdu translator and scholar Dr Aftab Ahmad, who has put up with far too many questions from me and answered all with great generosity. Jasdeep Singh possesses an amazing depth of knowledge about Punjabi language, literature and folklore and I am deeply indebted to him for all his help. Musharraf Ali Farooqi and Dr Mohammad Taqi know seemingly everything there is to know about Urdu and Persian, and both have been very generous in their thoughtful replies to my cries for help. Once again, Dr Allauddin Mian came through in a pinch when I sought arcane bits of medical knowledge from 1930s' Punjab. Anupama Kapse helped me understand the passages on early Indian cinema. Other helpful friends from Twitter and elsewhere: Salman Hussain, Awais Athar, Alok Ranjan, Saurabh Gupta, Sadhana Gupta, Nalini Sahay, Rahul Asthana and Jesse Knutson. Many thanks to my IRL friends and family for their help and support as well, particularly my husband, Aaron, my daughter, Serafina, and my dearly departed cats, Otto and Ignatz. Though Jenny Linsky, Madama Butterfly and Princess Leia were not familiar with Ashk's work and had never assisted in a major translation before, they've quickly learned the ropes and helped shepherd the book to completion.

Last, but by no means least, immense gratitude to Neelabh, Ashk's son, who sadly passed away as I was completing the translation. Neelabh, who was himself a gifted poet and translator (this is the man who translated Arundhati Roy's first novel into Hindi, with the brilliant title *Māmūlī Chīzon kā Devtā*), was the greatest expert on Ashk's work, having worked with his father and edited for him for many years. He told me in the year before his death that his father had been his literary mentor, and that he missed him every day, despite Ashk's irascible temperament. While completing the manuscript for the translation of the first volume of Ashk's series, *Falling Walls*, I had the good fortune of sitting with Neelabh for several days, going over countless questions that truly, only he could answer. He was full of anecdotes about the books, and about his father, while always exercising his right to distance himself from the work. Apprenticing with someone of such an immense literary ego was not easy for him, and he sought always to differentiate himself from his father, developing an irascible temperament of his own along the way. Nonetheless, he was always willing to help me, willing to ponder my endless questions, and happy to discuss thorny problems of translation. In my email drafts box sits an unfinished message to Neelabh with a fresh set of questions for this translation. It's an email I never sent, but still can't bring myself to delete. Such messages are not the same as yellowing leaves of stationery inscribed in pen and ink, but such is the digital age. This translation, then, is dedicated to Neelabh's memory, in gratitude for his help and encouragement.

Author's Preface

The characters in my novel *In the City a Mirror Wandering* have inhabited my mind for years. One could even say they had actually become an obstacle to my writing. Whenever I thought of writing a new novel, they always blocked my path. I am relieved now to feel finally lighter for having put them down on paper.

I first started writing the novel in 1957. That year, I had gone to Dalhousie in hopes of writing the whole novel there. But I was so captivated by the beauty of the place that I ended up just writing poems instead. All the same, once that mood ran out, I again put my hand to the task and wrote five chapters. But for the next three years, I couldn't get any further, no matter how hard I tried. Every year I attempted to complete the book, but I was only able to write seven more chapters.

I was so distressed by the slow pace of the novel that when I became the chairman of the Assam Hindi Sammelan in 1961, and went to Tinsukia (Assam), I took the manuscript along with me. I had thought that after my tour in Assam, I'd stop in Kalimpong and not return until I'd finished the novel. But I did not find the climate in Assam salutary. I fell ill in Shillong and had a fever by the time I reached Kalimpong. My wife wanted me to return and recuperate, then go elsewhere to write. But I stayed on and, despite my illness, finished the book in one and three-quarters months. I couldn't sleep at night for coughing, so I slept by day and wrote all night. Although my health deteriorated even further due to this pig-headedness and my old TB grew a bit active again, I have no regrets. I have complete faith that had I returned without finishing the book, I wouldn't have been able to write it for many years more and that this would have become a source of relentless anxiety.

But was it right to undertake so great a risk for the depiction of such a mean, mediocre, lower-middle-class life? It's possible my critics will read it and ask this very question with sarcasm and disdain. I have no answer for them. I can only describe my own compulsion to write it.

I am heartily grateful to my comrades Surendra Pal, Virendranath Mandal and Kaushalya, who helped me greatly in preparing the press copy. I regret that because of my current ill health, I was not able to do as much work on it as I usually do. There must be some errors remaining. I hope that sympathetic readers, on hearing of my plight, will not judge the book for any small errors. As always, I welcome their suggestions.

25 March 1963

To the reader who expects every work of art to teach him something, I submit that a good work of art does not teach anything directly, but that those inclined to learn will learn a great deal. There's a saying in Punjabi:

Ikkanāñ nūñ dittī rabb ne
Ikkanāñ ne sikkh layī
Ikkanāñ nūñ jo na āyī
Jyūñ patthar būnd payī

That is, there's one type of person who's born already knowing everything from God; another learns (by observation or study); and then there's the third type, off whose mind knowledge rolls like drops of water from a rock.

In order to gain something from another person's impressions and experiences, one must keep an open mind. Those who have been born knowing everything and those who can't learn anything won't get much out of this novel. This novel is intended only for the middle group (of which the writer considers himself a member as well), and he's found that most readers fall into this category. It is into their hands that he hesitantly presents this book.

Morning

Morning

1

Chetan had fallen asleep quite late that night. A host of thoughts swirled in his mind like blades of grass caught in a whirlwind. Words and sights from Neela's wedding, of no apparent significance—tiny details that had shaken him—entered his thoughts again and again. Conversations he'd had with Neela, Meela, Sheelo and Ranvir echoed in his ears, and he began to hear his own voice mingled with the others. He'd jerk his head and turn over; again he'd try to fall asleep, but those same sights, incidents, conversations would return . . .

Much of the night had already passed when the cloudy sky burst open and it began to pour. In the relentless slapping of the rain a lament arose from the sheets of tin that covered the metal railing above the courtyard. Chetan's attention was drawn to this monotonous wailing, and soon the pounding rain began to calm the storm in his mind. His eyelids grew heavy and he was enveloped in a deep sleep.

*

He might have slept quite late the next morning, had he not become conscious of a grunting sound in the early hours. At first the grunting sounded like a far-off pounding on the door to his consciousness; then he began to have a sort of dream, in which he saw a strange, horrifying beast, with the head of a sheep and the body and gait of a bear. The beast chased after him, grunting. The door to his consciousness opened suddenly and he awoke with a start.

The rain had long since stopped and the clouds had cleared, but all about the roof, sparkling clean after the torrential downpour, danced the sort of light that bursts forth with the sudden blossoming of the sun in a cloudless, blue, monsoon sky. The night's downpour had filled the air with a cool moisture, and Chetan had wrapped the covers around his head, his face—everything. When he awoke with a start and pushed them from his face, his eyes filled with the glare of sunlight. His neck was a bit sweaty. He glanced around the room for a moment as he wiped his neck with his hand. A breeze blew through the screens that hung from the large arches on each side of the rooftop room and water dripped down the bricks from the roof above. His wife, Chanda, lay beside him, in a deep sleep.

He wondered if it had been her snoring that had woken him. But she never snored. All the same he leaned over and listened near her nose—she was breathing evenly. There wasn't even the slightest hint of a rasp.

Chetan pushed aside the covers but didn't get out of bed. His eyes were fixed on his sleeping wife. Her large, round eyes were closed, her coarse hair lay strewn across her forehead, her lips were chapped, her round, plump cheeks looked as dry as stale bread rolls, and a little bit of spit was pooled in the left corner of her mouth. Suddenly he thought of Neela's glowing face when she had come to see him before getting into her palanquin, jingling with jewellery and weighted down with bridal clothing. He suppressed a sigh, jumped up and walked out of the room.

Chanda started from his movement, but didn't sit up; instead she turned over and went back to sleep.

Outside, two bricks lay on the dividing wall that joined the two roofs (the wall had been made with a view to adding a third storey,

4

but the means of building a third storey had not yet materialized and the only use for the wall at the moment was to separate the two roofs). Chetan saw oily handprints on the bricks and drops of oil on the lower roof. He now realized what had woken him and what the grunting noise had been! His younger brother Parasaram must have been doing his exercises here. Every morning he did one thousand push-ups and one thousand sit-ups. The drops must be sweat from his brow and the grunting must have been the sound of his laboured breathing. Chetan ran to the cement bench to test his theory and peered down at the neighbourhood well below. He had guessed correctly. Parasaram was filling a pot of water at the well, with only a loincloth covering his fair, muscular body. Whenever he finished his exercises, he always took the pot to the well and filled all the water for the house before resting. When he exercised, he kept his lips pressed shut, and when he did push-ups, he made a loud grunting noise as he lowered his body, as wrestlers do at the *akhara*. It must have been this grunting sound that had woken Chetan.

He stepped back. The bench was not wet, but quite chilly. He lay down on it, on his stomach. He rested his left cheek on the cold surface. A pleasing shiver ran down his spine all the way to his feet. He let his right arm dangle from the bench. His side stuck to the rounded edge and a cool tingling ran through his body, but he felt very happy. He continued to lie there silently without moving. He closed his eyes with pleasure . . . but that pleasurable feeling reminded him of lovely moments spent with Neela and, as he lay there, eyes closed, he lost himself in those memories.

*

He stands at the Basti tonga stop with his friend Mulkraj. He's come to secretly take a peek at his future wife as she walks home from school. Just then, school lets out and groups of girls begin to

5

emerge . . . A girl of about twelve or thirteen, surrounded by friends, her books in her hands, walks by slowly and deliberately, as though unaware of her own beauty. As she passes by she glances flirtatiously at Chetan. Chetan's heart pounds. He glances hopefully at his friend Mulkraj. Mulkraj shakes his head. That's not the one . . . and Chetan wishes he could go home without seeing his future wife after all.

*

After seeing his plump, dowdy future wife and not caring for her, he returns, on his father's orders, to see her formally—at the home of the social reformer Master Nandalal. His eyes are downcast with embarrassment, but when he looks up, his heart starts pounding again—that same girl is sitting near his bride-to-be . . . that same flirtatious, lively girl with the deliberate gait . . . and for that one instant, Chetan sees only a part of her face: that row of pearly teeth that makes her playful eyes sparkle.

*

He is sitting at his wedding feast, but he's paying no attention to the food (the reformer Master Nandalal has forbidden the singing of obscene wedding songs by the women) as his eyes search the deserted ramparts of the house for those playful eyes, delightful as streams of cool water.

Most of the groom's party has finished eating and stood up. None of the boys teases Chetan; no girl stitches his coat to the dhurrie; no one hides his new shoes. Listless, he stands up as well. He starts to put on his first ever pair of patent leather pump shoes but then he stops. That same girl has lifted the chick blinds on the veranda and emerged, scattering her smiles about her like so many blossoms, a thicket of girlfriends close behind her. 'Jija ji, tell us a

6

chhand!' . . . 'Jija ji, tell us a chhand!' And he learns that this girl demanding a nonsense wedding couplet is his sister-in-law—the daughter of his wife Chanda's paternal uncle—Neela.

And gazing into Neela's eyes, he recites a chhand:

Chhands come, chhands go badum-bum-bum-a-teela
I forgot all of the chhands when I first saw Neela.

And he recollects the poem by Ella Wheeler Wilcox:

You are the moon, dear love, and I the sea:

The tide of hope swells high within my breast,
And hides the rough dark rocks of life's unrest
When your fond eyes smile near in perigee.
But when that loving face is turned from me,
Low falls the tide, and the grim rocks appear,
And earth's dim coast-line seems a thing to fear.
You are the moon, dear one, and I the sea.

*

After his wedding, he is lying in the rooftop porch at the home of his in-laws. Neela comes and places a magazine in his lap.

'Read this, right here!'

She puts her finger on one line on the page. Chetan reads it—it's a sentence from a dialogue in a story:

'How can I say I don't love you?'

He reads the sentence to himself. Neela gazes at him with a strange look that plumbs the depths of his heart, and before Chetan can respond she rushes off, hugging the magazine to her bosom, turning once to look back at him.

*

A moonlit night after a full day of rain, and a small cloud like the wing of a partridge. A cool breeze blows. He lies on the roof at his in-laws'. Neela sits next to him and he watches her, entranced. She begins to stroke his hair slowly and lovingly with her fine fingers, and suddenly, without thinking, she cries, 'Jija ji, your hair is so soft—it's so long and curly!'

Chetan doesn't respond. He takes Neela's hand in his and, closing his eyes for a few moments, he lies there silently. Then he says, 'I was thinking, Neela, about how I came to see Chanda twice, and both times I saw you.'

'I saw you both times as well, and I can also tell you what suit you were wearing the first day when you stood at Basti Adda.'

*

And those letters he had written ostensibly to his wife from Lahore, but were secretly meant for Neela:

> . . . before, my heart was sad and barren, like a centuries-dried-up sea that no longer knows the sensation of waves and the rippling of water. Destroyed by its emptiness, it stared fixedly at the sky. Then you smiled from some corner of that sky, a tiny new cloud throbbing with life, and the sea overflowed its banks.

And:

> I've broken my silence and burst into song. I feel such joy suffuse my being, as when a beggar suddenly discovers some

hidden treasure. And haven't I discovered a treasure—the
priceless treasure of beauty and love? But I tremble with
fear—what if this treasure is somehow snatched from me!

*

Chetan suddenly propped himself up on his elbows. 'You idiot,' he cried out to himself. 'That treasure was snatched from you, you idiot! Because you were worthless, you were a coward, you were mean-spirited. It was your own stupidity that got her snatched from you and handed over to someone else.' He wished he could beat his head against the bench. But instead he lay there for a few minutes, staring into the void. Then he took a deep breath and relaxed again . . . He thought about the wedding of his distantly related sister-in-law in Alawalpur and an incident that had occurred there became magnified manyfold before his eyes in its minutest detail.

*

Chetan lies ill in a rooftop room. He has a high fever. His throat is swollen. His wife can't come to him. She sends Neela instead. The children are kicking up a racket in the room. Chetan has a terrible headache. 'For God's sake, get them out of here!' he cries out feebly.

Neela scolds the children and chases them away. She shuts the door and pulls the chain across, and comes to sit at the head of his bed. He moans with pain. She slowly starts to massage his head. Chetan is half asleep. Neela's enchanting voice pours into his ears like a peaceful tune—sweet music coming from somewhere very far away.

She runs her fine fingers through his long curly hair and says, 'Jija ji, your hair is so beautiful, long, black and curly!'

9

And she asks, 'Tell me, Jija ji, how did you get these curls? Did you curl your hair yourself or did it happen naturally? My hair can't do that. My hair is long, but it's not curly.'

And she takes her braid and shows it to him so he can see how soft her hair is, how long, but not curly.

Chetan takes the soft cool braid in his hands, burning with fever, and slowly unplaits it, and the long, black, soft, fragrant tresses fall across his face. And Neela cries out, 'Jija ji, you've undone my braid!'

She pulls her hair back but Chetan won't let go. And Neela doesn't really try to free her hair. Chetan takes those soft, dense tresses in both his hands and spreads them over his face—Neela leans over him . . . so close . . . so close . . . that suddenly he has a powerful urge to take her in his arms and kiss her. But he just kisses her hair. And that too in such a way that Neela doesn't notice and she continues to speak, talking about how she won't get married, and why do people get married at all if they regret it so much later? And she tells him of the tragedy of her elder sister Meela's marriage. And suddenly she caresses his face and says, 'Jija ji, you're growing a beard, why don't you shave?' And she laughs, 'Shall I get a razor and do it myself?'

And she caresses his lips with her hand and says, 'Jija ji, your lips are chapped, shall I put a bit of butter on them?'

Chetan places his hand on hers and presses it lightly to his lips.

*

When he's feeling a bit healthier and is better able to think properly, he calls for Chanda.

'I've been sick for four or five days now. I've had such a fever—did you even ask about me?' he asks.

10

'Why do you ask? I'm always keeping track of you. What are you having problems with? Neela's here . . .'

'Neela . . . Neela . . . Neela . . .' he explodes and adds, almost yelling, 'You should be sitting by me!'

'You don't know,' says Chanda in a meek and emotional voice. 'If I sat next to you, people would talk. The women in this family will say anything. Neela . . .'

'What I'm saying, Chanda, is that you're crazy,' he retorts with annoyance. 'Neela's not a child any more. She's fourteen or fifteen and I . . . Don't you see I'm a man! A weak man!'

Chanda bursts out laughing. 'You were scaring me. But I'm not scared of that. She's my little sister. So what if she's my uncle's daughter? I've always considered her a sister. Her honour is in your hands. She's playful, she can make little mistakes, but you can't.'

And she gazes at her husband with boundless, generous faith as she strokes his brow.

*

And the result of this faith is that when Neela comes to him again with milk and then chases away the boys and sits at the head of his bed to serve him, she leans him against her and props him up with her arm, and he suddenly takes her in his arms and kisses her, and he is not able to forgive himself. In the evening when Neela's father comes to see him, he hints at everything that has occurred.

And quickly, Neela's marriage to a middle-aged military accountant is arranged and Chetan watches as his beloved treasure, which had come to him unbidden, is transferred to another.

*

11

He sees Neela holding out her thin, pale arm over the drain in the courtyard; the leeches on her wrist have sucked her blood—that wrist, thinner than before, yellowish, but even more beautiful than ever—like a blossom flowering in a rocky cave. He has tried to forget the Neela he had known, but she has lodged somewhere deep inside him. She gives him an abrupt 'Hello.' After Alawalpur this has been their only interaction. Has he come from so far away, all the way from Shimla, just to hear this dry 'Hello'? But when he hears she is marrying a widowed military accountant in Rangoon, something begins to gnaw at him. He tries to talk to her, but doesn't get more than a brief word or two in response.

'How are you, Neela?'

'I am well!'

'Neela, you look ill.'

'No, Jija ji!'

'Neela, you're going so far away.'

'Yes, Jija ji!'

'Neela, are you angry with me?'

'No, Jija ji!'

He wants to speak openly with Neela before being separated from her; he wants to lighten his soul and beg her forgiveness, but he doesn't get a chance and walks irritably upstairs to the room on the roof. After that, he doesn't attempt to speak to her.

*

Farewell. Music plays outside. Chanda comes upstairs several times to tell him Neela is leaving, and that he should give her *shagun*, the bridal gift. But he won't move. He decides he'll go quietly and place the shagun in Neela's hand when they've walked on a bit, when she's veiled and seated as a bride. But suddenly his heart begins to pound—Neela is coming upstairs jingling with jewellery and weighted down with bridal clothing.

'Namaste, Jija ji! Please forgive me my mistakes!'

'Neela, forgive me . . .' and he bows down at her feet.

'Jija ji, what are you doing!' She lifts him up and runs off, suppressing a sob.

*

Chetan slowly beat his head against the bench two or three times—he felt as though he were being stabbed. He turned over and lay flat on his back. But it was seven or so in the morning, and a sharp, shimmering sunlight had already spread across the roof. His eyes could not take the glare. He turned over again and lay down as before, letting his arm dangle from the bench. Then those same sights, those same conversations, those same words, began to spin through his head once more. But this part of the bench was shaded by a curtain. The curtain's shade, so close to the sharp monsoon sunlight, made the cement pleasantly cool. His exhausted, tense mind relaxed with the pleasure of that cool touch. He dozed off.

But he wasn't able to stay asleep for long. Suddenly he was startled again and sat up for a moment, his legs dangling foolishly. He'd had another dream . . .

He saw . . . he saw . . . it wasn't a bench . . . Neela was lying there, wearing that same glittering clothing, and her fair cheek pressed against his own. He sat up.

The sunlight had reached that part of the bench as well and his body was growing hot.

He couldn't stay here . . . he couldn't stay . . . He would run off to Lahore again. Oddly irritable now, he got up, ran into the room and shook his wife awake.

'It's getting late. You're still asleep. What will Ma say?'

Chanda rearranged her dishevelled clothes and sat up on the bed. 'I've been up so many nights,' Chanda replied. 'I was sound asleep.'

And she smiled bashfully.

When he saw that exhausted face and those dry lips parted slightly in a bashful, sad smile, Chetan felt overcome with a flood of compassion, and something made him take her head in his lap and kiss her brow.

2

Chetan kissed his wife and even walked her downstairs and explained to Ma that they had slept late because they were so exhausted by Neela's wedding; he even laughed as he said this, but secretly he couldn't stop himself from feeling annoyed. He was finding it difficult to remain in the house for even a moment. He got ready quickly and went outside.

By the well, he ran into Jagdish, commonly known as Disa—one of the Chowdhrys—walking along foolishly, his mouth agape. Time was, the Chowdhrys had had quite a bit of clout. They'd owned shops selling Muradabadi pots in Chaurasti Atari and made money too; but nowadays Chowdhry Badhawa Ram and his younger brother, Chowdhry Sulakkha Mull, were famous—not just in the mohalla, but throughout the city—for their addiction to opium. Sulakkha Mull had no children and Badhawa Ram had four daughters and two sons. The girls' weddings had broken him, and the boys weren't the least bit educated. Disa was a draughtsman at the court and his younger brother wandered about as a vagrant under the tutelage of Sarna Debu, learning the ropes of hooliganism. Chetan wanted to avoid Disa, but Disa came up and hugged him. 'When did you get home, brother?' he asked.

Chetan hadn't even had time to reply, when Disa added, 'Amichand's become a deputy! The results came out in the papers yesterday. I found out in court.'

'How's your draughtsmanship going?' replied Chetan, as though he hadn't heard him.

But Disa wasn't listening to Chetan. 'Come on, let's congratulate him,' he said, throwing his arm around Chetan as he tried to get him to turn towards the *bhuvara*.[1]

Chetan recalled running into Amichand at Shimla's Scandal Point, where Amichand had behaved as though he'd already become a deputy before the exam results had even come out (Chetan had approached him, crying out, 'Hey, Amichand, what are you doing here?' He'd held out his hand warmly, but in response Amichand had only reluctantly held out two fingers, a far-off smile on his face). Chetan wanted to respond with some biting remark, when Amichand himself appeared, coming from the bhuvara clad in a white shirt and trousers. His neck was a bit stiff and he was gazing straight ahead, as though he could see them, but didn't choose to. If it had been the old days, Chetan would have gone up to him, shaken his hand and congratulated him. But now he just glanced at him quickly and looked away again.

Disa left Chetan and went over to Amichand. Disa wanted to go up to him and embrace him, but the future deputy collector, who'd gone from being known as just 'Amiya' to being called by his full name, Amichand, was now coated in the sort of armour that would rob a mere draughtsman of the courage to attempt such informality. So Disa just said, 'Hello, brother! Congratulations!' and laughed delightedly.

Amichand responded to Disa's hello without looking at him—he just moved his lips slightly—and walked right past without stopping. He didn't think it proper to say anything in response to the congratulations. But Disa followed him. It almost

---

[1] A narrow, dead-end lane.

seemed to Chetan as though Disa were wagging his tail though he didn't have one.

'The bastard is kissing up to him, as if Amichand's going to turn a damn draughtsman into a sub-collector,' joked someone sarcastically behind him.

Chetan turned and looked—Shyama, one of the Jhamans, was coming from the bhuvara. The Jhamans were Brahmins. There were two Brahmin houses at the other end of the bhuvara, a little beyond where Amichand's brother, Amirchand lived. Three Jhaman families lived in the three-storey house, one door of which also opened out into Khoslon ki Gali. The other one-storey house belonged to Pandit Gurdas Ram, whose son, Pyaru, and grandson, Debu, were noted *goondas*, known not just in the neighbourhood, but throughout the city for their thuggishness and hooliganism. The Jhamans were Amichand's neighbours (and therefore hated him), and anyway it had been thus since the very beginning between the neighbourhood's Khatris and Brahmins.

Shyama walked up to him.

'This Amiya hasn't just been made a goddamn deputy, but these people think they're up in heaven now,' he muttered angrily, waving to Chetan as he walked quickly by. 'When he came home last night, Amirchand was saying that when Uncle Telu comes back to the neighbourhood, he'll bust his head open. I'm on my way to Mandi to get Uncle Telu. We'll see whose head gets busted!'

Chetan had returned to Jalandhar after a long absence. He was unaware of the current obsessions. He wanted to stop Shyama and ask him what the dispute was between him and Amirchand but, for one thing, Shyama was in a hurry and, for another, the thought of Amichand and Amirchand vexed him, and besides, he did want to go see his old classmate Anant right now. So he didn't stop Shyama; when Shyama turned towards Harlal Pansari's shop, Chetan went towards Barhaiyan to see Anant.

*

Anant was still lying on the charpoy on the open roof when Chetan woke him. The sound of Chetan's knocking had roused him, but by the time his mother had unfastened the chain and Chetan had made it upstairs, he'd turned over and started dozing again. Chetan shook him when he got there, and Anant wrapped himself in the sheet, adjusted his *tahmad* and sat up, still sprawled out on the charpoy.

'Oh, hi, when did you get back from Shimla?'

'I got here three days ago but it was my sister-in-law's wedding. I went to Basti as soon as I got here! I got back just last evening.'

'So she's deserted you, has she?'

Chetan sat quietly and stared at the open sky. High above, a vulture circled round and round, in tighter and tighter loops with each turn. Chetan followed it with his eyes.

Seeing that this topic was a sore spot for Chetan, Anant changed the subject. He laughed slightly and asked, 'How was Shimla? Did you see Amichand there . . . ?'

Chetan's gaze was still fixed on the vulture. 'It was great!' he responded distantly, as though from way up in the sky where the great bird circled. He didn't respond to the part about Amichand.

'He won the competition!'

Chetan stared up at the sky.

'So how is your "Mahatma" anyway?'

'Which Mahatma?' asked Chetan suddenly, turning his gaze from the sky.

'You know, that doctor, Kaviraj Ramdas, the one you were so full of praise for after you first met him that you dedicated your book to him . . .'

18

Anant hadn't even finished what he was saying when Chetan chuckled, 'Oh, that Mahatma . . .' He was about to use an obscenity, but his eye suddenly fell upon Anant's mother standing close by, her hands on her hips.

'Hello, Aunty, how are you?' he turned and asked her with a rueful laugh.

'My, my,' she said. 'You just spent three months in Shimla but you look even sicklier than before!'

Chetan wanted to curse the weather in Shimla with a few 'sweet words' but all he said was, 'No, Aunty, the weather there isn't beneficial to everyone; the air is quite heavy. I lost my appetite completely, and my stomach was always bad.'

'Then rest here a few days; you've come home from a high mountain. Your cheeks are sunken.'

'He's fine,' said Anant. Turning to Chetan, he said, 'What our mothers and sisters think is, if you say someone looks healthy you'll invite the evil eye, so they'll say a buffalo looks healthy if it looks as thin as a blade of grass.' And he chuckled.

But Anant's mother felt she'd done her duty, and went back down the hallway without listening to her son's critique.

Chetan felt as though he needed Aunty's sympathy more than Anant's sarcasm. The three months of life in Shimla spun before him . . . when he'd bathed outside in the cold and worked day and night, sometimes deep into the night in that close, dark room. All the walking he did was from home to the dhaba, or from the dhaba to home, especially on those days when he was busy writing Kaviraj's book for him . . . and his health really hadn't been good.

'No, my health has actually got worse,' he said sadly. 'Aunty is right.'

And sitting there, Chetan told Anant the entire story of his stay in Shimla.

Anant chuckled even louder.

19

'You're an old fool!' he cried. He paused for a moment, then asked, 'What happened to that story collection of yours, the one you were going to publish with Kaviraj's help, which you wanted to dedicate to him?'

'The very first thing I'm going to do when I get back to Lahore is tear up that dedication.'

'Then how will you get it published?'

'Even if the story collection doesn't get published for the rest of my life, I still won't take his help, nor will I dedicate it to him.' He stood up.

Anant stood up as well. 'Sit here for five minutes,' he said. 'I'll just get ready. I have to go to Chowk Sudan. I'll go with you as far as Atari.'

Just then Aunty returned and asked, 'Do you want lassi or milk?'

Before Chetan could say anything, Anant had draped a towel around his shoulders and, stopping on his way to the bathroom, he called back, 'No, Ma, we'll get lassis at Ramditta's shop. Don't worry about it!'

'You've come back after so many days, you will stay for a while, won't you?' asked Aunty, her hand on her hip.

'No, Aunty, I would have left today, but Ma said my father might come home today. So I'll just stay for one day. But I'm leaving tomorrow.'

'Oh yes, you're a Lahorite now, what do you care for Jalandhar these days?'

And Aunty returned to the kitchen. It was hard for Chetan to remain sitting there. He began to stroll around the roof, but after making just one round, he felt alarmed . . . His thoughts were again caught up in a storm, so he went into the kitchen to extricate himself from them. Aunty had filled a ladle with ghee and onions and was holding them over the fire, waiting for

20

them to turn red. Chetan's eyes were glued to the onions as they slowly swelled, then turned red around the edges, then dried up and turned brown, as though it were something he'd never seen happen before, while Aunty told him of her back pain, so when Anant arrived, Chetan heaved a sigh of relief and stood up.

3

'Oh, hello there, Chetan bhai, how are you?'

Chetan turned and saw that it was Badda.

He and Anant had come out from Khoslon ki Gali and were walking towards the bazaar when Badda leapt forward, slapped Chetan on the shoulder with his wide hand and asked how he was doing. Chetan was not in the mood to run into Badda. He felt quite distracted. Anant had to go to Chowk Sudan and Chetan had thought he would go meet up with old friends and, if possible, take a turn through Puriyan Mohalla and Kot Kishanchand as well.

'When did you get back from Shimla?' asked Badda.

Chetan stopped. 'So, Badda, how are you?' he asked.

Badda's real name was Nihalchand. He was around the same height as Chetan, but with a slightly broader build, a wide forehead and salt-and-pepper hair, despite his youth. He wore a dirty kameez and patched tahmad.

'Great, thanks,' he said, smiling slightly.

'So, did you take the Matric again this year?' asked Chetan.

'Did he take it!' retorted Anant, with a mischievous laugh. 'This fool actually did something amazing. He passed in the second division.' And he gave Badda an appreciative slap on the back.

Badda grinned widely. Chetan was just about to congratulate him when someone called out from behind: 'Ask him his roll number.'

The three of them turned around and saw Hansa of the Jhamans, who lived in the same gali as Badda.

'Why, it's 4229!' blurted Badda.

'And Debu Kana says you said it was 4226 at first. When he asked around and found out that was someone else's number, you told him it was 4229.'

Suddenly Badda stopped. He grimaced, his nostrils flared, his lips began to tremble and, cursing Debu Kana fulsomely, he cried out, 'That mother— is lying!'

They had turned from the gali towards the bazaar, where Ramditta the sweet-seller's shop sat right across from Harlal Pansari's grocery. Actually, in Kallowani Mohalla, there were three galis, two chowks, and one long, wide gali, through the middle of which flowed a narrow drain. This gali turned to the left at the end of Bajiyanwala Bazaar. Ramditta's sweet shop was right at the beginning of the gali, to one side, and Harlal Pansari's shop was on the other side. There were two more shops after those two, in which only Harlal Pansari's goods—sacks of grain, canisters of ghee and oil, etc.—were stored. The first chowk was called Andon (short for Anandon). This was where Chetan's home was. From there, the gali grew rather narrow and curved to the right. At the beginning there was a kiln, where Jwali Mehri roasted chickpeas and corn kernels. A little beyond this, to the left, was a long closed gali, Khoslon ki Gali, where Badda lived, and beyond that, along the right side for quite some distance, all the way to Barne Pir, were a series of walls, the backs of Muslim homes, none of which had doors that opened on to that side of the gali. After Khoslon ki Gali, to the left, there was a house where two families lived. In one section lived a widow who had five sons. Since the widow was very quarrelsome, the people in the neighbourhood called her *Gidhari*, or 'the Vulture', and they called her children, 'the Vulture's Children'. In the other house was another widow, but she was remarried. Her husband was an ordinary superintendent, but she had been a child widow, from an important family. She'd moved to the mohalla after her remarriage. She was educated, dark-skinned and had a beautiful singing voice, so people called her *Koyal*, or 'the Cuckoo'. She had three daughters and two sons, all of whom were called 'the Cuckoo's Children'. Next to this house was Barhaiyon ki Gali, at the start of which was Anant's home. A bit farther ahead, to the right, beneath a large neem tree, was the tomb of Barne Pir, the arch of which was built into the wall. There were sconces here for small clay lamps, and at night devotees would light many lamps at once. Chowk Chaddhiyan was to the left. The gali on the other side passed by the houses of this chowk and met up with the bazaar. From Barne Pir, a road went straight through the Muslim mohalla and came out into Chowk Qadeshah. Right here in Chowk Chaddhiyan, directly across from Barne Pir, was the home of the astrologer Daulat Ram, whose son Debu was the neighbourhood's most famous goonda. He was a bit squinty-eyed so he was also called Debu Kana, or 'Squint-Eye Debu'. Beyond Barne Pir, where the street curved above the chowk, was the gali where an old classmate of Chetan's, Laloo Baniya, lived; this had come to be called 'Baniyon ki Gali'.

Arriving at Ramditta's shop, Chetan ordered half a paav of barfi and asked the sweet seller to make him two large glasses of lassi, requesting that he beat the cream well, then add the ice and water.

Chetan placed the dish of barfi in front of Anant, then popped a piece into his own mouth and looked Badda over from head to toe. He wanted to ask Hansa and Anant why they were bugging this poor guy, but couldn't say anything in front of Badda.

'Yesterday Laloo Baniya was saying that the number 4229 didn't even appear in the paper,' observed Anant, as he popped the bits of barfi into his mouth. He glanced at Chetan and added, 'You work for a newspaper, yaar, did you see roll number 4229 in the Matric results?'

'What are you talking about!' Chetan nearly retorted. 'Does a newspaper editor remember all the roll numbers?' But he saw a glint of mischief in Anant's eyes; Anant looked over at Chetan and winked subtly.

'It was! How could it not be?' cried Badda. 'I'll go get it and show you.' And he ran off toward his gali.

Chetan watched him running off, then laughed slightly and said, 'Badda is exactly the same; he hasn't changed a bit, except in terms of passing.'

'Who says the bastard passed?' asked Hansa of the Jhamans, chuckling loudly. 'When Badda took the exam this time, he didn't even tell his mother his roll number. When the Matric results came out he went to his mother and told her the good news— that he'd passed in the second division. His mother can't tell the difference between A and B. Her eyes danced with joy. "Your name is in the paper?" she asked. "Not my name, my roll number is printed right here," Badda told her. "Look at this, it's my roll number!" And the fool put his finger somewhere on the list. His mother borrowed a rupee from the Khoslas and distributed sweets to the whole neighbourhood.'

'The son of the whore and the smuggler's horse, both overeat and are lazy of course!' interjected Ramditta, thereby enriching their knowledge with a fresh saying as he churned the lassi, a look of boredom permanently affixed to his face. Though he laughed as he spoke, the boredom continued to cling to his person.

No one paid him any mind. 'You know Debu Kana, that son of a bitch,' said Anant. 'Somehow he found out that the roll number Badda said was his actually belonged to someone else. Who knows if he actually found it out or was just bluffing, but Badda immediately changed his story and said he hadn't said that number at all.'

Hansa of the Jhamans guffawed at this and clapped his hands together.

*

Badda was two years older than Chetan and had studied two grades ahead of him in the same school. His mother, Prasanni (Prasann Kumari), had become a widow when she was young and, like the other widows, she had great faith in holy men. She had numerous brothers-in-faith. Partly with their help, and partly by her earnings spinning and skeining cotton, she managed to educate her son, and she dreamt of making him an important officer one day. In her view, this boy of hers was brighter and wiser than all the other boys in the mohalla. As she sat in the gali and spun or skeined cotton with her neighbours, Badda would sit in his own doorway or a neighbour's, and amaze her and the other ladies with his dazzling intelligence. He remembered everything: who was born when in the mohalla; who married when; who died when—all the days, dates and times of all incidents and accidents. He knew the train schedules, the dates of holidays, the comings and goings of the mohalla, everything about everything. Often, when the date of some holiday or some incident or accident in the mohalla would be in doubt or a topic of debate, Badda would demonstrate his point with proof, and his mother and neighbours would be astonished at the brilliance of his intellect and memory. He had no shortcomings whatsoever and his mother liked to say that Nihalchand was a boy who was like the girls. There was no doubt about this. All day long he sat with his mother and her friends, and his mother would periodically praise this or that fine quality of his. So when he failed the Matric the first time and told his mother that his paper had been very good, but that he'd had a fight with the invigilator who either hadn't sent his paper forward or put a blank notebook in its place, his mother immediately believed him and announced to all the neighbourhood that her boy would have passed with very good scores but that the 'ingilator' (Badda's mother was very fond of using English words she'd heard from her son in conversation) had made enemies with him and switched his notebook.

But Badda stayed back the second year as well. That time he'd saddled his school teachers with all the blame, saying they were against him and didn't instruct him properly. He told his mother he wouldn't pay fees to the school any more, and instead take the exam privately; he'd pass in the first division and show everyone. And from then on, he'd either studied at home or sat among the gali women. From then on his nickname became Badda.

He took his first private exam the same year that Chetan took the Matric. In the English paper, there was a story filled with blank spaces, and one was to fill them in to complete the story. The gist of the story was *'Ram rakkhe use kaun chakkhe'*—or, no harm shall come to him whom God protects—and it went something like this:

Prince Hira Singh was defeated by his enemies in a fierce battle and fled. On his way home, his horse died. Night had fallen, so he hid in a mountain cave. His enemies came and searched for him, but, thanks be to God, in the midst of this, a spider had woven a web over the mouth of the cave. Two enemy soldiers came to the cave as well. One proposed searching for the prince inside the cave, but the other, on seeing the web by the light of his torch, rejected the proposal, saying that if the prince had gone in, the web would have been broken. They went off to look for him elsewhere instead and the prince's life was saved.

In the textbook from which this story had been taken, there had also been printed a dialogue between a spider and a fly. The spider spins a beautiful web and calls out to the fly, praising its beautiful wings and enchanting voice, but the fly does not get caught in the web.

In the evening, when Chetan had seen Badda at Ramditta's shop, he'd asked him, 'How did your paper go?'

Badda grinned widely and slapped his hand on Chetan's, saying, 'It was so easy. There was that conversation between the spider and the fly. I answered that question first. I bet I got at least nine points out of ten on that one.' (Badda had read the word 'spider' and written his answer based on that. How he'd answered the rest of the questions, one can only imagine.)

Chetan smiled to himself at this, but he shook Badda's hand warmly nevertheless and only replied, 'You killed it, yaar, I just wrote out the story of Prince Hira Singh.'

Chetan told Anant and his other classmates what Badda had done. They had taken the Matric exam at the same time. All of them slapped Badda on the back and assured him that his paper would be the very best of all, and all of them had just given the wrong answers, and Badda told his mother the news and Badda's mother joyfully told the women of Khoslon ki Gali the news, and from that day on, she began to light lamps at Barne Pir.

But Badda failed that year as well.

After that, he entered all the schools in Jalandhar and tried to do the Matric, but the year Chetan did his BA, he failed yet again. This was the eighth year he had taken the exam. He had no job and his primary occupation was sitting among his mother's friends expressing his priceless views on mohalla politics and enhancing the knowledge of the gali women on numerous topics as well as performing small chores for them. In the gali, he was famous for being a 'son-like-a-daughter', and in Andon Chowk, for being 'more womanly than the women', but he was perfectly happy and didn't care about either of these epithets. In the meantime, he'd acquired skill in cards and *chaupar* and usually he joined up with card and chaupar games at Laloo Baniya's house, at Pandit Banarsidas's shop, in the chowk at Papadiyan Bazaar, or on the open cement platform in front of the Shiva temple at the Dharamshala. No hero's eyes could have shown greater concentration than Badda's as he dodged the blows of his enemies while playing cards and chaupar.

*

Ramditta had finished making the lassi and given a glass each to Chetan and Anant, then began to scrape the pot with a spatula.

Hansa of the Jhamans was saying, 'The funny thing is that the results came so many months ago, but the fool never even shows anyone his certificate. Uncle Telu Ram talked to Lala Jalandhari Mull Yogi ji and arranged a job for him, he praised Badda and also said he'd passed the Matric in the second division, but when Lala Jalandhari Mull asked for the certificate, Badda never showed his face there again.'

'Look! Did my roll number get printed in the newspaper or not?' Badda called out from the bend in the gali.

Chetan drank down his lassi and placed the glass to one side, then picked up the newspaper to take a look. It was an old copy of the *Tribune*, very carefully folded. One spot on the list of private roll numbers for the Matric had been marked in red pencil. Chetan read it: it was number 4229.

'Look, does it say 4229 or not?' asked Badda, pointing at the number again and again.

Although just a few minutes before, he himself had wanted to tell Anant to stop teasing the poor guy, Chetan put out his hand. 'Congratulations,' he said.

Badda grinned widely as he grasped Chetan's hand in both of his. His nostrils flared and his eyes shone; he glanced very proudly at Hansa.

'Take this newspaper and show it to Amichand; if he becomes a magistrate, he'll make you his record keeper,' suggested Hansa sarcastically.

'And you won't even need a certificate,' added Anant.

'I'll show him, I'll show him, why not?' responded Badda, sticking out his neck defiantly.

'Oh, even if he made you a chaprasi, that would really be something.'

And everyone guffawed.

Just then, Ramditta jumped down from his shop, cursing, and ran after someone in the direction of Chowk Kharadiyan, still holding his metal spatula dripping with milk.

'What happened?' Chetan asked Anant.

But Anant didn't know himself.

Everyone dashed off in that direction.

4

Chetan had seen Ramditta sitting at this same shop ever since he
could remember. In the past few years, the hair at his temples had
grown white, the boredom on his face had increased, and one of
his front teeth had weakened and broken, but otherwise the rest
was all the same—his round cap jammed down on his head, his
coarse, filthy, too-short pyjamas stitched from the same fabric,
his legs that turned out slightly like the points of a compass from
sitting all day, his strangely stiff back and his awkward gait . . . his
entire person bore a striking resemblance to his clothing. Chetan
couldn't imagine Chacha Ramditta wearing anything else.

Chetan had called Ramditta 'Chacha', or 'Uncle', since his
childhood. This was partly because he too was a Brahmin and
partly because his mother had taught him and his brothers that
whoever was the same age as their father or two or three years
younger than him in their mohalla should be called 'Chacha'.
Since he called him Chacha, he also felt a sense of kinship with
him, and when people teased Ramditta, he didn't like it.

But just as he had ribbed Badda without even really wanting
to, in the same way, despite calling Ramditta 'Chacha', and feeling
sympathy for him, Chetan sometimes joined in on the jokes being
played on him.

Since his childhood, he had heard many things about
Ramditta's past that were etched in his mind. The first was that

Ramditta's wife had been very beautiful and innocent. Ramditta had beaten her a great deal, but when their first child was born (the baby was stillborn) and she fell ill from post-partum fever and died, he had pounded his head against the walls and cried like a baby. The other was that when he began to try to get remarried, Pandit Gurdas Ram had interfered. What happened was that Ramditta had hoped to remarry sooner, but since there weren't any elders in his home, no one insisted, and then, when people did come to see him a couple of times thanks to Harlal's efforts, Pandit Gurdas Ram had said things that not only stopped that particular marriage but future ones as well. The door to marriage was shut forever for the poor man.

Chetan was very young when he heard this story about Ramditta from his mother, and ever since then he'd felt a strange loathing towards Pandit Gurdas Ram.

*

Pandit Gurdas Ram had four sons. The eldest, who had died recently, had lived in Bilga (from whence his paternal grandfather had come to Jalandhar). The second was an astrologer; the third had passed the Matric and become an employee at the audit office in Delhi; and the fourth was a goonda famous not just in the mohalla but throughout the entire city.

Pandit Gurdas Ram was of medium height and extremely muscular. He was fair, with large round eyes. He always held a stout *lathi*, a wooden staff, in his hands. Chetan had heard from his mother that he was quite adept with a lathi. He was rather old by then, and Chetan had never seen his lathi feats, but he'd heard from his mother that he had once walked in a groom's procession with his patrons, when thieves had surrounded them. Pandit Gurdas Ram had single-handedly confronted them with his lathi and not only saved the groom's party from getting robbed, but also wounded several of the attackers. Pandit Gurdas Ram would sometimes come and sit at Harlal Pansari's shop with his lathi in the evenings and Chetan would glance at him and imagine those days when he wielded the lathi with such force.

Ordinarily, Chetan should have felt respectful on hearing of great feats of bravery, but for one thing, he loathed Pandit Gurdas Ram's two sons—the astrologer Daulat Ram and Pyare Lal (who was known by the name 'Pyaru Goonda', or Pyaru the Hooligan)—and for another, ever since he'd heard about how he'd stopped poor Ramditta from getting married, a seed of resentment towards the elderly lathi aficionado had grown in his mind.

*

This seed might not have grown into a tree if he hadn't seen him at a Brahmin feast eating as though he'd been hungry since birth.

*

Chetan had heard many stories from his Khatri friends of Brahmins eating four or five seers of kheer each. It was perhaps for this reason that the Brahmins were called dogs by the Khatris, but he had never believed it, thinking instead that it was simply due to the enmity which was common between the two castes. No one in Chetan's home was a heavy eater. Alcoholism had dried up his father's hunger, but his father's father, his Dada, who had lived in the country his entire life and was quite hearty, never ate more than four chapatis with his meals. Although his great-grandmother Gangadei had fulfilled all priestly obligations, Chetan's Dada was a patwari and his father a station master, so priestly duties had more or less stopped in his family. Chetan's mother didn't care for accepting priestly alms either. One reason for this was that on holidays, the Khatris gave out as alms to the Brahmins whatever fruits were wasted or leftover in the bazaar, or whatever cloth or pots were selling cheap. (Chetan's mother believed in always giving high-quality donations and when she gave alms, she gave everything to just one household so that the children could eat until they were full, unlike the Khatris of the mohalla, who gave out just one piece of fruit to each Brahmin household.) Secondly, Chetan's mother thought that eating second-rate food given as alms made the intellect second-rate as well. On festival days when portions of feast food came for the children, Ma made excuses on their behalf as much as she could. But Dada said that one should partake in such feasts respectfully; if one didn't, people would say that the Brahmins had grown snooty just because they'd started earning a bit of money.

In the gali of the Baniyas there was a man named Ruldu who used to serve a feast to the Brahmins with great devotion during Shraddha, and all the voracious Brahmins in the city longed for an invitation. He was delighted to feed high-born and non-greedy Brahmins and he always made sure to invite Dada, who never turned him down. One time, when Chetan was perhaps studying in class six, Ruldu had invited him along with Dada. Chetan had heard so much praise for Ruldu that he was quite eager to see for himself what the feast at his house was all about.

Ruldu's house was right where Baniya Gali meets the bazaar. Small seats were set up on a porch inside the doorway, across a small courtyard. Ruldu stood in the doorway with a pot and bucket. Whenever Brahmins came, he would wash their feet with his own hands and bring them to the porch and seat them.

Large metal plates were set out before them. The first course to arrive was a small shining brass bucket of full of kheer. For some reason, Chetan had a great aversion to kheer, so he took only one ladleful. But yes, he certainly did notice that the kheer was very handsomely made—the fragrance of basmati rice and pure ghee rose from it, there was less rice than usual, and the milk was creamy like *rabri*. After eating a couple of spoonfuls of kheer, he began to watch the other feasters. When the server with the bucket of kheer reached Pandit Gurdas Ram, and he started to ladle the kheer on his plate, Chetan watched with astonishment as Pandit Gurdas Ram asked, 'Do you only feed Brahmins kheer with ladles?' He grabbed the bucket from his hand and poured the whole thing on to his plate. When his plate was completely full, he handed back the empty bucket and began enthusiastically slurping up the kheer, shovelling it into his mouth with his entire hand.

Chetan was quite offended at how loudly he ate. When the guests had finished the kheer and began to eat puris and vegetables, Pandit Gurdas Ram took a second helping of kheer.

Chetan sat and waited for the feast to end a long time after he'd finished his puris, so he could receive his ceremonial donation and thereby enrich his savings (which he was collecting in order to buy a toy on Diwali) by one anna. For him that one anna was much more important than the entire feast.

He assumed that Pandit Gurdas Ram would stand up now that he'd finished off the kheer. Maybe he wouldn't eat puris and vegetable *tarkari*. But his astonishment knew no bounds when after eating so much kheer, Pandit Gurdas Ram consumed ten puris and didn't pay the slightest heed to the jokes and teasing from the others waiting for him to finish.

Chetan dozed off as he sat and waited. He awoke with a start when Pandit Gurdas Ram belched upon the completion of his meal, thinking it must be the sound of an ox belching. Then Pandit Gurdas Ram got up rubbing his belly, and belched even more loudly as he smoothed out his large white moustaches with a greasy hand.

There was something about that gesture that inspired in Chetan a strong loathing for him, and he decided, above all, that he would never again attend a feast, and if Dada forced him to, he'd find out first whether Pandit Gurdas Ram was invited or not.

But slowly, Ma convinced Dada that going to feasts was unbecoming to the honour of his son, and so Chetan escaped this misfortune.

*

As far as Ramditta's engagement went, Ma told him that a couple of Brahmins had come to Jalandhar from the town of Bilga with a proposal. Harlal Pansari had praised Ramditta's gentlemanliness greatly and they had even given him the shagun, but because Pandit Gurdas Ram's son lived in Bilga as well, they thought it right to greet him on their way back.

When Pandit Gurdas Ram found out that they had given their daughter's shagun to Ramditta, he acted very pleased. He grinned widely and said, 'You did very well, the poor fellow's been a widower some four years now, and if he gets married, Daulat's [his elder son, Daulat Ram's] wife will get some rest.' And he explained to the newcomers that the two of them lived in two parts of the same house, and informed them that Daulat and his wife had tried to help Ramditta get married many times, with no success.

'Why, is there something wrong with him?' one member of the party suddenly asked.

'Well, gentlemanliness and innocence can be flaws as well,' Pandit remarked philosophically. 'What use is so much gentility when he suffers a financial loss every year?'

'But Harlal says . . .' one of the Bilga people began.

'Why wouldn't he?' Pandit Gurdas Ram interrupted. 'He's lent so much money to Ramditta. He won't be free of that shop in this lifetime. Yes, if he gets married and sells off the jewellery from the dowry, there is a chance.'

And Pandit Gurdas Ram laughed slightly. 'What can I tell you? Ramditta is such an honest man. But Daulat once told me he has some flaw in his blood. When he got married, I told him he should get himself cured. Our Pandit Shyam Ratan is a great hakim; he even said he'd give him a couple of pills and he'd get better. But he didn't pay me any heed, and see—not only did the child die, but the wife passed away as well.'

Pandit Gurdas Ram laughed again at Ramditta's foolishness.

'So did he get cured or not?' asked one of the Bilga men. His tone was oddly anxious.

'He won't do it,' said Pandit Gurdas Ram laughing. 'He's so innocent, he thinks the death of his child and wife were acts of God . . . Oh yes, brother, sure, they're acts of God, but God also gave us this "brain" we've got in our skulls so we can use it.'

And after those Bilga Brahmins touched Pandit Gurdas Ram's feet and left, they never returned again. Ramditta had to stop right in the middle of his wedding preparations. Around a year later, they found out that same girl was getting married to Pandit Gurdas Ram's nephew.

*

There was nothing about Ramditta's appearance that would excite much love towards him, but for some reason Chetan felt a deep sympathy and affection for him. It might have been his meekness, or his deep conscientiousness (which made him never dilute the milk in the slightest and ready to fight anyone who accused him of such—the boys of the mohalla only did it to tease him), or his foolishness which always made him lose money; Chetan had never analysed it. But he was fond of him.

Once Ramditta's engagement was broken, no other matches came for him. The syphilis rumour that Pandit Gurdas Ram had started spread so far afield that no family ever came with a proposal again.

'Who knows if he's even ill,' Ma had remarked, bringing up the topic of Ramditta one day. 'If he had any such illness, it's been so many years, it won't break out again.' And referring to Pandit Gurdas Ram's bad deed, she remarked sadly, 'Brahmin against Brahmin, dog against dog.'

But this wasn't just a Brahmin flaw. The people of Jalandhar's Kallowani Mohalla were like the man who punches himself in the eye to create a bad omen for his neighbour. Every last one of them was mired in the same filth and they couldn't stand to see anyone rise above it or flourish. If two wanted to come together, there were always four to break them apart. This was not just the case with the Brahmins, but with the Khatris as well; if a proposal came for someone, everyone else would do their best to ensure it didn't come to fruition. They'd praise the boy in front of everyone, grinning widely, but in private conversation they'd pass a couple of remarks regarding the boy's intelligence or character, or the mother's bad character, or the father's financial situation, in order to sow the seeds of doubt in the minds of those bringing the proposal. This was why the elders always made matches secretly. But Ramditta's parents had died when he was still a child. He had no elders to speak accurately on his behalf. Harlal Pansari felt sympathetic towards him (perhaps because he was his neighbour, or because Ramditta was so innocent) but despite his best efforts, Ramditta simply could not get married.

As he grew older, Ramditta's desire to start a family grew day by day. The people of the mohalla frequently managed to steal his milk and cream for months on end by promising to arrange his marriage. And despite having been robbed before, he'd go ahead and do it again.

Whoever felt like robbing him would just come to his shop and sit, and casually drink a lassi or eat some pakoras a couple of times, then ask in the course of conversation, 'So, Chacha Ramditta [strangely, even people his age called him "Chacha"], how old are you?'

'I turned twenty-nine last January,' he'd say.

And then the person would express sadness that Ramditta hadn't yet remarried and advise him that he should, with a few sayings in Hindi and Punjabi such as: 'A house is only happy with a wife'; 'Without a wife, a house becomes haunted'; 'Brief is the distance between a bachelor and a madman.'

That day, Ramditta would mix plenty of extra cream in the man's milk or lassi, or fry his pakoras extra crispy.

Then a few days later, the person would tell him that the daughter of his distant relation (or friend) had come of age, and that he thought it would be wonderful if Ramditta married her. From that day on, Ramditta would stop taking money from him altogether.

A month or two later, Harlal Pansari, who kept track of Ramditta's accounts due to the loan he'd given him, would get wind of this. Not only would he scold him, he'd also ask the mohalla man what he was doing stealing from a poor man.

But Ramditta would end up getting robbed again, despite putting his hand to his ear and swearing not to do it again.

His desire to remarry was so powerful and he was so cheered at the slightest hope, that one time when Chetan's mother had casually asked him how old he was, out of sympathy, and he had said that last January he'd turned twenty-nine, and Ma, praising the beauty and accomplishment of his first wife had said that he should get remarried now, Chetan noticed that that day, Ramditta had added an extra paav of milk to the daily seer for no reason.

This weakness of his was known not just to the mohalla's adults, but also to all the children. Chetan himself had once casually asked him, 'Hey, Chacha Ramditta, how old must you be by now?'

'I'm six years younger than your father,' he replied.

This was his style of replying to boys. He'd mention the boy's father, or uncle, or older brother, and tell them that he was twenty-nine or thirty.

But as he grew older and began to lose money by giving out free milk and pakoras, Harlal finally sat him down in the quiet of his warehouse and explained that he had no well-wishers in the entire mohalla. These people would drink his lassi and his milk, they'd eat his pakoras, but they would not give him their daughters or sisters to marry. 'Look, you won't get married this way. Let me do your book-keeping for a few years. Right now I look over your books sometimes to get my money back, but from now on, I'm going to watch your accounts until you've saved up three or four hundred rupees.'

When Ramditta asked what would happen to that money, Harlal explained to him, 'Look, you're my age. If I'm thirty-nine, then you must be thirty-nine too. As long as these people from the mohalla are around, they won't give you a young unwed girl, but if you spend three or four hundred rupees, you can get a child widow from a widow ashram.'

Ramditta was now so eager to get married that he immediately agreed, and for the next three years, he turned over all his earnings to Harlal. Not just that, he stopped indulging the freeloaders. If some thief brought up a girl with him, he would tell him to go and talk to Harlal. And slowly people stopped asking his age and suggesting new proposals.

When Chetan was studying in his first year of college, he heard one day that Ramditta had brought home a new bride. Ma told him the good news the moment he came home, and he immediately put down his books and ran over to the bazaar. On his way home from college, he hadn't even paid attention to what was going on there.

Ramditta was not at his shop. Chetan was walking back when he saw him coming from Chowk Chaddhiyan. He was walking along jauntily, wearing a Stetson and new long-cloth pyjamas.

'Congratulations, Chacha Ramditta!' Chetan cried out.

Ramditta grinned in response, and Chetan liked seeing his smile despite the one broken tooth.

'Here you've brought home a new bride and you haven't even fed us any laddu!'

'I'll bring you some, I'll bring you some. You go home, I'll bring some right away.'

And Chetan had just washed his face and hands and started to eat when Ramditta arrived with a tray full of laddus.

'I've brought them to you very first of all,' he said laughing.

*

But this marriage did not agree with Ramditta. Less than two months had gone by since he'd brought his new wife home after paying the widow ashram three hundred rupees. One day, after noticing that his shop had been closed for several days, Chetan asked Harlal about him and learned that Ramditta was very ill.

Chetan was quite eager to see this new wife of Ramditta's. Although a child widow had previously married into the mohalla

43

among the Khatris (though they only learned this years later), and one of the Khatris' young widows had with great fanfare set up house with her younger brother-in-law, the superstitious mohalla was generally against widow remarriage. Although the women of the mohalla had secretly found out about Ramditta's wife, no one had openly gone to meet her. Even Chetan's mother didn't think it right that a widow had come to his house.

One Sunday, when he had the day off, Chetan decided he'd go and see Ramditta after lunch. He'd forgotten to ask Harlal what illness afflicted Ramditta. It was summer, and it hadn't started raining yet, so seasonal illnesses such as smallpox, typhoid, dysentery, cholera and other such things had spread throughout the city; or maybe Ramditta, after hungering for a wife so long, had overdone it. The Punjabi saying came to Chetan's mind:

A poor Jat found a cup
Too much water so he drank
His belly bloated up
He fell down with a clank

Perhaps Ramditta was in the same state as that poor man.

The first house in Chowk Chaddhiyan in front of Barne Pir was Ramditta's. Actually, the astrologer Daulat Ram lived with his family in the front section, with windows opening towards Barne Pir, and Ramditta lived at the rear. The doorway of the house opened on to the chowk. When Chetan got upstairs after feeling his way along the darkened doorway and up the even darker stairway, he saw that Ramditta lay on the charpoy in his room. There was a string of pearl jasmine around his neck, another hung from the head of his bed, and another was tied to the neck of the clay pot lying nearby, and Ramditta was moaning with high fever.

Ramditta was very happy when he saw that Chetan had come to inquire about his sickness. He motioned for him to sit. Chetan quietly sat down on the edge of the charpoy.

'Tell me, Chacha, how is your health?' he asked.

Ramditta shook his head to indicate that he was in poor shape. He ran his tongue over his dry lips.

'What's wrong?' asked Chetan.

Speaking slowly between moans, and using gestures, Ramditta told him he'd had a high fever for many days. Today Choti Mata had graced his throat. It was *motijhara*.

Chetan realized Ramditta had typhoid. In typhoid, tiny pearl-like bumps break out in the throat. The people of the mohalla called this Choti Mata or motijhara, and just as they did nothing to cure smallpox, they did nothing for this either. They simply performed a ceremony to appease the goddess, or Mata, with garlands of pearl jasmine and put the same garlands on the patient.

'Your Chachi has taken very good care of me,' said Ramditta, looking to the left. 'If it weren't for her, I would have died. She saved me.'

Chetan glanced in the direction Ramditta had glanced. To the left, in the dim light, sat a very ugly middle-aged woman on a stool. Chetan pressed his hands together in greeting from where he was sitting.

But all of his enthusiasm was destroyed. For some reason he had been eager for Ramditta's wife to be extremely beautiful. Perhaps because he'd heard so much from Ma about how beautiful his first wife had been, he hadn't pictured him with an ugly wife (although Ramditta himself was extremely ugly). And seeing this woman who called to mind the saying 'Camel, oh camel, what part of your body is straight?', he felt disgusted and vexed, and after talking about this and that for a little while, he stood up.

'If you need anything, let me know and I'll bring it over,' he said. He murmured a sort of farewell to Ramditta's wife and left. When he got near Barne Pir he stopped under the cool shade of the neem tree and took a long breath of freedom.

And Ramditta was not yet altogether healthy, he'd just started to go and sit at the shop again, when one day, he went home to eat and came back beating his head. He told Harlal he'd been robbed. Not only had his wife herself run away, but she'd taken all the clothing and jewellery with her.

Harlal scolded him, reminding him he'd told him not to show his new wife the clothing and jewels of his first wife until he'd been married a few years; why had he given her the jewels?

Then Ramditta told him weeping that he hadn't shown her any of his first wife's things initially, but she'd cared for him like an angel during his illness and this had overwhelmed him with gratitude, so he'd brought out his first wife's clothing and jewels and placed them at her feet.

'Then what are you crying for? When you don't listen to reason of course you'll get cheated!' replied Harlal angrily.

Despite his anger, he felt sorry for Ramditta's state and did his best to find the 'child widow' for him, but she was nowhere to be found. They went to look at the widow ashram, but learned it was a travelling ashram; they arranged four or five marriages in one city, then packed their bags, pulled down their signboard and set off for another.

This incident affected Ramditta so strongly that it cured his obsession with remarrying. He again owed Harlal two hundred or so rupees, so he quietly got back to work without talking to anyone about it. He wouldn't answer anyone's questions, and if anyone asked about his second wife, he'd start swearing at them.

In the midst of this, the boys of the mohalla learned that now Ramditta turned irritable when asked about his age—he'd pick up his spatula or his ladle and chase after them—so they'd found a new method for amusement. The more annoyed he got, the more fun the boys had teasing him.

After having his home thus destroyed for a second time, a helpless look clung about his face. His lips hung slightly open, his broken front tooth looking quite hideous, and his face was twisted into a permanent grimace.

*

As he followed Ramditta towards Chowk Kharadiyan, the past few years passed through Chetan's mind, and he had only just entered the gali when he saw Ramditta walking back, twisting the ear of a small boy with one hand and threatening to spank him with the spatula in his other hand.

'What happened, Chacha?' asked Anant suddenly.

'This son of a bitch is asking my age,' said Ramditta irritably. 'Why don't you ask if he's planning to give me his sister or his mother?' And he quoted a Punjabi saying as he twisted the boy's ear: 'Some people think they're born knowing everything.'

He was about to spank him with his spatula, when a boy cried out from behind, in Chowk Kharadiyan:

'Hey, how old are you, Chacha Ramditta?'

Ramditta let go of the first boy and ran after the second one. But the other boy ran into the gali and perhaps went and hid in his house.

Ramditta couldn't catch him and when he returned, he was cursing the boy and all his ancestors before him. In the meantime, the milk had boiled over the sides of the pot. Someone yelled to him from the shop, so he stopped chasing the boys and rushed back. When he arrived, he sprinkled the boiling milk with drops of water and sat down, cursing like a sailor at those boys and their parents, and began stirring the pot again with his spatula.

*

Although the others were enjoying Ramditta's irritation, Chetan was filled with a strange combination of pity and aversion. He paid Ramditta for the lassi and barfi and walked toward Chaurasti Atari, pulling Anant along with him.

5

'If Ramditta's shop weren't at the entrance to the gali, the boys wouldn't even bother,' said Anant, walking along with Chetan. 'He curses at them four or five times a day. These damn boys keep coming after him.' He smiled widely, perhaps at the thought of Ramditta's foolishness. But Chetan had fallen completely silent. His heart, heavy since morning, felt even heavier.

Anant kept talking about Ramditta's eccentricity and his idiocy, but Chetan, despite hearing his words, wasn't really listening. He responded, 'Unh huh, unh huh,' to everything Anant said, still wrapped up in his own thoughts. Both Ramditta's future and Badda's distressed him. As he thought of the two of them, he imagined the life and the future of the entire mohalla as well, and he wished he could go back to Lahore by the night train and forget all the baseness of his mohalla in the vast sweep of the hustle-bustle of the city.

But his feet continued to move towards Chaurasti Atari and he walked along, holding on to Anant's hand.

As they reached Chaurasti Atari, Anant said suddenly, 'Okay, brother, I'm off now. I have to go over to Chowk Sudan. Go on over to Hakim Dina Nath's; make sure to ask him for me whether he's had his moustaches completely shaved by now or not.'

And Anant chuckled loudly. Then he said, 'If he has another child next year, he'll have to shave off his ears too.'

And he began to laugh some more.

49

Hakim Dina Nath had been their classmate. When he studied with them in class eight, he had been hearty like his father and uncle, and like them, he'd had enormous moustaches. He'd been married quite young—in Class Eight—and after he'd passed middle school, he began to work at the shop with his father and uncle. After just one year, he had his first son. In the eight years since then, he'd had five children, and not only had his wrestler-style physique grown weak, but his enormous moustaches had also thinned out and become wispy. Anant liked to say that if Dina Nath had one more child, he'd have to shave his moustaches off completely, and then all he'd have left to trim would be his ears. Hakim Dina Nath's sixth child had been born this year, and that's what Anant was referring to.

But Chetan did not join in this crude joke with Anant. He was still caught up in his own thoughts. When Anant stopped laughing and shook Chetan's hand before taking off, Chetan suddenly said, 'Chacha Ramditta's gone half mad.'

'In two years he'll be fully mad,' Anant guffawed loudly and, shaking Chetan's hand just as hard, he added, 'After all, you call him Chacha, so that should embarrass him a bit.'

Chetan liked this joke even less. 'Okay, I'll see you this evening,' he said and, shaking Anant's hand slightly, he turned into Papadiyan Bazaar.

*

But he couldn't get Anant's joke out of his mind. Like a thorn, it dug deeper and deeper into his heart and that invisible pricking brought to mind his great uncle Phalguram, so like Ramditta, who now appeared before him like a jinn in the *Arabian Nights*.

*

50

All three of Chetan's grandfather's brothers had been crazy. The elder two had passed away before Chetan was born, but Chetan had known the youngest, Chunilal, who was well known by the name 'Crazy Chunni' throughout the city.

Chetan's father had once broken his crazy uncle's nose in a fight. Chunilal wandered the galis of the city, with his sunken nose and scarred upper lip, totally naked, his teeth chattering, constantly drawing men of wood and iron in the air with his hands, then making them fly away. If anyone gave him bread, he ate it; otherwise he was usually lying down, in the sun or shade, whatever the weather. Whenever he felt thirsty at some odd time, he'd go to the well. Otherwise, when the committee water carrier arrived in Kallowani Mohalla behind the sweeper to wash the drains at three or four in the afternoon, Chetan's crazy uncle would squat before him with his palm cupped before his mouth and the water carrier would turn the opening of his leather pouch away from the drain and pour it into his palm until his thirst was slaked, and then Chunni would be on his way, teeth chattering, tracing his men of wood and iron in the air. He was famous not just in the mohalla but throughout the city. Often women stricken with sorrow and pain, as well as speculators and gamblers, would surround him to learn their fate. He would usually sit silently and stare stonily into space or curse at them, but sometimes when he was comparatively alert, he'd tell them whatever came into his head, and people believed that whatever he said was the truth. Chetan had even heard from his grandfather that once Chunilal had locked himself up in the rooftop room of their old house for forty days, when it was still a ruin, in order to bring Lord Hanuman under his power. He chained the door shut, locking himself in, and told his mother, great-grandmother Gangadei, that no one was to disturb him until the time was up, or his austerities would be destroyed.

51

He was Gangadei's youngest child and of all her sons, she loved him the most. He was a hearty young man; she was petrified at the thought of him locked up in that room for forty days with no food or water. Several times a day she went upstairs and placed her ear against the door and listened to him intoning his mantra. She managed to keep herself under control for thirty or so days out of a desire for her son's success. She continued to hear his voice in snatches, but when on the thirty-third day she heard nothing at all, she raised a commotion in the mohalla and broke down the door.

Then—this is what Chetan's grandfather told him—Lord Hanuman slapped Chunilal across the face and knocked him unconscious, and he cursed Gangadei, saying, 'Go! You will never enjoy the good fortune of this son! Whensoever you come before him, he will be insane!'

Although Chetan's grandfather always said that if his mother had only been patient a few more days and his austerities had not been destroyed, Chunilal would have had Lord Hanuman in his power, it was widely believed in the city that Chunilal had indeed attained power over Lord Hanuman, and whatever words emerged from his mouth became the truth. The Kapoors of Bohar Wala Bazaar were devout followers of Chunilal's. They had clothing made for him, and in winter they had quilts stuffed for him (he'd always give the clothing away to others and wander about naked regardless of the season); they would trap him, give him food and drink and look after him in every way. They had complete faith that all their success in business was due to his brilliance.

But Chunilal had no consciousness of their business or even their existence. The entire city belonged to him, and he wandered about all day long. In summer, he'd fall asleep on the stoop of some shop in the open bazaar or on the front steps of someone's home, and in winter, he'd take refuge at a kiln or tandoori oven.

Yes, whenever he was in his right mind (and the odd thing was that whenever great-grandmother Gangadei went with her grandson, Chetan's father, to far-off stations, Chunilal's sanity returned), he'd show up at the Kapoors'. He'd be wearing clothing and he'd do skeining work at their shop.[2]

Chetan had gone there once when his mother had asked him to. He had bowed down to his great-uncle, fearfully, and his great-uncle had given him a blessing as well. Throughout the whole hour Chetan was there, he simply saw Chunilal quietly doing his work—not once did he say anything to anyone.

But this was after the death of great-grandmother Gangadei. During her lifetime, this youngest great-uncle of Chetan's remained consistently insane. Once, when Gangadei had arrived in Jalandhar suddenly, someone told her that her son was completely sane, and busy untangling skeins at the Kapoors. Gangadei did not pause long enough to take a breath or drink a sip of water. She ran right over there, but it seemed the moment he saw his mother, Chunni felt the slap of Lord Hanuman on his cheek (this was the explanation Chetan had heard), and he ripped off all his clothing and went running off, drawing wood and iron men in the air, his teeth chattering away.

Chetan's grandfather always said that after that, Gangadei never went to the Kapoors' shop. She was satisfied with the thought that even if she didn't see her son, he was happy and healthy. But all the same, Lord Hanuman, the All-Knowing, always knew when she arrived in Jalandhar, and straightaway, he slapped Chunilal across the cheek and Chunilal would turn up stark naked to torment his mother. Because of this sad state of affairs, Chetan's father finally took his grandmother to live with

---

[2] Skeining, or *patphera*, involves wrapping skeins of silk around the knees to untangle the threads.

him permanently, and there she died, at some far-off station. After her death, Chetan's great-uncle was never insane again. And when he died, the Kapoors called for his wife and gave her his earnings of three hundred rupees.

Crazy Chunilal had a son named Phalguram, who had been a postman in Miyan Mir. He hadn't studied beyond Class Five and Chetan's father had helped him get a job there before Chetan was born. Phalguram didn't marry and he lived with his mother. In a fit of madness, his sainted father had set fire to the veranda and enclosed porch that were their portion of the house in Kallowani Mohalla, so Phalguram's mother had moved out to live with her son. When Chetan's father had had the house completely rebuilt, he'd purchased the veranda and porch from Phalguram for four hundred rupees. The veranda still lay in ruins, making their new house look blind in one eye.

During the time Chetan's father was thinking of rebuilding the house, he'd called Phalguram to Jalandhar. Chetan had been small then. He was studying in Class Five or Six. That was the first time he'd seen this uncle of his. Phalguram was sturdy, tall and broad like his father; in his uniform he looked less like a postman and more like a soldier to Chetan.

Chetan learned from his mother that Phalgu was the name of a pure river and that his uncle had been born after his mother had gazed upon that river. He wanted to joke with his uncle when he met him, so he lay in his lap in that same roof-top room (the house was still old then) where Phalguram's father, Chunilal, had attempted unsuccessfully to attain power over Lord Hanuman, and asked him, 'What is your name, Uncle?'

Chetan had thought that if his uncle replied, 'Phalguram,' he'd say, 'But that's not a good name, Phalgu is the name of a river, and Ram is an avatar, put the two together and it's not a name at all.' His own name was so much better—Chetananand—

54

and he would astonish his uncle by telling him the meaning and interpretation of his name, including the *sandhi* that joined the letters, as heard from his father. But his uncle picked up Chetan's slate, which lay nearby, and wrote out a name in the Urdu script that astonished him. He wrote:

Chichchal Khan, Chichchalawal Khan, Jahijjatbijjat Bijli Khan, Sher Bahadur Aiyye Khan.

Chetan actually had a hard time sounding out the name and his uncle ended up reading it out loud to him.

'This is your name?' he asked suspiciously.

'Yes.'

'But your name is Phalguram.'

'I've given up that name, this is my name now.'

And then he told Chetan to say the whole name fast, which he simply couldn't do, even after several tries.

In the evening, his uncle took him out for a walk, and although he treated Chetan to several types of sweets, he also frightened him terribly, because he took him wandering about looking in two or three cemeteries for some fakir dwelling there. Chetan didn't let it show, but inwardly he was terrified.

*

Walking along in Papadiyan Bazaar, he recollected each and every detail of that uncle he'd seen years ago, and the two or three days he'd spent with him. Taken altogether he didn't dislike his uncle, although he wasn't fond of being taken along to wander about cemeteries every day.

After that, there had been no news of Phalguram for years. Then, on the birth of Chetan's youngest brother, when Ma told

Chetan to write the joyous news in a card to Phalguram, he had written to his uncle in beautiful handwriting, addressing him with great respect. The response came by return mail and Chetan was quite alarmed when he read it. In the upper portion of the card were written just two words over and over: '*Ya rab, ya rab, ya rab*: Oh, Lord . . . oh, Lord . . . oh, Lord,' and after this was written one more line:

> *Yaad-e-ilahi mashghul*
> Engaged in contemplation of the divine
> —Phalguram (AKA, Sher Bahadur Aiyye Khan)

When he read the card aloud to Ma, she smote her brow.

'When will we be rid of this problem in our family?' she asked. 'Will there always be some lunatic in our home?' Because of Chetan's grandfather's crazy brothers, his family was known as 'the crazy clan'. The pain in Ma's voice was plain to Chetan.

Chetan's brothers took the card from Chetan and took turns reading it. Everyone laughed uproariously, and Bhai Sahib declared that some day soon they would hear that Phalguram had ripped off all his clothes, just like Great-Uncle Chunilal, and was wandering about naked.

And when, three years later, news came from Miyan Mir that Chetan's great-aunt (Great-Uncle Chunilal's wife) had passed away, and Chetan's grandfather went to Miyan Mir and returned to tell them that Phalguram had gone mad, no one was surprised. Dada ji said he'd lost his mind long ago, but as long as his mother was living, he had stayed on at his job; when she died, he performed her last rites, then said goodbye to his job: he went into the office, tendered his letter of resignation, ripped off his clothes and run off, crying '*Ya Hussain, ya Hussain!*' Chetan's grandfather went to great trouble wandering around for two days looking for his nephew, but he must have boarded a train to somewhere as there was no trace of him anywhere in the city.

*

The joke Anant had made standing in Chaurasti Atari alluded to Chetan's uncle Phalguram. As he walked along in Papadiyan Bazaar recalling Uncle Phalguram, Chetan thought, 'Anant's right, though. What real difference is there between Ramditta and Uncle Phalguram anyway? It's possible one day Ramditta will leap from his shop, ripping off all his clothes!'

His wasn't the only family with lunatics in the neighbourhood. Jagtu, of the Jhamans, who had died just two years ago, had also been crazy. Chetan remembered something that had happened years ago—a hullabaloo had suddenly broken out in the neighbourhood one afternoon, and the women seated on their low stools in front of their homes in the chowk, spinning and carding at their spinning wheels, had picked up their skeins and gone and hidden indoors. Later he learned that Jagtu had gone mad and ripped off all his clothes and run off towards the bazaar from the bhuvara, totally naked, ranting and raving.

One of the Jhamans had said, 'No, he's not crazy, he just drank too much liquor and wasn't in his right mind.'

His mother had called him upstairs to tell him not to go to the bazaar at all. But Chetan went into the open sitting room on the second storey, and from there he caught a few glimpses of Jagtu. He was waving his arms as lunatics do, and yammering curses; first he ran stark naked from the bazaar towards the bhuvara, then, perhaps because the door to his own home was still locked, he ran back towards the bazaar. The memory of his skinny, milk-white body flashed before Chetan's eyes like lightning.

57

Jagtu, who had always been so silent, who had always walked with his eyes to the ground as he passed through the mohalla on his way to and from Mandi, was now swirling about shamelessly like a tornado. Who knows how long he would have continued to terrorize the mohalla, but Amichand's elder brother, Amirchand, had caught hold of him, brought him to the Chowdharain's doorway and beat him so brutally that he ran from the mohalla again and never returned.

And a few chapters of the books he'd read while ghostwriting for Kaviraj Ramdas swam before Chetan's eyes. He sighed. In this deprived, illiterate mohalla, where lack of education and culture held sway alongside hunger and thirst, where young unmarried men spent their whole lives full of longing, what else would they become besides dishonest gamblers—adulterous, profligate and insane? Was it any surprise that illnesses settled in for generations, hollowing out each generation in their wake? Often when an unmarried man married after a considerable delay, he'd have already fallen prey to sexual diseases, and if a young widower didn't remarry, he'd end up falling victim to such illnesses as well, and wander crazed from gali to gali.

*

Deep in thought, Chetan reached the triangular chowk of Papadiyan Bazaar, when suddenly his attention was arrested by two shopkeepers fighting over a game of chaupar in the corner.

This particular chowk in Papadiyan Bazaar was quite small. The shops on the right side veered away from the bazaar, then turned straight again, to form a sort of a triangle by which the right side of the bazaar was turned into a smallish chowk. To one side, at the edge of the bazaar, Salho (Saligram) was rolling out papads in front of his shop. First he made balls of the dough from mashed lentils and chickpea flour, and set them out. Then he coated them lightly in oil and rolled them once each with the rolling pin to flatten them out. After that, he picked them up a second time and rolled them into a ball and threw them on to a nearby mat. His heels rose slightly as he squatted and pressed them out. After rolling out the papad, he'd toss it on the mat and then plant his heels on the ground again.

Inside the shop, his boy Melaram was washing the dal in baking soda, the odour of which had spread throughout the chowk. Wherever there was sunlight in the chowk, papads had been spread out on mats, the rolled black pepper peeping out like tiny eyes. Dyed dupattas and turbans fluttered lightly in the breeze from a clothesline stretched across the chowk by the corner dyer, Chiragh, and right in front of Salho the papad maker, Relu was grinding dal on the grindstone of the bazaar. He wore only a loincloth and undershirt and the sinews of his arms and shoulders were taut.

Although the papad makers were engrossed in their work and it was still early in the morning, there was a notable lack of excitement in Papadiyan Bazaar. In the rest of the shops—there were a few goldsmiths, a tobacconist, Moghar the plumber's shop (who was still called Moghar Patphera although he'd given up skeining work years ago), and Dwarka's cotton and tape weaving shop—all was still and the owners of these shops were taking part in a chaupar game set up in the corner.

Chetan saw that Chiragh the Dyer and Moghar Patphera were the ones actually playing the game—although, at that moment, they were fighting as they played—while the rest crowded about them in a ring. Among these, he saw Daulat Ram the astrologer, his long braid knotted up, clad in nothing but a cloth printed with the name of Ram wrapped around his waist and wooden sandals. Since the chaupar cloth was spread out below Dwarka's shop, he

59

was seated right on his stoop, wearing a dhoti that ended a bit above the knees, his sacred thread across his naked torso, baring his yellow twig-like teeth in a grin and enjoying the game.

Papadiyan Bazaar was never an exciting bazaar anyway, but what with these chaupar players leaving behind all worries in this world, utter dullness reigned. However, this wasn't the only bazaar like it. In Jalandhar there were (and still are today) countless such bazaars where games of cards, chess, or chaupar carry on from morning to evening.

*

When Chetan, tangled up in his memories of the lives of his uncles, neared the chaupar players, he heard raised voices and, looking up, he saw Moghar Patphera suddenly take off his shoe and smack Chiragh over the head two or three times in quick succession.

Chiragh was a pale young man. Handsome, pointy-brown moustaches adorned his face. He wore a trailing parrot-wing turban on his head, a striped boski kameez and a tahmad around his waist.

With the very first blow, his turban fell off. For a moment, he stood there stunned, then cursing fulsomely, he leapt towards Moghar. But the astrologer held him tightly in his arms, remonstrating with him. A couple of people grabbed hold of Moghar as well.

Chetan asked an onlooker what had happened.

Then he learned that Chiragh and Moghar had each bet a seer of milk on the turn. Moghar had won all seven pieces; only one had ended up in the house of hell. All seven of Chiragh's pieces had died, but in one hand he had killed two twelves, two fourteens and two sevens, and not only had he boldly freed one of his pieces and won, but he'd also given a beating to Moghar's one piece lying in hell. And he didn't let that piece of Moghar's rise again. If Moghar lifted it up, he'd beat it down. Finally Chiragh beat all seven pieces. Each player had only one piece remaining. But by ill fate, Moghar ended up in the house of hell again and Chiragh beat him, and Moghar was mortified and pulled off his shoes and hit him.

Moghar claimed Chiragh had won the piece through trickery; his piece had also come into the house of hell, but he'd moved one house back. And not only had he won the game by trickery but he had also sworn at him, crying, 'This isn't skeining, it's chaupar! It's not something your average riff-raff can pull off!' That low-down dyer had had the nerve to swear at Lala Moghar Mull and taunt him, crying out, 'Let go of me, let's see what he's got!'

Chiragh probably wouldn't have calmed down and would have knocked a few more heads together, but Daulat Ram the astrologer leaned his shiny oily braided head near Chiragh and said, 'Now, brother, if the only thing that will calm you down is taking revenge, why don't you hit me with your shoes!'

And as soon as the Brahmin bowed his head before him, Chiragh's anger cooled. He bent down and touched his feet. As he stepped over to his shop, he swore at all the other shopkeepers and called them impotent—they only knew how to win—and then, cursing himself even more roundly, said he'd sooner sleep with his own mother than play with any of them again.

'What a vow that good-for-nothing's made! But he'll be back to playing again in two days!' Chetan thought to himself and, casting a glance of revulsion at all of them, he continued on his way.

Whenever he came to Jalandhar and happened to pass that way, and saw the games of cards, chess and chaupar, he thought to himself, 'How can these people waste so much time?' He was

61

astonished at the lack of ambition and ineffectiveness in such people in comparison with his own ambitions and hard work. Sometimes he envied them too. He wished he had no worries whatsoever, that he had no sense of responsibility, that he had no desires and that he could happily play chaupar all day long like them. But he shuddered to imagine such an aimless existence. He felt that even if he wanted to, it was beyond him to live that way. He wouldn't even last two days . . . and the image of Hakim Dina Nath swam before his eyes—a man who had intelligence, a powerful means to rise above his station, and one whose struggle had always given Chetan inspiration, yet nonetheless, still struggled away in Jalandhar . . .

*

As he walked over to Dina Nath's shop, the last several years passed before Chetan like the colourful clouds of a monsoon evening.

6

Dina Nath, who was known only as 'Dina' or '*Thallu jariye da puttar*'[3] before he attained the title 'Hakim', was quite wise even in boyhood. He was just a few years older than Chetan, but right from the beginning, Chetan had got along very well with him.

Dina Nath's father, Thallu Ram, and his uncle, Dal Chand, regularly went to the akhara. They had at least warded off the sense of laxity one got from their names in terms of their physical forms. They were of medium height, fair and fit, with large round eyes and handlebar moustaches—yes, in terms of their mental acuity, it was a different story, but you can't expect sharp minds from goldsmiths! Dina Nath also exercised at the akhara, but he had a much sharper mind than either his father or his uncle. He adored reading. Chetan was just in Class Six when Bhai Sahib started reading novels rented from Mahantram Booksellers in Bhairon Bazaar. Watching him and secretly reading the books he brought home, Chetan also developed a fondness for reading. Whatever spending money he got, he saved up to rent more novels, and he and Dina Nath would read together whatever books he brought home.

First, he read *Chandrakanta*, then he read *Chandrakanta Santati*, then *Bhoot Nath* and then *The Arabian Nights*. One day he

---

[3] The son of Thallu, the maker of inlaid jewellery.

was standing at Mahantram's shop, just flipping through books, when he saw a book with the title *Magic of Bengal*. He brought the book home. He read the secrets to many magic tricks, but he couldn't figure out how to set up a single one. Then he showed the book to Dina Nath. Dina Nath kept the book for only two days, but he must have noted down numerous tricks in that short time, because after that, for the entire month, he showed Chetan a new trick every single day.

One morning, on the way to school, when Chetan went to get him in Gali Barhaiyan where he lived in the house opposite Anant's, Dina Nath produced a colourful ball from his pocket with a piece of twisted cotton string threaded through it. Dina Nath pulled one end of the string, then stretched each end of the string in his hands until it was taut. Chetan watched with astonishment as the ball balanced atop the string, near Dina Nath's finger and thumb. Then Dina Nath whispered a mantra to himself: 'Go, son!' and the obedient ball swung around to the bottom. Dina Nath again commanded, 'Stop!' The ball stopped. Whenever Dina Nath commanded, the ball would move; when he told it to stop, it stopped.

Dina Nath astonished the other boys with his magic all day at school, and Chetan kept asking him for the secret of the trick.

He recalled how he had threatened him for days, until Dina Nath finally came out with the secret . . . Although the string was pushed through the top of the ball and came out the bottom, the hole wasn't straight; inside the ball it came together at a 120-degree angle. If the string was at all loose, the ball would spin around, and when it was stretched taut, it would tremble to a stop.

'I had to ruin several balls before I got the formula right,' Dina Nath told him joyfully. 'The holes have to be equally long on both sides and they should meet exactly in the middle of the ball.'

'That's it?' asked Chetan, paying Dina Nath's joy no heed. He'd thought perhaps the whole thing really did work on the strength of the mantra.

The next week, Dina Nath showed him an even more interesting trick. He held out his left hand in the shape of a half-moon, with one card in it. Chetan saw that it was the queen of hearts. Then he took just a pinch of ash in his other hand, sprinkled it over the card and, crying 'Vanish!' he waved his right hand over it. The queen of hearts was transformed into a matchbox; Dina Nath took a match from it, lit it, then blew it out.

Chetan was amazed. 'Show me again!' he cried.

Dina Nath put both his hands behind his back. The next moment, that same queen of hearts was in his left hand. Chetan was staring at him hard to make sure Dina Nath wasn't sneakily hiding anything from him. But in the blink of an eye, he'd sprinkled the pinch of ash on the card, waved his right hand over it, and the queen of hearts became a matchbox again.

When Dina Nath finally told him the secret after several days of threats and grovelling, Chetan was disappointed again. The card that was in Dina Nath's hand was a completely ordinary small, thin card. Dina Nath had cut one side of the matchbox cover off and glued it to the back of the entire card. The box filled with matches he kept hidden in the fist of his right hand and when he waved his hand from below to above, the card stuck to it and became a matchbox.

'That's all!' said Chetan. 'That trick was even easier than the first one.'

'Oh, it's an easy trick?' Dina Nath made a face. 'If it's so easy, how come you were beating your head for so many days; how come you couldn't figure it out?'

'It's not easy to guess,' retorted Chetan, trying to make himself feel better, and he asked Dina Nath to prepare a trick just like it for him.

Two or three weeks later, Dina Nath showed him an even more amazing trick. He took out a completely new deck of cards and shuffled it thoroughly, then told Chetan that he should shuffle it himself and take out a card. Chetan shuffled the deck thoroughly and took out a card. It was the nine of diamonds. 'Light it with a match,' said Dina Nath.

'But then you'll be one card short.'

'Burn it!'

Chetan nervously set fire to the new card. When it had turned completely to ash, Dina Nath picked up a framed glass box filled with sand. Shaking it up and down, he showed that there was nothing else in it, then took a pinch of ash from the card and sprinkled it over the box. After this, he placed the box against the wall and, murmuring a mantra, he began to wave a handkerchief over it. Chetan's eyes popped out when he saw that slowly the curtain of sand disappeared and the same shiny new nine of diamonds appeared in the glass box.

When Chetan finally learned the secret to that trick after many threats and entreaties, he was even more disappointed than before. Every single card in the deck had been the nine of diamonds. There had already been a card in the frame. While they were talking, Dina Nath had turned the frame over and the sand had started to slide down.

All these astonishing magic tricks turned out to be exactly the same. Chetan would be excited by the trick when he first saw it, but when he learned the secret, he'd completely lose interest. Although he learned several of the tricks from Dina Nath, and had even been praised by the boys in the neighbourhood for them, he was no longer as thrilled by magic tricks as he had been at first.

Then one day, he took out a book from Mahantram Booksellers called *Treasury of Spells*. After reading just the first chapter, he decided he would develop exceptional hypnotism

66

skills and astonish Dina Nath. He drew a circle with black ink on a blank piece of paper and stuck it to the wall before him, following the instructions given in the book. He closed the door, lit a candle, spread out a mat, knelt down and focused his gaze on that circle. He thought the paper might be a little too high; it was written in the book that the ink circle should be directly in front of one's eyes, so he lowered it a bit. Now it was a little too low. Then he put it up a little higher and, feeling fully satisfied, he went and sat on the mat again and focused on the circle. Staring unblinkingly at it, he began to count to hundred. When he reached ten, he blinked. The second time he blinked at twelve, the third time at fifteen. Each time he got a little further. When he got up after an hour, he felt quite happy—although his eyes were watering—because he was making good progress according to what was written in the book.

But on the seventh day, he was forced to end his training. His eyes were smarting. It was summer. His already weak eyes were strained from staring so hard in the dim candlelight in that humid room. When he found no relief despite applying zinc lotion around his eyes for three or four days—in fact, his discomfort had only increased—Bhai Sahib took him to see Dr Jivaram.

Dr Jivaram was not a real doctor. He'd spent his entire life as a compounder at Mayo Hospital. Upon his retirement he'd moved to Kot Pushka, opened a dispensary on the ground floor of his house, and started calling himself a doctor. He wrote the prescriptions himself and prepared the medicines as well. After examining Chetan's eyes, he said he had trachoma. He'd have to perform a 'caustic touch', he said, and advised him not to read in poor light and not to read lying down, otherwise his eyesight would be ruined. He sat down on a stool and told Chetan to sit on the floor and lean his head back in his lap. Dr Jivaram was a sturdy man. His lips were shaded by huge white moustaches. He wore a loose-fitting shirt and a huge turban on his head. When Chetan leaned his head in Dr Jivaram's lap and looked up at him, he felt nervous. Then Dr Jivaram touched each of his eyes with the caustic. Although he rinsed out Chetan's eyes with cold boric water after the caustic touch, Chetan began to whimper with pain. He felt as though his eyes had been touched with burning embers. He returned home from Kot Pushka with the help of Bhai Sahib, almost a blind man. Dr Jivaram had said he should have the caustic touch administered one more time, but Chetan never went back. Instead, he got a prescription from Hakim Nabi and had a package of barberry root extract, musk and camphor made up by Jeetu Attar, the compounder and, lying in the dark in his room, he applied a poultice of these to his eyes for a whole week. After fifteen days, when his eyes got better, he was rid of the hypnotism bug as well.

*

But he wasn't about to give up so easily. He was still in search of something by which he could prove his greatness to Dina Nath. One day, when he was reading *Treasury of Spells,* he leapt up after reading the final chapter. In it was recorded a method by which one might gain control of one's *humzaad.* When he read the title of the chapter, 'Controlling the Humzaad', he didn't really understand what a humzaad even was, but there was a description right at the beginning explaining that it was a powerful being born at the same time as every man, which lives within him. If it emerges and you take control of it, it can execute any task you wish—it can give you information, increase your salary, make it rain, tell you the secrets of another's heart, tell you about another person's life, help you cross a river, make the woman you love fall for you, bring you delicious food, defeat your enemy, bring you success in court—in short, the humzaad can perform whatever task the practitioner wishes.

Chetan read the chapter several times. It didn't seem all that hard to control the humzaad and, as he read the book, he became more and more convinced of this. The chapter was written in such a way that little boys and poorly educated people would automatically believe what it said. It explained how many days of practice it would take for the humzaad to appear; if and when it appeared, which conditions you should accept from it, and how you could make it your slave, and so on. It was written in such detail that you automatically came to believe it. Chetan's childish imagination took flight as he read that chapter. It fluttered about on airy wings. Dina Nath's magic tricks would look so measly in comparison with the control of a humzaad. Whenever he read the book, his humzaad would appear before him in his imagination, hands bound, like the jinn in Aladdin's lamp and do anything he asked in the blink of an eye.

Finally, he resolved to do it.

It was summer vacation. The boys of the mohalla would get up early and go for walks on Cantonment Road. They bathed in the deep, bricked tank under a thick stream from the Neeli Kothi well. It would be difficult to attain control of one's humzaad in the presence of so many boys, Chetan thought, so he decided he would go to Chuparana and bring the humzaad under his control in solitude there. He tied a new loincloth made on a Tuesday around his neck like a muffler and, wrapping a paan leaf very carefully in paper and placing it in his pocket, he set out confidently for Chuparana.

But the fashionable people of Adda Hoshiarpur and Kot Kishanchand all took their morning strolls to Chuparana. There was quite a crowd there in the mornings. In some spots, people were doing callisthenics; in others, yoga. Elsewhere, there would be people discussing their neighbourhoods, city or national politics, and in other spots, they'd simply be enjoying scandals to combat the day's boredom. For this reason, Chetan chose a well half a mile beyond Chuparana for his austerities. He'd gone that far several times before with his friends. He did feel fearful about going beyond Chuparana alone, but the very first condition for controlling the humzaad was courage, and it was written in the book that the seeker should choose a spot where no interruption would occur during his austerities, so he reached the well a little before sunrise. As he bathed in preparation, the sun came up. Then, just as it was written in the book, he put on his loincloth and stood in the sunlight with his back to the sun. He turned his feet to the right. It was difficult for him to stare unblinkingly at the throat of his shadow with his neck turned. But he concentrated very hard and kept his gaze fixed, as he repeated over and over to himself—'Oh, humzaad, come speak with me!' It took him about an hour and a half to stare at the shadow of his throat seven times and at the sky seven times while continuously summoning the humzaad, as was written in the book.

It said in the book that after practising daily for ten days, the seeker would begin to have very strange sensations—he might feel as though a storm was coming, or as though a tree had cracked and was about to fall on him; sometimes beautiful young women would attempt to lead him astray—but the seeker should continue his austerities without being moved in the slightest. All these phenomena are caused by the humzaad in order to distract the seeker and test him. On the twentieth day, the humzaad would come and stand silently before the seeker. The seeker should also remain silent and continue with his austerities. After a few days, the humzaad would ask the seeker for some paan leaves. The seeker should not give it any paan leaves until the humzaad promises to come under his control. However, the seeker should

70

only accept this promise after much thought, because sometimes, even when the humzaad says it will come under his control, it sets extremely difficult conditions that are not within the power of the seeker. For example, it might say, 'I am prepared to become your slave, but you will have to feed me until I've had my fill,' or 'You must remain pure forever' . . . Obviously it's not within the power of the seeker to meet such conditions. Then a few days later, the humzaad will set an easier condition. The seeker should immediately agree to it. But before giving the humzaad the paan leaves and making it one's slave, the seeker should definitely get it to agree to two conditions—the first is that it should never come unless the seeker calls for it; the second is that the seeker can be freed of the humzaad whenever he wishes. If he doesn't demand these two conditions, the humzaad will make his life intolerable—it'll be hanging around twenty-four hours a day, or in old age, when the seeker's power and strength have grown feeble, it will not only make it difficult for him to live, but even after he dies he'll have no peace.

On his way home from Chuparana, Chetan's imagination took wing. He imagined himself with all phases of the penance completed in the blink of an eye. He imagined the humzaad coming to stand silently before him. Then for the rest of the way home, Chetan imagined demanding conditions of it and extracting promises. As he imagined bringing the humzaad under his control, Chetan's face lit up with indescribable joy . . . he had no idea how he'd managed to walk such a long way in that crackling sunlight. The magic only broke when he entered his mohalla and his mother asked where he'd been. It was so late already and his stroll had lasted forever.

When Chetan lay down after eating, his neck felt horribly stiff and his calves and feet were quite achy.

*

71

It was the hottest part of the summer. The sun came out at six or six fifteen, and its rays were harsh even that early in the morning. His body would start to burn from standing naked in the harsh sunlight, but he would only return home each day after one and a half hours of austerities. When he lay down at night, he'd imagine his shadow, his gaze focused on its throat, summoning the humzaad. On the seventh day, he started to have a slight headache and his eyelids felt a bit heavy. Then he realized that he'd been wrong to decide to undergo penance in such hot weather. He should have chosen weather that was neither too hot nor too cold, when the sunlight wasn't just to be tolerated, but actually felt nice. But at the same time, he felt that the more hardship he had to endure, the more quickly the humzaad would come under his control, and he recalled the tale of Raja Uttanapad's son, the devout Dhruv. If he could undergo such severe austerities that the god Vishnu was forced to fulfil his heart's desire, then Chetan was certainly old enough to do the same. Besides that, it was written in the book that there would definitely be some results on the tenth day, so he decided to himself that no matter what, he would do penance with great devotion for ten days and see if the sensations described in the book happened to him or not.

On the tenth day, when he began his penance, he heard no voices, no storm blew, no tree fell over, and no fairy came to distract him. He had a terrible headache—he felt as though his temples would burst, and someone was continuously banging on his head with a hammer. He finished his penance, threw the paan in the well and put on his clothes. He could barely walk on his way home. He felt nauseated by a sharp pain and his right eye was watering. He walked home massaging his temples with his thumb and forefinger, went into his room downstairs and lay down on the floor.

When he didn't go upstairs to eat and didn't respond to Ma's calls, Ma came down to his room. He lay on the floor, unconscious with fever, repeatedly mumbling, 'Oh, humzaad, come speak with me!'

When, after seven days, the intensity of his fever had lessened somewhat, and Ma asked him why he kept shouting 'Humja! Humja!' Chetan was alarmed—what if the humzaad had slapped him and he had gone crazy, just like his great-uncle Chunilal? But he didn't see the look of someone who has just seen a lunatic in the eyes of Ma, Dada, or Bhai Sahib. He was able to think clearly, in fact, in even finer detail. He felt like telling Ma the complete truth. But what if it alarmed her? So he kept quiet and when he was up to getting out of bed, he went downstairs to his room (his mother had brought him upstairs to the veranda because of his sickness) and hid that 'treasury' of spells. At first he thought he'd tear the book to shreds and stuff the pieces in the stove, but then he held on to it as a memento of his own foolishness.

*

And it was because of this illness of Chetan's that Dina Nath became a hakim instead of a jeweller.

*

What happened was that although Chetan's fever went down, his headache lingered on. Either he had become very weak, or because of standing continuously in the sunlight and staring unblinkingly at his shadow, he'd caused himself mental stress. Whatever the case, every second or third day, he'd feel a hammering in his head; he'd get dizzy as he walked around and he'd be about to fall over. One time he had been squatting for a long time while talking to

Ma, and then, when he got up, darkness suddenly fell before his eyes and he felt dizzy and fell to the floor.

When he came to after a few minutes, there was a pain in the back of his head, and he felt a lump when he touched it. And his face was damp when he ran his hand over it. Perhaps Ma had sprinkled his face with water and was sitting anxiously beside him. He sat up quickly to tell her there was no reason to worry. But he felt very weak.

Ma took him to Dr Jivaram and to Hakim Nabi Jan, and to Rajvaidya Durga Das as well, but Chetan found no relief from his headache. He'd get temporary relief from medicine but then a week or two later, the pain would begin again and his temples would start to throb so terribly that he'd burst into tears. Then one day his Dada brought him a book from his old friend Shyam Ratan (who was in the thread trade, but was a hakim by hobby)—*A Treasury of Medicine*—and he told Chetan's mother he'd found an amazing remedy for headaches in there. Chetan should be fed kheer made of musk melon seeds for seven days.

Ma was astonished and she asked Dada via Chetan what musk melon–seed kheer was like. Dada read the book and said that actually it was just kheer made with rice but it was cooked in musk melon–seed milk.

There was no shortage of melon seeds in the house: On the dark night of Ekadashi, Chetan's mother always ordered five to ten seers (depending on how generous she could afford to be) of melon to be given as alms. Chetan and his brothers also got quite a bit of melon to eat, and melons came to them from the homes of their patrons as well. The seeds of the melons were not thrown out but tossed into a clay pot. When enough had collected there, Ma put them in a brass sieve and scrubbed them clean. The pulp came out of the sieve and flowed down the drain and only the milky-white seeds would remain. These she'd dry on a cloth spread out on a charpoy in the sun. When there was no other work, or if there was some gathering to attend, women of the mohalla would bring tiny baskets that contained a few seeds wrapped in a damp cloth. The women would chat and hull the seeds with small wooden tongs. When she had free time, or rather, when she had time to go visiting in the gali or the neighbour women would come to her house, Chetan's mother would also hull the seeds while chatting. Sometimes when she made halwa or kheer, she would add the hulled seeds to them.

That very evening, Ma soaked some poppy seeds and oat bran as per Dada's instructions. There weren't that many hulled melon seeds in the house, so the next morning she put two fists of whole seeds in a basin along with the poppy seeds and oat bran that had soaked overnight, and then she pounded them thoroughly, added some water, strained it through a cloth and extracted the milk. She put the dregs in the basin again and rubbed them with a stick. After grinding and rubbing them two or three times this way, all the milk came out. Then she threw out the dregs and strained the water from the oat bran and mixed it with the milk. After that, she ordered half a seer of cow's milk from Ramditta's shop and poured it in and heated it over the fire. When it had cooked a bit, she added some basmati rice and after a little while she added two large spoonfuls of pure ghee and five or six small cardamoms, ground. Ma started work on the mixture early in the morning. At around one in the afternoon the kheer was ready. Chetan was feeling hungry. The kheer tasted delicious to him—so delicious that afterwards, whenever he thought of it, the fragrance came back to him.

Ma fed him kheer for seven days. And truly, after that, he never had such a headache again. When Dina Nath found out that Chetan's grandfather had a book with a remedy that had brought him comfort, he begged him to ask his grandfather for it. Chetan did, and Dina Nath began coming to his house every evening. He would sit and read the book and note down remedies. Sometimes Chetan would read them out and Dina Nath would take notes.

They had not yet finished the book, when one day, Dina Nath gave Chetan's Dada a small vial of digestive powder. He let Chetan, his mother and his brothers taste a bit of the powder as well. Chetan's Dada tasted it and remarked, 'This has ammonium chloride in it.'

'There are a total of twenty other ingredients besides ammonium chloride, Dada ji,' replied Dina Nath proudly.

Chetan's Dada belched loudly. 'This is useful for flatulence,' he said.

'You won't find a better powder for digestion than this,' said Dina Nath. 'If Uncle Dal Chand hadn't helped me, it wouldn't have been made. It took four days to prepare. Grinding up all the different ingredients, then weighing them out according to measurements and mixing them. If you ever have a digestive complaint, let me know. I'll make it for you right away.'

After a few days, Aunty Purandei's children came down with whooping cough in the Jhamans' gali. When none of the hakims or doctors were able to do anything (what could they do when no one could cure it anyway—the neighbourhood was poor and medical treatment cost money), Dina Nath concocted a medicine following a remedy he'd noted down from *A Treasury of Medicine*. He bought some small long peppers from the grocer's shop. He got a goat's liver, tore it open with a knife and stuffed it with the long peppers. He placed the liver in a clay pot, sealed it with flour mixed with water, and cooked it in a one-hundred-dung-cake fire. Then he opened the cover of the vessel and carefully separated the long peppers from the liver. He ground them up and made powder packets to give to Aunty Purandei and told her to have her children lick them with honey. Whooping cough is a tyrant and can cause discomfort for months. When the children found relief, Dina Nath became the honorary hakim of the neighbourhood. Whoever had discomfort would go straight to Dina Nath, and he would make them medicine.

He enjoyed his work as a hakim so much that goldsmithing became an annoyance. He'd set diamonds and pearls into jewellery with his father and uncle and work with gold as well, but he used all his spare time to read books on Yunani medicine and prepare medicines at night. He started subscribing to a journal of Yunani medicine from Lahore, from which he learned that he could not only study medicine through a correspondence course but he could also pass the Hazik exam. For the next four years, through relentless toil, he not only passed the Hazik exam, but came in first, and he also attained the rank of gold medallist. The very next day after passing the exam, he hung a large, heavy sign in the middle of the bazaar in front of the jewellery shop (although it was still just a jewellery shop), on which was written in both English and Urdu:

Hakim Lala Dina Nath, Hakim Hazik (Gold Medallist)

But the jewellery-making business and the medical business could not coexist side by side. There wasn't enough room in the shop. The two teapoys out front were for Thallu Ram and Dina Nath, and Uncle Dal Chand sat inside the shop. There wasn't even any space for the patients to sit. And the demand for gem-setting had been decreasing for a couple of years. Then Dina Nath rented out two sitting rooms in Rayzada Khushwant Ray's house, which opened out into Bajiyanwala Bazaar, and established his dispensary there.

When Chetan had come to town for his own wedding, he'd also visited Dina Nath's dispensary. A curtain divided the sitting room in two. Outside was Hakim Sahib's table, a small box of medicines and a book rack. On the other side of the curtain there was a bench, covered by a dhurrie, a sheet and a bolster. A stethoscope also hung from a peg there . . . 'Hakims check a patient's urine and pulse,' thought Chetan to himself. 'What does he want with a stethoscope?' But then he thought that perhaps Dina Nath was also learning how to be a medical doctor alongside his hakim practice. When he mentioned this to Anant, he burst out laughing. 'Dina Nath doesn't put the stethoscope on people's chests, he places it on their stomachs,' Anant had said. 'The bastard is a total fraud.' But Chetan didn't believe Anant. He had unbroken faith in Dina Nath's intelligence and honesty.

The pharmacy was in the other sitting room, which Dina Nath's father Lala Thallu Ram had taken charge of. One morning when Chetan passed through the bazaar, he found Lala Thallu Ram sweeping the sitting room. Thallu Ram was simultaneously the dispensary's chaprasi, counter clerk and accountant, and Dina Nath had become 'Hakim Sahib'. Even Thallu Ram now called his own son 'Hakim Sahib'.

But the dispensary couldn't survive for more than a year. The thing was that Dina Nath had imitated Delhi's Hamdard Pharmacy and Lahore's Kaviraj Ramdas in opening a dispensary. He'd forgotten that there's a world of difference between Delhi and Lahore on the one hand, and Jalandhar on the other. And then the folks in Kallowani Mohalla, Chowk Chaddhiyan, Rasta Bazaar, Kot Pushka, Chowk Qadeshah, and Chowk Kharadiyan, all of whom Dina Nath needed in order to run his dispensary, were used to Hakim Nabi Jan. They took their prescriptions from Hakim Nabi Jan and had them filled by Jeetu Attar in Panjpir. Hakim Nabi Jan was a royal hakim. He received a monthly salary from several princely states. He took handsome fees from the rich, but for two hours every morning and evening, he saw poor people for free and wrote out prescriptions. Why would those who had been going to him for years get prescriptions from Dina Nath and buy his expensive medicines? Slowly the people of the mohalla began to complain that that bastard Dina Nath was a thug . . . after all, he's just a jeweller, isn't he? And everyone knows a jeweller will skimp on gold even when making jewellery for his own mother. That's what everyone was saying in the mohalla. And on top of that, as soon as the dispensary opened, people in the mohalla started to speak of themselves as Dina Nath's brothers or his uncles, and began to consider it their right to take loans from him and not pay him back. The result of all this was that in just a year, Dina Nath had to close the dispensary. But there was also another reason for this: he'd learned how to make vinegar from water from a book similar to *The Treasury of Medicine* in order to fill a shortfall and, after making enough doses of it, he began to sell it cheaper than real vinegar. Finally, he got caught. This gave him a bad reputation and forced him to close up shop.

And now Dina Nath was back in that same old shop again. His father and uncle did the same work they'd always done in their shop in Lal Bazaar. Dina Nath's seven- or eight-year-old son opened the shop every morning and tidied it, and Hakim Sahib would come and sit down about half an hour after the shop opened.

Since Dina Nath was devoted to medicine and refused to return to goldsmithing no matter how many times his father told him to, he'd put up a signboard with the added title '*fida-e-tib*' or, 'Devoted to Medicine':

Hakim Lala Dina Nath, Devoted to Medicine, Hakim Hazik (Gold Medallist)

But Anant always called him *Mama-e-Tib*, or 'Uncle Medicine'.

7

'Tell me, brother Chetan, when did you come from Lahore?'

Chetan was walking along, wrapped up in his thoughts, when suddenly he stopped. Hakim Dina Nath was seated to his left at his old shop in a suit and shoes, instead of a kameez and pyjamas, at a small table and chair, smiling through wispy whiskers (Chetan was astonished).

If Anant had been with him, Anant would have asked, 'Hey there, Uncle Medicine, what's your latest scam?' At the thought of Anant, Chetan said to himself, 'Tell me, Hakim Sahib, I heard you had a son, congratulations! Now give your wispy whiskers a break!' . . . But he wasn't in the mood to joke. Silently, he climbed the wooden step into the shop.

Before, when Dina Nath had worked with his father and uncle inlaying jewellery at this same shop, there were burlap mats spread out for sitting on and no steps whatsoever. When Chetan and Anant used to stop by on their way home from school, then college, they'd sit on the mats and let their legs dangle from the shop; but now the spot where the mats had been was adorned by a table, chair and bench, so a wooden step had also been installed for climbing up into the shop.

Chetan entered the shop, shook Dina Nath's hand, and went to sit on the bench against the wall across from him. He didn't respond to his question, but said instead, 'Congratulations, Hakim Sahib, Anant just told me you've had a son.'

'Congratulations to YOU, congratulations to YOU,' Dina Nath's fair complexion reddened slightly as he said this and his smile was tinged with embarrassment. But Chetan wasn't happy. He saw that Dina Nath's cheeks were sunken, the lids of his large, bulging cowry-like eyes had grown heavy; his long, thick handlebar moustaches, which he'd once been so proud of—pointy enough to pierce a lime, and which up until two years ago had been as thick as pump shoe laces, now hung limp beneath his nose. When he smiled, lines formed on either side of his mouth, from below his nose all the way down to the sides of his chin—and he wasn't yet twenty-five.

'Tell me, how's it going?' asked Chetan hesitantly.

'Thanks be to God,' he said, his smile contracting slightly, as he drew out the A in 'thanks'. Then a long sigh suddenly escaped his lips, 'But this isn't the right place for a good hakim.'

'All places are equal for the man with a healing touch,' said Chetan. 'People will come from Delhi and the south to be healed by him, whether he's in the desert or the jungle, the village or the city, on a soft cushion or at the plinth of a well.'

'If patients come to see someone, have him treat them, and they find relief, then he will become famous and people will learn that he has the healing touch. Here, a patient comes to my place one day, the next day they go to Nabi Jan, and the third day they go to Durga Prasad. And of course, whoever does come wants free medicine,' Dina Nath added with some irritation.

'To get famous, you have to distribute free medicines,' said Chetan. 'There must be some medicines that are cheap and can be given out for free—the kinds for digestion, constipation, purgatives and so on. Let people fill the expensive prescriptions with the compounder. Hakim Nabi Jan . . .'

'Arré bhai, I know all this . . . but right at the beginning I made the mistake of opening my dispensary in my own neighbourhood. People have drunk seers of violet sharbat and essence of bugloss and not a single bastard has given me one paisa, and on top of that they swear at me.'

'A brilliant man like you should set up shop in Lahore,' argued Chetan. 'And your medicines should be made famous throughout India with advertising. Already your whooping cough medicine is infallible . . .'

Dina Nath only sighed deeply.

And Chetan told him the story of Kaviraj Ramdas, how he'd got his Kaviraj degree, made his dispensary famous all over India on the strength of advertising, written *Marriage Secrets* and sold lakhs of copies, and how the people who read his books came immediately to his dispensary, whereupon he fleeced them forthwith.

'You're so brilliant,' said Chetan abandoning the more formal term for 'you' as he spoke. 'You know so much more than Kaviraj; you're devoted to your work. But you're just sitting here rotting away. Jalandhar is too small for you. Come to Lahore and start a practice there.'

Hakim Dina Nath's eyes opened wide. For a moment he sat and stared into the void, as if lost in a dream world. Then he got up and took a manuscript from the cupboard.

'I have also written a book for married couples. Take a look, the style is so much better than Kaviraj Ramdas's *Marriage Secrets*, and there's much more information in it.'

'If Dina's book is printed, a hullabaloo will break out in the medical community!'

Chetan turned to look. Dina Nath's uncle, Dal Chand, stood nearby, with his big round eyes, handlebar moustaches and innocent, plump-cheeked face.

'Where did this idiot come from?' thought Chetan to himself, but aloud he said, 'Namaste,' and pressed his hands together. He added, 'Tell me Chacha Dal Chand, how are things?'

'Arré, has anything ever been bad for me, that it would be so today?' laughed Uncle as he smoothed out his moustaches. 'I get up at dawn, I still do one hundred push-ups and sit-ups, I work hard all day and sleep soundly at night. I never touch Vanaspati ghee, and eat only milk and ghee from my own cow.'

He set one foot in the shop, scratched his thigh and began to explain the harm that can come from using Vanaspati ghee, and the benefits of pure milk and ghee, as though he were an elder, when he was actually only five or six years older than his nephew Dina Nath.

*

Uncle Dal Chand had been like this from the beginning. Dina Nath had started working at the shop after passing the middle school exams, but Chetan and Anant were in the habit of making a point of sitting in the shop with Dina Nath for a while if they went home through Mohalla Mendruan, Mitta Bazaar and Padiyan. Dina Nath had left school, but he continued to study his neighbours' textbooks, especially science. Chetan and Anant still did not know much science. They hadn't yet started studying it, when one evening Dina Nath showed them a science trick. He placed two small glasses filled with a white watery substance on a teapoy. He then took a white paper and wet one end of it in one of the glasses. It turned red. He dipped the other end into the other glass, and it turned blue. Chetan looked on astonished. How could a white paper change colour in a white watery substance? He just could not understand it.

Then one day, Dina Nath made a crystal and showed it to them. Chetan asked him where he'd learned all this.

Dal Chand had replied for him, 'This is all the magic of science. Even at this age, Dina can perform amazing feats your science teacher probably doesn't know. When he grows up, he'll be an important scientist.'

And that day, Uncle Dal Chand explained at length what can be done with chemistry and how Dina Nath would one day turn copper into gold.

When Dina Nath started doing magic tricks, Uncle Dal Chand began giving speeches on magic; even Thallu Ram would sometimes jump into the middle of the speeches. When Dina Nath took up compounding medicines, his father and uncle augmented everyone's wealth of knowledge on the topic of medicine. Thallu Ram did not interfere as much as Dal Chand, but both of them suffered from this affliction, and Chetan felt quite irate when he was forced to listen to what those two had to say rather than what Dina Nath was saying. Finally, one day, he got so annoyed, he said to Anant, 'After all, Dina Nath's the one studying medicine, but Thallu Ram and Dal Chand seem to have become doctors without studying anything at all!'

'I'll fix those sons of bitches,' said Anant.

In those days, they were studying for their intermediate FA degree. One day, on their way home from college, they saw Dina Nath seated at the shop as always. After talking about this or that for a couple of minutes, Anant asked, 'Dina, is there any cure for haemorrhoids?'

Dina Nath looked through a book and read out a very long recipe.

Then Thallu Ram pushed the cheap frames of his glasses on to the bridge of his nose (they had slipped down while he was working) and, leaving off work, he remarked, 'A moneylender had bleeding haemorrhoids and was in a wretched state from continuously losing blood. All the hakims and vaidyas around tried to cure him, but it came to nothing. One day, he was travelling to another village on urgent business, when he stopped at a well along the way to rest a bit. A sugar-cane crop grew in the nearby field, the long stalks of cane waving in the breeze. They were tended by a tenant farmer. He cut down fifteen or twenty stalks of sugarcane and presented them to the moneylender. The moneylender did feel a bit thirsty, and some of the cane was quite sweet and juicy, so he sucked them all dry. Then the farmer said he would harvest a whole bundle of them and send them home with him on his way back.

'That evening, the moneylender did not bleed. The next day, he sucked the sugar cane some more, but the corners of his mouth were skinned from too much sucking, so he stopped after five or ten tastes. That day too he found relief from his sickness, and there was no end to his astonishment when he found his haemorrhoids were completely cured.

'One day the town hakim came to the village to see a patient. He had previously cured the moneylender many times. After seeing the patient, the hakim went to see the moneylender as well and, after greeting him, he asked after his health.

'"My problem has disappeared," the moneylender, who had been completely cured in just a few days, told him enthusiastically.

'"But how?"

'"By sucking on sugar cane."

'The hakim wrinkled his brow. For a few moments he was lost in thought. Then he said, "Yes, there is one kind of bleeding haemorrhoids which can be cured by sucking on sugar cane."

'"Then why didn't you tell me?" complained the moneylender.

'"Because there was no hope of finding the right kind of sugar cane,"' said Thallu Ram, imitating the hakim's voice in a theatrical manner.

'"But of course you can get any kind of sugar cane," said the moneylender.

'"Well, let's go to that well where you sucked on the sugar cane," said the hakim.

'Then the moneylender enthusiastically took him to the field in the company of a couple of other villagers. The hakim told the farmer to dig up the spot where the sugar cane had been harvested. Everyone was astonished when they dug up a dead hooded snake. The farmer told him that one day he'd found a snake in the porch, which he'd killed and buried right in this spot.

'Then the hakim said to the moneylender, "You are lucky, sir, that you were given the sugar cane from this soil to suck on. This cure for haemorrhoids is written in the books; come to town and I'll show you. If a black-hooded snake remains buried somewhere for two months, and sugar cane is planted there, then the person who sucks on that cane will find relief from the most intractable of bleeding haemorrhoids. I would certainly have told you this cure, but where would I have found such sugar cane?"'

After telling this story, Thallu Ram looked at his son and his friends with great pride and, hitching up his dhoti slightly, he jumped down from his seat and went a slight distance to squat over the drain and urinate.

Then Uncle Dal Chand smoothed out his moustaches. 'But I can tell you an even easier cure for haemorrhoids than this,' he remarked.

Chetan nudged Anant with his elbow.

'It's like falling off a log,' said Dal Chand. 'Get a bitter white radish. Don't peel it, divide it into four parts, sprinkle it with salt, hang it upside down by the leaves. When all the liquid drains from it, eat it. In just one week, you'll get relief from the bloodiest of haemorrhoids.'

'Did you cure your own haemorrhoids that way?' asked Anant, picking up his books and stepping down into the bazaar.

'I cured your father's,' growled Dal Chand, and he hurled a particularly vehement curse Anant's way.

'You must have cured your mother's because my father never had that problem,' called out Anant, and then added, preparing to run, 'Amazing how there's only one goldsmith that's studying hikmat, but the whole family's turned into hakims.'

'You come back here, your mother's—' Dal Chand picked up a nearby anvil, jumped over their seats and, hurling the stones of curses after Anant, leapt into the bazaar. But in the midst of this, Anant had got quite far away and was running as fast as he could without looking back. After chasing him a short way and flinging curses after him, Uncle Dal Chand returned panting.

Chetan and Anant stopped when they got to Har Lal the grocer's shop and laughed long and hard.

*

Dal Chand was narrating the benefits of pure ghee and Chetan was staring at him fixedly. He'd always envied such men who experienced all emotions the same way, who considered whatever came before them to be ordained by fate and took it in stride, who harboured neither ambition nor envy, who were satisfied with just a little, who ate, drank and slept comfortably, and when the time came, aged like ripened fruit. Chetan had always noticed a peculiar innocence bordering on idiocy in Uncle Dal Chand's eyes. And sometimes he was jealous of this innocence. It was this innocence that made him so idiotically self-confident. Dal Chand would never believe that anyone could be smarter than him. He had unbreakable faith in the truth of his own words. And he was like those flowers floating in the waters of a lake that neither know the depths of the lake nor the loftiness of the sky, and flow along laughing and smiling. Then some wave comes along and swallows them and they drown, smiling all the while.

Ever since he'd known Dal Chand he'd seen him smiling happily like this. It was as though a light, cool, unchanging breeze always blew within him, and he had never experienced any rattling or gusting gales. Whenever Anant teased him, the two of them changed their route and went home via Lal Bazaar for a few days. After ten days or so, when they again came to sit by Dina Nath, Dal Chand would have forgotten everything. They thought he was a moron, but sometimes Chetan envied him his simple nature.

Telling them the benefits of pure ghee and the detriments of Vanaspati ghee, Dal Chand added, 'Now I'm in the habit of eating hot chapatis slathered in pure ghee with a bit of sugar. In the winter, I continue to eat ghee and sugar . . .'

'The elders have also said,' Desraj, the jeweller seated at the shop across the way, left off his work to interject, 'eat sugar with ghee, bring the world to its knee.'

'Well, who knows if I bring the world to its knee—all I do is bring home my earnings—but I for sure eat sugar with ghee,' said Dal Chand.

And he continued, 'So yes, as I was saying, I'm in the habit of eating chapatis slathered in ghee, with a bit of sugar. That's what I take for dessert after dinner. A few days ago, I went to a friend's house in Phagwara. Now, what can I tell you, at the start of dinner, I asked for a spoonful of ghee on the last roti with a bit of sugar.

89

'When I was done eating and tore off a bit of the sugary bread, I just didn't take to it. All the fun of eating was spoiled. I felt nauseous. "What kind of ghee is this?" I asked.

'"Pure Vanaspati," they said.

'And the result was that now, as soon as I put ghee and sugar on my chapati, I remember the Vanaspati ghee I tasted in Phagwara, and I start feeling nauseous.'

'Arré bhai, one day everyone will eat Vanaspati ghee. When there's not enough food for men, who will feed the cows and buffaloes?' asked Desraj from across the street. 'I've just started using Vanaspati.'

'By then I'll be gone,' Dal Chand retorted, smiling to display his pearly teeth in the garden of his moustaches.

'It'll happen in your lifetime, mark my words,' replied Desraj, standing up on the stoop of his shop and stretching in a prophetic manner.

'Okay, brother Chetan, be happy!' said Uncle Dal Chand, ignoring Desraj and patting Chetan on the back. 'If you're in town again, come by here too.'

And he set off, carefree, grinning from ear to ear.

*

After Dal Chand left, Dina Nath opened his book and said, 'I've called it *Marriage: Home-Making or Home-Wrecking?*'

But Chetan stood up. He wasn't interested in hearing anything at all about the problem of marriage. 'Look Dina Nath, I'll come by tomorrow and listen carefully. Right now I have to go and see a couple of friends.'

And he held out his hand.

Hakim Dina Nath stood up as well.

He took Chetan's hand in both of his and, pressing it warmly, he smiled and said, 'Definitely come by tomorrow, don't forget.'

For just a second, Chetan's eyes were fixed on the two wrinkles that started on each side of his nose and stretched to his chin, and then he said, 'No, no, I'll definitely come.'

And he stepped down from the shop and even tossed a greeting Desraj's way as he continued on his way.

8

A bit ahead, before Tunka the dhobi's shop, were the lock-and-key smiths. They poured molten iron into moulds to make locks and keys. The boy who worked with the blacksmith would pump air with the bellows from the side into the pine coals beneath the crucible in which the metal melted, while the blacksmith prepared the mould. When the mould was ready, he'd remove the upper portion and shake the dirt mixed with sand from the mouth of the lower portion. The shape of the key would be dug from the middle of the mould. He'd draw a line from the mouth of the mould to the key with an iron awl. After fixing the upper portion in this same manner, he'd use a cotton swab to take some of the sand mixture from a clay pot and sprinkle it over the mould, then bind it tightly and prop up the anvil with his foot, lift the crucible with tongs, and pour the melted metal into it. Smoke would begin to rise from the mould and the smell of burned spice and sand filled the air. Then he'd place the crucible back on the stove, put more pieces of metal in it, place the mould on the wooden platform, pound it a couple of times with his fist, open it and lift out the upper portion with a practised hand. The cast key in the lower portion would sparkle, and a line running from its top to the mouth of the mould formed a sort of metal mound. Then, having lightly knocked both sides of the mould a bit, he'd take them in his hands and flip them over so that the key would fall out, but the sand in the mould would not move at all. After this, he'd lift the key with the tongs, and dunk it into a small clay jug filled with water. There'd be a hissing sound. The smell of smoke and metal would rise and fill the nostrils. Then he'd separate the metal ridge with one blow of the chisel and hammer, toss the new key to the right on to the pile of new keys and, separating out the burnt sand mixture, he'd knead it again and pour it into the mould.

He didn't know why he was so attracted to this process, but whenever Chetan was on his way home from school or college alone, he'd stop there for a long time, watching the locks and keys being made. Sometimes the keys were already finished and the blacksmith would be picking them up from the pile one at a time and cleaning them off with a file. His hands moved at the pace of a machine and Chetan would watch transfixed. Sometimes he'd be binding together the top and bottom portions of the locks. The process that he'd watched again and again always seemed new to him. The freshly minted shining keys lying in their moulds always looked like newborn babies and when the blacksmith cut the thin plate between the lump on the mouth of the mould and the key, it was like snipping the umbilical cord.

When Chetan left Hakim Dina Nath's shop, he thought the blacksmith would probably be making locks at that hour. He'd stand for a few moments and watch, and that odd smell of burnt sand and burning iron and water all mixed together would fill his nostrils.

And indeed, the blacksmith was preparing the mould and the molten metal was turning red in the crucible on the stove. Chetan had just stopped there when Anant slapped him hard on the shoulder.

'Hello there, all done with your Uncle Medicine?'

'But you were going towards Lal Bazaar.'

'I'd meant to see Tirth in Chowk Sudan, but he wasn't there, so I thought I'd go and see Billa—he's living in a room in Bohar Wala Bazaar these days. I didn't find him either, so then I came this way. Did you see Dina Nath?'

'Yes.'

'How's he doing? Has he shaved off his moustaches or not?'

'He hasn't, but if things keep up like this he'll soon do it.'

Anant laughed. 'Why?'

'The state of Hakim Hazik Hakim Dina Nath, Gold Medallist, seems a bit dire.'

'Now he wants to earn money by fraud,' said Anant. 'How's a practice going to run on fraud? I wouldn't be surprised if he ended up in jail one day.'

'Why?'

'Because ever since the dispensary in Bajiyanwala Bazaar failed, he's been putting out ads under the names of several fake companies and selling fake goods in the style of Shera and Company. Planchettes, fake cameras, watches and who knows what else . . . he thinks no one knows. One of these days, he'll get caught, and then all his tricks will be revealed . . . We don't speak any more, otherwise I'd tell him, you jerk, you got your medical degree so fast; practise for nine or ten years and you'll become famous on your own. You're not the kind of genius that can become Thakur Dutt Multani in just two days. If you were going to be such a fraudster, what was the point of studying medicine!'

And Anant laughed.

'I advised him to go to Lahore and open a dispensary. He knows so many recipes. He should just advertise that medical knowledge of his, then he'll become famous like Kaviraj Ramdas.

95

Kaviraj came to Lahore and started a practice in just the same way.'

'How many children does Kaviraj have?' asked Anant suddenly.

Chetan fell silent for a moment; the question was so rude. Then he replied, 'He had only one son at the time. Now, after fourteen years, he's had another.'

'The guy who can wait fourteen years to have a second child is the guy who can become Kaviraj Ramdas. Dina Nath's had five kids in eight years. If he goes to Lahore, whose daddy will he cry to? Thallu spends whatever he earns on liquor. Who would raise Dina Nath's kids here? Who told that son of a bitch to quit jewellery-making and become a doctor? If he wanted to cheat people, why didn't he stick with his original profession?'

And Anant guffawed loudly. He slapped Chetan on the shoulder and asked, 'Where are you going now?'

'I was thinking of going to see Nishtar.'

'What are you going to do at that squint-eye's place? Come on, let's bring Debu Kana and Badda along. Debu is more of a squint-eye than Nishtar. Let's play a few rounds of chaupar. We'll get the two of them to fight and then watch the fun.'

'I'm not in the mood.'

'Being in a bad mood isn't going to bring your sister-in-law back.'

'Shut up.'

Anant chuckled. 'It's time to move on to greener pastures. Out of sight, out of mind, that's my motto.'

'You've always been a womanizer.'

'And you've always been a fool.'

Anant went on his way, guffawing loudly. Chetan stood there for a moment, feeling defeated. He saw that the blacksmith had pounded the mould a couple of times with his fist and lifted out the upper portion. In the lower portion sparkled the new key, fresh as a baby.

The key . . .

Chetan watched for a few moments, unblinkingly. But though he stared, he didn't see a thing. He sighed deeply and went on his way.

9

'Anant was right though,' thought Chetan as he walked along. 'No matter how rudely he speaks, there's some truth to what he says.' What was the reason for his uprootedness, after all? Wasn't it Neela's wedding? And what if she hadn't married? What if she'd continued to adore him? He didn't have the courage to leave Chanda—to make Neela his own. He didn't want to betray Chanda either, but he still wanted Neela's love. On the one hand there was Anant—completely unconflicted! He felt no sort of dilemma whatsoever. He was uninhibited in love; Chetan recollected a few of Anant's romances. Two servant women had worked in the mohalla, Jwali and Mirchan. They both had young daughters, Akki and Ambo. Both liked Chetan. Akki was very beautiful. Ambo wasn't beautiful, but she was young and attractive. Whenever Chetan went to fill water at the well or bathe, and one of them was fetching water, they would always beg to have their pots snatched, and they'd speak flirtatiously to him while he held on to their pots. But Chetan never went beyond that. When he told Anant about them, Anant cooked up many schemes for him. And when Chetan wasn't able to put any of these into play, Anant pressured his mother to hire a servant to fetch water for them. When he no longer wanted the first one, they hired the second one and he told Chetan at length how he'd snared the girls one by one. Anant believed women were good for one thing only, and a man who doesn't make proper use of them doesn't deserve to be called a man. Forget all this lovey-dovey nonsense!

And then there was Chetan's father. His beliefs were no different from Anant's. Chetan had heard him discussing this topic with his friends many times in his childhood. When necessary, he even used religion to bolster his case. What sort of man shrinks from women when they come to him for protection? Krishna cavorted with the milkmaids in Braj. He loved Radha, who was the wife of another. When Rukmini summoned him, he carried her off, and when, after defeating Jarasandha, he had to marry sixteen thousand princesses, he did so without hesitation.

Far from marrying her, Chetan hadn't even been able to requite Neela's love; even when he desired her with every particle of his being, he'd kept his body under control. How he had punished her with his innate clumsiness. He was timid . . . a coward and a fool!

But then he thought of his mother. How his poor mother had suffered because of his father's prowess! He thought of Lacchma—skinny Lacchma, with her complexion the colour of wheat, her bold eyes, her sharp features—the wife of his father's sergeant friend Mangal Sen and his father's mistress.

Ma had once told him the story of Lacchma with great sadness. She had been the child widow of a Kalal family—toddy collectors—from Urmar Tanda. When Mangal Sen had been head constable there, he'd gone to her home on a search for some case; their eyes had met and that was it. In the middle of the night, she removed her sari, tied it to the window and climbed out naked. She ran off with Mangal Sen and moved in with him. Chetan's father had been the assistant station master of Urmar Tanda at the time. She had hidden in their house for many days. Then Mangal Sen got a transfer and took her with him.

But she never left Chetan's father. On many occasions, he had given her his entire salary. Chetan remembered the First World

War, when his father was station master at Koyta. Sacks of wheat were going for twenty-one rupees then. They could only afford to make one vegetable dish at home, and often they had to eat just onions with their chapatis. They were also in quite a bit of debt. Whenever his father sent his salary home, he'd tell them to send a sack of wheat to Lacchma's house as well.

Ma didn't rate her any higher than a prostitute. How could a girl from a Brahmin Mishra home accept food from the hand of a low-caste Kalal? When his father brought Lacchma to their home, and she ate right there inside the house, Ma would prepare the food, but fast herself. She'd do her utmost to avoid touching Lacchma. If she did touch her, she'd bathe afterwards and wash her clothes.

One time—their house had not yet been rebuilt—his father came from somewhere bringing Lacchma with him. He also brought a bottle of liquor. Lacchma poured it out for him with her own hands. Ma served them dinner. Then Chetan's father, extremely drunk, ordered that the new sari that had come to Ma as a gift from her father's home (Chetan's maternal grandfather had sent a sari and sweets for the festival of Teej) be given to Lacchma. As if Chetan's father ever bought anything for Ma. Chetan had hardly ever seen Ma wear a nice silk sari. This one was from Benares. Although Ma was indifferent to silk clothing and usually didn't wear it, every six months or so she'd open the trunk just to gaze at her silk saris and imagine the day when her sons were grown and getting married, and her heart would be gladdened at seeing them adorn her daughters-in-law. She'd carefully stored this sari in the trunk as soon as it came to save it for Bhai Sahib's wedding. She harboured no hope that her husband would spend even one paisa on the bridal gift.

But she had never refused a command from her husband. With pangs in her heart, her eyes brimming with tears, she brought out the sari. Lest that Kalal woman touch the clothing she was wearing, she wrapped her own sari tighter and tossed the new one into Lacchma's lap. Chetan's father had beaten her severely just for that. He grabbed her by the neck and made her bow down before Lacchma again and again; her forehead burst open from hitting the ground and gushed with blood, and she fell unconscious.

Chetan laughed bitterly. Was that how little the god Krishna valued women? And he thought of Ram's character . . . whenever Chetan's father invoked Krishna to cover up bad conduct, Ma told him the story of Ram. Ravana had abducted Sita, but Ram continued to think only of her. There is no mention of any other romance anywhere in his long forest exile. Surpanakha had approached him, attracted by his beauty, and was shunned (if Anant, or his father, had been in Ram's place would they have ignored her? Perhaps not). Then when Ram himself exiled Sita to the forest after the victory in Lanka, he continued to remain alone. He subsumed his loneliness in his kingship.

Did Ram love Sita?

Did Ram love himself?

These two questions came suddenly to Chetan's mind. But he wasn't sure of the answer. Hadn't the ancient storytellers conceived of the two ideal temperaments in the form of these two ideal men? This is what made them complete. It seemed to Chetan that the middle-class people around him were bound to these two extremes; this is what motivated them. None among them could become Ram or Krishna completely. As far as others were concerned, he couldn't be that certain, but he himself wavered between these two poles like a rose in the eye of a storm. His father's hot blood flowed in his veins, as did his inconstancy, but so too did the coolness of his mother's blood and her restraint. Whenever he thought about Neela, he saw Chanda in his mind's eye, and then Ma's silhouette would rise

up before his image of Chanda and his heart would fill with
boundless pathos and he'd shudder at the mere thought of
causing Chanda trouble.

*

Daal[4]—Do not rise so high, oh heart
Those who raise their heads get killed

Chetan stopped. To the left, at the shop of Tunka the dhobi,
a *baitbaaz*—a singer of Punjabi couplets —hand to his ear, was
singing a couplet in a highly melodic, passionate voice that echoed
far off. After singing two lines in a softer tone, he raised his voice
again for the next couplet:

Daal—Do not rise so high, oh heart
Those who raise their heads get killed

Those who grow vain
Never attain their heart's desires

The ditches can engulf the skies of toil
The hillocks stand high and dry, wailing

The flowers blossom but briefly, T.C.[5]
Once thrown in the pot, their essence is extracted

---

[4] *Daal* is the fourth letter in the Urdu alphabet. [Daal is actually the eleventh letter
in the Urdu alphabet, but the first letter in the fourth *group* of letters, which must
be what Ashk meant by this footnote. This poem is part of the 'Si-Harfi' genre
of Punjabi poetry described in *Falling Walls* by Ashk, thus: '*Si-Harfi* = A series
of *bait*s in which each bait starts with each letter of the Urdu alphabet.'—*trans.*]
[5] T.C. are the poet Tarachand's initials.

Chetan's attention turned away again. Wasn't Neela's situation like that of a flower that is punished for two hours of blooming by being plucked and thrown into a boiling cook pot!

Darkness shadowed his eyes. Anguish stirred within him.

The singer's voice was filled with such pain . . . and Chetan was thinking: Here, flowers are plucked before they even get the chance to bloom. The gardener who plants them plucks them too, then hands them over to some worthless character. No matter how much Pandit Deen Dayal loved his daughter, Neela, no matter how much he adored her, he was still the one responsible for strangling her . . . Neela . . . Neela . . .

Was her vanity for her own beauty really so great that fate deemed it proper to pluck her up and toss her away? She probably hadn't even been conscious of it!

And he found that he wasn't actually sad that Neela had got married at thirteen or fourteen; that the bloom had not even had a chance to blossom before it was plucked. What made him sad was that she'd married a middle-aged man and that the reason for this marriage was actually Chetan's own idiocy, cowardliness, childishness and insecurity. He could not get that incident in the room atop the house in Alawalpur out of his head, for which Neela now suffered the punishment. He didn't know how to atone for his sin and he could focus on nothing. If Neela had married Trilok, or some other young man, perhaps he wouldn't feel as troubled as he did now. He'd be happy, despite his distress. But now . . . now . . .

Daal—Why such sorrow, oh heart?
Is there anyone who does not suffer in this world?
The world is like a wayside inn
Every guest that arrives is suffering

The singer had thrown down another couplet . . .

And so people are satisfied by their sorrow. Knowing that sorrow is irresistible, they surrender their weapons before it and consider it best to accept their fate as unchangeable . . . And he set out . . . a sort of ball of rebellion rose inside him and stuck in his throat. Was it necessary for the world to remain simply a temporary resting place? For there to be nothing but sorrow? For man never to change the circumstances that bring him sorrow, never to break with the traditions that he himself created; never to create joy? The world is a halting place, sorrow is necessary, and so people will patiently drink it down and live with it? They will simply soldier on. Neela will endure sorrow patiently, her father will endure, he himself would endure, Chanda would endure, and who knows where this cycle would come to an end, or perhaps it never would. His head spun with a rush of anger, he walked straight through the bazaar, head down, like a dust storm that emerges from the galis and bazaars and churns along but does not flip off roofs, or knock down houses, or cause the clouds to rain. When he lifted his head he found he was passing below Nishtar's house. He stopped, looked up and called out.

'Nishtar . . . Nishtar!'

When no response came, he walked through the doorway, climbed the stairs, and knocked loudly on the door.

'Nishtar!'

10

'Come in, sit down, my brother will be here soon,' said a small girl staring at the ground as she opened the door.

Chetan walked across the courtyard and sat down on a filthy chair in Nishtar's room, but nearly fell over. The chair was missing a leg. It had been propped up against the wall, balancing on its remaining three legs. In order to stay seated, one had to keep the back against the wall, and Chetan had pulled it out slightly to sit down.

The girl suppressed a smile with great difficulty and remarked ruefully, 'I've told my brother to get it fixed many times. Someone's going to break their head open one of these days; but he doesn't ever listen to me. Sit over there on the charpoy or push the chair up against the wall.'

'No problem, no problem,' said Chetan, relieving some of his embarrassment by pushing the chair against the wall. He sat down, picked up a newspaper from the charpoy and began to fan himself.

The girl ran to get a fan, and set it down quietly in front of him. These actions seemed to have left her out of breath. Eyes downcast, she asked, 'Shall I make you lassi or shikanji?'

Chetan was acquainted with Nishtar's financial situation, but in a Punjabi home (especially before Partition), it was unheard of not to serve a guest lassi or sharbat.

'No, just bring me some cold water from the pot,' Chetan replied, picking up the fan.

The girl went away. She was twelve or thirteen. She wasn't beautiful like Neela, but she wasn't ugly either. Like Nishtar, her left eye was a bit squinty, but where Nishtar's squint made him look ugly, hers made her more beautiful . . . 'Was Neela's fate written on her forehead, or was Chanda's?' thought Chetan. 'There is no other fate for lower-middle-class girls. Who knows when things will ever change? Perhaps when they are truly free, when their situation is better than that of sheep. One shake, one strong shake, and these walls imprisoning the middle class will collapse. True, the independence movement has brought some outside their homes, but how many? Maybe not even one per cent.'

And Chetan imagined a full cloud full of bashful raindrops, each wondering which drops would leave first. One would fall, then another, then the rain would descend in torrents.

'Perhaps the women jumping into the independence movement are like those first drops of rain,' thought Chetan.

He thought about his own neighbourhood. During the movements of 1921 or 1931, not one woman had left the house, not one had gone to jail. Many had not even seen a rally. If they were asked 'Do you want freedom?' perhaps none would even have been able to reply.

Chetan sighed deeply.

'Here you go!'

Chetan lifted his head. The girl stood before him with a glass of *kacchi* lassi in her hand. Chetan wanted to ask, 'Why this formality?' But he didn't say anything. He took the glass from her hand and nearly drank the whole thing down in one gulp.

The girl stood still, her eyes glued to the ground, and when he was done drinking, she took the glass and went away.

'Will Nishtar be long?' he called out.

She stopped but didn't turn around. 'He said he was coming right back when he went out,' she replied, as though speaking to the floor. 'He didn't eat before going out. He must be on his way back.'

And she went away.

Chetan looked all about the room—it was a small balcony he'd visited a few times before. A charpoy scattered with books and papers was set along the left side of the room. Then there was a broken teapoy and the three-legged chair (the one on which he was now seated, somehow). On a tablet resting on the teapoy lay some papers, pen and ink, and the new issue of *Sadaqat*, which Chetan had picked up in his nervousness, then tossed aside when the fan had arrived. To the right side, on the wall above, was a stack of files for *Sadaqat*.

Chetan picked up the issue of *Sadaqat* again—it was a six-page Urdu weekly. The name of the journal was written on the front page in a flowery style that looked especially vulgar to Chetan. Beneath the title was printed a couplet:

Oh to dissolve into fidelity!
Indeed I shall wipe out all falsity

And beneath the couplet was printed in thin Arabic letters the name 'Nishtar'.

'As though without the name, the people reading this couplet would think it must have been written by Iqbal,' Chetan laughed to himself.

His gaze travelled further down. Inside a long, rounded border was written:

Owner-editor Nanda Lal 'Nishtar' Hunarvi

Chetan chuckled to himself at both these titles. First at 'owner' (Nishtar must consider this pamphlet to be no less than the *Tribune*), then at 'Hunarvi' (so Nishtar had also joined the ranks of Hunar Sahib's pupils. First 'Abr', then 'Rehmat', now 'Hunar'— who knows how many more gurus Nishtar would follow!).

*

Chetan was in Class Six when he first saw Nishtar, who was still 'Nanda Lal' back then. He still remembered that evening. The Non-cooperation Movement had been in full swing. When he'd got up that morning, he'd seen Rayzada Khushwant Ray, the adopted son of the late Ray Sahib Dayal Chand who lived in the house across the way, writing in beautiful letters with chalk above the old, flowery, shisham-wood door frame of the medieval brick house:

> *Supporters of non-cooperation should not come here asking for foreign clothing, or a court case will be opened against them.*

Chetan didn't understand the meaning of 'non-cooperation', so Bhai Sahib told him that Mahatma Gandhi had urged people not to work with the government—that was what non-cooperation meant. The whole country was on fire. Schools and colleges were closing. People had given up wearing foreign clothing, they had quit drinking liquor—all this to destroy the trade of those damned money-grubbing English.

His brother told him all sorts of things he didn't understand. But that day when he went to school, the first bell had not yet rung when he saw all the boys running out of their classrooms. Someone must have said something in the hallway that made them all get up and come outside. He followed them. Outside the schoolyard a huge crowd of boys had gathered in the field. Someone was standing on a stool giving a speech on the other side. Chetan couldn't see or hear a thing as he stood behind the oldest boys. Then a loud slogan echoed through the crowd—'Long live!' and everyone shouted as one—'The revolution!' And the crowd took off towards Adda Kapurthala beyond the police line— singing *Vande Mataram* and chanting 'Long live the revolution!' Chetan was at the very back—he'd seen his teachers standing by the school gate looking oddly helpless and embarrassed.

Chetan couldn't make out the entire song. But he heard one refrain again and again that reached him like a growing wave:

Oh Gandhi, he was put in prison too
And gave us homespun cotton

After this refrain, they'd yell 'Long live!' at the top of their lungs and Chetan cried out 'The revolution!' with the others.

From Adda Kapurthala they went to Imam Nasiruddin, then Bara Bazaar, then Bohar Wala Bazaar, then Bhairon Bazaar . . . thousands of people joined the procession, to the point that Chetan could no longer even hear the people singing up ahead. He felt tired too, so when they got near the statue of Bhairav, he left via Gali Tamakhiyan and came home through Papadiyan Bazaar.

In the afternoon, he had been playing chaupar with Badda, Debu and Hansa when suddenly they heard cries of 'Long live the revolution!' and the national anthem again. They rushed outside, abandoning the chaupar game. They'd only reached the well, when a volunteer appeared from the direction of the bazaar. He held aloft the national flag, and behind him came other volunteers wearing homespun kurta pyjamas and Gandhi caps, singing the homespun anthem and holding a sheet by four corners that was so weighted down with foreign-made clothing that it touched the ground.

They stopped when they entered the chowk of the mohalla and spread the sheet out on the ground. Two volunteers got on the plinth of the well and began to sing, and everyone joined in. Although it had been ten or eleven years since Chetan had heard that song, he remembered the first verse even today:

Wearing a homespun gown
Blowing the trumpet of civil disobedience
Loading the cannon-balls in the spinning wheel

Shoot cotton-balls at Lancashire
 at 'Shire
Shoot cotton-balls at Lancashire

Everyone will do as Gandhi says
Everyone will wear the shroud on their heads
Many a Jallianwala could happen again

Take out your rifles, and tell this to Dyer
 to Dyer
Shoot cotton-balls at Lancashire

Even after so many years had gone by, Chetan still remembered how the singers' faces glowed with a peculiar martyr-like zeal. Listening to the song sent chills down his spine, and as it ended, Bansi leapt up and joined in shouting 'Long live!' and Chetan shouted with the rest of them 'The revolution!'

After giving a brief but brilliant speech, the leader of the procession went from door to door asking for foreign-made clothing. It was a poor mohalla, and people didn't have much clothing; no one was going to tell them to donate their silks to burn in the bonfire. The housewives mostly gave old torn clothes. Even when all they got was a foreign-made rag, the neighbourhood echoed with cries of 'Victory to Gandhi Baba!' and 'Long live the revolution!' Chetan ran to his mother, who gave him a very old silk lehnga that looked quite new (since she saved up all her expensive clothing for her future daughters-in-law) and Chetan was proud as anything when he brought it to the leader. When the procession turned from their homes towards Rayzada Khushwant Ray's mansion they found the heavy shisham door closed. Then someone saw the notice written in chalk—

Supporters of the non-cooperation movement . . .

Someone else cried, 'He's a toady!' and the people of the mohalla joined the cry with the processioners, 'Yes he is!'

They wailed, 'Death to—Khushwant Ray!' and 'He's a toady—yes he is!', beat their breasts and cried out their slogans of 'Victory to—Gandhi Baba!' and 'Long live—the revolution!' Then the members of the procession continued on their way, carrying the heap of foreign clothing and singing their song, and Chetan followed.

After the procession had passed Harlal Pansari's shop, it made its way through Bajiyanwala Bazaar and was passing beneath the sitting rooms of Khushwant Ray's mansion, which opened out on to the bazaar, when all of a sudden, the upstairs windows opened and the Rayzada's elder wife (he had two wives, the first was from Jalandhar's Sondhi family, which was quite prominent in the independence movement, but since she had no children, the Rayzada had got married a second time, to a woman from a poor family) threw down a silk sari with a brocade border. And from one end to the other, the bazaar rang out with cries of 'Victory to—Mahatma Gandhi!' and 'Long live—the revolution!'

Chetan followed the procession outside the city, half a mile or so beyond Kot Kishanchand, to the Gandhi Pavilion. The Gandhi Pavilion was actually a wide, dried-out water tank, which was also called Nadiram's tank. Brick stairs led down into the tank from all four sides. A rally had taken place there the first time Mahatma Gandhi had come to Jalandhar and since then, it had been called the Gandhi Pavilion, and that's where all Congress rallies had taken place. Chetan felt exhausted from walking so far. The steps of the tank were completely packed. Such an enormous crowd had gathered from different neighbourhoods, it seemed as though the entire city was there. Chetan wanted to go up front and sit near the stage, but he couldn't see any empty space anywhere. He was so exhausted it was difficult for him to take another step, so he sat right down on an upper step. There were no microphones in that era, nor had a platform been built to fill up half the tank. The enormous, dry Nadiram tank looked like the stadiums of ancient times, but the speakers were accustomed to giving speeches at the top of their lungs, and when, after the singing of *Vande Mataram*, a small boy came on stage, and the chairman of the rally introduced him, even Chetan, seated on the topmost step, could hear his voice. The chairman praised the wisdom of young Nanda Lal, his power as a poet and his love of self-rule. Mother India was proud of such worthy sons, he said, who jump into the independence movement at such a young age, and he expressed the hope that the day was not far off when Mother India would be freed from the chains of slavery, and the name Nanda Lal 'Azad'—*freedom* (that was Nanda Lal's nom de plume in those days)—would echo in all corners of the nation. And he asked Nanda Lal to read his poetry.

Before reading his poem, Nanda Lal said a few words. His voice didn't reach Chetan, but Chetan certainly noticed that it bore no trace of anxiety at all (Nanda Lal must have been just a year or so younger than him) as he addressed that enormous crowd. He exuded amazing self-confidence. When he'd finished his brief speech before reading his poem, the crowd applauded as loudly as possible and shouted 'Long live the revolution!' and Chetan felt quite envious of him.

After his speech, Nanda Lal began reciting his poem with great enthusiasm. Chetan couldn't hear a single line, but he saw that after each verse the audience applauded and shouted, 'Long live the revolution!'

After Nanda Lal's poem, two or three leaders gave speeches, followed by the chairman. But Chetan heard and saw nothing else. He kept thinking about that boy's face and the applause of the audience.

Just then, he noticed that there was a pile of foreign clothing in the centre of the tank; oil had been sprinkled over it and it was being set on fire—and right at that moment, he heard cries of 'Police!' 'Police!' and the people sitting on the top steps suddenly stood up. Chetan saw uniformed police marching up behind him, lathis on their shoulders. They climbed on to the broken pillar made of medieval bricks, which at one time must have held up one side of a gate. Then Chetan saw a dark-skinned Muslim wrestler-type police inspector with a baton in his hand make his way down the path through the spectators (on one side were women and on the other were men) to the stage, and behind him a division of lathi-armed police climbed down the stairs. He watched as the police inspector stepped on to the stage and said something to the people there that made them stand at once. He took a step forward, they stepped back, and Chetan saw the lathis begin to swing. Chaos broke out. Chetan had no idea when he jumped from the pillar in that chaos and climbed up on to a farmer's sleeping perch overlooking the field across the street.

The next day when he heard that twelve men had been wounded in the rally and thirteen arrested, including twelve-year-old Nanda Lal 'Azad', his heart filled with respect and envy.

Nanda Lal was given a punishment of three months' hard labour. After he was released, Chetan sought him out and made friends with him. Later, when the self-rule movement had died down and the Hindu–Muslim riots began, the Mahavir Dal was born and the two of them became members together. Chetan started reciting Punjabi couplets as well and they both played the flute in the Mahavir Dal band. Nanda Lal was first the pupil of the Punjabi poet 'Abr' and when he became the pupil of the Punjabi Poetry Association leader Ustad 'Rehmat', he changed his nom de plume again, this time to 'Nishtar', and took Chetan with him and made him Rehmat's pupil as well. Rehmat was a dyer and his pupils were primarily the city's drifters: unemployed, lower-middle-class boys. Chetan's own middle-class sensibility would not allow him to wander about with such a low-life, ignorant dyer, nor to kiss up to him in his capacity as poetry mentor. He went to Rehmat's place a couple of times and also participated in the Mahavir Dal poetry gatherings. Then he, like most of the educated students of his social class, began to take an interest in Urdu poetry and only greeted Rehmat Sahib from a distance. After that, he met Hunar Sahib and, in his heart, he made him his ustad instead.

*

'So Nishtar has become a pupil of Hunar's as well,' he said to himself on seeing the title 'Hunarvi' next to Nishtar's name on the weekly. He wondered what couplets Hunar Sahib had recited to Nishtar as his own.

And he turned over the first page of *Sadaqat*. On the very next page was printed a poem by Janab Nanda Lal Sahib 'Nishtar

Hunarvi'—called 'Sorrow and Poverty'. Chetan had heard this poem of Hunar Sahib's before. Hunar Sahib had reeled Chetan in, in just one sitting, by reciting short verses in the style popularized by the Urdu poet 'Hafiz' Jalandhari. Whenever he took on a new pupil, Hunar Sahib would have the pupil write that very same poem under his own name and publish it in some lesser known journal. Several years ago, that poem had been published under Chetan's name by Munshi Girijashankar in his journal *Girija*. At the thought of *Girija*, Chetan recalled Munshi Girijashankar's hippopotamus-shaped moustaches, and how, since no one pays much attention to the placement of the diacritics *zabar* and *zer* in Urdu, he used to read '*Girija*' as '*Garja*' or 'thunder', and had thought it a very odd name for a monthly journal. When Hunar Sahib had submitted the poem to Munshi Girijashankar under Chetan's name, he had thanked him, smiling through his enormous whiskers, as though he'd offered him not just a poem, but dues for a yearly subscription.

As he sat there, he cast a cursory glance over the poem. As soon as his eye fell on the final verse he had to smile:

What is an old woman's heart anyway, that fills with grief
The hearth of her home already long extinguished, but
> There is fire in her heart
Now it is like night, there is a dark sky
> There is one lamp
Empty of oil, its wick dry
Enduring every pain and sorrow, she says today with 'Nishtar'
> What a terrible thing is poverty!

All that was different was that 'Nishtar' had replaced 'Chetan'; otherwise it was exactly the same poem. Chetan was astonished at how much he'd liked it at the time, and that he'd actually submitted it for publication. And all those poems and couplets—they were devoid of feeling, of experiences; just simple mental exercises that hadn't been touched in the slightest by real life and which rang completely false, like Hunar Sahib's own life.

As he sat there, Chetan felt that the past few days had aged him. He'd been accustomed to living in an emotional fantasy world, but now he'd come to know the reality of sorrow and joy, and this one incident—Neela's wedding—had given him new insight.

The poem filled two entire columns. In the other two columns was printed a story by Janab 'Hunar', Nature Writer. He'd heard this story the first time he'd met him. It had been printed before in a little-known Lahore weekly and a monthly, and now it adorned the pages of *Sadaqat*.

The famous Urdu short-story writer Devdarshan used to write 'Nature Writer' after his name so frequently that Chetan had begun to have his suspicions about his 'nature writing'—and Hunar . . . Chetan recollected him reading the wedding song for Neela's wedding . . . how he'd compared a middle-aged, sunken-cheeked groom to the full moon . . . He crumpled up the issue of *Sadaqat*, threw it in the corner and got up to leave.

*

Nishtar's sister was seated to one side in the courtyard, reading a novel perhaps. Her pose suggested extreme concentration. Her eyes were strangely wide and watery.

'Hunar Sahib didn't come by?' he asked, as though addressing the door frame.

The girl started and quickly hid the book behind her back. She looked as though someone had caught her stealing. For just a moment she stared at him alarmed, then leapt up.

118

Chetan repeated his question.

'If anyone came, I didn't see them,' replied the girl, staring at the ground. 'But he didn't eat before he went out. He said, "I'll be right back."'

'Okay, so tell him Chetan came by.'

And he walked quickly across the courtyard. The darkness on the stairs had slowed his pace and he had to feel his way along as he descended.

11

Just after the point where Papadiyan Bazaar meets Lal Bazaar by way of Gali Patpheriyan, on the left side, there's a tiny, narrow lane full of twists and turns that goes to Juttiyanwallah Chowk. This was the gali where Nishtar's home was. When Chetan came out of the doorway, he stopped for a moment. He couldn't decide which way to go. He had absolutely no desire to go back home. He didn't feel like seeing anyone from his mohalla. 'Amichand's a deputy commissioner now' (the people in the neighbourhood had made him a deputy commissioner effective immediately): There was nothing else they wanted to discuss besides that, and just hearing Amichand's name made Chetan think of the Scandal Point incident. What he wanted to do was go some place where he could completely forget about Neela's wedding, his own pain, Amichand becoming a deputy collector, and his feelings of inadequacy in that context. He had no hope of sympathy from Anant. He'd just give him a couple of derisive pokes, and if he went to Dina Nath, he'd be forced to hear his entire epic, *Marriage: Home-making or Home-wrecking?* which was why he'd come to Nishtar's home—to avoid both Anant and Dina Nath. He had thought he could listen to Nishtar's new poems and his vain boasting; he'd hear about his schemes and, if he was in the mood, he'd say to him, 'Yaar, sing me a few verses from *Heer Ranjha*.' Nishtar sang *Heer Ranjha* in a lovely melodious voice and

Chetan wanted to hear that passage where the villagers force Heer into her bridal palanquin and set off:

> As they lifted the palanquin, Heer screamed,
> They're taking me, Papa, oh, they're taking me away!

Chetan had been turning that passage over and over in his mind. He wanted Nishtar to sing it while he listened quietly. He knew this desire was no better than reopening his wound, but just as picking at a scab can be oddly pleasurable, it made him happy to hear that passage from *Heer Ranjha* and use it to imagine the sight of Neela's leave-taking. When Neela had come to see him before her departure, and Chetan had bowed at her feet to ask her forgiveness, she had said, 'Jija ji, what are you doing!' She had lifted him up, then fled, suppressing a sob, and he'd no longer had the courage to go downstairs and look her in the eye. He didn't even go to give her the shagun. Chanda was the one who gave the shagun for him, and afterwards, she came and told him that Neela's eyes had overflowed with tears as she was leaving; she had been beside herself with grief, and hugged everyone as though she didn't want to leave and was being forced to go . . . 'After all, how old is she? She's just a child,' Chanda had said. And this reminded Chetan of Heer's leave-taking:

> Heer says—Papa, put me down,
> the Kahaars have lifted the palanquin, they're taking it away!
> Oh, Papa, you used to give me whatever I pleased
> Where have those days gone?
> I rested in your tree-like shade, like a traveller
> I had hardly four days of peace
> I leave now, after sorrow, joy, disaster

Forgive my sins, oh Papa
I am leaving after just five days in your home

When Nishtar sang it, that passage stayed with him all day. But now that Nishtar had become an Urdu poet, who knew if he even sang *Heer Ranjha* any more, thought Chetan, and he shook his head with displeasure. At first he felt like going by way of Bara Bazaar to Imam Nasiruddin, but he doubted he'd run into any friends there. He could go to his old school via Adda Kapurthala and say hello to some of his teachers, but he did not have one good memory associated with that school. He turned back, crossed the gali and stopped for just a moment—should he go to the right or the left? First he thought he'd walk by Jaura Gate and Rainak Bazaar and come out by Kutchery and Company Bagh. 'But what's the point of all this aimless wandering?' he thought. 'Why not go to Bohar Wala Bazaar via Qila Mohalla and end up in Puriyan Mohalla?' Puriyan Mohalla . . . Kunti. Memories of the flickerings of his first love; and he turned to the left. Just then he heard the loud melodic voice of a Punjabi *bait* singer:

Who can know the sorrow hidden in my heart?
The world looks at me and smiles
A wildfire blazes inside the ocean
But you can't tell on the surface

He stopped and turned. A few lay-about Punjabi poets sat at the poet Rehmat's shop, across from the moneylenders' shops, in the direction of Jaura Gate. There was also a gathering just across the way, at Bansi the vegetable seller's shop. Chetan had completely forgotten about the existence of either of them. He turned back towards them quickly. The poet was singing:

The louse is eating the wood from within,
But the paint remains unharmed
Darling, the fire of pining is also hidden
and burns deep inside

Quite a few passers-by had gathered round when Chetan got there. He went and stood behind them.

'Wonderful, wonderful! Wah, wah! How true, how true!' sighed one listener delightedly—'Darling, the fire of pining is also hidden!'

*

Before Bansi and Rehmat had come, Lal Bazaar had been famous because of Billa Saraf the moneylender, who had declared bankruptcy three times and whose relatives had taken over half of Kot Pushka, but since the arrival of those two, the bazaar had become famous for them. Chetan didn't know which of the two had arrived first. For as long as he could remember, or at least, since he'd started writing poetry himself, he'd seen them both there. Before he'd ever met them he used to listen to couplets at their shops. There weren't just card, chess and chaupar games in the open market in those days, there was also *baitbaazi*—Punjabi poetry matches. Billa Saraf became famous much later, but after the 1921 Movement, Bansi and Rehmat were the most famous, not just in the bazaar, but throughout the city.

Whenever Bansi appeared, abandoning his vegetable business, wandering about the city ringing a copper bell in one hand and carrying a wooden hammer in the other, people understood that a national movement had begun. The strange thing is that when the Congress movement began, Bansi forgot all about his shop and roamed about from morning to evening, from gali to gali, mohalla to mohalla, announcing the news, rallies, processions and meetings related to the movement. When it came to national service, this was what he considered his responsibility and he became quite skilled at it.

'Sisters and brothers . . .'

When his voice echoed all around after the ringing of his bell, the children of the galis and mohallas would gather around him. He was of medium height, with a broad forehead, innocent eyes and smiling lips. He wore a (usually wrinkled) Gandhi cap on his head and a homespun Bengali kurta with high pyjamas—he'd smile when he saw the children, then announce enthusiastically:

'This evening at five thirty, the Congress Committee will hold a wonderful rally at Nadiram Talab, where Syed Ataullah Shah Bukhari will give a powerful lecture. This is the same Ataullah Shah, who joined the Congress with Maulana Mohammed Ali and Shaukat Ali, and whose lectures are hugely popular in Punjab—what a speaker! His words are gems. He makes people laugh, he makes them cry. Before the lecture, the poet Jhumman will recite his new baits, and bring a new flavour to the proceedings!'

And another long clanging of the bell . . .

Sometimes Bansi did not speak one word on the stage, but when he was making his announcement, he'd string couplets together like so many pearls. And at the Congress meetings, even in those days when the movement was in a lull, Bansi's skill played no small part in rallying whatever size of crowd that gathered.

But not a word came from his mouth on stage. One time in Qila Mohalla—his own chowk—there had been a meeting. He publicized it throughout the entire city, and the crowd was chock-a-block, but he couldn't even say what he'd said in his announcements in order to introduce the speaker.

*

By contrast, the poet Rehmat hadn't been influenced at all by the national movement, although several of his pupils had gone to jail in the Congress movement, and he also helped them with their nationalist poems, even writing them where necessary. He had become famous because the city's greatest goonda—the very first to enter the self-rule movement in 1921, and whose baits spread like wildfire—was his pupil. He spent his own energy dyeing clothing; wandering about with young boys, a kameez and tahmad hanging from his skinny, wasted body, a trailing turban on his head, and his arms and hands dyed to the elbows; and preparing young men for the baitbaazi at the Harvallabh Festival or chairing the poetry gatherings there. Wherever Punjabi poetry recitations were held, for Ramnavami or Janmashtami, Eid or Muharram, he was the chair of the Doaba Punjabi Poetry Association.

As he thought of Rehmat Sahib, Chetan recalled a particular incident. At the Dharam Sabha (Mai Hiran Gate), a huge poetry recitation had taken place under the auspices of the Doaba Punjabi Poetry Association. Chetan didn't remember what the occasion was, all he remembered was that that enormous space had been absolutely jam-packed. Although Chetan had been in college, and had started writing in Urdu by then, he still enjoyed Punjabi poetry, and if it was a good reading, he always went. He'd heard Lahore and Amritsar's most famous poets were taking part in this one.

Two chairs had been placed behind a table on the stage; on one was seated Ustad Rehmat, his skinny frame attired in a tahmad and kameez, with a long-tailed turban on his head. His arms, resting on the table, were dyed to the elbows. On the other chair sat the successful doctor Captain Doctor Bhagwan Das, of Bhairon Bazaar, in the role of Session Chair. He was a hearty man with huge pointed moustaches and a proud and handsome face, wearing a Gandhi cap and matching suit. Chetan spent a long time mentally comparing the two of them as he sat in the front row: Ustad Rehmat looked a complete mouse compared to Captain Doctor Bhagwan Das.

Captain Doctor Bhagwan Das would state the names of the poets, and then Ustad Rehmat would rise and introduce them. Each poet would read a poem, then the audience would applaud and cry out 'Wonderful, wonderful!', as they listened to two poems each from their favourite poets. Just then Captain Doctor Bhagwan Das called out the name of Sardar Ishwar Singh of Lahore.

Ustad Rehmat rose and stood to the right of the table as he introduced the poet:

'Sisters and brothers, you've probably heard of the English's Tangore . . . '

(At *Tangore*, Chetan started—English's Tangore—but then, from the next sentence, he realized that Ustad Sahib meant the great poet Rabindranath Tagore.)

'At this time the English poet Tangore is known throughout the world. He has brought glory not just to Bengal, but also to all of Hindustan. The poet who is about to come before you now is no less than Tangore. He is our Punjabi Tangore.'

After he'd introduced the poet, Rehmat turned, looked behind him and said, 'Please come forward, Sardar Ishar Singh ji.'

And a slender Sikh poet, about thirty years of age, came forward and recited a poem in a thin voice:

127

Oh ill-fated one, you sleep deeply
Your husband stands outside
Open the door immediately!
Never again will you hear the sound of a knock
Why have you fallen?
You've fainted—
Open the door!
Come now—the spring of love is flowing
Take a dip in its waters
Open the door

The poet was saying something very deep about *darshan*—the mystical qualities of the gaze—in the style of the great mystic poet Bulleh Shah, using the ill-fated beloved, sleep and the husband as symbols, but how could ordinary people understand such deep philosophy? The poem's refrain was 'open the door', which sparked the audience's imagination in numerous ways. They had listened to two or three couplets, and the poet had only just recited the *qaaffiya*—the rhyme before the last word of the line—when the audience shouted out in unison—'Open the door!' Instead of paying any attention to the poet's words, everyone was waiting for the refrain, and when they heard it, they'd all shout in unison, 'Open the door!' and some would even burst out laughing. Not yet one quarter of the poem had been finished when someone seated in the back called out loudly, 'Come on and open that door, lucky lady, that guy's been standing out there forever!' The audience erupted in laughter and instead of reciting the next verse, the Punjabi 'Tangore' quietly went and sat back in his place.

*

Daal—Why such sorrow, oh heart?
Is there anyone who does not suffer in this world?

There was a long *taan*, and a supple voice full of pain—Chetan moved forward in the crowd a bit. The poets were not at their shops and their pupils were engaged in baitbaazi practice as they waited for them:

Oh heart, why do you pine?
But who in the world doesn't feel sorrow?
There's no time for complaining
This world is but a momentary stop on the road
And all the guests who come here are full of sorrow
All the Hindus and Muslims who come are sorrowful
Oh beloved, the truth is hard to see
But truly the whole world is sorrowful

'Fantastic! How true—truly, all the world is sorrowful!' one listener enthused.

The poet let loose a new couplet:

Laam—The days of friendship are behind us
Nowadays will we find friends only rarely
Love all you want
The earth will only get worse, nowadays

Chetan felt as though someone were saying this to him on Neela's behalf:

Tell me, friend, again wanting evil for a friend
Because that's the way of the world nowadays

Oh stars and moon keep your love by your side

That time is not today and truly those friends remain

The poet had written the couplet about friendship, but Chetan twisted it towards love. He'd fallen in love with Neela and because of that, she'd been sent across the sea to the prison of Rangoon. That was a nice sort of love he'd committed . . . and he turned his steps away from the crowd . . . but a self-rule-loving poet seated at the shop of Bansi the vegetable seller began to sing 'Toady Baccha' to the tune of Motiram's *Baarah Maase*— 'Twelve Months':

Chetra[6]—

Get this in your head, you toady, our rule will come for sure

Your lords, the English, they'll have to leave, their motives are impure

Death calls for everybody's head, it does, whether nobleman or king

If you don't serve our nation well, your name won't mean a thing

Baisakh—

You've forgotten to be a patriot and turn your nose in the air

You dress too fine and eat too much, a fatted lamb you are

You live in a palace up on the hill on this earth we all must leave

Toady child, listen dear, in the end, we all must leave

For a while the crowd listened to the parody of Motiram, but the intensity of the movement had dimmed. People were talking

---

[6] [*Chetra* and *Baisakh* are the Punjabi names for two months in the Hindu/Sikh calendar. The song 'Baarah Maase' presumably had a verse for every month of the year—*trans.*]

130

of turning the country into national governments. They had no interest in cursing the toadies of this world. The crowd began to thin. Chetan was walking on ahead, when someone slapped him hard on the shoulder from behind. Chetan turned.

'Oh, Hamiiid!'

'Well, hello, Chetan brother, what's up?'

In the old days, Hamid would not have asked after him without cursing at him or calling him a lover of his own mother. But Chetan didn't notice this slight formality in address and, giving up on the thought of going to Puriyan Mohalla, he embraced him.

12

Hamid and Chetan set off for Hamid's home at Jaura Gate, arms draped around one another's necks, but after just a few steps, Hamid freed himself from Chetan's arm. He said nothing; first he removed his own arm and, when Chetan didn't get the hint and continued to walk along with his arm around Hamid's neck, talking all the while, he slowly dislodged his shoulder from Chetan's arm and separated from him as they entered Jaura Gate. His face showed no emotions and he didn't slacken the pace of conversation, but Chetan noticed the gesture and his feelings were deeply hurt.

*

Although Hamid had studied with Chetan from the first year of college, his subject and section had been different. It was in the third year that he'd attracted Chetan's attention, and he did it in such a way that Chetan found himself increasingly drawn to him. He was slender, refined and cheerful. If Chetan observed any flaw in Hamid it was that his upper row of teeth was slightly turned in, and Chetan did not much care for the way he looked when he smiled. Although he knew that Hamid was a very intelligent, bold and outgoing student, his smile made him look oddly sycophantic just because of that flaw in his teeth.

In the first and second years, all Chetan knew about Hamid was that there was a handsome Muslim student in the other section, and since he was intelligent and quick-witted, the college bullies couldn't get to him. They hovered around him but they couldn't touch him. Chetan was himself partial to beauty. In those days, when his head had yet to be turned by the opposite sex—even before he first encountered Kunti at the Sheetala fair—he was very fond of beautiful boys of his own age or slightly younger. He liked being near them, talking to them, making friends with them, and if none of this was possible, just gazing at them from afar made him ecstatic. Once, early one morning, long ago, maybe he was studying in Class Nine or Ten, he'd gone to bathe at Neeli Kothi on Anant's insistence. The citron and orange trees on either side of the gate were in blossom and the air was fragrant with their scent. When they got to the bricked tank, Chetan's heart missed a beat. A fair, handsome boy was bathing there.

Chetan had been to Neeli Kothi four times before. But each time he'd been terribly fatigued. Neeli Kothi was in the direction of Company Bagh, nearly two miles from Kallowani Mohalla. At that intersection with the main street, which nowadays goes towards the radio station, the left fork veered towards Neeli Kothi. Chetan didn't know how its name had come to be Neeli Kothi or 'blue mansion'. A Saraf family in Bara Bazaar had had the mansion built. There was an open paved area in front of the mansion and a garden in the corner to the left side, where there was a tall wheel-well that filled the deep, bricked tank with its wide stream of water. At the edge of the tank, there was a small room with coloured-glass windows for changing one's clothes. In the hot season, it was satisfying to bathe in the tank beneath the thick well stream. No one lived in the mansion now. Perhaps a son of the owner had had smallpox, and the owner had built this house so his son could live in the fresh air, or just so he could bathe and wash in the morning, but the boys of Kallowani went there nearly every day in the summer. Sometimes the gardener did not hitch up the oxen to turn the wheel, so the boys took turns yoking themselves up and bathed until ten or eleven in the morning.

The road to Neeli Kothi ran along both sides of Company Bagh. If he was not with Pyaru or Debu, Chetan would go by the street on the far side of Company Bagh which went by Lala Dayal Singh's mansion, and which the boys of Kallowani Mohalla called Neeli Kothi Street. This street wasn't deserted like Grand Trunk Road. Bungalows had been built almost all the way to Neeli Kothi and the road didn't seem as long. But if Pyaru or Debu came along, then they'd go on the big road closer to Company Bagh. There was a dense jungle between the large street that went to Neeli Kothi and Grand Trunk Road. It was full of bushes, hills, ditches and countless trees, such as peepal and crown flower. Under the leadership of Debu and Pyaru, the boys would journey far into the woods to answer the call of nature. They'd play games and set strange conditions. The sun would get higher and higher in the sky, but they still wouldn't be done, Chetan would grow exhausted and bored. And usually someone or other would fight with Debu or Pyaru, and someone would get beaten up. On his return, Chetan would always vow never to go back.

But one particular day, neither Debu nor Pyaru came along. Anant was there, a couple of other boys were there, and after relieving themselves in the fields, they quickly reached Neeli Kothi. The handsome boy was perhaps with his older brother or a young uncle—Chetan saw a tall, thin man with a wheat-coloured complexion wearing a loincloth who was getting a massage; he had some sort of scar on his right leg. Perhaps he was the one for whom the mansion had been built. The beautiful boy was bathing openly right near him in the tank. Chetan and his companions stopped short because the owners were using the tank, so they didn't have permission to bathe.

He himself stood to one side, watching the boy the whole time. He was quite fair, with a body soft as butter. Chetan didn't want to stare, but he found it hard to look away. And after that day, Chetan began to go to Neeli Kothi long before the other boys—sometimes alone, sometimes with a friend—but the beautiful boy didn't come every day. If Chetan didn't see him he felt listless. He learned the address of the boy's family's shop, and walking by there in the evenings, he'd sometimes catch a glimpse of him and feel electrified. He wanted to be able to sit near him somehow, to talk to him, but his shyness was always a barrier. If Pyaru had been in his place and set his heart on a boy, he'd have caught him somewhere or other—on the way from home to the shop or from the shop to home. He'd have staked out the front of his shop and whenever the opportunity arose, he'd have tripped the boy, and when he would start to cry, Pyaru would put his arm around him and behave affectionately or threateningly, telling him that if he avoided him he'd be beaten. But all these styles seemed barbaric and bestial to Chetan. And just one glance gave him enough enthusiasm to read and write and perform other tasks.

One evening during that time, he had gone to Chowk Sudan on an errand. It was evening when the trunk sellers surrounded the large area of the chowk, and there was a crowd, everyone standing shoulder to shoulder. Chetan was trying to slip through the crowd when suddenly his foot got stuck. Just ahead of him, he saw an extremely beautiful, fair boy with sharp features, wearing a silk kurta and a fine dhoti so white it looked washed in milk, walking along with his brother or father. Chetan had never seen such a beautiful boy in the city; it was impossible he wouldn't have seen him at rallies, or in galis and bazaars, at fairs put on by the Arya Samaj or other religious organizations, or in the tournaments held on the grounds of the government schools.

'He's definitely come from somewhere outside because even his clothes don't look Punjabi,' thought Chetan. But that was what he thought later. At the time, his heart just pounded and he stood rooted to the spot. All night long that face swirled around in his mind. Later he learned the boy's name was Rajat. His father had been Punjabi. He had been an executive engineer. Most of his work had been in UP and he'd married there. Just a few months before, the father had died, so his wife had come to Jalandhar bringing the children with her as they had property in Kot Kishanchand . . . Chetan began going to Kot Kishanchand every evening.

Kot Kishanchand, that is Kishanchand Fort, is one of the twelve neighbourhoods on the outskirts of Jalandhar. At some point of time these were estates. There were walls around the outside, with a large gate and a fort. In the corner of the Kot Kishanchand wall, where there had once been a tower with gun holes set in it, Rajat's mother had built an outside door and stairs in the round part and turned it into a sitting room. Chetan had established a friendship with a neighbour friend of Rajat's living in Kot Kishanchand and the first day he went into that sitting room he felt like a poor country boy who has suddenly been granted permission to enter the palace of the empress. Everything in that round room, the tables and chairs, the divan, the couch, the pictures, the curtains, looked like they were from some other world. When Chetan sat down, Rajat's sister brought tea. The tea set, the netted cloth with the pearl fringe over the milk jug—it was like Chetan had arrived in some heavenly abode. They hardly ever drank tea in his home, and when they did, it was from glasses. He and his brothers would gulp down their tea holding the hot

137

glasses in the cuffs of their kameezes, crouching near the stove in the kitchen.

Chetan was unable to speak to Rajat that evening, nor to his younger brother or sister. He just listened to their delightfully polite conversation. He felt jealous of all those boys who went there every evening and when he came home, he lay awake until late at night thinking about every word and gesture made by Rajat, his younger brother, Lalit, and his sister.

But Chetan hadn't felt this way when he first saw Hamid. After seeing Kunti at the Sheetala fair, an imperceptible change had occurred in him. He would walk below Kunti's window, and although sometimes he went as far as Kot Kishanchand in the evenings, and even saw Rajat there, Chetan no longer felt the same attraction to him—in fact, he even laughed when he thought about how he used to stare at him! (Although Rajat was still just as handsome, the *saraaf*'s son had turned out strangely soft and flabby.) Chetan couldn't believe he used to go all the way to Neeli Kothi early in the morning just to catch a glimpse of him and then make a round of the shoe bazaar by way of Chhati Gali in the evening. It astonished him that he could have been in love with a boy with a name like 'Ambarsariya Mull' (which was how they pronounced Amritsariya Mull).

Although his heart had not pounded when he'd seen Hamid, he certainly did like him. Chetan only found his smile unattractive, especially whenever he grinned. Chetan didn't try to make friends with him, as he'd already grown out of that phase of enjoying talking with young men just to gaze at their beauty. But when the College Union was set up in the third year, and Hamid took part in the debates, Chetan saw there was no one who spoke more persuasively than him in the whole college. He was elected the head of the College Union after the very first meeting as a result of his speaking, and Chetan had become especially interested in him.

But it was while they were acting in *Mrs Manjri* that he'd got close to Hamid. A production of the play *Mrs Manjri* was staged on the occasion of the annual meeting of the Arya Samaj (college section). Chetan played the role of Ray Bahadur Janakidas and Hamid played the orphaned Muslim youth. Although Chetan had acted very well and the audience had praised him too, he himself was transfixed by Hamid's performance. He wasn't surprised at the success of the play. He had been moved by his acting even during rehearsals. The drama was being directed by their English teacher, who'd come with a second-class MA from Government College, Lahore, and who had also begun the Union and the Drama Club at the college. But Hamid was the one who ran the rehearsals. At the rehearsals, Chetan got to know Hamid well, and he learned that he wasn't just a good actor and speaker, but also very well read. It was during those rehearsals that Chetan and Hamid had become close friends. There could be no doubt that Hamid was very well read in both Urdu poetry and English, but Chetan had one talent that Hamid didn't. Although he didn't know that much Urdu or English poetry, he was a born poet. Despite the fact that Hamid knew Shelley and Keats, Wordsworth and Browning by heart, just as well as he did Iqbal and Tagore, Hafiz and Akhtar Shirani, he couldn't write a single line of poetry, whereas Chetan, despite not having such command of these poets, wrote couplet upon couplet, poem upon poem, with ease. And whilst Chetan greatly admired the breadth of Hamid's reading, Hamid had nothing but praise for Chetan's natural-born genius. And the two of them grew to be close.

One day after the play, Hamid brought Chetan to his home, and his smoky room full of newspapers and magazines and books left a lasting impression on Chetan's mind.

Hamid's home was to the right, off a small yard where Jaura Gate opens out from a narrow gali and Rainak Bazaar begins. Chetan never went into the women's quarters and of the men's quarters he saw only Hamid's room—which was neither especially small nor particularly large (if it had been any smaller, it would have been more like a storeroom). From the outside it looked as though it were built of baked bricks, but the walls inside were made of mud, with built-in shelves crammed with books and newspapers and magazines. There was no furniture in the room, just a low, square writing desk in the middle, with a dhurrie next to it, extending all the way to the wall. The dhurrie was spread with a filthy checked-linen sheet and two large bolsters. Stacks and stacks of newspapers, magazines and books lay about on the seat and the cloth, as well as in the corners of the room. The piles of reading matter had no small hand in making the room appear even more cramped than it was.

Chetan had heard that Hamid was the son of the Dewan of the Nawab of Khairpur. But his clothing was utterly ordinary. He was handsome, so he looked good in an ordinary kameez and pyjamas, but Chetan certainly was surprised sometimes. Seeing Hamid's room, he was even more surprised. Much later, he learned that the Dewan of Khairpur kept a famous Jalandhari prostitute in his home and that Hamid was her son. Hamid's father had married three or four more times after that—and Hamid's mother had been shut up in the walls of that house the whole time. She received a fixed income every month, which was what the two of them lived on.

The moment he set foot in that room, Chetan learned the secret of Hamid's vast knowledge. While Chetan didn't own even one book of his own, Hamid's room was crammed full of newspapers, magazines and books. Since Hamid didn't live far from Kallowani Mohalla, Chetan began to go daily to his home after that day and he spent quite a bit of time in his company.

Hamid smoked a great deal and when he smoked near Chetan, his head would start to throb, but in his greed to take advantage of Hamid's companionship and consume all the reading material at his house, he didn't mind the headaches and slowly became accustomed to the smoky room.

*

But perhaps Hamid and Chetan wouldn't have become such close friends if Chetan had not got him Meenakshi Ramarao's photo (which Hamid had attempted to get, unsuccessfully) and thus impressed him deeply.

*

Meenakshi was the MA-pass daughter of a judge from Madras. The cinema director Advani had gone to Madras for an outdoor shoot, where he'd met the judge and his daughter, and there he'd persuaded her to work in his upcoming film. Until that time, only prostitutes, illiterate girls from poor homes, or Anglo-Indian girls worked in the movies, but as soon as talkie films entered the scene, the Anglo-Indian girls were completely cut out of the business. Actresses like Sulochna, Madhuri and Savita (it may be that to this day, no other heroine has surpassed her in beauty) may have reached the peak of their genius, but they were suddenly useless just because their Hindustani accents sounded too English. And not every beautiful prostitute could be a heroine once microphones were introduced into films; talkies also demanded better acting and facial expressions, bringing about a demand for new, educated girls in the industry. Meenakshi was not only an MA and beautiful, but she was also the daughter of a judge, and her interest in cinema created a huge splash in film magazines, which were full of interviews with her. Her quotes, remarks and photos were being printed right and left. Chetan somehow had the impression from her remarks that she was not that attracted to films or to acting, but rather that it was the film director himself who had drawn her into the industry. He saw a photo of Advani—he was a handsome, well-built young man with a broad forehead and large, round eyes. He'd come from England just a few years earlier, after getting an education in film directing. And Chetan wasn't surprised when, a few years later, Meenakshi Rama Rao became Meenakshi Advani. But at that time, Advani Sahib was garnering much praise for bringing such an educated girl into the movies.

Chetan wasn't particularly fond of Meenakshi. She didn't blossom with youthfulness like his favourite actresses Sulochna and Zubeida . . . She had a wide face, a broad forehead and slightly sunken cheeks with jutting cheekbones. Certainly her lips were thin and lovely and there was intelligence in her eyes, but although her face looked intellectual, there was no youthful attractiveness about her. Chetan was so smitten with the carefree beauty of Sulochna that his heart beat quicker just seeing a picture of her. One day he had seen a picture of Sulochna pinned up in a paan shop. The paan seller had torn it from a weekly newspaper, cut out her silhouette with a pair of scissors, pasted it on a piece of paper and had it framed. Chetan had stopped in the bazaar and stared at it for a long time. Then he'd asked the shopkeeper if he would sell it. The shopkeeper asked him for one rupee. One rupee seemed a small price to Chetan for such a valuable item. With much ingenuity, he managed to save up one rupee, fearing the whole time that someone else might make off with the picture. In the meantime, he went once every day to gaze at it. After he bought it, he hung it up in the small room next to the sitting room (where he'd set out a dhurrie, a bolster, covered by a linen sheet on the floor, and a small, low desk for writing and reading, just like Hamid).

But Hamid liked Meenakshi much better than Sulochna. 'It's not her intellectualism,' Hamid had said, 'but the nobility she exudes. Sulochna and Zubeida may be beautiful, but they look vulgar.'

Chetan did not agree with him. Sulochna may have been playful, but she looked every inch an empress. She was shapely and tall as a cypress, with delightfully sharp features; her eyes were large and round, and radiated a peculiar mixture of warmth and haughty distance—'How could a vulgar woman possess such qualities!' Chetan felt bitter, but he smiled to himself ironically at Hamid's loathing for vulgar women—he who was himself the son of a prostitute. He thought of a cutting response, but all he said was, 'Then you should put up a picture of Meenakshi in your room.'

'I'm not cutting a picture out of some magazine,' Hamid had retorted, and he told Chetan how he'd written a letter to Meenakshi in English (Hamid was quite proud of his English) and was hoping to receive a picture soon. And he would only hang an autographed photograph in his room.

When two months had passed after this conversation and no response had come, let alone a picture, Chetan asked about it one evening, and Hamid told him morosely that he'd written to Meenakshi and she hadn't responded.

Who knows what got into Chetan. 'If you're that keen on it, shall I get a picture of Meenakshi for you?' he asked.

'How will you get it?' asked Hamid, surprised. His eyes widened and his lips parted slightly to reveal the inward-pointing row of teeth. For a few moments he looked Chetan up and down, then his expression changed to sarcastic contempt. 'He's going to get her picture when I couldn't,' he thought, and after staring at Chetan incredulously, he burst out laughing loudly.

Chetan was bewildered. Somewhat annoyed, he replied, 'You'll get your picture. Now step aside.'

And after talking about this and that for a few minutes, he left. Hamid's sarcastic laughter had enraged him and he had decided that if he couldn't get Meenakshi's photo, he'd never go to Hamid's house again.

Actually, a strategy had suddenly occurred to Chetan when he saw Hamid's despondency, and it was his faith in that strategy that made him promise to get the picture for him. Meenakshi was not just a successful heroine, but also an MA—and she was also the daughter of a judge. There was no way she'd send her photo in response to a letter from some third-year student, but he strongly believed that if a young lady were to write to her, and if she too were a graduate, and a lady author to boot, Meenakshi would feel compelled to respond. And Chetan decided that he would write a letter in the guise of a lady writer; he'd praise the style of the essay Meenakshi had written on the art of Director Advani, he would agree with the content, he would write of his high hopes for Indian films thanks to Director Advani, and about how he'd definitely raise the status of Indian films thanks to his knowledge and experience attained abroad. And after writing all this, at the end, he'd ask Meenakshi for a signed photograph, assuring her that he would write about her in northern magazines.

As he thought about all this, Chetan pondered what his lady writer's name would be. He thought up several names but none sounded real to him. He wanted a name that was simple and one that he liked. After some thought, he chose the name 'Chanda'. But since Chanda was going to become a writer and she'd have to have a nom de plume, he named her Chanda Devi 'Kumad' or 'night-blooming lotus', and he wrote a letter to Meenakshi under that name. Although he consulted a dictionary many times and wrote simple and fluent English, he wanted to make sure there were no errors. If he'd been writing a letter to someone else, he'd have gone to Hamid, but he didn't want Hamid to get even a whiff of what he was up to. He went to Amichand. Amichand corrected his letter, but he objected to Chanda's nom de plume. 'It shouldn't be spelled "Kumad", it should be spelled "Kumud",' he said. 'But then Kumud is masculine; a woman shouldn't have a masculine nom de plume!' He changed Kumud to the feminine form, 'Kumudini'.

Chanda Devi 'Kumudini', BA—it sounded grating to Chetan. The name 'Kumudini' could also be used on its own and, for just a second, he thought that instead of Chanda Devi he would just make the name Kumudini. But Kumudini didn't sound simple enough. After some thought, Chetan left the name as it was. In the midst of this, he saved up one rupee. He bought a lovely, fragrant, pale-pink writing pad—foreign—and a matching pink envelope from Bhairon Bazaar. Then he copied out the letter in pretty handwriting on two sheets of the paper. He wrote Meenakshi's address on the envelope and for the sender's address he wrote, 'Chanda Devi "Kumud", BA, Kallowani Mohalla, Jalandhar City (Punjab)' and mailed the letter. That same day, he went to the post office and told the postman that if any mail came for Chanda Devi 'Kumud', Kallowani Mohalla, he should throw it into his sitting room.

Chetan had so much faith in the likely success of his scheme that when he received a reply from Meenakshi a mere seven days later, and a large autographed photo printed on expensive glossy paper to boot, he wasn't a bit surprised, although he was quite pleased. He went to Hamid's place that very evening and tossed the packet with the photo on to the writing desk before him. 'Here!' he said.

Hamid opened the packet, took out the photo and just stared at it. Then he turned it over and saw that on its back the following words were written in English:

For Chanda Devi 'Kumud'
With love,
Meenakshi

'Who is this Chanda Devi Kamadd?' asked Hamid suddenly.

'Not Kamadd, *Kumud*,' said Chetan laughing. 'That's Chanda's nom de plume. In Hindi, "Kumud" is what they call a lotus that blooms at night.'

But Hamid was still not able to pronounce it correctly.

'But who is this Kumudd?' he asked.

'Do you want to eat a mango or count the trees?' asked Chetan with excitement. 'Frame this picture and put it on the wall so it's before your eyes at all times!'

But Hamid wouldn't let the matter drop until he'd heard the whole story from Chetan. When he learned the truth, Chetan's prestige increased quite a bit in his eyes and their friendship reached a more equal status.

*

But Chetan and Hamid weren't equals. Chetan knew this perfectly well himself. Though he'd won Hamid's respect by obtaining Meenakshi's picture, Chetan had none of his command of a wide variety of subjects—society, culture, politics, philosophy. He had talent, but Hamid had knowledge. Chetan had that spring that bursts forth from rocky terrain on the strength of who knows what rites undertaken in a previous birth. He needed endless streams of study and experience so the spring wouldn't dry up and would

146

continue to flow to form a great river. Hamid had those streams in his possession, and after winning his friendship, Chetan decided to make those streams his own as well.

Hamid liked to read Western philosophers such as Plato, Aristotle, Schopenhauer, Kant, Hegel, Nietzsche, Bergson and Russell and he often quoted Aristotle and Schopenhauer in conversation. Chetan tried to have a go at this field as well, so he borrowed Plato's famous book, *The Republic*, from Hamid, but for some reason, he found it extremely boring. After reading just a few pages, he began to feel sleepy. Theory and philosophy bored him, whereas novels, stories and poetry robbed him of his sleep at night. The very next day he returned the book. Then Hamid recited some of Tagore's poems in English (of which he had two collections) to him, and Chetan was engrossed in them for weeks, filling entire notebooks with prose and poetry written in the same style. He also translated Tagore's plays *Karna and Kunti* and *Natir Puja* through the medium of English, and even attempted to write a one-act play about the Buddha in imitation of those.

Although Chetan had heard the names Hafiz Jalandhari and Iqbal from Hunar Sahib, he actually studied them in the company of Hamid. He'd read so many of Hafiz Jalandhari's poems at Hamid's house—'*Apne Man men Prīt Basā Le*' ('Bring the Beloved into Your Heart'), '*Dil Hai Parāye Bas men*' ('My Heart Belongs to Another'), '*Jāg Soz-e-Ishq Jāg*' ('Awake, Oh Passion of Love, Awake!')—and memorized them. Hamid also knew Iqbal's ghazal by heart:

Kabhī ai haqīqat-e-muntazar nazar ā libās-e-majaz men
For once, Oh awaited reality, reveal yourself in material form

. . . as well as the poem '*Nayā Shivālā*', or 'New Temple'. He'd sway back and forth, singing:

Sach keh dūn ai Brāhmin, gar tū burā na māne
But tere butkadon ke sab ho gaye purāne[7]
I'll tell you Brahmin, if you don't object
All the idols in your temple have grown old

And Chetan memorized all those ghazals and poems of Iqbal and
Hafiz as well. One day, when Chetan went to Hamid's place,
he said, 'Have a seat, I'm going to recite something from a new
romantic poet for you. I don't think we've seen his like in Urdu.'
    And before Chetan could ask the name of the poet, Hamid
began in his zeal to recite:

Oh love, take me somewhere, take me from this place of sin
from this world of hate, from this existence filled with hatred
from these sensual people, from this sensuality
    Take me somewhere else, far away
    Oh love, take me away
I am a priest of love, you are my beloved Krishna
You are my beloved Krishna, this is the boat of love
This is the boat of love, you are its oarsman
    No worries at all, take me away
    Oh love take me away somewhere
Now I am leaving this merciless world
Now I am turning away from callous friends
Now I am breaking whatever hope I had
    No, I cannot take it any more, take me
    Oh love, take me away somewhere
Injustice is the enemy of free thought
The killer of aspirations, the thief of hopes

---

[7] [This line is quoted incorrectly by Ashk. The line should read: '*Tere sanamkadon ke but ho gaye purāne*'—trans.]

It is the slaughter-house of feelings, it is the graveyard of emotion
    Come let's go somewhere away from here
    Oh love, take me away somewhere

In those days, Chetan loved Kunti with all his heart. Since Kunti
had become engaged to the pundit from Sham Chaurasi, he knew
he had no hope of his love ever amounting to anything, but this
had not diminished his feeling in the slightest, nor his bittersweet
pain, despite the despair that loomed. He too, with the poet,
wished to escape to some place far off from this 'world of hate',
where there were no social bonds, where there was no deception
of fate, where there were no narrow-minded human natures and
customs—he'd be there, his lover would be there too, and the
God of Love . . . and Hamid recited the stanza of the poem:

    Perhaps there's a place on the other side of the world
    That has longed for centuries to see a human face
    That is awash with solitude
        If such exists, then take me there
        Oh, love, take me away somewhere

So it seemed to Chetan that the poet had said exactly what was on
his mind! And from that day, he and Hamid became fans of the
author, the poet Akhtar Shirani. Not only did he note the poem
down in his notebook, he took down the complete address of the
monthly journal edited and run by Akhtar Shirani, *Khyalistan*—
'Idealand'—(in which the poem was published) so that he might
himself save up to order that journal somehow.

    From that day on, the two friends threw over the old poets and
became Akhtar Shirani fans. Iqbal stirred the mind, but Akhtar
stirred the heart and took the readers' hearts far from filth into the
'valley of light', where the 'foothills of the mountains' were filled

149

with 'exhilarating breezes' and 'pure moonlit nights'. Just as film fans memorize every detail of the lives of their favourite actor or actress—the loves, marriages, break-ups, remarriages—they knew all about Akhtar Shirani's love life, which they embellished in their imaginations, then used to impress their friends. In those days, Akhtar Shirani had started writing poems addressed to a young lady named 'Salma', and all sorts of conjectures were being made about 'Akhtar's Salma' in Urdu literary circles. Some said that Salma resided only in Akhtar's imagination, others said that no, she actually lived in Lahore and wrote poetry herself. Whatever the case might be, Chetan just adored some of the sonnets and poems written about Salma, especially—

I've heard my Salma will come at night into the valley . . .

And—

Having placed my heart with Salma, I have become disgraced with all the neighbourhood girls

In those days, Chetan kept a separate notebook in which he wrote down only those poems by Akhtar Shirani about Salma. There weren't that many of them, but Chetan refused to write anything else in the notebook.

And for the two final years of college, Chetan and Hamid were practically inseparable. Chetan wrote stories in those days, he tried to write some plays too, and with Hamid's help, he not only made a fool of the owner of the local cinema house (through the medium of Chanda Devi 'Kumud'), but they also pulled the wool over the eyes of the owner-editor of a famous film magazine from Lahore, G.R. Oberoi. Oberoi not only published 'Kumud's' articles, he also sent her books on film writing and a photo of himself, and attempted several times to come to Jalandhar to meet her (Chetan always put him off). After doing his BA, Hamid left for Aligarh for his LLB, and Chetan went to a daily newspaper office in Lahore . . . and today they'd suddenly met again.

*

After removing Chetan's hand from his shoulder, Hamid walked along at a slight remove from him while telling him rather loftily that he hadn't ended up doing an LLB; the Lucknow radio station was opening, they'd needed a programme assistant, and he had been selected in an interview.

'But I heard there was only a radio station in Delhi so far . . .'

'No, just this January another one opened in Lucknow. Only five candidates were chosen from five hundred applicants. Even some England-returned people applied, but I got the highest score in the interview.'

'Well, you are knowledgeable,' said Chetan.

And Hamid told him that the All India Radio controller, Fielden Sahib himself, was among the interviewers and that he was very pleased by his interview (he didn't mention that he also had a powerful recommendation from a member of the Counsel of the Viceroy [due to the influence of the Nawab of Khairpur]). Hamid told him at length what questions had been asked in the interview and how he'd answered them. In the midst of this, he laughed and smiled several times, and Chetan noticed that although his upper row of teeth was still turned in a bit, he no longer looked obsequious when he smiled, but condescending and light-hearted instead.

After telling him about his interview, Hamid told Chetan all about his work, about how he ran the entire station. The director was Sindhi, and an English professor at Delhi University. He didn't know a word of Urdu. He was an absolute fool, and Hamid was the one who did all the work at the station—he was the one who set the schedule, produced the dramas and arranged the talks, and he had not yet made a single scheduling error. In the next ten years, radio stations would open in ten cities in India and if he didn't become the station director during that time, then his name wasn't . . . at this last, he slapped his hand to his chest.

Chetan listened and listened—*schedule, talks, errors*—he didn't understand a thing he was saying. He wasn't even really sure what radio was. He'd heard a radio station had opened in Delhi. Apparently someone would say something in the studio, do some singing, and all this could be heard in Chandni Chowk. Sound boxes were affixed to pillars in the park across from Divan Hall and one could hear speeches, songs and dramas on them.

Suddenly he asked, 'When will a radio station open in Lahore?'

'Plans are afoot, but it will take three or four years.'

*

By now, they'd reached Hamid's home. He stopped in the bazaar, just outside the compound, and held out his hand. But suddenly he realized he'd just been talking about himself the whole time. He took Chetan's hand in his own and asked, 'What are you up to these days?'

Chetan wanted to tell him that he was working at a famous newspaper, that he'd been in poor health and gone to Shimla for three months, that his sister-in-law had got married so he'd come back earlier than expected . . . but Hamid's stature had grown so much that as he talked about himself, Chetan felt terribly diminished. If Hamid had brought him into his old room, offered him sharbat or something to eat and acted like an old friend, perhaps Chetan would have said something about himself, but first off, he'd been offended by him removing his hand from his shoulder, and then he'd felt distance in the way Hamid spoke (although he was speaking quite openly), and when he'd held out his hand outside his home, it seemed to Chetan that he was not an old friend he'd been close to for two years, but rather a careerist climbing the steps of the future while treading upon the past . . . and diminishing his own importance even more, he said, 'Oh, I'm just a translator at a daily paper: I got sick and found some temporary work in Shimla, so I went there. I'm on my way back to Lahore now. I don't plan on staying at a newspaper; I'll just do some part-time work so I can get an MA.'

And before Hamid could let go of his hand and turn away, Chetan gave his hand a slight shake and went on his way.

13

Although clouds had gathered in the sky, the sunlight had somehow tricked them and burst through their ranks to fall squarely on one's head. It was extremely hot and humid, and there was the usual huge crowd in Rainak Bazaar . . . But after shaking hands with Hamid, Chetan walked along, head down, not noticing anything—not the humidity, the heat, or the crowd. His feelings of insecurity that had been gnawing at him since morning due to Amichand's contemptuous regard (or disregard) had now increased several-fold thanks to Hamid's behaviour, and by now they completely overshadowed his senses. He had tried to hide or forget his feelings of inferiority by going to Anant's, and Dina Nath's, and Nishtar's, but he'd found peace nowhere. He kept thinking about how he needed to go to Lahore immediately, quit his job at the daily paper, somehow get himself enrolled in an MA course, pass in the first division, do a doctorate, become a professor at a college, and write book after book—so many books that the sun of his brilliance would spread its rays not just throughout this country but others as well, and when its light reached his officer friends wearing down their seats in the stifling darkness of their offices, constrained by the fetters of their slavery, they'd at last get a sense of their own inferiority.

Amichand might have been his classmate, he might have been his contemporary, but between Chetan and him there had always been an invisible wall, and although when necessary Chetan went to see him, and Amichand also came to Chetan's sitting room, there had never been any depth to their friendship. And then Amichand had gone to Government College, Lahore, after passing the FA (as his father, Lala Maniram, assistant post master, had taken an advance from the government from his pension and arranged to send him there), following which the distance between the two had only grown. But he had been with Hamid for two years. Those deep chats in Hamid's smoky room, those debates on the acting of Sulochna and Zubeida, those schemes to hoodwink Oberoi or Lala Mohan Lal, their joint appreciation of Iqbal, Tagore, Hafiz and Akhtar Shirani . . .

'But friendship occurs between equals,' he said to himself, and a bitter smile spread on his lips. 'When one friend rises up, he no longer thinks of the one below. If I too were to become programme assistant today, Hamid would embrace me as before, and if I became a programme director, that old obsequious grin would return to his lips!'

Chetan wanted to tell Hamid about G.R. Oberoi, about how a friend of Oberoi's had told him that it was Chetan who had been writing to him under the name of Chanda Devi 'Kumud', and how he had never looked Chetan in the eye again. He also wanted to tell him that he'd seen Akhtar Shirani at a mushaira, and he wasn't at all handsome—he was of medium height, roly-poly, with a puffy face; he sported Ronald Coleman–style trimmed moustaches; it had been clear from his tiny little eyes that he was quite drunk . . . He'd come to the mushaira inebriated and hadn't let anyone else recite. He wanted to tell him about Hunar Sahib, about his editor Dhanpat Rai, BA (National) . . . Privately, he patted himself on the back for not telling Hamid anything, for only giving his hand a light shake, and for going on his way before

Hamid had had a chance to let go of his hand and turn towards his house.

*

'Arré bhai, where are you running off to like a blind man?'

Chetan felt someone right in front of him put a hand on his shoulder and he stopped and lifted his head—'Nishtar!'

'I heard from Hunar Sahib you were here; we were thinking of going over your way.'

Chetan looked over and saw that Hunar Sahib and his own brother-in-law, Ranvir, were seated in a shop that sold strips of cotton tape for weaving the string beds of charpoys; they were practically drowning in giant spools of cotton wool, string and charpoy tape. He wished there was some way he could flee from there, but Ranvir came leaping from the shop as soon as he saw him.

'Come in, Jija ji! Come in!'

He grabbed Chetan's hands and practically dragged him inside.

14

'Come, brother Chetan, please meet this gentleman—Mr Rudra Sen Ariya!' called Hunar Sahib, mispronouncing the name 'Arya' in the Urdu style. 'There can be no other businessman in the entire city as devoted to literature as he.'

And Mr Rudra Sen 'Ariya', who was seated upon spools of cotton charpoy tape the size of wheels, grinned.

'And this is Chetan! He's my pupil, but he's becoming a master in his own right,' laughed Hunar Sahib foolishly. 'Have a seat, brother, have a seat!'

It was extremely humid in the shop. Despite the fact that the table fan was whirring at full speed, the huge quantities of cotton wool, string and charpoy tape created an oddly stifling odour. Chetan would have preferred to stand outside. 'I won't sit down,' he said, 'I'll wait for you outside, why don't you come out here!' But Rudra Sen Arya picked up two of the tape spools and tossed them in the other corner. He wiped the sweat from his ox-like neck with the end of his thick, homespun dhoti, and told him to have a seat where the breeze from the fan would fall directly on him. Then Hunar Sahib pulled him over by the hem of his kurta, so that he ended up sitting down, even though he didn't wish to.

Once seated, Chetan cast an apathetic glance at the literature-loving businessman: he was of medium height, with a fair complexion. He had the short, stocky frame of a villager; short, dry, salt-and-pepper hair; large teeth in a wide mouth; and a filthy sacred thread wrapped around his neck that peeped out from his homespun undershirt. He wore a dhoti around his waist, which was growing dirty from its continuous use as a handkerchief. Sitting there upon the piles of tape, this man didn't appear to have even a remote connection to literature.

'I was just about to recite my translation of the Gita to Mr Rudra Sen Ariya. I've translated the verse about becoming immortal that occurs in the second section, into ordinary, easy-to-understand language, so that one can grasp the entire meaning without any intervention. You know the verse, right? *"Na jiyate mriyate . . ."*'

Rudra Sen Arya laughed, 'Not *jiyate mriyate*,' he said, and he sang the verse with perfect Sanskrit pronunciation:

Na jāyate mriyate vā kadācin
Nāyaṃ bhūtvā bhavitā vā na bhūyaḥ
Ajo nityaḥ śāśvato 'yaṃ purāṇo
Na hanyate hanyamāne śarīre

'Okay, listen—from that same verse,' said Hunar Sahib. 'You keep reciting the *Sanskreet* (Hunar Sahib's pronunciation of "Sanskrit") verses, then I'll recite the translation in Urdu verse. I don't actually know *Sanskreet*, but do note how much one can grasp of the original verses and what simple language they've been rendered into, without adding or subtracting anything from them,' and he said to his host, 'Please recite that same verse one more time.'

And Rudra Sen Arya recited the verse once more with great concentration.

Then, explaining that this is what is said about the *jīvātma* or the soul, Hunar Sahib began reciting in a melodic voice:

Neither is its birth tied to time
Nor is it in danger of dying any day
Once it is, it continues to be, unchanging
Unborn, eternal, unending, ancient
It is not mortal, like the earthly body
It does not die, as this body does

'Wow! Wonderful, wonderful!' cried Rudra Sen Arya in praise, and he sang the next verse, swaying slightly:

vedāvināśinaṃ nityaṃ ya enam ajam avyayam
kathaṃ sa puruṣaḥ pārtha kaṃ ghātayati hanti kam

And Hunar Sahib recited:

Arjun, son of Pritha, listen to what I say
He who knows it to be immortal
Who is convinced of its continued imperishability
That it has no match in indestructability
Whom will he kill, or have killed
When its existence is eternal

Rudra Sen Arya started to recite the next verse, but in his enthusiasm, Hunar Sahib kept right on singing:

Just as old torn garments
A man discards for new
This soul breaks its bond
With the old, tired body

A weapon cannot cut it
Fire cannot burn it

161

Water cannot dampen it
Wind cannot dry it

'Wonderful, wonderful, absolutely wonderful!' cried Rudra Sen Arya, as he swayed and wiped the sweat from his face with the edge of his dhoti. 'You've translated the verses into such simple poetry!'

'It's easy enough to recite couplets in difficult Urdu,' remarked Hunar Sahib proudly, 'but it's not that easy to render the deep thoughts of the Gita in simple language.'

He grinned, and looked over at Ranvir and winked.

'If this simple Gita of Hunar Sahib's gets published, people will memorize it and go about singing it like *Heer Ranjha*,' said Ranvir.

'It's not a question of earning money,' said Hunar Sahib. 'I wish to deliver this sermon by the god Krishna to every home. Now that I've translated the second section of the Shrimad Bhagavad Gita into Urdu poetry, my plan is to publish it and hand it out for free at the annual Arya Samaj festival. I've also decided to gift it to a literature-loving Gita fan.'

'What greater literary fan could there be than our brother Rudra here?' Ranvir suggested. 'He loves the Gita so much he won't even take food or drink without reciting from it first, and he knows the entire thing by heart.'

'You must definitely publish it!' cried Rudra Sen Arya enthusiastically. 'It's not just service to the faith but also to the nation. Today India is under foreign rule, but there is still one thing that makes her hold her head high before the whole world, and that thing is the Bhagavad Gita.'

'I'd publish it in the thousands and distribute it,' said Hunar Sahib helplessly. 'But you know, my younger brother's legal case has ruined me. The bastards kept ten thousand rupees' worth of jewellery, not to mention all the clothing given as a bridal gift. I've come to Jalandhar to sue them. I thought there could be no better way to alleviate our suffering from hanging around the courts than to render the second section of the Shrimad Bhagavad Gita into Urdu poetry.'

The air from the fan was hitting the front of Chetan's body squarely, but a river of sweat flowed down his back. He could no longer tolerate sitting there. 'Come on, why don't we go stand outside?' he asked Nishtar, pulling on his hand as he stood.

'Sit, sit,' said Hunar Sahib. 'We're just about to leave.'

But Chetan pulled Nishtar up and stepped out of the shop and down into the bazaar. Even though the air was stagnant outside as well, Chetan felt much relieved in the open air.

He placed one foot on the stoop of the shop and asked, 'What's Hunar Sahib got himself mixed up in now?'

Nishtar's squinting eye sparkled with laughter. 'Arré bhai, you know his younger brother, Gopal Das? He got married not long ago to Labbhu Mehndru's daughter from Mitta Bazaar. Not only did they have three sets of jewellery made for her, but for show, he also placed his wife's jewellery and that of his older brother's wife among the gifts to the bride. The girl stayed at their house one night, then never came back again. She says the boy is impotent and she won't live with him. She's kept all the jewellery and clothing, and now the case is making its way through court.'

'Is that really what happened?'

'Only God knows the truth, but people say that Gopal Das went to his in-laws and brought some holy man with him. Now, who knows what happened but the girl has refused to go back. Hunar Sahib's elder brother went himself and placed his turban at the girl's feet, but she wouldn't budge. And now the girl's elder brother has opened a general merchandise shop in Lal Bazaar. Hunar Sahib says it's all thanks to his jewellery . . . Whatever the case, that's why Hunar has to come to Jalandhar every few days, and the literary world here has become especially exciting as a result.'

Although Chetan already knew the answer, he asked, 'You haven't started reciting couplets in Urdu now, have you?'

'I have.'

'So you've become Hunar's pupil, then?'

'I haven't stopped writing in Punjabi,' said Nishtar with embarrassment.

'Have you become Hunar's pupil or not?' Chetan demanded.

But before Nishtar could respond, Hunar Sahib came outside and said enthusiastically, 'Rudra Sen is prepared to pay fifty rupees for paper but he says he'll buy it himself. He's a merchant, after all, the bastard!'

'But you promised to buy us lunch at the Khalsa Hotel,' said Nishtar.

'Well, hold on, I'll be right there,' said Hunar Sahib. 'You call Ranvir.'

Nishtar called out to Ranvir. When he came outside, Hunar Sahib went back in.

'I came by to hear you sing *Heer Ranjha*,' Chetan said to Nishtar.

'Then I'll sing it for you. You're here now.'

'I might leave today.'

'We'll say goodbye to Hunar Sahib now and go and sit somewhere.'

Just then, Hunar Sahib and Rudra Sen Arya came out. Hunar Sahib took Rudra Sen's thick hand in his own thin, fine fingers, and pressed it warmly as he grinned and thanked him profusely. And when they were some distance from the shop, Hunar Sahib took a five-rupee note from his kurta pocket and showed it off to Nishtar.

164

15

Hunar Sahib was describing at length his plans for rendering the Upanishads in simple Urdu after finishing his translation of the Shrimad Bhagavad Gita; as he walked along, he told humorous anecdotes in entertaining and idiomatic language without pausing for commas and periods, and Chetan was wondering how they were going to get rid of him. Hunar's idea was that they'd first go to the Khalsa Hotel on Kutchery Road for lunch and put to use Rudra Sen Arya's contribution for the simple translation of the Shrimad Bhagavad Gita. After that, the three of them would go and pay their respects to the head of the Doaba Widows' Aid Society on Mandi Road—that is, the 'Gandhi of the Doab', Mahatma Banshiram ji 'Karmath', editor of the weekly journal *Widows' Aid*. To go to Mandi and not pay one's respects to Mahatma Banshiram ji was absolute impiety in Hunar Sahib's religion—especially considering the fact that he'd opened not just the doors of his weekly to Hunar Sahib and his pupils, but also all the windows and ventilation slats. Mahatma Banshiram may have been the editor of *Widows' Aid* in name, but the real editor was Hunar Sahib. He not only wrote poetry for the journal, but he also obtained suitable essays and stories for it. And he also spread the word about the publication amongst his acquaintances and convinced them to become subscribers. He didn't actually get any compensation for his 'good deeds', not even a cup of tea for journeying from so far away. No, for him, this was Service to the Nation, and what greater joy or satisfaction could there be than to offer one's art in service to the nation? Of course, it was also true that ever since he'd taken on the unofficial editing of *Widows' Aid*, the number of his disciples had steadily grown in Jalandhar, Hoshiarpur and the surrounding towns and rural areas, and if his disciples wished to render their guru any services or gifts in the traditional manner, who was he to deprive them of this happiness? He'd promised Mahatma Banshiram ji that when he finished translating the Gita, he would publish it serially in *Widows' Aid*. This was why he wanted to go to the widows' ashram first after the Khalsa Hotel. Ranvir was after him to give him a poem to publish under his own name in this week's *Widows' Aid* for sure, and although Nishtar had a journal of his own, he too wanted his creations to be printed regularly in *Widows' Aid* . . . And thus, though Hunar Sahib was ostensibly going with his two pupils to pay his respects to Mahatma Banshiram, he was secretly going there to figure out how many columns were left for him and his pupils in the journal after the collection of pieces related to widow remarriage. After that, his plan was to go to see Mandi's famous broker Lala Jalandhari Mull ji 'Yogi'. Chetan had never met Lala Jalandhari Mull, but he'd certainly seen him at a few rallies. When Lala Jalandhari Mull's father was living, and Jalandhari Mull ji passed the middle school exam after failing four times and began working at the family business, he used to write poetry in Urdu. He'd taken the pen name 'Sarfarosh' or 'Brave One', and his nationalist poems had been published in a collection under the title *Patriotic Longings*, on the dedication page of which was printed a couplet by Ramprasad 'Bismil', the martyr of the Kakori Case:

The longing for sacrifice is now in our hearts
We shall see if it lies in the arm of the killer

Below that was written in large letters:

In sacred memory of the immortal martyr Ramprasad
'Bismil'

On the facing page was a photo of 'Sarfarosh ji': he was of medium height and quite pudgy; he had a short, thick neck; a large pimple on his right cheek near his nose; and an inky-dark complexion. He looked less like a poet in the photo, and more like the wrestler 'Kalue Pehlwan' in a Gandhi cap. During the Congress movement, he'd been sentenced to two years' hard labour. During this hardship, his father had fallen quite ill. By the time Sarfarosh got out of jail, his father had passed on to his heavenly abode. No one saw Sarfarosh at Congress rallies again after he returned from jail. When his father died, he took over the family business, got married and had five children in five years. But despite all this, he continued occasionally to express his feelings in couplets. In jail, he'd not only studied Vedanta philosophy, but he'd also taken on the title 'Yogi'. Lately, he'd been going home less and spending more time at the shop. After work, he'd go upstairs to the rooftop room which had a spacious terrace outside. His friends would visit, and Yogi ji would explain the mysteries of the Vedanta with great love and devotion. He had stopped wearing a Gandhi cap and now wore a kurta and dhoti dyed in red ochre. They didn't get dirty as fast and they also matched his new title. He looked after the affairs of the shop with detachment. He worried not about consequences, good and ill (or so he said), and he awaited the time when his sons would themselves take over the business and give him leave to pursue his yogic practices full time. It was

167

Yogi ji himself who had inspired Hunar Sahib to come up with the idea of translating the Upanishads into simple Urdu.

*

'Perhaps Hunar Sahib will present his translation of the Upanishads to "Yogi ji",' Chetan thought to himself, but he was interested neither in 'The Gandhi of the Doab' nor 'The Yogi of Mandi'. Although he'd enjoyed the hoodwinking of Rudra Sen Arya to a certain extent and his sadness had diminished somewhat, when Hunar Sahib had robbed the man of five rupees, he recalled how he himself had been robbed of the same sum by Hunar Sahib the very first time he'd met him. When he'd gone to see him off at the station, Hunar Sahib had asked him for the money claiming he'd left his wallet at home. The moment he remembered that incident, Chetan immediately felt bitter, and he recalled all of Hunar Sahib's prior offences—right up to the reading of the poem at Neela's wedding—and wished he could get rid of him somehow.

Just at that moment, they reached the open area where Rainak Bazaar meets Bazaar Sheikhan. Suddenly, he noticed the enormous signboard of Hoshiarpur Cycle House, and he saw that his boyhood friend, Harasaran, was seated out front, fitting up a bicycle. He called out from far off, 'Hello, Saran!' and rushed over. To Nishtar he explained, 'I'm going to hang out here for a while, you all can keep going.' But Nishtar went and stood right near the shop, and Hunar and Ranvir stood a few steps away from him.

*

He and Harasaran had been studying together in Class Eight when Harasaran's father had retired and started a small bicycle shop in Rainak Bazaar. There had been only a couple of bicycles there, apart from a fairly large number of tyres hanging up in the shop, and Harasaran's tall, hearty father, with his long moustaches and thick convex glasses, sat and repaired bicycles wearing only an undershirt and undershorts. After just a year, he had taken over the large shop next door, and Chetan saw that Harasaran's elder brother, who had had a job as a clerk somewhere and who might not have been quite as tall as his father, but was just as hearty, and whose moustaches were not quite as long, but still very thick, and who wore the same thick eyeglasses, was seated outside the shop fixing tyre punctures. Harasaran was strongly built like his father and brother, but a bit rougher around the edges. He had smallpox scars on his face and thick glasses as well—something about the composition of the faces of the two brothers and their father always seemed coarse and dishevelled to Chetan. There was nothing fine or elegant about them. But nonetheless, Harasaran had been quick in his studies. He always came fourth or fifth in class and had wanted to study to the MA level.

But work at the shop increased so much as he approached the Matric that his father demanded he stop studying any further and come and work with him. Chetan was going to a rally with Anant at the Town Hall one day on their way home from college (they'd decided to attend the rally when they'd reached Imam Nasiruddin, so from Bazaar Sheikhan, they'd come straight out towards Rainak Bazaar), when he saw Harasaran on one side of the street next to Hoshiarpur Cycle House, hands and face blackened with grease, repairing a puncture. He'd just called out 'Hello' to him from his cycle, but in his heart he pitied his friend who had sacrificed his glowing future to fix punctures in cycle tubes.

But over the past five or six years, Hoshiarpur Cycle House had spread to the shops around it—they'd knocked down the dividing walls and made one large fancy shop, in which hung the shiny frames of bicycles, handles and tyres, and ready-made cycles. Although the father had stopped fixing punctures and fitting out cycles, both the brothers still put bicycles together with their own hands. They hired boys to fix the punctures, inflate tyres and make small repairs. And they themselves didn't hesitate to do this work either when necessary. 'So that's why they've made so much progress so quickly,' thought Chetan, as he watched Harasaran for a moment fitting together a bicycle. Harasaran's kameez stuck to his back with sweat, there were black spots on his face from wiping the perspiration with his grease-covered hands and the hem of his kameez—and he felt respect for his friend and thought about how he had no right to pity him. Had Chetan really accomplished anything amazing by finishing his BA? He himself didn't make more than fifty rupees a month . . . he passed his days in profound want and was trying to feed his ego by puffing up his own accomplishments, while all his friends were making great strides and coming out ahead of him.

*

As soon as he saw Chetan, Harasaran left off fitting the cycle and jumped down from the shop. Wiping off his filthy grease-covered hands with the equally filthy hem of his kameez, he held out two fingers with embarrassment and said, 'Yaar, my hands are dirty.'

'Well, at least they're dirty from labour and sweat, not from the blood of your brothers.' Chetan was thinking of Amichand's hands, which were about to commit untold atrocities against his fellow men at the behest of the English. He grasped Harasaran's hand warmly.

Harasaran felt pleased by his praise. The sparkle in his eyes was not visible through the thick lenses of his glasses, but a wave of joy ran across his coarse peasant face.

'This labour is all that's written in my fate. God hardly gave me the sort of brilliance that you have,' he said smiling, and told Chetan that since they belonged to the Congress Party, they subscribed to *Bande Mataram,* and he had read all of Chetan's stories in the weekly editions, and not just he, but his brother and father all liked them very much.

He turned and called to his father, who was inside the shop counting newly arrived frames; then, bursting with happiness, he introduced Chetan to him.

Harasaran's father was even more pleased than him and, pulling forward a chair for Chetan, he said, 'Harasaran is always singing your praises. We're so fortunate to see you today. Come in . . . come in . . . Purify our shop for a few moments with your presence!'

He laughed happily, his clean teeth sparkling in his dense moustaches, and with that, all of Chetan's feelings of inadequacy, gathering since morning, all his depression, his shame, his listlessness, his sense of failure, his feelings of ill fortune, evaporated into a mist in that fresh breeze.

Let Amichand and Hamid and all his friends become officers, let them earn thousands of rupees a month, he would be satisfied with his own poverty a thousand times over! He was an artist, and they all appeared downright impoverished in comparison—a bunch of elephants plodding about in small circles! By contrast, he was free—a tiny bird soaring through the expanse of the sky as he sang. Sure, an elephant in captivity gets his belly filled, and the bird has to peck among the seeds to assuage his hunger, but how could the trudging of an elephant bound in chains compare to the soaring of a bird? And he felt electrified by ineffable bliss.

He decided that he would sit a few moments in Hoshiarpur Cycle House and tell Harasaran and his father about his experiences; he'd tell them his dreams, his techniques, his ambitions and the possible obstacles in his path; he'd tell them of his firm decision to remove those obstacles and arrive at his goal. He could have stopped there, but he didn't; his own sense of self-importance grew manyfold. 'I'll come again,' he said. 'Punjab's famous poet Hunar Sahib and his other friends are with me right now.'

'Invite them too . . . invite them too!' said Harasaran's father, beaming, and he called out to the servant to set out chairs, and told Harasaran to bring four glasses of shikanji, and he again courteously urged Chetan to invite his friends . . . 'We're just uneducated folk; it's not often that we get to see great individuals such as you! What can we do for you? Of course it will be as insignificant as Sudama's grain of rice was to Krishna . . .'

And he laughed.

Chetan decided to call Hunar Sahib, Nishtar and Ranvir over. That way, the topic of his stories published in *Bande Mataram* could be brought up in conversation as they drank shikanji, and then Hunar Sahib, Nishtar and Ranvir could learn how far his fame had spread and where all his fans were . . . But he didn't have to take the trouble to call them. Before he could turn around, Hunar Sahib slapped a hand on Chetan's shoulder from behind, and said, grinning, 'Arré bhai Chetan, introduce us to your friends as well!'

Chetan started and introduced him to Harasaran and his father, and since this could only augment his own importance, he praised Hunar Sahib fulsomely, forgetting all his hatred for him. Hunar Sahib came in and installed himself upon a chair. He seated Nishtar and Ranvir to his right and left, and began narrating a steady stream of entertaining anecdotes . . . When Harasaran brought the glasses of shikanji, Hunar Sahib was reciting his simple translation of the Shrimad Bhagavad Gita to Harasaran's father. He took the glass without slowing his pace in the slightest. He'd recite a couplet, then take a sip.

Chetan was waiting for him to finish talking so he could bring up his stories published in *Bande Mataram*, but that auspicious moment never arrived.

*

Hunar Sahib might have sat and recited poetry to them until evening, but Ranvir and Nishtar were both extremely hungry, so suddenly, he stood up. Just then, he remembered Chetan. So he fulsomely praised Chetan's artful short stories and said that he had the potential to really do something in the field of poetry as well. If Chetan hadn't left Jalandhar, or if he himself hadn't come back from Lahore, that potential would already have been fulfilled. He thanked Harasaran's family for their hospitality and their love of literature and, promising to visit them again soon, Hunar Sahib clasped his hands together and pressed them to his forehead.

'*Vande Mataram*—hail Mother India!' he said as he stepped down from the shop.

Chetan tried to say something in an indistinct voice about how it had got late and now he'd go home, but Hunar Sahib wrapped his right arm around him and pulled him forward. He wrapped his left arm around Ranvir and Nishtar together, and set out on his way.

As they started walking, he suddenly recollected himself and turned his head to thank Harasaran and his father, and assure them he'd be back to see them soon.

*

They had only just turned on to the big road towards Zila Kutchery from the intersection of Grand Trunk Road, when Chetan saw the three goondas, Debu, Jagna and Billa, installed outside the Khalsa Hotel. Chetan was perplexed: How was it possible that all three of them were in the same place at the same time, with no fighting?

Afternoon

16

Of those three goondas, Debu and Jagna were from Chetan's own mohalla, and Billa lived somewhere inside Khingra Gate, in Naiyon ki Gali or 'Barbers' Gali', a lane which had become known throughout the city on account of Raja Khairayati Ram. In Jalandhar, a barber was known by the title 'Raja', and his wife was known as 'Rani'. Khairayati Ram was the barber for the most important Khatri homes in the city. In his boyhood, he had even shaved his own patron, but the advent of the safety razor had deprived him of that occupation. Now it was his job to deliver the news of weddings, deaths, festivals, feasts, or mourning to the friends and relations of his patrons. But this task was usually handled by his Rani on her own. Instead, Khairayati Ram had opened a school just outside Khingra Gate, where the sons of all the city's moneylenders came to study. The school only went up to Class Four, and history, geography, Urdu and English were not taught there—Khairayati Ram only taught moneylending. Moneylending is the language of ledgers, and in just five years, Khairayati Ram brought the students to such a level in their arithmetic that a young man sitting for maths at the BA level couldn't compete with a Class Four-pass boy from Khairayati Ram's school. In ordinary schools, on reaching Class Four, boys can remember up to ten times ten with some difficulty, or if they're really advanced, up to ten times twenty, but in Khairayati

Ram's school, Class Four-pass boys memorized up to one hundred times one hundred, and could add, subtract, divide and multiply enormous sums. Khairayati Ram gave them formulas to memorize such that any boy who passed out of his school and went to sit at a shop would have no trouble keeping a ledger book at all. For this reason, those shopkeepers who wanted to seat their sons with them at their shops always sent them to Raja Khairayati Ram's school.

Khairayati Ram was a solid-looking man of medium height with salt-and-pepper moustaches and a drooping left eye. His ample frame tended towards fatness, and he wore too-short pyjamas, a kameez, a thick coat of checked cloth, and a low-wrapped turban. But he was the guru of moneylending and the city's businessmen knew this, so they accorded him respect. Instead of calling him Raja Khairayati Ram, they called him Master Khairayati Ram. Khairayati Ram only went to important patrons' homes on special occasions to give out invitations. Although his Rani would take the entire ceremonial gift, he considered it an obligation to his patron to fulfil his duty as barber in this observance himself. For this reason, the more the fame of his school grew, the more he cut himself off from his patrons.

Then one day, word got out that a rally of all the city's barbers had taken place under the chairmanship of Master Khairayati Ram, and that they had passed a resolution that only barbers who cut hair had the right to call themselves 'Nai' or 'barber'. Those in business could be addressed by the title 'Lala', and those who taught could be addressed as 'Pandit'. According to Arya Samaj philosophy, one did not become a Brahmin or a Khatri by birth, but rather through occupation, and since Master Khairayati Ram worked in education, he announced that he was now a Pandit. There was much rage over the barbers' proposal in Sanatan Dharma circles and the Sanatan Dharma Khatris and Brahmins even threatened to challenge their barbers, and declared they'd have to wash their hands of their patronage. Some poor barbers even grew fearful and decided to stick with the title Raja, but Khairayati Ram left his patrons and didn't leave off calling himself 'Pandit'.

Khingra Gate used to bring to the minds of city dwellers Master Khairayati Ram's school and the barbers' movement, but in the meantime, ever since Billa had entered adolescence and earned his stripes among the goondas of the city, it was his name that first came to mind at the mention of Khingra Gate. Master Khairayati Ram had grown old and the new crop of boys didn't even know about his movement, and every second or third day, Billa's name was heard in connection with some conflagration or other.

Billa (whose real name was Hari Kumar and whom people used to call 'Hariya') was about two years younger than Chetan and of a similar build to Chetan's younger brother Parasaram: he was hearty, handsome and muscular. Chetan recalled that years ago, when Hariya studied in Class Five or Six, he'd been skinny, pale and delicately beautiful, with eyes like a cat's—a bluish brown. That's how he'd ended up with the nickname 'Billa', or 'tomcat'. Chetan had also liked him very much when they were small. Once or twice, on the pretext of calling for Khairayati Ram, he'd also tried to go to Billa's house, but goonda boys would always surround him, and in those days, getting close to him was tantamount to getting one's head bashed in. Also, for some reason, he never had liked his tawny eyes. Ma's saying that you should never trust someone with cat's eyes had always made Chetan wary of him. Hooligans from every school in the city used to circle by Khingra Gate. Once, on the road going to Adda Hoshiarpur, right in front of Khingra Gate, there was a huge showdown over Billa between two bands of goondas that resulted in two stabbings and two busted heads; the police had come and the case had dragged on for months.

Then, as Chetan watched, skinny Billa began going to the akhara in the company of a wrestler boy from school, and in just two or three years, he became so muscular and such a powerful fighter, that instead of being followed around by boys, he was the one doing the following and he was the one bashing in heads. He failed his exams two years in a row in Class Eight, and did the same for Class Nine. When he couldn't get through Class Ten in two years, he quit school. Now he ran speculation games and paid the police copious bribes. He did get caught, but he was released every time. He was getting fat and he was the most notorious goonda in the city.

*

Jagna lived right near Kallowani Mohalla. He was the son of the priest at the dharamshala in Chaurasti Atari. There was a Shiva temple in the dharamshala, to which worshippers came for daily darshan. They'd make offerings, complete a circumambulation, round their lips and make an 'ololo' sound with their tongues, call out 'Bum bole!', ring the bell and press their foreheads on the threshold, and go home contented. Many offerings were made on Shivaratri, and contributions were gathered for the dharamshala at every shop in the bazaar. Next to the temple there was an old two-storeyed house made of medieval bricks. In the upper storey lived the priest and his family—two girls and a boy. There were four rooms in the lower storey, where grooms' parties stayed during weddings. There was a garden next to that, with an akhara. Quite a bit of income came from the dharamshala. The priest was not very educated but he certainly wished for his only son to read the shastras and to carry on in his place. Because the priest himself was uneducated, the atmosphere at the dharamshala was not conducive to study. The mohalla's layabouts played cards, chess and chaupar on the wide front terrace of the dharamshala all day long. One group would go, then another would come, and from morning to evening, this sequence would be repeated. Then, during Diwali, there would be gambling, but only under the patronage of the priest. Once, when Chetan had gone to get his father, he'd seen men gambling with cowry shells in the light of a hurricane lantern in the downstairs room at the back.

Mohalla enthusiasts (principle among whom was Pandit Shadiram) commissioned performances of the Raslila in the dharamshala and waved money at the boys dancing in the roles of Krishna and Radha as though they were prostitutes dancing at a *mujra*.

What with this atmosphere, Jagna wasn't able to study past middle school despite his father's best intentions, and even at that young age, he'd already adopted all the 'good habits' of smoking, drinking, theft and gambling under the patronage of Kallowani's most famous goonda, Pyaru. He'd been going to the akhara since he was a child—and cards, chaupar and gambling were a regular affair in his home. Since childhood he'd acted as a representative for his father at the Diwali gambling gatherings—that is, when the priest had smoked too much ganja and fallen unconscious, he'd stay up all night and keep the bank open. In the morning, he'd give half the money to his father and with the other half he'd go to the cinema with Pyaru and Debu and other friends, or they'd feast on roghan josh or shahi korma at one of the hotels on Station Road. And it was at these hotels that he'd become addicted to carousing at a young age as well.

It had already been three years since he'd failed middle school, when his father, the priest, passed into the next world. He'd married off his elder daughter before his death, so Jagna assumed his father's post with the help of his younger sister and mother. His mother and sister were in charge of cleaning the temple, and he took half of the offerings from them. During his father's time, there had only been gambling during the days of Diwali, but under Jagna's rule, there were gambling parties day and night. The residents of Kallowani Mohalla and Chaurasti Atari had earlier used the dharamshala jointly to hold meetings. Harlal Pansari took donations and had bathing taps installed there. The people of the mohalla went there to bathe in the mornings, and a curtained area had been set apart for women. This was why they went to the temple—both to bow their heads before the deity and to bathe. Those who didn't have extra room in their homes would spread out dhurries and mats there for visitors who came for weddings or to mourn the passing of a relative. The women would come there to bathe after performing the funeral rites. When, under Jagna's rule, the hooligans of the city began to frequent the dharamshala twenty-four hours a day, it became a cause of great hardship for the people of the bazaar and the mohalla. Someone harassed someone else's mother or sister, and then the mohalla people stopped giving donations. When that had no impact, the leaders of the mohalla and the bazaar held a meeting and passed a proposal to expropriate the temple and dharamshala from them. They raised donations in the bazaar and filed a complaint in court. Since the case was underway in those days, Jagna went with his four friends and hung about the courts, and since everyone was boycotting the dharamshala, he turned it into a centre for gambling and carousing.

*

But Chetan found Debu's personality much more interesting than those of his two colleagues.

*

182

Debu had one squinty eye. When the people of the mohalla spoke of him contemptuously, they added 'kana' or 'squint-eye' to his name. His father, the astrologer Daulat Ram, had been one of the minions of Chetan's father, Pandit Shadiram. Daulat Ram's education had consisted of just three or four years of study in the field of moneylending, but he'd spent the greater part of his life in the skeining business, or patphera. During Chetan's childhood, Jalandhar was famous for silk-dyeing and sateen. Raw silk was dyed in large vats and pots. There were scores of boilers for dyeing. When the water was drained off after the dyeing, an odour spread throughout the gali and all the drains ran with colour. When Chetan would come home from his primary school in Qila Mohalla, he often covered his nose with his sleeve to avoid the stench. The loose, dyed skeins would be sent into Patphera Bazaar, the skeining market. Two skeiners would sit across from one another on stools. One would wrap a dyed silk skein around his knees and then spread his knees apart. Then he would move his knees from left to right, letting go of one thread at a time. The other would wrap each thread around his own knees to create a skein, just the way a kite-fighter creates a skein with his pinkie and thumb from string cut down from another's kite. The men formed the skeins so rapidly that Chetan would be transfixed, standing in Patphera Bazaar for hours watching the skeining of fine silk thread.

Sateen—the silken fabric woven on Jalandhar's looms—was so thick and lovely that it was sold far and wide. Coloured threads of silk were cross-woven together to give an amazing impression of sunlight and shade. Wide sateen skirts or ghagras, and suits were usually stitched for weddings. But when cheap, machine-made silk threads and fabrics started coming from abroad, this Jalandhari handicraft was finished. Not only did sateen stop being made, but silk-dyeing work came to an end, and Patphera Bazaar lay deserted. After that Pandit Daulat Ram took up the work of his forebears—family priesthood. Upon becoming a priest, he began sitting in the company of Qila Mohalla's famous astrologer Pandit Atma Ram, and one day he marked his forehead with three lines of ash, made a knot in his braid, wrapped a shawl printed with the name of Ram over his naked upper body above his dhoti, and announced that he was an astrologer. All the same, Chetan knew perfectly well that this respected astrologer, despite saying 'No, no,' at Chetan's father's parties, partook nonetheless and, despite shaking his head in refusal, 'drank' when Pandit Shadiram forced him to (but only when three or four friends pressured him into it). Chetan had seen astrologer Daulat Ram's 'refusals' and 'acquiescences' when performing waiter duties at his father's parties. Daulat Ram would say, 'Look, Shadiram, don't force me! I went to Haridwar and left all this behind me. Why are you making me partake in sin with you?' or 'Look, I'm not the same Daulat Ram any more, I'm a priestly astrologer. You're a Brahmin too, but you're even worse than the *mleccha*s—the non-Hindus— leave me to my piety!' and Chetan knew what he was getting at. Upon the respected astrologer invoking 'mother— Haridwar' and dharma and karma, Pandit Shadiram would order his comrades to shake all the Haridwar and piety from the bastard! And two or three of them would leap up and descend upon the pious astrologer, while Pandit Shadiram would personally force the glass to his mouth—the astrologer's shawl imprinted with the name of Ram would fly off, his sacred thread would become a noose around his neck, they'd hold him down from all sides, and then he'd take a sip of wine as though under extreme duress. But then, when he'd glance towards the glass again, all tied up like that, his eyes would become thirst personified. His thirst seemed to bubble up like steam when the cover of a pot is suddenly removed. Chetan would watch the steam of longing bubble from his eyes and overflow on to every part of his face as Daulat Ram laughed and whimpered with feigned anger. And when he'd take the first sip, he'd cry out, 'Get away from me, you've destroyed all my dharma earned over all these years!' And he'd take hold of the glass, shove his restrainers aside and sit up, forgetting all righteousness. Oh, how he'd lash out at Pandit Shadiram and his other colleagues with the filthiest of curses expressed in the purest Punjabi as he lifted the glass to his lips.

Sometimes, when he returned home from these parties in the middle of the night, he'd be singing in a voice that sounded like a busted drum:

Oh my Ram, I am your sinner!

The next day, he'd roundly curse Pandit Shadiram and his depraved comrades, keep a fast for penance and recite prayers. Whether he actually fasted and prayed, Chetan didn't know, but he made sure to announce as much to all passers-by, while seated at Harlal Pansari's shop.

Chetan never did understand why Daulat Ram, if he really was such a pious man, showed up at Chetan's father's house the moment Pandit Shadiram came into Jalandhar. Why didn't he just steer clear of the parties instead of later paying the price by fasting and praying?

His wife—Debu Kana's mother—was a strict and quarrelsome woman. And it was also well known in the mohalla that she beat her husband. How affectionate would a woman who beat her husband be towards her own children? Thus, as a result of this 'boundless affection' of his mother's, Debu had grown accustomed to slaps across the face and punches to the back from infancy. (Some parents do believe in the philosophy that a child's bones are strengthened from beating, and their lungs from crying.)

When Debu fled from this 'affection' of his mother's, he always ended up with his young uncle, Pyare Lal, who was himself adept at rendering bones thoroughly steely.

Pandit Gurdas Ram's youngest boy, astrologer Daulat Ram's younger brother and Debu Kana's uncle, Pyare Lal, aka Pyaru, was one of those youths who was born from his mother's womb a goonda. Chetan remembered that ever since he'd been conscious, Pyaru had been the chief among the mohalla's mad, wayward boys. When he was studying in Class Two and Three, Pyare Lal had been just a couple of classes ahead of him. Because he was older, he took everyone under his patronage and performed all sorts of mischief. If anyone refused to do as they were told, then, in his words, he'd 'mould' them, that is, he'd beat them senseless. Chetan usually avoided his group, but living in the mohalla, he did sometimes end up with them. He remembered two such incidents from his childhood days quite clearly.

*

It was summer and small, unripe mangoes were in abundance. It was fun to eat the tiny mangoes with salt, but since he would be scolded at home if he was seen with them, and told that his eyes would be inflamed and his throat would get sore, Chetan used to go out to Company Bagh or to the fields outside the city with the other mohalla boys, where they'd pay no heed to the sun or the hot *loo* wind, to the dust or rain storms, and pick up the fallen mangoes, or knock them down with stones—Pyaru and Debu both had such good aim, their first or second shot would fell the fruit, whereas the rest of them threw stones that usually fell two to three yards on either side—then they'd sit in the shade of a tree, peel, cut and salt the mangoes, and eat them. Their eyes smarted and their throats felt sore, but neither of these afflictions could deprive them of the supreme pleasure of eating those tiny fruits.

One morning on their way to school, someone proposed they go and pick mangoes from Tikka's garden.

Pyaru wasn't in the mood to go that day. 'Those mangoes have started coming into the market to be sold by now,' he said. 'What's the point of picking them from trees? Come on, I'll just get you some along the way.'

In those days, most of the bookshops were in Bohar Wala Bazaar, but there were two large vegetable shops there as well, at the turning from Mitha Bazaar towards Bohar Wala Bazaar. It was morning, and there was a large crowd at the shop. The basket of green mangoes lay right on the ground. When they were still at a distance, Pyaru called out, 'How much for the mangoes today?'

The vegetable seller was busy. 'Two for a paisa,' he responded as he weighed out the other customers' merchandise. Then Pyaru cut through the crowd and arrived at the basket of mangoes. He winked subtly, and Debu came up behind him.

Pyaru boldly picked up a pair of mangoes and handed them back to Debu, who distributed them to the other boys. When every boy had got mangoes, he held up two more in his hand and showed them to the vegetable seller from the crowd; he handed him one paisa and then took his disciples off to school.

Another time he took all his comrades out for muskmelons. The melon market was in Chowk Imam Nasiruddin. Melons were stacked up in piles there, surrounded by crowds of customers. Pyare Lal sneaked into a circle of customers crowding around one such pile. They were nice melons and the crowd was dense. He went and squatted in front. Debu, who was his lieutenant in such matters, slipped into the crowd and sat behind him; Jagna went behind Debu and stood slightly stooped over. Pyaru picked out two large melons and, stroking them, called out to the shopkeeper,

187

'How much for these?' The shopkeeper's attention was elsewhere. Then Pyaru rose slightly and rolled the melon through his legs. Debu pushed the melon through his legs to Jagna, and Jagna passed it to the very last comrade who took it across the bazaar and gave it to the boy sitting at Charat Singh Corner.

Pyaru, after pushing one melon to the back, selected another one, and when he saw that the shopkeeper wasn't paying attention, pushed it through his legs and picked up a third.

On the day of Nirjala Ekadashi, Chetan went with his Dada to get melons from the market, and Pyaru and his gang came too. Since Debu had already told him what they would do, Chetan watched him as Dada purchased the melons.

After Chetan left the market with his Dada, he saw them all in Lal Bazaar, picking up the melons, pounding them in two with their hands and eating them exactly as villagers do . . .

*

But Pyaru didn't just do all this, he did many other things as well: he smoked cigarettes and beedis, sang vulgar songs, played dirty jokes on boys and cursed obscenely, or rather, he educated his disciples in all forms of obscenity. No one in his group ever had the nerve to contradict him or he'd beat the dissenter to a pulp.

The thing that astonished Chetan was Pyaru's courage. Especially in terms of stealing—it was second nature to him to go out to Bara Bazaar with his band, wait until the fruit seller's attention was elsewhere, then nick apples or pomegranates or bunches and bunches of bananas. Not just that: a typical exploit of his would be to go to a fair, stand in a crowd gathered around a sweet-seller, hold up one rupee and show it to the sweet-seller a couple of times, then put it in his pocket; after that, he'd take puris (without paying any money), then get the change back from the sweet-seller. It wasn't that he never got caught; if he got caught, he'd quietly put the stolen item right back, but if the sweet-seller cursed at him or scolded him, he'd haul off and sock him, declaring that he was being falsely accused of theft. Because of all the fun that could be had during such activities, Chetan wanted to go with him too, but for one thing, he was afraid of getting beaten by Pyaru, and for another, he was afraid of getting caught and dishonouring the name of his station master father. He also knew that if his father found out that he'd stolen something, he'd bury him alive. As with all fathers who have seen every kind of sin, Chetan's father too wished to see his sons become completely virtuous, good boys (although he'd never said so).

But Debu faced no such difficulty. He found ever new happiness in wandering about with his uncle. Sometimes his uncle would beat him mercilessly for some minor infraction, but Chetan had never seen tears in Debu's eyes even after so much thrashing. His mother had made his bones so strong in his infancy that nothing could affect Debu, even if his uncle walloped him so hard that his hand started to hurt . . . and his uncle saw to it that this 'worthy' nephew of his became proficient in every art. Yes, Debu did have one shortcoming, but it wasn't in his uncle's power to make it right. Although Pyaru's skull too was stuffed with hay in place of brains, his hay was a bit of a higher class than his nephew's (he could never be called knowledgeable or intelligent, but he was definitely rather cunning—he noticed suitable opportunities in fighting. If an opportunity wasn't favourable, he'd avoid it). Debu had no capacity for reflection whatsoever. He'd leap into a fight heedless of all consequences. He didn't worry at all if his adversary was strong or part of a group and because of this, he'd been badly thrashed many times, and many times, after they'd found out about it, he'd been brought back in a semi-conscious state. But as soon as he got healthy again, he'd grab his opponents one by one and beat them up, taking revenge so thoroughly that others, finding him alone, wouldn't have the courage to raise a hand against him themselves.

*

Chetan remembered two incidents related to Debu in particular, because he himself had played a role in both.

*

The first incident was from those days when Debu's wife was extremely ill. The thing was that, like his uncle, Debu was not very educated. His uncle had failed the Matric. Debu had got stuck at Class Five, although he'd managed to plagiarize his way through to the third division, and just as the uncle had been married off the moment he'd failed school, so too had the nephew. This was the only solution the parents of Kallowani Mohalla had for improving their sons—marriage! Then, although the boys were ruined even more by this, and went on to produce ruined offspring, they believed this to be the fate of Kallowani Mohalla, and tricked themselves into believing that they'd fulfilled their duty as parents now, and if all that was fated in old age was enduring hardship at the hands of their sons, what could be done?

Debu's wife was beautiful. But a beautiful wife could not tie Debu down. Whether his wife was lovely or not she had only one use for Debu, and he worked her fully for it. He didn't believe he had any other duty as a husband. If he had known better, he wouldn't have believed this, but he didn't know any better. Debu's negligence and his mother's atrocities dragged that innocent girl into the embrace of tuberculosis in only two short years (when the people of the mohalla had glimpsed her charm as the palanquin

190

was lowered, they had declared that Debu must surely have given a gift of pearls in his previous birth). She lay on a charpoy by the window of the room on the Barne Pir side, and coughed and coughed, and sometimes passers-by below would be seized with terror when they heard her.

Although he'd never done anything for that sickly wife of his, one evening, Debu saw some Muslim boys playing *chikri* in the shade of the neem tree at Barne Pir. He mentioned his wife's sickness to them and demanded they not make any noise and told them to run along from there.

There were Muslim neighbourhoods on three sides of Kallowani Mohalla—the entire district beyond Barne Pir was Muslim. Who could bloody well stop them from playing chikri near the Pir's tomb? When they ignored what he said, he immediately picked up the board and turned it over, cursing at them all the while. The game pieces scattered all about. The Muslims surrounded Debu, who was alone.

Chetan had been visiting from Lahore for two days. He was talking to someone in the mohalla, when a small boy came running and asked where Chetan's brothers Parasaram and Shankar were (Parasaram and Debu had been in the same class and because they both frequented the akhara, they were great friends; in the meantime, Shiv Shankar had started going to the akhara as well).

'What's wrong?' asked Chetan.

'There's a fight going on at Barne Pir between Debu and the Muslims.'

Chetan knew both of his brothers. They didn't hesitate in the slightest when it came to fighting; so, wanting to avoid them getting their heads busted open, he ran over himself to put an end to the matter instead.

He had just made it to Jwali Mehri's kiln, when he saw that Debu was standing with his back to him, surrounded

191

by a semicircle of four or five boys, who were preparing to crush him.

Just then, Debu turned around and cast a glance back at the sound of Chetan's footsteps, or to see if anyone from the mohalla was coming (from such a distance he couldn't have gathered in that one second who was coming, but it was enough for him to know that someone was). The next moment, he climbed on top of one of the boys and knocked him backwards, and then the whole group fell upon him.

Debu actually had an amazing knack for grabbing his adversary by both legs and knocking him flat with lightning speed: he'd lift him up by both ankles and the next moment, his opponent would fall to the ground, bang, flat on his back. Debu's grip was so powerful that his opponent just couldn't move. If he grabbed the legs of the boy whose turn it was during kabaddi, he wouldn't let him drag him even two inches, let alone reach the line. And he'd knocked over the boy who was threatening him the most among all those surrounding him. When Chetan got there, he saw that one boy was beneath Debu, and the rest were pounding on him from above, but he still had the first one pinned.

Just then, Chetan saw a boy come from the gali across the way, carrying a metal rod, with which he slapped Debu's thigh twice in quick succession.

Debu didn't notice it any more than a man would notice a fly alighting on his leg. When the boy raised the metal rod for the third time and was about to hit him on the head, Chetan, who had come to make peace, got angry—'There's only one of Debu and so many of them, and they've brought a metal rod against him,' he said to himself, and he leapt up and grabbed it from the boy's hand in one shake and hit him hard across the lower back with it.

192

Before the boy could turn and jump on Chetan, Parasaram, Shiv Shankar, Hansa of the Jhamans, his brother Mansa, and Badda all arrived and saw Chetan swimming in a sea of feet and fists. Shiv Shankar went in first and pinned back the arms of the boy fighting Chetan.

As soon as he had been kicked and punched, the boy bent over; Debu let go of him and turned to confront them. Debu leapt up as they all brawled, kicked the boy lying down hard in the buttocks, and went and grabbed the rod from Chetan's hand, smashed two of them in the head and sent the rest scurrying with a beating.

*

The other time he knocked out Billa himself.

*

What happened was that during the Matric, Chetan used to visit the home of a boy from Bazaar Charat Singh. He was actually a couple of classes behind him, but he was a scout in Chetan's group, and they would come home from scouting together. Chetan would drop him off at his house, then come home through Imam Nasiruddin and Bara Bazaar, crossing Chhati Gali. This friend of Chetan's was rather handsome. Well, he wasn't so much handsome as he was delicate. He was a classmate of Billa's. Although Billa had no interest in scouting whatsoever, for a few days, he'd been playing with his friends outside on the street or on the police line after school, and when Chetan and his friend were leaving school after scouting, he'd tag along behind them and hover about outside the other boy's house all evening. One day, when they arrived in Chowk Mendruan, Billa cracked a dirty joke

193

about him. When Chetan tried to reason with him, he elbowed him out of the way and took off.

Chetan had left his friend and was walking home angrily when he ran into Debu. Debu had a length of wire bunched up in his hand and was singing lustily, albeit in a fairly crass voice:

Oh you girl, lovely as Lakshmi
I'll only drink water from your hands!

'Hello there, what's up, Bhapa ji!' Coming near Chetan he fondly slapped his hand on his shoulder.

Since Chetan was two years older than him, Debu called him 'Bhapa ji', or 'big brother', whenever he was in a good mood.

And anyway, their fathers were also thick as thieves. Chetan called Debu's father 'Chacha ji' or 'uncle', and Debu called Pandit Shadiram 'Chacha ji' as well, and according to Pandit ji, the two were closer than a pair of brothers.

'Yaar, your friend is totally harassing us,' Chetan said suddenly, on finding him in a good mood.

'Who's harassing you, his mother's— . . .' Debu let slip a curse and twirled his bunch of wire around.

Then Chetan told him what Billa had done, and said, 'Even with you around, your friend is disrespecting your elder brother; it's not an insult to me, it's an insult to you!'

'Let's go, then!' cried Debu, cursing Billa fulsomely.

Chetan turned back and retraced his steps. Billa was wandering about Bazaar Charat Singh. They went over to him, and Debu, without saying a word, smacked him hard and, motioning towards Chetan, asked, 'Why did you shove this bhapa of mine?'

Billa had no idea what was going on. He thought Debu was joking, so he reeled off a few 'extremely sweet words' in the service of that 'bhapa'.

But when, at this, Debu hauled off and socked him in the nose, and blood sprayed from it, Billa pinned Debu down.

Although Debu went to the akhara regularly and did push-ups and sit-ups and was also extremely courageous, Billa was sturdier than him, and knew better wrestling manoeuvres. In just five minutes he had Debu pinned beneath him.

By this point, quite a crowd had gathered. But no one had the courage to break it up. Then, when Billa grabbed him by the neck and started ruthlessly bashing his head against the ground, a brick somehow made its way into Debu's hand. Either an onlooker had given it to him or he'd just managed to reach for it himself. Though he was still pinned to the ground, he managed to smack the brick against Billa's head. Seeing both of them covered in blood, people broke them apart.

Both of them were swearing horribly and saying that they meant to kill one another but Chetan, imagining the unfortunate outcome of such a fight, spent a good deal of time reasoning with them and calming them down, and managed to cajole them into shaking hands. Billa acknowledged Chetan as Debu's elder brother and apologized, and Debu in turn apologized to Billa, and the two of them, heads busted, set off arm in arm to get bandaged up by Hakim Dina Nath in Papadiyan Bazaar, with Chetan in tow.

17

Chetan smiled slightly to himself as he recollected that incident in Bazaar Charat Singh. The Khalsa Hotel was at the crossroads, to the left. As Chetan arrived in front of the hotel, arm in arm with Hunar Sahib, he wondered whether or not he should part with the group.

'What are you up to, Bhapa ji?' asked Debu on seeing them standing in front of the hotel. He held out a hand to greet them.

Chetan shook his hand and told him that he'd gone to Rainak Bazaar, then run into Hunar Sahib, so he'd come over here with him. He let go of Debu's hand and introduced them to one another. 'This is one of the premier poets, not just of the Doab, but of the entire region, and his memory is so amazing that he remembers not just his own work, but the entire oeuvres of other poets as well,' he said, and of Debu, he remarked that he was like a little brother to him—the elder son of Chacha Pandit Daulat Ram, the astrologer, and that he was amazingly fearless.

Although Debu's squinty eye shone on hearing his praises sung, and Hunar Sahib beamed, Chetan chuckled to himself at the slight touch of irony in his praise (which hinted at the reality of the special qualities of each).

Debu told Hunar Sahib that he'd seen him before and had even heard his couplets in a poetry gathering. He nodded and smiled and held out his hand to shake Hunar Sahib's, at which

Hunar Sahib grinned and, bowing slightly, pressed Debu's hand warmly between his own.

Then Debu introduced his acquaintances, and Hunar Sahib his, at which Billa came forward and, smacking Nishtar hard on the shoulder, he asked Hunar Sahib, 'Since when have you made this squint-eye your pupil? Has he stopped keeping Rehmat's bed warm?'

At this, all of them laughed as though Billa had made a wonderfully clever joke. Nishtar glared at Billa with rage through his drooping eye, but at that same moment, Billa filled his lungs with a deep breath and stuck out his broad chest. Nishtar looked down.

There was an enormous crowd at the Khalsa Hotel (it wasn't really a hotel, nor was it a restaurant; it was just a popular dhaba—a roadside eatery—but you could get wonderful tandoori parathas there, and pork, mutton, keema, koftas, the Mutter Paneer Special Dish and yogurt lassi). There were a handful of other dhabas of this type, but the Khalsa Hotel was known for its expertise and the prices were reasonable. Hunar Sahib peered into the large room, where the customers were stuck together at the dirty benches and tables despite the heat and humidity. The charpoys arranged beneath the tree outside were also packed: there sat Jats, kameezes unbuttoned, broad chests dripping with sweat, fanning themselves with the tails of their turbans; youths dressed in undershirts and tahmads; and law babus, wearing suits despite the heat . . . He turned to Chetan and said helplessly, 'There's nowhere to sit!'

'Will you take something to eat?' asked Debu, suddenly coming forward. 'Here you go, we'll make some space right away.'

He cast a glance over the charpoys—on two were seated Sikh Jats, on one were two or three babus from the court, and on the fourth, some youths—he went over to the youths and demanded that they clear off.

Debu spoke in a rather harsh, authoritative tone, such that two of them immediately stood up, but the youth in the middle, who was comparatively stronger than the other two, and who wore only an open kameez and tahmad, stayed seated as though no such thing had been said to him.

'Please, take a seat!' urged Debu to Hunar Sahib, paying no attention to the seated youth.

But before any of them could come forward, the seated youth grabbed the arm of one of his friends and indicated that he should sit back down.

His friend was now half standing, half sitting, when Debu stepped forward, grabbed him by the arm and turned him around.

'I told you to clear out, but now you're sitting down again,' he said.

Now the seated youth stood up, raised his shoulders slightly, stuck out his neck, and took a few steps forward. He rolled up his sleeves and glared at Debu, enraged.

'Why aren't you letting us sit here?'

'This charpoy is reserved.'

'Who's it reserved for?'

'For this *baap* of yours,' Debu motioned towards Hunar Sahib.

And a ringing slap landed on Debu's cheek. Before anyone could say anything, Debu leapt forward, as was his wont, shouting a horrifying curse like a slogan in the air, and dived at the youth, grabbing him by both ankles and lifting him up. The next moment, the boy was in the air and then flat on his back, with Debu sitting on his chest.

'Oh, oh,' said Hunar Sahib. He snapped the end of his homespun dhoti and stepped forward to free the boy, but Billa, without saying a word, put out his arm and motioned for him to go and sit back down on the charpoy.

When the boy for whose sake the fight had occurred came forward to free his pinned comrade, Billa stopped him as well, as if to say, 'If you have to fight, then fight me. It's an even match, just let it happen.'

All the other charpoys emptied out in the blink of an eye. The people eating inside, the people walking by—everyone gathered round. The lower middle classes, whether due to their difficult life struggles, severe unemployment, laziness or boredom, will gather to watch any spectacle in a heartbeat . . . and Billa and Jagna didn't allow anyone to break it up.

But the boy didn't stay down long. He grabbed one of Debu's arms, pressed it down and started to twist it in such a way that despite pushing down on him with all his might, Debu fell over. Now the excitement of the crowd knew no bounds.

'Great! Great!'

'Pin him!'

'Spin him like a top!'

Some of the onlookers praised him; some began egging Debu on and suggesting manoeuvres.

'Get him in a leg hold!'

'No, get his neck between your legs, trap him and turn him!'

And Debu did throw him: clamping his neck between his legs, he twisted around and was on top again.

The spectators were beside themselves with glee.

'Amazing! Bhai, amazing!'

'He knows all the moves, bhai, how did he get out from under? He must have taken a beating at the hands of a master.'

Perhaps that youth not only knew better moves than Debu, but was also stronger. He got out from under Debu and came up again, and this time, despite the crowd going wild and egging Debu on, he didn't let him get up. He began to press him into the ground.

Just then, a police officer noticed the crowd that was growing by the minute and entered the crossroads. Billa grabbed the boy's hand and pulled the two of them apart (he didn't care especially about the officer but Debu was getting beaten).

'An officer is coming,' he said.

Debu got up and brushed the dirt from his sweaty clothing (though it couldn't be brushed off without drying first). He told Billa sadly that he'd broken it up for no reason; he was about to make that guy see stars in just one move.

'That's fine, but do you want to go and sit down now or make him see stars?'

Debu walked over to the charpoy. Nishtar and Ranvir had sat down on it and Hunar Sahib was about to sit down as well, when that same youth returned and said, 'This charpoy's ours, please get up!'

This time, Billa stepped forward. 'Go on, go sit somewhere else. Why are you quarrelling? This is our guest, a famous poet.'

'If he's a famous poet, then bring a charpoy from home. Whether he's a poet or the baap of a poet, he can't have this charpoy. We were sitting here first.'

Billa replied slowly, suppressing his anger as he emphasized each word, 'Oh, son of a wrestler, what are you getting so worked up about?' (Seeing him glancing over at the policeman and starting to roll up his sleeves, he took it even further.) 'Take a look at that policeman. Police don't scare easy. Consider this charpoy and this hotel ours, not your father's.'

The youth was about to haul off and punch him, but Billa stepped forward, picked him up and threw him on the ground, then stood by silently, hands on his hips.

The youth got up as soon as he fell, and leapt upon Billa like a tiger. Billa grabbed him by one arm and one leg and threw him even farther and then went and stood quietly near his head.

When the youth stood up again, practically insane with rage, Billa threw him even farther.

Secretly, Chetan felt quite angry with Debu and Billa. First, they'd committed theft, then made a display of their arrogance. If the other fellow had the charpoy first, why should he leave it? All his sympathy was with the young man. He was sure that if they'd cajoled him, told him that these poet types had come from out of town, they're guests, we need space for them, he'd certainly have given it up. It seemed entirely unjust for Hunar Sahib or himself to sit on the charpoy. He got up and went over to the youth.

The youth had sat up on the ground, but he hadn't yet stood, and was currently trying to decide whether he should get up and jump on Billa again or just go away. Billa was much stronger than him. Chetan went over and said to him, 'Bhai, do take your charpoy back. There's no need to fight over such a small matter! We'll eat in a little while.'

Pleased by Billa's bravery, a Sikh Jat, fanning himself with the hem of his tahmad, called out, '*Basshaho*, come over. We're done eating. Seat your guests over here.'

And he stood up with his comrades.

But the youth refused to accept sitting elsewhere after getting beaten. 'No, no, sir, you go sit there,' he said to Chetan as he stood up. 'I'll deal with this Billa some other time.'

And he turned his back and went off to another dhaba. His friends went to join him, following at a slight distance. Chetan returned to find that Hunar Sahib had dragged the Jat's charpoy over as well and was sitting and fanning himself with the end of his dhoti, feet up.

Just then, Billa said to the hotel proprietor, 'Look, Sardar ji, we have guests, please serve us something special.'

'Don't you worry, Basshaho,' said the proprietor, pulling a cooked roti from the tandoor with an iron skewer and placing it in the basket. 'We'll serve you first-class eats.'

18

Nishtar and Ranvir very grandly ordered pork, *gurde-kapoore* and tandoori parathas. Hunar Sahib had quit eating meat when he'd started following Gandhi, so he ordered the Mutter Paneer Special Dish and the 'free dal' with two paisas' worth of spices sautéed in pure ghee thrown in. When he was giving the order, he said the phrase 'free dal' in a particular way, and then looked over at his companions and laughed. He was apparently hinting at a story about such free dal that was quite famous in Jalandhar. Chetan, whenever he ate at a dhaba, also had to chuckle when he thought of it.

The story goes like this: a Jat once came to Jalandhar from the far-off countryside in connection with a court case. When he got off the train, he felt extremely hungry. Right across from the inn was a dhaba. The dhaba owner was popping rotis into the tandoor one after another.

'Tell me, brother, how much for the rotis?' asked the Jat.

'Two for a paisa.'

'And the dal?'

'Dal is free!'

'Okay, then first just fill a bowl with dal for me!' the Jat had said, holding out his hands impatiently.

*

205

For just a second, it occurred to Chetan that he too should simply ask for a bowl full of free dal, just like the Jat. On the other hand, a dhaba owner could laugh at what the Jat had said, but what if he said something sarcastic when he saw an educated person like Chetan purposefully asking for such a thing? And what if he didn't understand the joke, and just filled a bowl with dal and handed it to him? What would he do with so much chana or urad dal and nothing to eat it with? If he went ahead and ate it, he'd have diarrhoea for a month . . . and he laughed to himself.

Ranvir had ordered a plate of pork for Chetan too, and next he wanted to order roghan josh, but Chetan stopped him and told him to get what he wanted for himself. 'I'm not getting pork,' he added and, after thinking a moment, he ordered a plate of mutter paneer and an order of dal with spice fried in ghee.

Chetan had never tasted pork. He did want to taste it, but the strange thing was that just imagining pork he thought of beef and his desire died out . . . At the thought of beef, he remembered Jamuna, the family cow that Chetan had always regarded with reverence and love in childhood. She was tall, pure white and young, but she didn't butt. She was extremely well bred. Ma had raised her like her own daughter. Although she referred to her as 'Mother Cow', she treated her with more affection than reverence. She spent as much time as she had to spare after doing the housework in caring for the cow. She'd prepare her feed by mixing chickpeas, cottonseed, wheat husks and who knows what else. She was absolutely attentive to her hunger and thirst. Because of this there was always plenty of milk, yogurt, butter, ghee and lassi in the house—it's a good thing, after all, that eating the flesh of a cow is forbidden. Would anyone eat the flesh of his mother or sister? And a shiver would run down his spine just at the thought . . .

'Jija ji, if you don't eat pork, then just get a plate of roghan josh,' suggested Ranvir. 'If not that, then get keema or kofta!'

'No, I don't feel like it,' said Chetan distractedly.

*

Chetan had only started eating meat in college, and that too, on Anant's insistence. He had been raised as a vegetarian, although his father ate meat and drank heavily as well. His mother had instilled an unspoken revulsion against meat in his heart. An incident from his childhood and a conversation with Ma about it had been etched forever in his mind . . .

He must have been about seven or eight years old. He'd gone to his father's station in Mukerian. Karim Khan, the switch operator, raised chickens there. One of his hens had given birth to chicks. Chetan just adored those tiny fuzzy chicks. After dinner, he'd take half a chapati and go outside, calling 'Here, here!' as he tossed pieces of it in their direction. The chicks would come running and cheeping as they leapt upon the bits of chapati. They'd pull them from one another's beaks and carry them off. At first, Chetan would have to toss the bits of chapati to call to them, but after a few days, on just hearing his voice, and later, on seeing him, they'd come hopping up. Chetan wanted them to nibble the chapati from his hand the way they did with Karim Khan's wife, Daani. Sometimes he'd toss them the bits of chapati, or he'd hold them up at a slight distance. Two chicks (which were perhaps male and therefore bolder) would jump up and nibble at the bits of chapati. Slowly, they began taking the pieces from his hand. But then one day, when he was late in tearing up the chapati, one came hopping on to his knee. Chetan's happiness knew no bounds. It began to nibble at a piece he held in his hand. As he watched, another also came

207

and sat on his knee and the two began to compete. Chetan was elated. What he wanted was for the other three chicks to come too, but they didn't have the courage. Chetan would call those two chicks every day and feed them in his lap. The hen—she was fluffy and round, and completely white, with a long neck and a spotless, fluffy chest—would stand at a slight distance, head up, excited, and the other three chicks would wander about near her feet. Chetan would sometimes throw her a piece as well. Then she would pick it up and the other three chicks would rush over. The hen would put the piece back on the ground. If it was large, she'd wave it in her beak and break it, and then the chicks would take it away. Chetan enjoyed all this immensely. He had come to love them so much that he decided to tell Ma to buy the chicks and the hen from Daani. When he told this to Ma, she scolded him, 'How can Brahmins raise chicks? This is the work of Shudras!'

Chetan couldn't understand this. When he insisted, Ma said, 'All right, I'll tell Karim Khan that the chicks will be ours. They'll stay with them, but they'll be ours. You can go over there and play with them as much as you want, but you can't bring them inside the house.'

But the next day, when Chetan brought his chapati out, he saw there was one chick less. When he went and asked Daani about it, he learned that she cooked one chick a day to make a stew for his father. Ma didn't allow meat to be cooked in the house. Pandit ji either went to the Kalals in the city or held a party in the evening in the switch operator's quarters. Daani was very beautiful. She served him liquor. She was the one who prepared the meat for him. What made Chetan extremely sad was realizing that Daani herself slaughtered the chicks she fed with her own hand . . . He ran weeping to his mother. 'Son,' Ma explained to him, 'all these people who kill living things, they are sinners. In this life, they eat the animals; in the next life, the animals will eat them.'

'But Ma, does that mean father's a sinner too?' Chetan asked suddenly.

Ma turned the response around, 'Son, he is your father. It's a sin to even think anything bad about him. His dharma is for him, ours is for us. Swear today that you won't kill living things and that you will never eat meat.'

And Chetan swore to it enthusiastically. But secretly, he decided his father must be a great sinner because of his cruelty.

*

But when Chetan was still a schoolboy, Anant had explained to him that if chicken eggs were not eaten and if chicks hatched from only half of the eggs a hen laid, there wouldn't be enough grain to feed them all. Anant had been eating eggs since childhood. By the time he reached the Matric, Chetan had tasted egg, but he still didn't touch meat until he was in college. In college, he did eat meat in Anant's company, but he couldn't enjoy it when he thought of that incident from his childhood and the oath he'd taken before Ma, and her sermons. Chetan had never enjoyed eating meat the way Ranvir and Nishtar did: their eyes lit up at the mere mention of pork, and when the dhaba proprietor lifted the brass lid from the pot to serve the meat on to their plates, Ranvir's mouth began to water. Whenever Chetan tasted meat, he felt as though he were committing a sin.

*

The plates had been set before them. Suddenly, Ranvir said, 'Jija ji, please, just take a little piece, why don't you?'

'No, no,' said Chetan, 'I don't like pork.'

'Have you ever tasted it?'

'No, just hearing the word makes me think of that filthy animal,' he said with irritation (he wouldn't tell those fools where his mind went at the mere thought of pork). 'It snuffles its snout around in filth. It rolls about in the drains. How can you people eat it?'

Nishtar laughed. 'Sometimes you say really stupid things, yaar. There's manure lying in the fields and wheat gets planted in that. But do we quit eating wheat because it makes us think of manure?'

And he picked up a piece of meat from his plate and placed it on Chetan's.

'There aren't any bones in this?'

'Why don't you taste it and see!'

The piece of pork reminded Chetan of a small slice of watermelon. There was a thick rind along the flesh, which looked like watermelon pulp. 'Just taste it and see,' he thought. He even picked it up. Just then he wondered—would he also just taste a piece of beef like this? Hamid had tried to get him to so many times. He put the piece back on his plate.

The thing was, though that argument had prepared him to eat meat, his upbringing was so strongly rooted in his subconscious that even when eating other kinds of meat, he thought about the problems with eating cow and pig meat, and although that argument gave the lie to his beliefs, he ended up losing the thread. He wouldn't eat meat at all, he'd decide. But then, people thought so many things were fine: lying, counting earnings from bribery as part of one's income, beating children mercilessly, earning money through questionable means by sucking the blood of the poor, killing women bit by bit, destroying generations with diseases such as syphilis—yet if someone were to find out that a certain person had tasted beef, he might be forced out of the neighbourhood, and thus Chetan would be compelled to think through several questions logically.

Maybe chickens were not that important, but thousands of poor people who couldn't raise cows or buffaloes raised goats; they only drank goat milk; for them, the goat is the mother and daughter, the way a cow is for Hindus. On the other hand, ever since he'd heard that Mahatma Gandhi only drank goat milk and when he'd gone to England to participate in the Round Table Conference, he'd taken a goat with him, he kept thinking about the difference between goats and cows. If it was a major sin to slaughter a cow or a calf, why wasn't it a sin to slaughter a goat, he wondered. He'd once asked his Sanskrit teacher this very question. His teacher had told him that we consider the cow to be like a mother because she gives us milk and ghee; her calves become bullocks, and not only do they carry loads but they also pull ploughs, and in an agricultural country like India, those beasts that pull a plough for us and plant seeds and prepare the crops for us are like our sons. And then, the cow is the sort of animal whose dung comes in handy not only for manure but also for dung cakes, and moreover it's pure, and Hindus smear the kitchen with it, and according to Ayurveda, cow urine is beneficial as a cure to scores of afflictions.

But when he got to college, several questions on this topic began to trouble Chetan. He'd often had no response in debates with Hamid and he could think of no answers himself.

First of all, cows give us milk, but then water buffaloes also give us milk, which is more nourishing than cow milk. If cow milk has some additional merits, then buffalo milk has other additional merits. Bullocks carry loads and pull ploughs, but so do buffaloes. So then, why are buffaloes not worshipped the way cows and bullocks are?

Then, as far as agriculture goes, when, thanks to scientific progress, tractors had begun to plough fields and trucks to carry loads, would there still be a special need for bullocks, and wouldn't the increased population of bullocks become a burden on the country? As for cow dung and urine being useful for medicines, well, science had made unimaginable progress, thus greatly diminishing the importance of the cow . . . And wasn't it better to send healthy livestock to dairies, have the animals properly tended, and get better quality milk and ghee made there, than keep sick and feeble cows, and bullocks caged up and . . . Was that true cow worship or was it what was happening nowadays, with cows growing old or hungry in cages, or wandering about freely in bazaars, carrying off the merchants' wares and getting hit with sticks in retaliation, and often walking about with terrible wounds . . . while day by day pure ghee was disappearing from the bazaar . . .

Chetan had read somewhere that in ancient India there used to be cow sacrifices—at the court of King Janaka of Videha, so much beef was cooked in the kitchen for the Brahmin guests that the drains ran with rivers of grease. Much later, during the time of Alexander's attack, the defeated kings had gifted him finely bred, fattened bullocks. Who knows when cow slaughter was decreed forbidden. There must have been some horrible famine. Thousands of beasts must have been offered up to the famine. At that time, buffaloes must not have been reared as domestic animals. Then, because of the necessity of the bullocks for agriculture, it was decreed that it was forbidden to slaughter them. This must have been publicized by the priests and become a part of religion . . . and over time, like scores of other social and religious customs, this had become one as well.

'Even if man is extremely vegetarian,' Chetan would think, 'why would he imprison a goat or a cow or a pig?' If no meat is harmful, then he couldn't understand why it was only to be given up because it was forbidden centuries ago under who knows what circumstances or for which reasons. Both the Muslim and Hindu approaches seemed wrong, but as the *sattvic* principles instilled in him by his mother in opposition to his father's *tamasic* tendencies since infancy were strong, whenever he began to think about this problem, he'd stop eating meat.

*

The piece of pork was still lying on his plate, and he was eating the dal and paneer with roti, lost in thought, when suddenly he started on hearing the people around him chuckling and laughing. Across the intersection, Debu had smacked a youth wearing a hat from behind; he'd knocked off his hat, and the youth had grabbed his collar and was about to haul off and punch him.

'That ass was bragging,' said Billa, pausing his laughter for a moment to explain to Jagna. 'There's no way he can pull this off. Just you watch; there's going to be a fight. He can't get out of it without a fight.'

And truly, as everyone watched, the youth slugged Debu in the temple with his drawn fist. Debu grabbed the other guy by the waist and tripped him. Just then, by ill fate, a tonga coming from the direction of the Mayo Hospital drove right over the youth's hat as it swerved to avoid them. The youth fell over, then got up, but instead of picking up his hat, he got tangled up with Debu and the two of them started wrestling in the middle of the street.

Jagna and Billa ran over. Quite a crowd had gathered. Somehow they sorted the matter out. Debu's kameez was torn. They managed to calm him down with great difficulty and brought him back.

What had happened was that the fight over the charpoys in front of the hotel a little while earlier had been gnawing at Debu.

213

If it had been a regular fight, Debu would have sent that youth on his way, and everyone would have ended up with a busted head, but since Debu had grabbed the guy's legs and knocked him over, and Billa had stopped others from coming to his aid, the fight had turned into a wrestling match, and perhaps the other guy knew wrestling moves better than Debu. Debu had felt jealous of the authoritative tone in which Billa had told the dhaba proprietor to take special care of Chetan and his friends after driving the youth away. If he had been the one to chase off the youth, he could have used that tone. He'd have been the one to direct the dhaba proprietor to serve his friends good food. And this was what had been eating at him. When he came back under the tree after dusting off his clothes and washing his hands, he told Jagna, to ease his shame, that he was going to knock the turban off someone walking by, and when he got caught, he'd apologize innocently; all this was second nature to him, he said. Perhaps Jagna hadn't been in the mood at that moment, or his attention was wrapped up in his court case, or his empty pockets were making him absent-minded—for whatever reason, he hadn't paid attention to what Debu had been saying. Just then a young man wearing a hat had walked by. And Debu, in order to mitigate his previous embarrassment and re-establish his superiority, had boasted that he himself would knock off the man's hat.

'You're going to get beaten, *sala*,' Billa had said.

'I can do it!'

'Or you'll beat him.'

'Not true!' Debu had said. 'I'll knock off his hat and he won't say a peep. If Jagna can do it, why can't I?'

Who knows what was going through Billa's head! Maybe he was in the mood to watch a spectacle. 'You can't pull it off, you ass,' he said. 'Only Jagna can do that kind of thing.'

And this had been the result of that taunt, which was what Billa had hoped for. 'What can't I do?' Debu had said, throwing back his head. 'There's nothing to it—knock off a hat, if he says something, apologize.'

'Then go and knock off his hat and show us.'

The youth was continuing on his way. Debu leapt after him.

'The sala's going to get beaten. Not everyone can do everything,' said Billa.

But Debu didn't hear him. He'd rushed off and, just as Jagna always did, landed a blow on the youth's hat from the rear.

*

When the three of them came back, they learned that when the youth's hat had gone flying off, he'd grabbed Debu by the collar, and Debu had apologized for his mistake—he'd thought it was his friend Hari! But at this, the youth had hauled off and socked Debu, and then Debu had got riled himself.

'Beta, that's why I said,' said Billa, smacking him on the neck, 'that you weren't up to the task. Jagna is the one who can do it better.' Then he turned and said to Jagna, 'Right, beta? Why don't you show us your stuff?'

In the meantime, Hunar Sahib and the others had finished eating. Hunar Sahib was under the impression that perhaps Debu and his friends were going to pay. When Billa had told the proprietor that they were their guests, what need was there to pay? And so they got up to go and watch Jagna's trick without having paid for anything. But Chetan took them aside and told them that these folks were all completely broke. They never have any money, and even if the dhaba people refuse, you should still pay. These guys can accomplish any number of other tasks, but not this one.

Hunar Sahib had thought perhaps the hotel owners would refuse to take money and say something like, 'No, no, how can this be, this bill is for them,' and then he'd keep his hands on that five-rupee note. But no such thing occurred. He asked for the bill. The proprietor told him the amount. He held out the note, and the man took it, then counted out the change and placed it in his hand.

At this point, Chetan thought he'd part ways with Hunar Sahib, when at that very moment, Jagna suddenly interjected, 'Okay, look at him, that gentleman walking by. I'm going to knock off his hat. You all won't laugh at all. Walk behind me, but keep your distance. If there's a dispute, he'll just yell at me.'

He was now totally in the mood, either because of Debu's lack of success or Billa's praise. He may only have been middle-school-pass, but he was wearing a really nice boski kameez and cotton trousers. He flew off with feet of wings.

They all followed him at a bit of a distance, and even Chetan, abandoning the idea of going home, went along with them.

19

Jagna continued to put his skills on display all the way to Company Bagh Gate, and his companions (Hunar Sahib's party had joined them) continued to follow along at a slight distance, chuckling so much it made their stomachs ache. Chetan considered it goondaism through and through, but Jagna pulled it off so cleverly that he was enjoying it despite himself. He kept bursting out laughing, at times completely forgetting his own sorrows. His sad thoughts had burrowed deep down somewhere, and the exuberance of the moment had taken their place. He too, with his comrades, had begun to enjoy the whole thing, and when Jagna, despite his best efforts, had ended up in a dispute with a round, bald gentleman near Company Bagh, he too descended to their level—unconsciously, unwillingly, even knowing Jagna's excesses all too well—and intervened on their behalf.

*

Although the youth Jagna had gone after from the Khalsa Hotel had walked quite a distance ahead, Jagna had caught up with him quickly, nearly flying along, and called out, 'Hey, Sohne, you bastard! I kept calling after you, are you sleepwalking?' And smacked him from behind.

The youth's sola topi flew off, and he turned to glare at Jagna, enraged. Jagna had evinced surprise mingled with regret. 'Oh, I am sorry!' he had said in English. 'I thought you were Sohan Lal. You look exactly alike from the back!' . . . And without giving him the chance to say anything, he leapt forward and picked up his hat. He removed a silk handkerchief from his pocket, dusted off the hat, then placed it back on his head with both hands. Patting him lightly on the back, he said, 'Please forgive me, please don't be offended,' and held out his hand.

'No matter, no matter!' the youth had said, shaking his hand.

'My name is Jagannath, everyone knows me at Chaurasti Atari. If ever you need anything, do think of me,' Jagna had said and, after shaking his hand, he had come back to the group.

Repeating that last sentence, Billa had said, 'If ever he needs a neck broken, he'll be sure to think of you.'

And he burst out laughing. That last sentence of Jagna's had cracked his friends up, and Hunar Sahib started coughing he was laughing so hard.

They all enjoyed this incident for a few moments, commenting on its various aspects; they had especially enjoyed the look of angry surprise that had appeared on the youth's face and the meek regret that had clouded Jagna's features. Hunar Sahib recited a couplet as a commentary on this meekness:

Who wouldn't die at this simplicity, Oh God
He fights yet doesn't ever hold a sword

Then they went in search of another victim. Just then, an elderly man appeared, walking towards the District Court—he walked with his head down, and wore a low-wrapped turban on his head, a long coat and pyjamas that ended just above the ankle. Billa motioned towards him. Jagna leapt forward. His friends also quickened their pace. 'Stay a bit farther away,' Jagna indicated and stepped forward.

The elderly man was walking along, head down, lost in thought, when Jagna softly smacked him on the shoulder and said very loudly, right into his ear (as if speaking to a deaf person) 'Chacha Bihari Laaaaal!' And the next moment he jumped in front of him and, folding his hands together, he cried out, 'Namasteeee!'

But the 'namaste' hadn't completely emerged from his mouth when he feigned realization of his mistake. 'Excuse me, excuse me,' he apologized, as he bent down to the man's feet and touched his knees, then patted his shoulders, and explained to him that he'd been mistaken; he'd thought he was his own deaf uncle Bihari Lal. After this, he begged his leave, pressing his hands together.

After the elderly man had walked some distance away, Jagna imitated his astonished expression such that everyone felt ill from laughing so hard.

*

It was fairly hot and even more humid. Everyone was uncomfortably sweaty, but in all this merriment they didn't even notice. They walked along cheerful as can be. There were some new two-storey houses on the street that went towards the General Post Office, after the District Court compound, across from Ray Bahadur Bhagat Ram's mansion. This row of two-storey homes went all the way to Company Bagh. Most of these housed new lawyers' offices. In the middle of the row, there were still a few empty lots as the row of houses was not yet complete. Right there, in one of the empty lots, a man was squatting to urinate by the side of the road. Jagna rushed over and, leaning down near his shoulder, he asked, 'Basshaho, what are you looking for?' . . . and the next moment, on seeing the man's shock, he cried out, 'Oh, you're peeing! Go ahead then! Pee! Pee!' He patted him lightly on the shoulder and came back, and Debu and Billa's eyes streamed with tears they were laughing so hard.

Chetan felt quite angry at his impropriety. What was this rudeness? But on the other hand, he couldn't think of a better way to eradicate the habit people had of squatting to urinate in the middle of the street and bazaar in Jalandhar. Although Jagna had only behaved thus for the sake of mischief, Chetan thought that whenever anyone squatted in the middle of the bazaar they should be interrupted in just this manner. If that were to happen to them once or twice, they would abandon the habit once and for all . . . and Chetan imagined people squatting to urinate into the drains of the bazaars and along the side of the road, and other people harassing them, and he involuntarily let out a chuckle. 'But how are ordinary people at fault?' The thought occurred to him the next moment: 'There's not a single urinal on this entire street. What's a man to do if he left his home hours before . . .'

'Oh yes, sir, that Ray Bahadur is amazing. He's the biggest criminal lawyer in all of India,' Billa was saying.

They were walking by Ray Bahadur Bhagat Ram's mansion. His mansion stretched along the right side of the street that went towards the General Post Office up to Company Bagh. He was a famous criminal-court barrister and his renown had spread throughout the country. Countless rumours had spread among the common people with regard to his erudition and cunning— some true, some false. Chetan, wrapped up in his own thoughts, hadn't heard how they'd got to that topic, but Billa was telling a story with great gusto—how Ray Bahadur had conducted a cross-examination and on creating the possibility for reasonable doubt on a minor point, he'd clearly proven innocent his client who'd been charge-sheeted under Section 302 and handed over to the sessions court. 'The murder occurred at night,' Billa was telling them, and the testimony of the comrade of the victim was the most critical. When he was conducting the cross-examination, Ray Bahadur asked him, 'So when the accused attacked with his accomplices, it was quite a while before sunrise, it was still completely dark?'

'"Yes, sir," said the witness.'

And Billa imitated Ray Bahadur's questions and the witness's responses exactly:

Ray Bahadur: You got hit with a lathi first?

Witness: Yes, sir!

Ray Bahadur: Where?

Witness: On the head!

Ray Bahadur: You got hit pretty hard?

Witness: Yes, sir!

Ray Bahadur: You fell and lost consciousness?

Witness: Yes, sir!

'"That's it, your honour, I have nothing more to say," Ray Bahadur said, and ended the cross-examination.' And Billa continued, 'But during the arguments, he tore the witness's testimony to shreds. If it was night, and if it was dark, and the witness got hit by the lathi, and the accused's lathi fell on him and he lost consciousness, then how did he know in that darkness that the victim had been killed by the lathi of the accused? And he raised doubts in the judge's mind, which benefited the accused!'

'He's amazing, Ray Bahadur!' said Debu, glancing over at Chetan with his squint-eye, but Hunar Sahib felt as though this was being said to him, so he said immediately: 'Yes, sir, Ray Bahadur's a genius, and geniuses are not born every day.'

Hunar Sahib then turned the conversation towards poetry and remarked, 'As Allama Iqbal has said . . .'

'For thousands of years the nargis flower
Has wept for being ignored
A true connoisseur is not born
In the garden every day'

Reciting the *sher*, swinging back and forth and praising the sher himself, he said, 'How truly Iqbal spoke—A true connoisseur is not born/in the garden every day—but Mir took up this notion with such ease . . .'

Do not consider me ordinary, understand, the heavens revolve
    for years
Then man emerges from the curtains of dust

'Do not consider me ordinary'—he repeated the entire couplet again, emphasizing each word, and then explained the meaning of both couplets to all of them. Then he began to explain their delicacy and refinement and his speech flowed freely.

Chetan could not figure out how Ray Bahadur's cleverness in criminal matters might be connected to these couplets, but Hunar Sahib knew full well that his audience were fools, and Chetan knew full well how easily he was able to impress fools. They'd reached the second gate of Ray Bahadur's mansion as they strolled along. Years ago, Chetan had seen Barrister Bhagat Ram standing at this very gate—he was a stout, stocky man, wearing a fancy, expensive suit (which included a waistcoat, according to the fashions of the times); he was bald, with puffy cheeks and bulging eyes. Chetan had always thought crafty men needed to be thin, but this man looked to him like the general manager of some large English firm. He had an oddly dreamy look in his eyes, and gazed at his companion as though he were gazing somewhere very far off as he spoke with him. Bhagat Ram might have been a great barrister, but Chetan couldn't quite understand whether he was that 'connoisseur' who could recognize the beauty of the nargis or that 'human' around whom the moon and stars wandered for years. These couplets could easily be applied to the Buddha, Jesus, or Mahatma Gandhi, who on seeing 'blindness' towards the poor recognized their light . . . Chetan was analysing those couplets to himself, and Hunar Sahib was giving a speech on the simplicity and depth of Mir's couplet in comparison to Iqbal's, when Billa grew bored and said, 'If we smack that bald guy on the skull, then we'll see.'

Hunar Sahib's speech stopped abruptly. Ranvir and Nishtar turned to look. Everyone focused their attention on a plump man, about thirty or so, wearing a fancy kameez and trousers, who was walking down the near side of Company Bagh.

'Watch, I'm going to do it right now,' said Jagna and he walked over.

The man's bald head shone in the strong sunlight. Jagna reached him quickly, and crying out 'Hey, Pumpkin!' he smacked the man's bald head affectionately as though he were hugging him, but the very next moment, he jumped away from him as though he'd been struck by lightning.

Perhaps nothing would have happened after that, and Jagna would have begged forgiveness as before, told him his address and returned, but Nishtar and Ranvir, who had walked up fairly close behind him, couldn't stop laughing, and the man grew suspicious that they'd intentionally played a prank on him. Jagna begged forgiveness again and again, but the man grabbed his arm. He didn't pull it and smack him since he was a gentleman, but he started yelling that he'd have him arrested.

By then, they'd all arrived on the scene.

*

223

Jagna was sticking his head out and saying that he wasn't himself bald, but if the gentleman would get satisfaction from slapping his skull, he should smack him not just once but four times if it made him happy.

On the face of the plump gentleman there was great anger, disbelief and indecision, which made him look hilarious—and Jagna looked so meek; he'd stuck his head forward in such a way that even Chetan had to smile.

'I've told this sala twenty times that he shouldn't smack friends from behind without looking first. He's done that to me many times as well. Please—take off your shoes and hit him four times so he'll learn for good,' said Billa.

But the shine in Billa's eyes and the smile on his face as he said this made the man even more apoplectic. It seemed to him that everyone was making fun of him.

'*I shall not take law in my own hands.*' In his anger, he had started to speak English poorly. 'I'm taking him immediately to the police station. I don't care if the policeman wishes to hit him four times with shoes or forty.'

Seeing that things were getting worse, Chetan came forward. He begged the man in English to drop it please. 'He made a mistake,' he explained. 'He's saying he's sorry, so please let it drop. What will you accomplish by taking him to the police? They're not going to hang him. If you do press charges, you'll have to drag it through the courts for months under the authority of code 323.'

'Who are you to interfere in this affair?' asked the man, also in English, as he waved his hand in the air with contempt.

Then Hunar Sahib came forward, wiping the sweat from his face with the edge of his dhoti, and introduced Chetan, explaining that he was a famous short-story writer, poet and journalist, and an editor at the newspaper *Bande Mataram*, run by the late Lala

Lajpat Rai. And Chetan introduced Hunar Sahib in English, and the offended gentleman was bewildered. Just then, a large amount of dust came blowing from the direction of the Lower Court and filled their eyes. In all this mischief and fighting, no one had been paying attention to the sky. A powerful cloud had arisen on the western horizon, and was now bearing down upon them.

Chetan glanced up for a moment and saw that a dust storm, black as the demoness Taraka, had covered the sky with its dark clouds just overhead. Before it flew a vanguard squadron of yellow and brown birds, followed by a dense black army of thousands more (as though they would be the ones to stop it), forming an arc in the sky and making a huge racket as they flew about.

Just then, two large drops fell on the moon-like pate of the aggrieved gentleman and he let go of Jagna's hand, enraged. After making them all feel ashamed for their poor behaviour, in English, he rushed off, and to escape the dust storm, all of them ran over to stand in the veranda of the building to the left which lay across from Ray Bahadur Bhagat Ram's mansion and had a sign on a pillar that read 'Hari Krishna, Advocate.'

20

'I have a buddy, Harjinder Singh "Tashna".[8] The two of us were together in the hostel at college. We recited couplets together and we made mischief together too.'

Outside, the rain poured down, and inside the veranda of Hari Krishna, Advocate, Hunar Sahib, seemingly unaware of the storm that raged outside, spoke on in a steady stream.

He had started off by discussing Jagna's mischief and the agitation of the plump, bald pumpkin-head, whose moon-like pate Jagna had so callously smacked, then quickly turned the topic to himself, and since he'd learned that his new audience had no comprehension of the finer points of poetry, and since he wasn't accustomed to hearing others speak, he'd begun to tell a tale from his college days.

'One day, we were coming back from seeing a friend off at the station, when we saw a holy man near the inn, on the city side—he had a beard so long it touched his belly, long matted locks down to his ankles (perhaps he'd added fake locks in with the real ones) and nothing on his naked body but a sandalwood tika! Who knows what got into Harjinder's head, but he said, "Hunar, why don't we perform some service for this Sadhu Maharaj!" And I said, "Yes, let's do it at once!" And I went up to

---

[8] *Tashna*=Thirsting one (the poet's nom de plume).

227

him, not worrying about getting my nice suit all dirty (I used to wear a suit in those days), and prostrated myself at his feet in the middle of the bazaar.

'The Sadhu ji's face lit up upon beholding such devotees. He lifted me up and asked, "Child, what troubles you?"

'"Maharaj," I said, "what troubles do students ordinarily have? I'm worried about an exam. I seek your blessings so that I can pass with good scores."

'The holy man patted me on the back and blessed me.

'Then Harjinder came forward and said, "Bhagwan, I have one request."

'The holy man looked up and smiled.

'"Maharaj," Harjinder said, "please accept a meal from me. It's time to eat after all. There's a pure Hindu hotel here with excellent food. Please come and eat a meal."

'"Oh, my, son," said the holy man. "I hardly eat at such places as hotels. If you wish to show your respects, then just give me a little something, and I will eat in your name."

'"No, Maharaj," Harjinder bowed low. "We feel such great reverence for you that we wish to serve you a meal at a hotel. If you accept this devotion from us, we will feel certain that you have blessed us."

'Long story short, we took the Sadhu Maharaj to a pure Hindu hotel. There were many fancy items on the menu, and we ordered one of each for the holy man and served it to him. Harjinder got a fan from somewhere and began to wave it like a fly-whisk. When platters filled with all sorts of delicacies arrived, the holy man's eyes began to shine and his mouth began to water. Then I asked, "You don't have rabri where you're from? The hotel owner said we could get some from the sweet-seller at the inn. I'll order some if you wish." I told Harjinder to take a bowl and run and get a whole paav of rabri.

'Harjinder picked up the bowl and ran off. How long could the Maharaj keep himself from tasting the delicious food while waiting for the rabri? He began to eat intently and I began to fan him. When Harjinder wasn't back in ten minutes, I said to myself, "Perhaps he couldn't find the shop." I put down the fan, picked up another bowl and went outside. Harjinder was standing right near the inn. We took an empty *ikka* to Adda Hoshiarpur and from there went straight to our hostel.'

'What happened to the holy man?' asked Ranvir suddenly; he had been drinking in every word that came from the lotus face of Hunar Sahib.

'That only God knows, or the hotel owner, or the holy man himself!' laughed Hunar Sahib. 'I didn't get up until he had started eating and rubbing his belly and patting his beard. I wrote a poem about that incident in those days too,' said Hunar Sahib. 'I don't remember the whole thing but I do remember the final couplet . . .'

After 'Hunar' left the hotel who knows what befell
the belly or beard or head of the matted-locked one

And he guffawed as Nishtar and Ranvir cried out, 'Wah, wah! Wow!'

'Asses!' Chetan muttered to himself, in reference to Ranvir and Nishtar. 'They probably think Hunar Sahib played that prank himself. He's so skinny, fair and fine—he was surely being harassed himself by mischievous boys. He must have learned how to make himself the author of pranks just the way he had learned to recite other people's couplets as his own, embellishing a little here and there.'

Hunar Sahib had begun telling tales of pranks he'd played in Lahore, but Chetan wasn't paying attention. He leaned against the pillar of the veranda, lost in thought, and began to watch the magnificent raging of the storm. The wind was strong; streams of water fell like slanted wires with the shine and sharpness of swords. The rain looked like it was attempting to fall straight on to the steps of the veranda, but was landing instead on the other side of the street. The area from the veranda to the street was totally dry. Chetan gazed steadily at the bent-over mango tree at the Company Bagh corner of Ray Bahadur Bhagat Ram's mansion. The two-storey house (where Chetan stood on the veranda) was blocking the wind from the trees in front of it, but the wind was hitting the corner where the mango tree stood with all its force as it whipped along Kutchery Road, and the lower court and the open yard of the Normal School alongside it—the gusts wailed as they plucked and pulled at the electrical and telephone wires; the storm had attacked the mango tree with all its might. The wind blew ceaselessly, giving the downward-bending branches no chance to return to their former state. Chetan was riveted by the sight. He had no idea if he'd been staring at the tree unblinkingly for ten minutes, or twenty, or half an hour. Then it looked as though the whole trunk was starting to bend over along with the branches and, as he watched, the mango tree came crashing down with a terrifying crack. It broke the gate and knocked over the electrical pole on to the cantonment road.

It was as though the storm had arrived expressly in order to knock down that tree. A little while later, its force dissipated. Tree branches began to swing, the wires of water changed to drops and then quieted down. Although there were still light clouds in the sky, the dense army of black clouds had passed by. Now there were soft puffs of breeze. They all stepped down from the veranda; Billa, Debu and Jagna shook hands with everyone and went off towards the Lower Court, and Hunar Sahib turned towards Company Bagh, as he had to pay his respects to 'The Gandhi of the Doab' at the office of the Widows' Aid Society. At first, Chetan had thought he'd part with them there, but the rain had washed the day clean. A lovely cool breeze blew, still carrying with it invisible drops of rain, and after Company Bagh, up to the turn towards Mandi, there were nothing but fields on both sides of the street that went above Ramjidas Mills. The thought of taking a stroll on that open street in such cool, rainy weather made even the company of Hunar Sahib and Ranvir tolerable, and when Hunar Sahib said, 'Come on, let's introduce you to Banshiram ji and Yogi ji!' Chetan did not refuse.

21

The Company Bagh street was quite wet. Water had pooled along both sides, so the four of them walked down the middle. Every time there was a puff of breeze, a shower fell from the trees. Chetan broke off a couple of leaves, rubbed them in his hands and inhaled them. The scent of eucalyptus infused his consciousness. Unripe fruit littered the whole street on the right side under the fallen mango tree, and little boys gathered it briskly. The street was empty along Company Bagh, all the way to the fork towards Mandi. The fields on both sides were full of water and a dense blue cloud had gathered in the sky to the right. Perhaps it was still raining hard over there. But the sky to the left was clear now. Hunar Sahib had become elated in that damp, expansive, freshly washed weather. He had a lovely voice and could do an excellent imitation of the poet Hafiz Jalandhari.

'Okay, I'm going to sing you a famous song by Hafiz,' he announced by way of introduction, and began to sing:

The morning has awoken in the east
    The darkness of the world is far
        But my heart is dark
The clouds have arisen in the west
    The drunken breezes roam about
Awake, oh, tavern-goers

233

Oh, drinkers and bartenders
　　　Mix the poison with the nectar
　　　My heart belongs to another
　The nightingale calls in a garden
　　　The nargis opens her eyes
　　　　The dew scatters its pearls
　The black cuckoo warbles in the mango
　　　A sob rises in my chest
　What if I go mad?
　　　The meek cries of beasts
　　　　Prick my every pore
　　　　My heart belongs to another

My heart belongs to another—Chetan sighed deeply—if his heart were his own, would he have been wandering about like an untethered camel since morning? He'd come home from Shimla after so many days, and run off to Basti as soon as he arrived; after returning from Basti the night before, he'd gone out wandering when morning came . . . His mother must be dying to tell him all sorts of things . . . Chanda must be waiting patiently for him to say just a few sweet words to her . . . she may have been quiet, but how many desires lay hidden in this silence? What was this fire that raged in his heart? Nothing attracted him. Nothing diverted him. If you thought about it, it was all absolute madness, complete idiocy. What had been his connection to Neela when he'd married Chanda? What right had he to desire her companionship? This was not the West, where, if he didn't get along with one girlfriend, he could just take up with another; if he destroyed one world he could simply start a new one . . . and now Neela was married too. She'd even departed, bound in the chains of marriage. How could desire exist without hope? Why didn't he think from the point of view of a married person? But he just couldn't come up with any answers; everything kept flooding into his mind, again and again. If he stayed at home and didn't come out and try to get rid of his sadness, he'd go crazy. But could he really get rid of it? It grew denser and coalesced deep inside him . . . What had happened to him . . . what had happened to him?

And Hunar Sahib was singing:

Who will tell me what affection is?
    What is the heart's truth?
        What is the pleasure in dying and leaving no trace
The heartless can hardly see it, only those who feel it know
Listen oh sage, the world is ephemeral, oh love, oh youth
        The *khas* grasses are aflame

'*The khas grasses are aflame*,' thought Chetan—not straw, grasses— they were smouldering, not crackling clearly, and they were giving off smoke.

*

Then Hunar Sahib began a new song:

Jingle jingle, the black clouds rain, drip drip the eyes do weep
In the seasons of Savan and Bhadon there are such days
    When the noisy droplets scatter songs
    When we strain our eyes hoping
    Waiting for the ones we love
In the shadow of our damp eyelids sleep broken dreams
In the seasons of Savan and Bhadon there are such days

And Chetan's heart filled with boundless sorrow at the gathering clouds, the damp weather, the rippling water-filled fields, the rain-drenched street that shone like molten silver, the intoxicating puffs of breeze. He wished he could just dissolve completely into this atmosphere, become a part of the breeze, puff along causing sorrow to fall like drops of rain, join in with the dolefully meandering clouds, and wander about from place to place.

Hunar Sahib was singing a poignant tune and Chetan began to listen, concentrating completely on the song:

> When the small black clouds do gather round
> in the rainy season I feel shaken without my darling
> They string the pearls of tears in eyelids again and again
> In the seasons of Savan and Bhadon there are such days
> The queen of rain does dance when
> she comes to the gardens full of youth
> We sow the seeds of sorrow in the fields of our hearts
> In the seasons of Savan and Bhadon there are such days

Just as Chetan had snapped and run from home in order to distance himself from the deep sadness he felt inside, he now felt frightened by these sorrowful songs. He interrupted abruptly, 'Why are you singing such sad songs, Hunar Sahib? It's such lovely weather, sing us a fun love song.'

And swaying along, intoxicated by the weather, Hunar Sahib replied, 'Here, listen to this:'

> Sing me a song, beloved, in the heavy rains of Savan
> Let love come to youth, let there be delight in words of love
> Sing me a song, beloved
> A song from whose sweet verses a Ganga of love bursts forth
> In the earth of the desolate heart, a river of light will burst forth
> Sing me a song, beloved

At the high note of the verse, Hunar Sahib stretched out the words 'Sing me a song' in such a tender tone that it lingered in the heart. Instead of listening to the song, Chetan kept waiting to hear the tone of the refrain. When that song was finished, Hunar Sahib began another. Chetan didn't enjoy it as much—there was depth in Hafiz's songs, sorrow, a delicate, sweet pain—but these other songs were quite light and shallow. He wanted to say to Nishtar, 'Why don't you sing some verses from *Heer Ranjha*?' but so long as Hunar Sahib didn't shut up, interrupting him would mean insulting him. And Hunar Sahib kept on singing—songs, ghazals, poems—but Chetan didn't hear a thing; on and on that same song by Hafiz—'My heart belongs to another'—echoed in his ears. He felt irritable and kept trying to get his mind off that song and on to something else—he kept thinking, there's so much to do in this life—one must rise above this aimless existence. He wasn't Majnu, nor Ranjha, nor Farhad. In Class Six, he'd read this couplet by Hali:

Oh love, you have often consumed entire countries and
    departed
That home where you first lifted your head, you ruined and
    departed

At which he'd decided to himself that he'd never get caught up in the whole love thing. But had he even known what love was then? And what use was love that had no resolution? And how could one love, if one considered the costs? So how could he have compared himself to Majnu now? What a fool he was.

And he walked along, tangled up in his thoughts, fighting with himself, making fun of his own idiocy, until they were just outside of Mandi, and he saw a large signboard that read, 'Widows' Aid Society' posted upon a new, half-built house that stood alone.

22

In the pages of *Widows' Aid*, the title 'Mahatma' was always printed before the name of Lala Banshiram. In a nondescript weekly in Lahore, one of his followers had even written an article titled 'The Gandhi of the Doab and His Domain'. Chetan had no idea who had given him the title of 'Mahatma'. He was also not so sure if Lala Banshiram possessed the intellect of Mahatma Gandhi, but it was true that Lala Banshiram had stinted nothing in becoming Mahatma Gandhi with respect to his appearance and demeanour—he was skinny like the Mahatma, though a bit taller, and when he walked along, with a hand on the shoulder of his secretary, Sister Saraswati Devi, he always bent over slightly; and like Mahatma Gandhi, he wore his dhoti a little above the knees. His two front teeth were broken and, in imitation of the Mahatma, he considered the wearing of false teeth to be immoral. He spoke very slowly. Like Mahatma Gandhi, he spoke Hindi with a Gujarati accent, though he was Punjabi, and he also placed a finger to his lips when he spoke, or sometimes when he was thinking, just like Gandhi ji. One year, during the Congress session, Lala Banshiram had found Sarojini Naidu standing outside Mahatma Gandhi's tent, which had made it particularly difficult for him to meet him. When Gandhi ji had entered the pavilion in order to take part in the Congress executive session, he had supported himself as he walked by placing one hand on

Sarojini Naidu's shoulder. Where was Lala Banshiram supposed to find a world-famous lady poet like Sarojini Naidu to be his bodyguard? The child-widow sister of a distant relation, Saraswati Devi, worked at his institution. With the help of the Mahatma ji, she'd even studied as far as the Prabhakar Exam. After returning from the Congress session, he had engaged Saraswati Devi as his secretary and bodyguard. Whenever people came to meet Mahatma Banshiram, they first met Sister Saraswati Devi. And whenever Mahatma Banshiram came out, she always walked with him, and one of Mahatma Banshiram's hands always rested upon her shoulder. She was also plump, like Sarojini Naidu. Otherwise, there was as much difference between her and Sarojini Naidu as there was between Mahatma Banshiram and Mahatma Gandhi.

Chetan had seen her in two or three sessions of the City Congress Committee in which there was quite a bit of heated discussion and debate. Mahatma Banshiram didn't say much, but when he did speak, he placed a finger on his lips, which was how Chetan learned how much he was actually worth. The patriot Lala Govindaram had total authority over the City Congress Committee. He didn't speak much, he worked hard, he organized strikes, participated in sit-ins and he went to jail. Mahatma Banshiram didn't want to do all this, because he'd taken on other constructive work according to the dictates of Mahatma Gandhi, but he also wanted to be the chair of the local Congress committee. Unfortunately, there was a greater need at that time for those doing destructive work rather than constructive work, so Mahatma ji had taken his institution to an inexpensive but spacious house outside the city, and when the movement was dormant, he took part in the Congress sessions as well. Before the Gandhi-Irwin Pact, when all the leaders of the city had gone to jail and people were annoyed that he remained outside, he too left his constructive work and went to jail for three months.

Whenever Chetan observed him, his persona seemed a crude parody of Mahatma Gandhi.

Actually, Chetan had not seen much of the world at that time. If he had, then he wouldn't have been so surprised, because in those days, there were people in every region of India imitating Mahatma Gandhi. Those people had no chance of measuring up to the intellect of Mahatma Gandhi, nor did they possess his compassion, his sympathy, his perception of popular thought, nor his understanding of the nation and society. All their effort went into shaving their heads, going about half-naked, keeping vows of silence, using natural remedies, eating boiled water-lily root, or potatoes, or yogurt, spinning, or making a display of their broken front teeth, and so on.

Since at that time even constructive Congress work was suspicious to the government, there weren't that many widows at Mahatma Banshiram's ashram. There were only two other women besides Saraswati Devi. Most of Mahatma Banshiram's work was publicity-related. This was why he had started his weekly and he ran it in such a way that the government would not shut it down, even as it propagated the Congress's constructive goals.

The house where Mahatma Banshiram's office was located was among those that had been built on cheap land outside the city for the lower middle classes, but the capital had run out before they could be completed. They climbed the stairs, from which the paint had peeled long ago, and Hunar Sahib told them to sit in the office of the weekly, to the left, while he himself went up to the roof on the right side, where Mahatma ji's ashram was located in the rooms on the lower storey, and where the constructive work took place: there was a school, a loom and spinning wheels where the widows were taught how to live independently.

The room Chetan entered with Ranvir and Nishtar was fairly large. There was a table and chair to one side. The file for this month's edition of the weekly lay on the table. Unsold copies of the weekly were piled along all three walls of the room. On the other side of the room, there was a bench. A thin layer of dust covered everything.

Chetan went and sat on the bench. Just then, Hunar Sahib returned from the roof, looking disappointed, but he managed with some effort to bring a smile to his face when he saw Chetan. He told them that Mahatma ji was observing a vow of silence and spinning.

'So?'

'Sister Saraswati Devi says we'll have to wait a little while,' Hunar Sahib clarified. 'Actually, Mahatma Banshiram doesn't just spin during his vows of silence, he also ponders how to take care of all his problems. That way nothing can interrupt his train of thought.' Hunar Sahib laughed. 'I'd actually forgotten that Monday is his day to observe silence. He's spinning right now, so he can only see us when he's done with that.'

'How long does he have left?' asked Chetan. 'If it's long, I'll be on my way.'

'No, no, stay; he'll be free in just fifteen minutes. Sister Saraswati Devi said he's already been spinning for forty-five minutes, and he always spins for one full hour by the clock. When he's free, we'll see him; after that, we can go. I'll have to come back at some point to discuss matters to do with *Widows' Aid*. From here, we'll go to Yogi ji's place. He's attained quite a bit of skill in yoga lately. If he's meditating and you go and sit quietly by him, you'll spontaneously start to feel the influence of his thoughts.'

'How can that be?'

'That's what's so amazing about yoga.'

242

'People should learn how to do publicity from you.'

'No, it's not a matter of publicity; he's just got a huge influence on me, bhai. I was so upset about this thing happening with my brother, but I was at peace after talking to him. I've promised him I'll present the nectar of the Upanishads before the public in straightforward Urdu poetry.'

And Hunar Sahib turned towards Ranvir and Nishtar. 'Look, yaar,' he said, 'I'm going to write a poem for the new issue of *Widows' Aid*. In the meantime, you two sort through all those slips of paper in the files where my poems and stories and other works are printed.'

Ranvir and Nishtar fell upon the weekly files like the obedient pupils they were. To pass the time, Chetan picked up the file from the table for that month's paper, and Hunar Sahib squatted on the chair and began to write a poem on the weekly pad placed on the table.

Chetan flipped through page after page, but his mind didn't alight upon anything. *Widows' Aid*, like the journals *Guru Ghantal* or *Paras*, wasn't the sort of popular weekly that would remind one of a carnival put on for the enjoyment of spectators with all sorts of interests and inclinations—a carnival where there are myriad forms of gambling; where tea, coffee and alcoholic beverages are sold; where there are caves of death; where there are small circuses; where there are stuntmen wearing burning clothing, who leap from five-hundred-foot heights into water; and most of all, where there are also holy men in a tent from a Himalayan cavern who will tell audiences the secrets to rising above life and death, joy and sorrow! *Widows' Aid*, on the other hand, reminded Chetan of the yearly session of the Gurukul, where one saw renunciants wandering about, heads shaven, or long, tangled hair free from the graces of oil and comb, wearing thick homespun clothing, sacrificial threads hanging about their necks, barefoot and bare-headed.

Everywhere you looked, there were Vedic sayings pasted up: on the walls, on the pillars. You'd only get hackneyed sermons to listen to, or hymns so ear-splitting, they'd damage your ears . . . Since this weekly was not sold in the bazaar it worried not about catering to the interests of the readers. It ran on subscription. Its customers were a captive audience. All the Congress committees in the district that had constructive centres had to buy it, and reports for all the constructive centres were printed in it; there were the Urdu translations of Mahatma Gandhi's *Navjivan* essays on the problems of women and untouchables; Mahatma Banshiram was the editor, and all the rest was written by Hunar Sahib himself or rewritten by his pupils—with a view to the Congress's constructive work . . . Chetan began to doze off after flipping through two issues. He'd been walking around since morning and although there was a breeze outside, it was quite humid in the room. He placed the *Widows' Aid* file across his face, rested his head against the back of the bench, and dozed off.

'There you go, it's done!'

Chetan started. Hunar Sahib had dropped his feet back to the ground, and held the writing pad in both his hands as he prepared to read the poem. Ranvir and Nishtar both jumped up when they heard his voice.

'Please observe the simplicity with which I have described the desires of a widow in just a few lines,' said Hunar Sahib, and he began to read the poem. Chetan also perked up.

> Life is full of restlessness
> A continuous torment
> Where weeping is hidden in every line
> Life is like a chapter of longing and grief

'Wah, wah!' Ranvir's eyes shone with praise.

'Amazing!' praised Nishtar. 'Recite it again.'

Hunar Sahib read the same verse again, then continued:

The sun was everywhere, once
The moon was everywhere, once
Life was full of light and music
There were the sweetest dreams, once
But now the pages are faded
Like a book with no charm
Every chapter a desert
And it is most distressing

'Wonderful! Wah wah!'

Ranvir and Nishtar began to sway. 'It's amazing how you've described the wasteland of a widow's life in so few words!' enthused Nishtar.

Hunar Sahib beamed and began to explain how his mind had been completely blank before sitting down at the table. He just sat down and picked up a piece of paper so that he would get in a 'topics dense as clouds are rushing towards me' type of mood.

And Chetan began to wonder—had Hunar Sahib truly just written this poem, or had he found it fitting after rifling through the work of some master. For just a moment, he watched him quietly—but he himself had seen him recite an entire ghazal or poem in a matter of minutes several times before. 'Why doesn't this man go back to Lahore?' he thought. 'He was fairly respected there and it's second nature to him to write the poems on contemporary problems in the Sunday editions of daily papers that everyone asks for, so what does he get out of writing the editorial for *Widows' Aid* or for the two-page *Sadaqat*?

'Tell me, Hunar Sahib,' he asked, 'why don't you go back to Lahore—here the flowers of your genius blossom in the desert.'

'Bhai, I took a one-month vacation and came here when my father died, then circumstances changed such that I was forced to take on the responsibility of managing the household and wasn't able to return.'

'But are you sitting at the shop in the village?'

'Can a free spirit like me not do the work of sitting in a shop?' he laughed. 'Besides that, I help my brothers as much as I can. Who can look after this court case that's going on right now besides me? I do think about Lahore, but "what to say of such desires that have turned to dust"?'

And he sighed deeply.

'But instead of writing for the papers here, you could be writing for the papers in Lahore.'

'I consider writing for *Widows' Aid* my contribution to service to the nation,' he said. 'As for the Lahore papers, wherever I used to write, "Dozakhi" has settled in and you know how I feel about him. Actually, when I was in Lahore, he saw the way I shut down all those people and complained horribly about it and that's why he wrote that essay against me.'

This Dozakhi was a famous poet in Lahore who wrote satirical columns and humorous poetry under an assumed name in the papers and magazines to earn extra money. Once he'd taken a poem of Hunar Sahib's and proven that he'd written it by plundering the work of four other poets, and ridiculed him terribly. Hunar had given his response (that he was sure would render him speechless), but no one was convinced, and in newspaper circles he was now considered nothing but a poet-thief. If he truly possessed a high class of original genius, he would submit new poems and work with unstinting labour to break through this gossip surrounding him, but he didn't have it in him to do the work required to write fresh material. He had in abundance the desire to attain cheap brilliance and the genius of being able to write ghazals or poems at a moment's notice, talents that are required for the 'Our Special Poet' columns that appear in daily Urdu papers. He'd read the complete oeuvres of all the poets: Mir, Sauda, Ghalib, Momin, Dagh, Atish, Asghar, Fani and Jigar. He had an amazing memory. He knew by heart ghazals of various masters written in one metre. And when he had to write on some contemporary problem (and in those days, amongst the special poets and satirists of rival papers there was daily ribbing—from which the readers derived a particular pleasure) he unknowingly used those poems by changing the refrain or metre or rearranging the words! But he was so used to getting praise every second or third day for writing ghazals and poems quickly, he was no longer in the habit of writing original material. Hunar Sahib was like an artist who takes refuge in commercial art to earn a living while still producing original material, and with the help of dozens of national and international journals, makes new designs daily for advertisers and then, when some details or colour-scheme or original idea is reflected in his own pictures, he considers it completely original and falls prey to self-deception.

As he sat there, Chetan gazed at Hunar Sahib with silent contempt and pity—'It's not written in the fate of this man to leave the mark of his talent on literature,' he thought. 'He'll write in these small journals and earn praise for his work from young whippersnapper pupils like Nishtar and Ranvir, and this will satisfy his ego. It's not in his fate to become a great author.' And he decided to himself that even if it took him years to write a good poem or story (he wasn't yet satisfied with his own works), he'd write original ones. Instead of stealing other people's experiences or ideas, he'd express only his own experiences—he wasn't going to plunder the wealth of others.

*

Hunar Sahib was reciting with great ebullience the poem with which he'd shut the mouth of Dozakhi, when suddenly Sister Saraswati Devi entered the room and announced that the Mahatma ji was now free and awaited them.

She arrived suddenly and stood before them with her plump body, her round face and her slightly protruding upper row of teeth. Chetan had been lost in thought; he started, and stared at her hard for a moment. Finding this fool staring at her so intently, she looked ill at ease. She pulled her sari border over her forehead a bit, grimaced, and returned upstairs, her sandals slapping.

Hunar Sahib got up and proposed they meet Mahatma Banshiram, and they walked upstairs to Mahatma ji's chamber; Hunar ahead, his disciples behind. Sister Saraswati Devi stood right inside the doorway to welcome them.

The room they now entered was even more unadorned than the first. That room had had a table, a chair and a bench; here, all these were missing. There was not a single picture or calendar on the walls. The whitewash had flaked off in several places and the bricks were bare—perhaps the paint had come off as soon as it had been applied—and the walls seemed to smile at newcomers with a strange disgust. A mat was spread out along the right wall in the middle of the room, on which sat Mahatma Banshiram ji. His elbow rested on the bolster and his legs were scrunched up in exactly the same pose as Mahatma Gandhi. He was writing something with a writing pad propped on his knees.

They greeted him, and Mahatma ji showed his broken teeth in response, motioning for them to sit down. Sister Saraswati Devi spread out a mat for them in front of Mahatma ji on which all four sat, although altogether only two of them could actually fit. Sister Saraswati Devi sat down on the stool near the door and began to spin silently.

Chetan and Nishtar were a bit farther from the Mahatma ji. Ranvir was sitting right next to Hunar Sahib. 'Yaar, what is this boring place you people have brought me to?' Chetan whispered into Nishtar's ear as he managed somehow to sit right against him.

He had whispered into Nishtar's ear, but Hunar Sahib overheard him. He turned and scolded him with a frown.

Mahatma Banshiram asked what he was saying, using a hand gesture.

'Chetan ji is saying,' Hunar Sahib grinned, 'that sitting here like this, you look just like Mahatma Gandhi.'

And he turned towards Chetan and winked slightly. Chetan wished he could burst out laughing. He stopped himself with great difficulty.

At this, Mahatma ji again smiled to reveal his broken teeth, and placing a finger to his lips, he assumed his thinking pose; he turned over the page on his pad and wrote: 'I can't even be compared to the dust on his feet.' And, removing a sheet of paper from the top of the pad (on which he'd already been writing something), he handed it to Hunar Sahib.

Chetan raised himself up slightly and read the sentence written on the pad over Hunar Sahib's shoulder. He wanted to say loudly, 'What you've written is one hundred per cent true!' But he managed to restrain himself using all his self-control. The boredom he'd felt for so long in Hunar Sahib's company as he waited for Mahatma Banshiram ji to finish his spinning was filling him with a need to liberate himself of all restrictions. But he managed to keep himself under control and sat down again as before, focusing his gaze on Sister Saraswati Devi's spindle so that his eyes wouldn't betray his secret.

After reading Mahatma Banshiram's reply, Hunar Sahib smiled appreciatively. 'But this is your modesty,' he said. 'People don't call you "The Gandhi of the Doab" for nothing.'

At this, Mahatma ji took the pad back from him and wrote a long statement to the effect that those people are the poor servants of Gandhi—like the twinkling stars swirling around the sun. If Mahatma Gandhi were before them, perhaps they wouldn't even be visible. They only shine in his absence and attempt as much as possible to give light in darkness with their twinkling glow. Just as he'd taken on his shoulders the task of improving the plight of the widows of his region and decided to spend his life in this work. If he could work towards the uplift of the widows and lost women of his region, he'd consider himself fortunate . . . etc. . . . etc. . . .

He handed the pad back to Hunar Sahib and again placed a finger to his lips.

Hunar Sahib read it and beamed as he praised Mahatma ji's service and sacrifice fulsomely. Then he said he was thinking of writing Mahatma Banshiram's biography: India was proud of her Gandhi, but the Doab was no less proud of its own Gandhi.

Chetan was getting bored. 'Who knows how much butter he's going to slather on here,' he thought to himself. 'Maybe he even gets something from Mahatma ji for editing the *Widows' Aid*—but why has he brought me along?' . . . And he stood up.

Hunar Sahib pulled on his sleeve and sat him back down, signalling that they would soon leave. Then he continued with his statement: the battle for independence was not just being fought by decorating 'temples to self-rule'. It was also being waged with the handle of the spinning wheel; with the thread from the spindle; on homespun looms; and for the liberation for women; and that the work Mahatma Banshiram had taken on as his responsibility was no less important than going to jail.

Having pleased Mahatma ji, Hunar Sahib added that he had actually come to discuss collecting materials for the new issue, but had forgotten about his vow of silence, so he would come back tomorrow. He then acquainted Mahatma ji with Chetan's brilliance and told him that Chetan would also write for *Widows' Aid* on a regular basis. With this, he said his goodbyes and stood up.

But then, as though he'd just remembered something, he kneeled back on the mat and asked if he could take home the issues of the weekly in which his own work had been published.

Mahatma Banshiram wrote on the pad that he'd already taken the files away twice.

Hunar Sahib replied that it was thanks to those that he'd already signed up two lifetime members of *Widows' Aid*, and that he'd promised himself he'd sign up one hundred new lifetime members for the weekly. He was taking these issues to Lala Jalandhari Mull ji 'Yogi' and, if God wished it, he too would soon become a lifetime member of *Widows' Aid*.

At this, Mahatma Banshiram smiled and very generously granted him permission to take the issues. He summoned Sister Saraswati Devi and wrote out instructions to her allowing Hunar Sahib to take the past year's files with him.

*

Fifteen minutes later, after they'd walked down the stairs, Nishtar and Ranvir were carrying the issues of *Widows' Aid* and Hunar Sahib was walking happily along as though he was making off with some great treasure.

23

There was a huge amount of mud in Mandi Bazaar, but there was not as much traffic on the paved street coming from above Ramjidas Mill. The street was sparkling clean after the rain. The office of the Widows' Aid Society was a furlong or so on the other side of Mandi Bazaar, so they hadn't seen any of the mud on their way there. Chetan could never have imagined that there could be so much mud on the street, or more accurately, in the bazaar, for such a distance. After wandering the sparkling streets of Shimla for three months, he'd forgotten how much mud ran in the galis and bazaars of his own city. The thing is, actually, that shops had begun to spring up suddenly on that street because of its proximity to Mandi—first on one side, then on both sides. And where the street going to the city from behind Mandi came out on the left side, the bazaar had grown quite dense because not only did the bullock carts coming to Mandi ply down that road, but so did the ikkas and tongas travelling back and forth, night and day, from the city to the station and the station to the city. And then there was so much other traffic as well—handcarts, hawkers, cyclists, pedestrians—and the street was so broken up, that with just a small amount of rain, the bazaar was no longer a bazaar, but a muddy swamp.

Hunar Sahib, however, was completely unconcerned about the mud. He was so pleased with his day's labour that the mud didn't even exist for him. His sandals might get stuck here and there, splats of mud might fly up and paint flowers and petals on his dhoti, and someone coming from the other direction might force him from that narrow path (where the mud tracked by the pedestrians had dried, and where they now walked, one behind the other) into the thin strip of mud in the bazaar, some tonga passing by from the bazaar might force him to climb on to the front step of a shop, but he noticed none of this. He did all these things as he walked along, talking continuously. If for a moment the thread of his conversation was broken by one of these obstacles, he'd overcome it, then take up the thread again right where he'd left off. Ranvir and Nishtar walked along with him, sometimes ahead and sometimes behind, holding the *Widows' Aid* files aloft. They responded, 'Hmm hmm,' to him, or contributed their own two cents here and there.

Chetan picked his way along behind them all, hitching up his trousers. Although the crease in his trousers had been completely erased since morning, first in the dust and then walking through the storm, they hadn't yet transformed into pyjamas although they'd certainly started to look like them. Nonetheless, Chetan was making every possible effort to save them, because this was his only pair, and he was afraid he would be forced to spend one more day in Jalandhar. But he had fallen behind his companions in this effort. Hunar Sahib would end up way ahead, stop, and wait for him to catch up; when he reached them, they'd set out again.

Suddenly, in order to jump from the path of a tonga, Chetan climbed into a shop on the left side. Just then his gaze fell on the other side of the bazaar, where the 'Mandi Soda Water Factory' signboard hung above a wide shop, and the memory of Chacha Fakir Chand's face rose up before his eyes. He looked down from the board, and saw that Chacha himself was seated on a stool to the left side on the front step of the shop, with one leg up on the stool and the other dangling. He was dozing, his head leaning against the large door.

Suddenly, Chetan felt incredibly thirsty. He hadn't drunk any water since eating tandoori parathas and mutter paneer at the Khalsa Hotel. He had even thought of drinking water at one point at Mahatma Banshiram's, but after seeing Sister Saraswati Devi and Mahatma Banshiram ji, he didn't have the courage to ask for any. When the tonga had gone by, he managed to lift the legs of his trousers somehow, and, avoiding the mire in the street, he crossed to the other side and stepped on to the fourth wooden step in front of the shop, where he cried out loudly, 'Namaste, Chacha ji!'

Chacha Fakir Chand started and stood up. He was of medium height, with a round body, pyjamas that fell to the ankles, a two-day beard, cropped salt-and-pepper hair, plump lips and a large cataract in his left eye. As soon as he saw Chetan, a tired smile appeared on his face and he said, 'Come, come, take a seat, have a soda.'

From the stoop, Chetan cast a glance at his companions. Hunar Sahib was walking along, enthralled with his own words. At first he considered calling out to him, but then he thought that he'd just drink a soda and catch up with them later, so he kept quiet and said, 'If you give me a fresh soda, Chacha ji, then we're talking.'

'Yes, yes, I'll give you a fresh one, a fresh one!' cried Chacha Fakir Chand, and he called out to his worker, 'Hey there, crank boy! Hey, you bastard, over here!'

*

Chacha Fakir Chand was among Chetan's father, Pandit Shadiram's, most intimate friends, of which there were four types.

255

The first type of friend was what Chetan's mother considered his *true friends*. Principal among these were Chowdhry Tejpal and Chowdhry Gujjarmal—both were tall, fair and hearty. Chowdhry Gujjarmal was stronger than Chowdhry Tejpal because he was a wrestler. His akhara was at Devi Talab. He had a saraf shop in Bara Bazaar. But he went to the akhara both before opening his shop in the morning and after locking up in the evening. Chowdhry Tejpal was a cloth merchant. His shop was right at Chaurasti Atari. Ma had told Chetan that both men had been heavy drinkers in their day, and key members of Pandit Shadiram's goonda party.

'But not everyone is like them,' Chetan's mother had told him one day. 'Now that they're married, they take care of their households.'

'Really, Ma, so they don't drink any more?' Chetan had asked.

'Chowdhry Gujjarmal doesn't drink, but I've heard that Chowdhry Tejpal takes a peg at dinner time,' Ma had said. 'Your father says Gujjar still drinks; that he's a coward; hides in his home and drinks, while acting like a community leader. But not everyone spends their entire lives ruining their homes.'

Chetan never forgot a particular incident with Chowdhry Gujjarmal. One day, Chetan's father had gone with him to Bara Bazaar so he could get him some fabric for a coat. After buying the fabric he went to see Gujjarmal at his shop for a few minutes. Chowdhry Sahib was seated as usual behind a small teapoy, applying gold leaf to a piece of jewellery set in lac on a small board. In a glass cupboard to his left lay some gold and silver ornaments. Gujjarmal set the board to one side and looked up.

'Come in, Shadi, have a seat,' he said.

Chetan's father did not sit down. He stayed where he was, resting his foot on the stoop, and told him he was stopping in Jalandhar for one night on his way from Banga Station to Dasuya, for Relieving; he'd come to buy cloth for Chetan, and he thought he'd drop by and see how Gujjarmal was doing.

'You must be about to retire?' Gujjarmal asked.

'Yes, in two years I'll have been in service twenty-five years, but I'm trying to make it last one more year somehow.'

'You'll be getting some kind of provident fund when you retire?'

'I'll be getting eight thousand rupees or so, but I owe three or four thousand.'

'If you take my advice you'll start a liquor shop with the rest of the money.'

Chetan stared at him with astonishment and laughed uncomprehendingly.

'And put up a signboard outside the shop—"All this is for me, not for sale!"' And he added in Punjabi, 'If someone comes to buy liquor, tell them—"I'm not letting anyone drink this, it's all for me."'

And Chowdhry Gujjarmal laughed, his tiny eyes shining with mirth.

Chetan's father began cursing at him straightaway. 'Sala, you're a fine kind of man, your wife has made an ass of you!' he cried, and he dragged Chetan off, cursing all the while. He continued to curse at his friend all the way to the shoe seller's chowk. But this sentence of Gujjarmal's stuck in Chetan's mind: 'I'm not letting anyone drink this, it's all for me.' And he imagined a liquor store with a signboard outside stating that the liquor there was not for sale, and he chuckled to himself . . . On their way there, Pandit ji had told him that Gujjarmal was his dear, dear friend. They'd played together; eaten and drunk together. He hadn't wanted to get married, the bastard. He just wandered about, a bachelor. Pandit Shadiram was the one who arranged his marriage and now Gujjarmal had abandoned him.

But Chetan's mother said that those two were his only true friends. Whenever they had the chance, the two of them would pull him together and advise him to take it easy; they bore the brunt of his curses but were never offended. Neither put him up to bad deeds, and if any misfortune ever befell Ma, she'd call on them and they'd always come without making any excuses or heeding Chetan's father's curses.

The second type of friend was completely selfish. Principal among these was Desraj. He was the worst lowlife of all Shadiram's friends. He'd loan him money, give him drinks, drink himself on top of that, get him to gamble, beat him, and then keep drawing interest from him for that sum: all these were regular activities for him. Sometimes Chetan's brothers wished they could beat him up and bash in his head, but Chetan's mother always stopped them from committing such a 'sin'.

The third type of friend was the likes of Pandit Daulat Ram, Mukandi Lal, Banarsidas—the sort of people known as *pichalgua* in Punjabi, or 'hangers-on'. When Pandit ji came to Jalandhar, they would all gather round—one would refresh his hookah, another would press his feet. As long as he remained in town, they'd eat and drink; then they wouldn't show their faces again, instead swearing at him behind his back, slandering him, and making every effort to harm his family.

Chetan and his brothers placed Harlal and Fakir Chand in the fourth category of their father's friends. Pandit ji entertained them no less than the others, and there couldn't be a party at Pandit ji's if Harlal or Fakir Chand were not present, but they never slandered him, and if Ma couldn't find Chowdhry Tejpal or Gujjarmal in times of crisis, she would call for one of them. Since Harlal had to look after his shop, he'd just have a peg or two and go on his way, and he never gambled except on the three days of Diwali. Fakir Chand had to look after his factory as well, but whenever Pandit ji came to Jalandhar he'd go over to the factory the moment he stepped out of the station. No matter how much work Fakir Chand had to do, Pandit ji would curse him roundly and order him to get up, and Fakir Chand would leave everything to his worker, the crank boy, and go off with him; he'd stick with him for as long as Pandit ji stayed in Jalandhar; he'd eat and drink with him, visit Bazaar Sheikhan, and do anything he wished.

Chetan had never heard him curse or speak loudly. He seemed to be the same age as Chetan's father, but he must have been a couple of years younger, because Chetan's elder brother called him 'Chacha', as did Chetan in imitation of him, and Chetan's father loved him as he would a younger brother. Although he had a soda-water factory, he hadn't got married until he was forty because of the defect in his eye. Then, suddenly one day, they found out that Chacha Fakir Chand had got married and his wife was coming to stay with them and she was going to have a baby (Chetan's father was working at Dasuya Station in those days and Chetan had gone there during his vacation). The small wooden room in their quarters was vacated for his wife. She was due to have a child in the month of Kartik, and since a child born in Kartik is considered inauspicious—it brings ill fortune to the home it's born into—Ma wanted Fakir Chand's wife to be placed elsewhere, but Chetan's father scolded her and swore at her, and demanded to know how he could place his sister-in-law in the servants' quarters. Fakir Chand was dearer to him than a brother. And after lecturing Ma for half an hour, he ordered her to do as he said and arrange everything.

Chacha Fakir Chand dropped his wife off and went away, and Chetan's mother was forced to shoulder the burden of looking after her along with managing the household.

The first day Chetan saw his wife, he just stared. She was so beautiful, it was hard to look at her: she was thin, of medium height, with long black hair, light dimples on her cheeks, teeth like pearls, large, round dreamy eyes, and a wide forehead. When she laughed, dimples formed on her cheeks.

'Ma, how did Chacha Fakir Chand find such a beautiful wife at his age?' Chetan had asked.

'If she weren't so beautiful, would she have become an unwed mother?' replied Ma contemptuously. 'When her father found out, he went looking for someone needy to unload her on to. Someone told your father and he thought of Fakir Chand. So he secretly called for him and got them married, and after they got married, he brought her straight here. When the child is born, they'll announce the wedding in Jalandhar and bring her there.'

The child was born in the month of Kartik and was sent off to some orphanage, and Chachi was brought to Jalandhar as a bride. Chetan's mother's idea was that such loose women are unlikely to stick it out in a marriage, but no one ever heard a complaint against Chachi again. After a year, a little girl was born in Chacha's home, who unfortunately took after her father rather than her mother, but at least one could be thankful she didn't have a cataract in one eye.

Nonetheless, Ma was never able to forgive Chachi—especially for setting up camp in her home during the month of Kartik! Whenever some new misfortune befell their home—if Pandit ji drank too much liquor, or lost at gambling, or wasted money in Bazaar Sheikhan, Ma would blame her for saddling them with the ill fortune of that Kartik-born child.

Whenever Chetan went to Chacha Fakir Chand's house, Chachi welcomed him warmly. He always liked her, and he couldn't understand what connection her having a baby in their

260

home, much less in the month of Kartik, had with their bad luck. His father already drank, already gambled and already visited Bazaar Sheikhan before she came.

*

After her second child was born, Chachi fell ill. Chetan was in his FA, when one day his father told his mother, 'Let's go, I'm going to take you to bathe at Haridwar.' And he applied for ten days' leave and railway passes.

Pandit ji had planned to accompany them to Haridwar, and then leave after ten days, and they would stay on there for an entire month. Ma was very pleased when she heard this. She pawned a large piece of jewellery and made plans for a pilgrimage. But right as they were leaving, all of her joy evaporated when she found out that Pandit ji was also bringing along Chacha Fakir Chand and his wife.

That was when Chetan had learned that Chachi was terribly ill. She had come down with tuberculosis. Pandit ji had heard from someone that there was a vaidya, an Ayurvedic doctor, in Kanakhal who had a magic touch, and he advised Fakir Chand to get his wife treated there. Pandit ji told him that Ma would stay with him for the whole month, and Chacha ji could look after her, but Ma knew that she'd be the one shouldering all the expenses, and she'd be the one doing all the looking after. And if there were any shortcomings, Pandit ji would be baying for blood.

When Chetan saw Chachi at the station, he couldn't believe his eyes: How could this be that same healthy young woman, beautiful as a fairy! Her complexion had turned completely dark. She looked like a small pile of bones. Chacha had to carry her. She couldn't stand up. She just slid to the ground when she tried to walk. She looked like a little girl. She smiled when she saw them and her pearly white teeth shone. That smile remained ever etched in Chetan's heart—so full of fear and sorrow!

As soon as they got down from the train, the pilgrimage priests surrounded them. One priest took down Pandit ji's great-grandfather's name in his ledger; that priest's home was near Har Ki Pauri. Chetan's mother, his brothers and his father stayed in two rooms, and Chacha Fakir Chand and Chachi stayed in one room right across from them. After taking her to the Kanakhal vaidya and arranging for medicines, Pandit ji went out in search of a bottle for the night's entertainment. But Haridwar was completely new to him. He didn't know where to get liquor, and he didn't feel right about asking people at a pilgrimage site. But Pandit ji was not about to accept defeat. He took Chacha Fakir Chand and went off God knows where, to the point that they didn't even return one night. Chachi's insides were in terrible pain. Ma put Chetan and his brothers to bed, then went and slept in Chachi's room herself, and she had to get up with her several times that night. The next day, around nightfall, Pandit ji and Fakir Chand returned from somewhere over by Bhimgoda, after covering pretty much the entire area, and he told Ma in a whisper that they'd gone to see Hrishikesh but weren't able to get back and so had stayed the night. They'd gone to see Kali Kamli Wale . . . but Chetan could tell from the paper-wrapped object they gave Ma to put away which deity they'd actually gone to pay their respects to . . .

The next day, when Ma asked him to take her to see Hrishikesh, he said, 'Yes, we'll go today.' But then he went out, taking with him that same bottle wrapped in paper, and was nowhere to be seen until evening.

And when, after ten days, Pandit ji returned to work, Ma heaved a sigh of relief. All she could think about day and night was how God would not forgive all this sin at a pilgrimage site. Now they'd come all this way, she wanted terribly to bathe just once at Har Ki Pauri but Pandit ji didn't even have the time to take a ritual bath. He'd get up at ten o'clock, by which time Ma was done with her bath in the Ganges and her prayers, then he'd go out to drink a glass of lassi, after which no one would see his face again until evening. But despite all this, he continued to take Chacha Fakir Chand and his wife to the vaidya at Kanakhal during those ten days and he did not leave Haridwar until he'd thoroughly arranged for her medicines.

*

When Chachi had arrived in Haridwar, Chacha Fakir Chand had carried her down to bathe in the Ganges, but after that, Chetan noticed that she'd sit on the steps of the house and pull herself down, step by step, cross a small portion of the bazaar and make her way to Har Ki Pauri. She'd go and bathe right there on the stairs, and change her clothes and sit there for quite a while before returning. And she'd make herself up fully, despite being nothing more than a skeleton. Chetan was astonished to observe her life force. And when Chacha Fakir Chand returned after a month, Chachi's body had filled out a bit and her complexion had changed back to a wheat colour. Six months later, when Chetan saw her looking just as healthy as she used to, he wasn't surprised.

*

Mandi Soda Water Factory had three rooms, all in a row. In the very last room was the soda machine. In the middle room were two large tubs of water: the first for the empty bottles, the second

263

for the full ones. There was also a cupboard in that room filled with small vials of essences and bottles of sharbat. The walls of the front room were lined with wooden racks, the middle shelves of which had been cut to fit the round ends of the bottles. This is where the bottles were arranged after they were filled. A small desk had been placed on a wooden platform in the same room, and this was used as a counter.

Chacha Fakir Chand went inside, picked up an empty bottle from the tub and asked Chetan, who had followed him in, what flavour he'd like—banana, orange, malted, vetiver or rose?

In those days, Chetan loved the light fragrance and sweet taste of rose. 'Rose!' he replied.

Chacha Fakir Chand then measured some sharbat into the bottle, and some essence, and went into the back room to place it in the machine. Chetan went and stood fearfully by the machine. As a boy, he'd loved watching the bottles filling with soda. He used to stand and watch it for hours in Bhairon Bazaar on his way home from school. Chacha Fakir Chand and the Khatri from Chetan's own neighbourhood, Shanno Chachi's brother-in-law-turned-husband, Chacha Mukandi Lal, had set up a soda machine there together. Soda machines were new to Jalandhar in those days. Chetan's father was the one who had arranged for the money and suggested his two friends form a partnership.

On his way home from Qila Mohalla primary school, Chetan would stop at the front step of the factory and watch the bottles filling with soda. Lala Mukandi Lal ran the machine. Chetan liked watching his pale arms and legs (his dhoti hiked up to the knees; his sleeves rolled up to the elbows) and his pale face, red with effort. Then one day, a bottle had burst while Chetan was standing nearby watching. In those days, soda bottles had a glass marble inside them, and Chetan's father considered it a mark of bravery to press down the marble in the neck of the bottle with his thumb and open it with just one smack of the other hand. Bets were placed at his parties as to whether or not the bottle could be opened in just one try, and a couple of rupees would always change hands. But since the marble couldn't come out of the bottle without breaking it, the bottles burst if they had just a tiny bit too much gas in them—especially in the hot season—and the task of filling them was fairly perilous. Although Lala Mukandi Lal had been turning the wheel of the machine, and Chetan had been standing down below in the bazaar, when the bottle burst, a piece of glass tore into Lala Mukandi Lal's cheek, leaving a large wound, and the marble hit Chetan on the forehead and bruised him. From that day on, Lala Mukandi Lal stopped cranking the handle and Chetan stopped watching the machine run.

Actually, usually when the bottles burst, Chetan and his friends were secretly extremely pleased—for one thing there'd be a loud explosion, and for another, the marble would pop out, and as it was of no use to the factory any more, they got to play with it. But he'd never imagined that his forehead could get busted by the marble when he'd stood so far from the machine, and from that day on, he'd always feared standing too close.

The crank boy began turning the handle of the machine. Chetan's heart pounded as he remembered that incident from his childhood. He felt fearful that the bottle might explode. But in just a moment a loud hissing sound came from the machine as the bottle was filled with gas; then it was filled with water, and Chacha Fakir Chand turned the machine and removed the bottle. He told the crank boy to run and get a paisa's worth of ice, and he himself filled a few more bottles in front of Chetan.

When the ice arrived, Chacha opened the bottle, poured it into a glass and gave it to Chetan. The tiny soda bubbles flew up his nostrils. He loved their sharpness and fragrance. But he sneezed hard and the glass nearly fell out of his hand. Then he stepped outside the shop, holding the glass in his hand. When he looked up, he started—Hunar Sahib, Ranvir and Nishtar were all standing down in the bazaar by the steps to the factory.

24

Chetan laughed slightly and remarked by way of explanation, 'I was feeling a bit thirsty. I saw the sign for Chacha ji's factory, so . . .'

'But we feel thirsty too!' interrupted Hunar Sahib with a chuckle.

'Come, come! Climb on up!' cried Chacha Fakir Chand enthusiastically. He turned to Chetan and said, 'Tell your friends to come on up!'

Without waiting for his response, he called out to the crank boy in Punjabi, 'Hey, you bastard, go get two more paisas' worth of ice, and open up three bottles of the rose for these guys!'

Hunar Sahib had already climbed the steps. 'No, no, I was just joking,' he said. 'Please don't trouble yourself.'

But before saying this, he glanced out of the corner of his eye to see if the crank boy had already gone to get the ice.

'No, no, no trouble at all!' objected Chacha Fakir Chand. 'Please consider this your own shop.'

Then suddenly Chetan recollected his duty. He introduced Hunar Sahib to Chacha Fakir Chand and Chacha to his friends.

'If Bau were here (Chetan's father's friends called him "Bau [short for Babu] Shadiram" or just "Bau"), he'd ask you to recite a couplet,' said Chacha Fakir Chand, referring to Chetan's father's colourful personality. 'He loves music and poetry. I don't really understand much myself.'

'What use is a couplet the ordinary man cannot understand?' cried Hunar Sahib. 'I consider simplicity and efficiency the greatest virtues of a couplet. I don't recite the "If you don't understand, God help you" type of couplet.'

Hunar Sahib dragged over a stool, sat himself down, and told the rest of them to sit on the stoop. Then he told Chacha Fakir Chand how he had rendered the difficult verses of the Gita into easy Urdu—this way the educated and uneducated alike could feel the Gita deeply with their hearts—'I'll recite some verses for you,' he said suddenly. 'See if you understand them or not.'

And, without waiting for a response, he recited that same translation of the Gita that he'd already recited to so many people since morning. The third time only Chetan was listening.

Chetan couldn't tell from his detached expression whether or not Chacha Fakir Chand understood any of it, but he listened intently and offered praise as well. It was in the midst of this that the crank boy returned with the ice.

'Chacha ji, since you have your own factory, why don't you order a maund or two of ice and keep it here?' asked Chetan. 'Do you supply bottles only to shopkeepers, not openly to customers?'

'I get an entire block every morning, beta,' said Chacha. 'There was such a rush today at twelve o'clock, all of it was finished off. It'll be delivered again in the evening.'

The crank boy in the meanwhile had washed and crushed the ice and put it into clean glasses. Then he opened three bottles and handed them each a glass.

The pink of the rosewater and that light fragrance! As soon as the glass reached his hand, Hunar Sahib swayed and recited a couplet in reference to his soda:

Sheikh ji, soda is not the daughter-of-the-grape[9]
Why have you grown anxious without reason?

This was a couplet Chacha Fakir Chand understood, and he praised it, as did Ranvir and Nishtar.

Well pleased, Hunar Sahib cried, 'Here's another!'

Love is like the bubbling of soda
Now you see it, now you don't

'Wah wah! Wonderful!' Chacha Fakir Chand was thrilled. When Hunar Sahib had emptied his glass, he ordered the crank boy to open four bottles of Vimto.

The brand Vimto had just come out in those days. An ordinary bottle of lemonade could cost only six paisas, but a Vimto was six whole annas. It tasted like Coca-Cola. Chetan felt uneasy. 'No, Chacha ji,' he said. 'Please don't open any for me.'

He had thought Hunar Sahib would take his hint. But he remained silent. His face shone at the mere mention of Vimto.

'How did you get rid of your thirst with just one bottle?' asked Chacha Fakir Chand. 'One time your father drank up an entire brass pot of lassi made for eight men all on his own.'

'All on his own!' chirped Hunar Sahib. 'How much lassi was that?'

'There must have been sixteen or seventeen glasses!' replied Chacha Fakir Chand and he began to tell the story.

'One day, we were coming home after exercising. It was summer. We were terribly thirsty. I dissolved some sugar and made one and a half seers of lassi in a small brass pot.

'"Yaar, put in some more water, I'm really thirsty," said Bau.

---

[9] The daughter-of-the-grape, i.e. liquor.

'"There's enough water," I replied.

'"Bastard, I'm going to drink that whole thing myself!" thundered Bau.

'There were eight of us. I had counted two glasses per person and put in enough for sixteen and one more on top of that. I was annoyed and said, "If you drink all that on your own, I'll give you a one-rupee reward!"

'And Bau didn't even ask, "Bastard, where will you get one rupee from?" He just picked up the pot and put it to his lips and he didn't set it down again until he'd swallowed it all down to the last drop.'

Although Chetan had no special love for his father, his chest swelled with pride on hearing this story and he looked around proudly at his companions.

By then the crank boy had opened the bottles of Vimto and filled their glasses. Chacha Fakir Chand presented the very first glass to Hunar Sahib.

Taking the glass, Hunar Sahib remarked, 'This reminds me of a couplet. It is a humorous one, but it might have been composed for Pandit ji himself:'

Even the ocean cannot quench my thirst
Oh cup-bearer, today pour me a whole pot of whisky

At this, he pretended his Vimto was whisky and put it to his lips lustily.

All of Chacha Fakir Chand's boredom had vanished. On just hearing the word whisky his face flushed with the thrill—'Wah, wah! What a couplet! If Bau Shadiram were here, he'd praise it. Truly, for him, even a jug is not enough.'

And Chacha Fakir Chand began to tell a tale about the time Pandit ji had put a bottle to his lips and finished it in 'just one gulp'.

270

Hunar Sahib licked his lips as he polished off his glass of Vimto. Vimto wasn't whisky but he felt a little buzzed all the same. He recited one more couplet:

Though thirst was assuaged by the cup
What's left is thirst for beholding you

After reciting the couplet with relish, he said, 'Chacha ji, we've slaked the thirst of our gullets but we will always be thirsty for conversation with you.' Having established an uncle-nephew relationship with him, he added, 'Now, whenever I come to Jalandhar, I won't leave without paying my respects to you.'

And he stood up and took out his wallet.

Chacha Fakir Chand took the wallet from his hand and placed it back in his pocket. He mentioned his friendship with Chetan's father, Pandit Shadiram, and his great debts to him and told him that when it came to Chetan's friends, they should consider this factory their own and come whenever they wished.

Feeling much pleased, Hunar Sahib assured him that if he wanted them to hand out any advertisements for Mandi Soda Water Factory, he should think of him; he'd prepare such a great ad in verse that people would be amazed.

And saluting his host with a 'Vande Mataram!' as he pressed his palms together, he stepped down from the shop. His disciples came after him, and Chetan too set off behind them after paying his respects to Chacha Fakir Chand.

25

Chetan again walked along behind his companions, hitching up his pants as before, as he carefully forged a path through the mud of the bazaar. His thoughts strayed from Chacha Fakir Chand to Chowdhry Gujjarmal, Tejpal, Desraj and his father's other friends . . . His father had a thousand faults, but nonetheless, his friends were prepared to do anything for him at the drop of a hat. Chetan wondered if he had any friends like that. And he realized that he did not have even one. There was Anant, but would Anant be willing to do anything for him as Chowdhry Gujjarmal, Lala Tejpal or Chacha Fakir Chand would for his father? When he thought about it, he felt the answer was no . . . But what had he himself done for Anant? Was wandering around together in school and college a sufficient basis for friendship? When Chetan thought about it, he felt perhaps it was not. Perhaps there was more giving and less taking in friendship. Whether it was Gujjarmal or Tejpal, Daulat Ram or Desraj, whether they liked Chetan's father or not, Chetan knew that if they needed something, any one of them could go to his father and he would leave no stone unturned to help them. Perhaps it was this sense that bound Pandit ji's friends to him. They knew in their heart of hearts that all his cursing was superficial, that whatever he owned was all for his friends . . . and dragging his feet through the mud of the bazaar, Chetan felt for the first time jealous of his father, who angered him but also terrified him, and for whom he even felt somewhere in his heart a deep hatred . . . He'd been wandering around since morning. If he'd had any intimate friend with whom he could share his feelings, who could understand his troubles, how much more relieved he'd feel if he could spend the day wandering around aimlessly with him, even if the friend did nothing else . . . but he had no such friend. He was completely alone. He'd seen nothing beyond himself to help him conquer his harsh struggle, and as long as we don't do anything for anyone else, how can we expect them to help us? One friend takes care of you, another helps with money, a third gives love. There's no greater fool than he who wants care in exchange for care from a friend, money for money, or love for love . . . Perhaps Chetan's father wanted nothing from his friends; perhaps he just wanted them to allow him to serve them and when he understood his friends no longer needed him, he avoided them. Now that Gujjarmal and Tejpal had settled down, and become white collar—respectable leaders of their own mohallas—Pandit Shadiram had also moved away from them, keeping company instead with those he could wine and dine, those for whom he could do favours and whose company filled his free time. The strange thing was that he still showed no hesitation in hosting friends who cursed him behind his back, and he knew they cursed him, too. 'I don't hold my hand out to beg from anyone,' he liked to say. 'If you're putting something in someone's hand, don't do it like this,' he'd spread out his hand as though waiting to receive something, 'but like this!'—and he turned his hand over and held his fingers together as though placing something in an outstretched palm.

*

The mud grew even deeper where the bazaar turned towards Mandi. It was as though there was no paved street at all today.

274

The wheels of the bullock carts had furrowed the street terribly. Not only had they formed two deep ruts down the centre, but they'd also gouged the street at other points, and the entire road now resembled a mason's mud pit. Chetan wasn't sure how he'd manage to avoid the mud and get to Mandi Gate. He walked along, placing his feet gingerly in the footprints of the other pedestrians walking back and forth along the sides of the street . . . and then somehow a new side of his father's married life occurred to him . . . His mother was devout, faithful and virtuous, but for the first time it seemed to Chetan that she could be the reason for half his father's profligacy . . . His father had started drinking in his boyhood. He was sociable, generous, a friend of friends. Ma had been raised in a Mishra home. In her religion, everything her husband did was sinful. Since he couldn't cook meat in the house, nor drink, he'd taken to staying out most of the time. His mother had once told Chetan that when she came as a bride, she hadn't allowed meat to be cooked in the house for several years. His father sang very well and he often stopped beggars playing the iktara or the sarangi in the street. After listening to their songs, he'd give them a couple of rupees instead of just a couple of paisas. Sometimes he'd invite the *mirasin*s to sing on festival days and wave money around before giving it to them the way men reward dancers. Ma thought this absolutely terrible. His father liked to sing tales; he'd get excited and belt them out. In Ma's opinion it was unforgivable to have tales sung in a house where there were children and, as soon as his father left, she'd gather up all the tales and lock them in the trunk in the dark hallway in case the children somehow caught a glimpse of them . . . and by the time Ma had figured it out, it was too late. A woman from a less devout home could certainly have straightened him out as the wives of Gujjarmal and Tejpal had . . . Chetan became thoroughly convinced that if Ma had allowed

275

his father to eat meat and drink in the house or if she'd cooked and served the meat herself, then his father wouldn't have gone out and wasted so much money . . . And Chetan was surprised that he'd never looked at his father's life from this perspective before. He'd thought of him as a sinner, a scoundrel, a cruel man, an alcoholic and a gambler, a carouser. But what was there in the house for such an impulsive man? He didn't believe in prayers and worship, fasting and customs and rules—their home must have seemed an enormous void for his art-loving soul, and if he ran out of the house just as soon as he came in, was that surprising? Ma always said that he was only awful towards his family members. The rest of the world had only good things to say about him, because he wined and dined them all, the whole world's children were his children, he treated only his own as though they weren't his . . . But perhaps that wasn't the case . . . If he could just ask his father . . . if his father could tell him—tell him about the mental process of his early married life . . . but it was still difficult for him to speak in front of his father . . . As he slid along in that mud-filled trough that was Mandi, Chetan imagined his devout, devoted mother who placed the greatest faith in fasting and rules, gods and goddesses, sin and virtue, and his uncouth, rowdy, sociable father. He imagined the early days of their married life, and whereas before, his heart only melted for his mother, for the first time a strange compassion welled up in his heart for his father—there must have been such a void inside him to make him always keep his buddies so close.

*

'Jija ji, Jija ji?'

Caught up in his own thoughts, Chetan was walking by Lala Jalandhari Mull's shop, when he started on hearing Ranvir's voice.

Hunar Sahib and his pupil were seated on the front stoop of the shop washing off the grime from their mud-soaked feet and shoes.

'Arré bhai, where were you wandering off to like a man who's blind and deaf? You see no one, you hear nothing,' Hunar Sahib called out.

Chetan turned back, still holding up both his trouser legs.

26

Shri Jalandhari Mull ji 'Yogi' was breathing in and out noisily and Chetan found it hard not to laugh. He got the impression that Yogi ji had sat down on the mat for his breathing exercises merely for their benefit. Downstairs, his accountant had told them that Yogi ji stayed at the shop until one o'clock; after that, he went up to the rooftop room to spend time in thought, reflection and meditation. He wrote down their names on a chit and took it upstairs, then returned and told them, 'Yogi ji is seated on his mat, please either wait here a few minutes, or go and sit quietly on the mattress.' Chetan was all for waiting downstairs, but Hunar Sahib said, 'Come on, let's go and sit upstairs. Then you'll see how when Yogi ji meditates, his lofty thoughts begin to have a spontaneous impact on those sitting near him.'

Hunar Sahib went up the stairs and spoke his name outside the door to announce his arrival. Then Chetan heard swift footsteps inside the room. It's possible he was mistaken, but it sounded to him as though someone had leapt up from somewhere and gone to sit in another spot. Yogi ji's little boy came out of the room and showed them in before going away. As soon as he entered, Chetan saw Yogi ji seated on his mat in the lotus position, breathing heavily.

Hunar Sahib—and Ranvir and Nishtar, following his example—prostrated themselves near Yogi ji's feet like devotees and then sat down on the mattress, and Chetan sat down behind them with his back against the wall. He did not hope for any thought connected to Yogi ji's meditation to pervade his mind spontaneously—at times, his gaze rested on Yogi ji's heavyset body, or his frog-like neck, or his shaven head, or sometimes on the blackish pimple below his nose on the right side of his cheek. And Chetan wondered what his own problem was: Why did he give himself a hard time instead of relaxing? He would have completely avoided coming here, but then again, he was secretly eager to see what 'Sarfarosh ji' looked like as 'Yogi ji', and he thought if there was any opportunity, a discussion might make him feel less dejected.

When he had been a poet, Yogi ji had looked more like a wrestler, and he didn't look any different now. He'd got fatter and his belly protruded. Gazing at his round belly, it occurred to Chetan that perhaps it was in fact this growing mid-section that had inclined him towards yogi-dom.

Chetan didn't put any faith in yogic practice. Since childhood, he'd had his doubts about it, and as there was no learned person in the house to resolve his doubts, and life had not given him the leisure to study this deep and mysterious subject on his own, he always took advantage of any opportunity to discuss it with those more knowledgeable than himself.

As Chetan sat there waiting for Yogi ji's concentration to break, he recalled numerous things he'd heard about yoga in his childhood.

*

Like most of the country's lower middle class people, he'd received some mixture or other of Indian philosophy (which included all sorts of rumours and superstitions from Hindu and Muslim cultures, fused with true knowledge) in his pabulum. From his childhood on, Dada ji had told him tales of rishis and munis—holy men who had attained powers from deep ascetic practices, and who, by performing austerities in Himalayan caves, managed to live for several hundred years . . .

Chetan always wondered how those rishis could live for several hundred years when ordinary people pass away by the time they reach seventy or eighty.

Dada had a simple solution for his doubts: 'On the day a man is born into the world,' he would say, 'Brahma (the Ordainer) fixes the day of his death. An accounting of man's every breath exists in Lord Yama's register and when his breaths are completed, Lord Yama's messengers come and take him away—he doesn't even get to take one breath more. Rishis and munis take as many breaths as the Ordainer has written in their fate, but when they cause their breaths to rise with yogic practice, they don't exhale for weeks, or even months.' And Dada ji would tell him the tale of Maharshi Bhrigu's son, Chyavan Rishi, who had sat in penance with his back against a tree for years and years. His entire body was covered over in grass and leaves, and ants formed an anthill around him. There were only two holes for his eyes in that pile of dirt. Then one day, the daughter of King Sharyati, Sukanya, came that way playing with a girlfriend. Thinking the pile of earth merely an anthill, she stuck a thorn into the hole, poking the rishi right in the eye, and his concentration was broken.

After Chetan grew up, he'd hear about the feats of the yoga-practising rishis and sometimes wonder what the point of such a life was. What's the difference between a life of yoga and death? Sometimes when he'd ask his grandfather such questions, Dada ji would tell him that the rishis and munis, once they'd attained complete mastery over their senses with yogic practices, would immerse their souls in the Supreme Soul, and although their outer eyes were closed during austerities, they opened their inner eyes. They learn the news of the entire world seated in their caves. After all, Sanjay, sitting in Hastinapur, told King Dhritarashtra the entire state of the war in Kurukshetra through the power of yoga alone. They don't just attain complete knowledge of the past and present, but of the future as well. It was these same omniscient rishis who had provided the details of the events to occur during the Kali Yuga, and they went so far as to reveal how many centuries, years, months and days the Kali Yuga would last, and when the end of the world would come. Then Chetan would wonder why the rishis and munis didn't become immortal like God once they subsumed their souls in the Supreme Soul and came to know every little detail about the past and the future; why didn't they attain victory over death?

Sometimes Dada ji would answer this question by telling him that God had kept just this one thing in his control, and he'd add, quoting the Punjabi saying, 'The cat taught the lion, and then the lion came to eat the cat.' And he'd append his own commentary: 'But the cat quickly climbed the tree.' And he'd explain, 'If God did not keep death in his own control, then wouldn't man try to finish God off?' And Dada would tell the story of Bhasma the demon, who pleased the god Shiva by performing severe austerities, and asked as a boon that he be given the power to reduce anyone to ashes by placing his hand on their head. When Shiva granted him the boon, he became determined to reduce Shiva himself to ashes. Shiva took a deep breath and ran. The demon chased him through all three worlds. Then he took refuge with the god Vishnu and told him of his distress. The god Vishnu assumed the guise of Mohini and bewitched the demon, tricking him into placing his hand on his own head, and thus the demon was himself reduced to ashes.

Chetan at once had all sorts of doubts after hearing this story: If God could deceive, then how was he an all-powerful God? He was a deceitful coward. And if Shiva was so powerful, then why didn't he assume the guise of Mohini himself and reduce the demon to ash? Why had he gone running to Vishnu? But he knew what the result would be if he kept poking at Dada ji with his questions. One time he'd called Ram a sneak for covertly killing Bali, and got a slap for that. Dada would never put up with hearing anything said against the deities.

And sometimes, on the topic of the inability of rishis to become immortal, Dada ji would say, 'Who knows how many immortal ascetics are sitting in the caves of the Himalayas right now, or have changed their appearance and are roaming this world! It's written in the Mahabharata that Ashwatthama was immortal; he must certainly be roaming the earth even today in some form or other.'

*

Dada ji was the one who told him about Raja Yoga or the path of meditation, but Ma had told him about Karma Yoga, the path of action, about how God gives good results for good deeds, and bad for bad. Not only does one accrue the results of one's actions in this lifetime, but one enjoys the fruit of the actions of this birth in the next lifetime as well. Those who are kings, rich and prosperous, enjoy themselves due to the merit of the good deeds of their previous birth; and those who are leprous and blemished, those who are born only to die, and those who die in an untimely manner after falling prey to accidents, have earned their deaths in this birth as the fruit of evil deeds in the previous one. And, Ma explained, this is why you should always do good deeds. Who knows what merits accrued through many lifetimes have forced the soul to undergo 84 lakh births before it reaches this human

283

birth! Man must attempt to attain birth for his soul in a human womb yet again, and not get stuck in the 84-lakh cycle.

Chetan would ask her why, if God gives man life and then immediately kills him off, does he give him a human birth at all, why doesn't he just give him some other kind of birth? 'Beta,' Ma would explain, 'this is what we call deepest hell—where the soul rots forever in rivers of blood and pus. A baby lives in blood and pus in its mother's belly anyway.'

'But Ma, the soul is changeless and immortal,' he'd say. 'Fire can't burn it nor water dissolve it. The senses find sorrow; when the senses sleep, then how will the soul find sorrow and how could blood and pus destroy it?'

This was his greatest doubt about Karma Yoga: How could man know whether an action he commits is new, and not just the result of some past action or karma? How can he know where the karma of previous births stops, and that of this life begins?

Ma was not able to give him any satisfying answers to these questions. Sometimes when his father would come home drunk and beat his mother, she'd say that she must have done evil deeds in a previous birth for which she was forced to endure hardships in this one. Chetan would ask, 'Ma, will father reap the fruit of these evil deeds of his in the next birth?' And Ma would cover his mouth with her hand because it was a sin for a son even to think bad thoughts about his father . . .

When he was older, he began going to hear Swami Satyadev's stories at the annual meetings of the Arya Samaj at Adda Hoshiarpur, and started noticing two terms in particular: 'disinterested action' and *moksha* or 'release'. Swami Satyadev's stories would go on for seven days. He was fairly old, but he was quite strong physically—there was dignity to his face and lustre in his voice. People came from far off to hear his stories. Although the girls of the lower middle classes who were mostly shut up in their homes took advantage of this opportunity to show themselves off, and the boys went to see them (and Chetan was no exception), sometimes he'd really listen to what Swami ji was saying, and he'd hear how man cannot rise above the hardships of this world by struggle and austerities, but rather he can cut the bonds of the cycle of death and rebirth by dissolving his soul into the Supreme Soul, and enjoying Supreme Peace. Through both Gyana Yoga, or the path of knowledge, and Karma Yoga, man can free himself from the bonds of life and death. We only achieve this birth through the fruit of the good deeds of previous births. If man undertakes actions attached to desire, he will surely reap the fruits in this life or the next, but if his actions are free of desire, he will not only reap no fruit from this in the next life, but also, the collected karma of previous births will be destroyed and he will attain supreme moksha, or release, becoming free of the cycle of rebirth and hardship.

When he was very young, and the atmosphere in his home was particularly bad, he'd sometimes consider performing severe austerities like Dhruva, and when God was pleased with him, he'd ask for a boon; he'd ask God to fix his father. When he got older and listened to sermons in the sessions of the Arya Samaj about rising above joy and sorrow, he sometimes began to wonder how he could do this as well. But there was no opportunity for yogic practice in their home. And when he got even older, he laughed at such foolish notions. The world had started to look lovely to him, despite the debased atmosphere of his home. He would take one look at Kunti and dissolve into pleasant dreams for days—and then this whole problem of cutting through the cycle of births and attaining moksha started seeming useless to him . . . and he began to wonder why everyone doesn't commit suicide if the world is so sorrowful and this birth in particular so difficult. Who has actually seen the cycle of rebirths? After all, one can't make it through the sorrow of this birth in the blink of an eye. Man cannot understand why bad people are happy and good ones sad—this is what made man imagine the actions of the previous life. When one reaps the fruits of past-life actions in this birth, one would definitely have to be reborn again in order to enjoy the fruits of the actions of this birth. But man can break the evil cycle in this birth itself—just cut the chains of life and become free of its sorrows. In the next birth if God again wants to give sorrow, then do it again. Around that same time he had read a couplet:

Your time for sorrow is now over, life, be happy
Whether or not the cage breaks, I will free you now

He liked this couplet so much that he had hummed it for several days.

His Dada ji always used to say that man will receive in the next birth whatever he was thinking of at the time of death. This is why they recite the Gita and the Ramayana at the bedside of dying men so that they will be focused on God and therefore gain release from the cycle of rebirth and attain moksha, and he told the story of Ajamil who was a great sinner, but when he was dying he called out to his eldest son whose name was Narayan, and just from that simple act, he attained moksha.

This story seemed entirely pointless to Chetan. If God is All-Perceiving, then surely he must know that this bastard is thinking not of me, but of his own son; why then did he free him? But he didn't say this out loud for fear of his Dada's curses. One day, when Dada ji was telling his younger brothers about attaining moksha by becoming free of the sorrows of this lifetime, Chetan had said, 'Dada ji, if this life is full of hardship, then why doesn't man end it? If he wishes never again to take birth as a human at the time of committing suicide, then he won't get that birth. What's the need for spending so many years in yogic practice and austerities when man can cut the bonds of existence in one minute?' He'd said the same thing in the weekly meeting of the Arya Samaj. In both locations he got more or less the same answer: that suicide is a sin. God has given us this birth, and only God has the authority to take it away. Dada ji added that if man commits suicide, then he will enter the womb of a ghost—his soul will not be reborn, nor will it 'attain God'; instead, it will wander about distressed.

But this gave rise to several more questions for Chetan:

How had God given us this birth? One's birth is the fruit of previous births. Karma is committed by man, so why can't he break the cycle?

And if God had given humans birth, then how is it not against his wishes to cut the bonds of the cycle of rebirth and attain moksha through Karma Yoga, or Bhakti Yoga (the spiritual path), and how is that not a sin?

And if God is All-Pervasive, All-Knowing and All-Powerful, then why had he created humans who commit evil deeds—why leave stars in the cosmos that have such an ill effect? And he'd recall Iqbal's couplet:

Agar kaj-rau hai anjum, āsmān terā hai yā merā
Tujhe fikre-jahān kyō ho, jahān terā hai yā merā

If the stars are crooked, is the sky yours or is it mine?
Why do you fret about the world, is it yours or is it mine?

Listening to the words of the Arya Samajis, the Sanatan Dharmis, Dada ji and Ma, he began to have doubts about the very existence of God. God was sometimes a cheater; sometimes a dissembler, sometimes a tyrant; he belonged to the poor, but he gave them endless trouble; he belonged to his devotees, but he gave them troubles as well, and tested them; he was all-powerful and pervasive, but he couldn't run the world properly . . .

Sometimes he'd say all these things to Ma laughingly, and she'd have no response for him, and she'd tell him that he didn't need to think about all this; his job was to attain knowledge, then enter into the householder stage of life and start a family; when he reached fifty years of age, he could do as he wished—he could consider knowledge and meditation, or enter the forest stage of life, or become a renunciant.

*

Chetan kept pondering all his doubts and the thoughts he'd had from childhood up to the present moment that had to do with creation and the Creator, and life, birth and death, and the cycle of rebirth and moksha, and of Raja Yoga and Karma Yoga. In the next room, a child who had quarrelled with someone or received a beating kept screaming '*Bhaiya ji*! *Bhaiya ji*! Brother! Brother!' The child kept coming to the door and whining (Hunar Sahib managed to calm him down with great difficulty and send him back). In the room on the other side could be heard the sound of women quarrelling continuously, but Yogi Jalandhari Mull's eyes remained shut; he was absorbed with supreme concentration in meditation. When he finally opened his eyes after about half an hour, Hunar Sahib got up again and touched his knees (although Yogi ji must have only been a year or so older than Hunar Sahib) and introduced Ranvir and Chetan to him. He knew Nishtar perfectly well, as they'd read poems together at the Congress meetings.

He greeted Chetan from where he sat, slightly meekly, politely, grinning from ear to ear. Then Hunar Sahib said with a smile, 'I was just telling Chetan as we came up the stairs that if Yogi ji happens to be absorbed in meditation, you'll see the wonder of his charisma—people sitting nearby are spontaneously influenced by his virtuous thoughts.'

27

'Ah!' said Jalandhari Mull, quite pleased at Hunar Sahib's remark about the silent influence of his meditation on people sitting nearby. His cheeks spread in a satisfied grin and his jet-black face shone. Then suddenly, he asked Hunar Sahib, 'So what influence did they have on you?'

Chetan found this question exceptionally foolish, but Hunar Sahib replied, grinning back at him, 'I kept thinking about those things you'd told me. I've rendered some verses of the Gita into straightforward Urdu poetry for practice.'

'Great!' Another gleam flashed in Yogi ji's eyes.

'The thing is,' said Hunar Sahib, 'the problems of the Upanishads are very complex; rendering them in simple poetry is like chewing on chickpeas made of iron, so I chose the second chapter of the Gita for practice. If you wish, shall I recite it?'

'Yes, yes . . . certainly, certainly!' Yogi ji assumed the half-lotus pose.

With great zeal, Hunar Sahib recited the same verses he'd already recited to Rudra Sena Arya, Harasaran's father and Chacha Fakir Chand.

Yogi ji was very pleased. Chetan had thought he wouldn't say anything else besides 'Great,' but he freely praised Hunar Sahib and gave a prophetic blessing, to the effect that the Almighty God would surely give him power to render the deep knowledge of the Upanishads into simple Urdu poetry, thus delivering the utmost worth to the people.

Then Chetan scooted forward.

'Yogi ji, you were fairly prominent in the Congress movement,' he said. 'What happened to alienate you from service to the nation? I've heard you haven't gone to any Congress meetings in years. Did you truly experience great hardships in jail?'

Chetan had apparently caused him some distress. But Yogi ji was not perturbed. 'Jail is not your sister's home, bhai,' he answered carefully. 'But it wasn't as if I was given too much trouble by others. We didn't get newspapers or political books to read in jail. By chance, I studied religious texts, and for the first time I got the sense that in this vast universe man's existence isn't equal to even one thousandth of a particle—who does man really think he is? Who knows how many worlds like ours there are in this cosmos, and in the boundless immensity of creation, who knows how many more cosmoses there might be? There are suns thousands of times larger than our sun, and stars millions of times greater than our earth. When the existence of our earth alone is like a particle in this vast creation, what is man's existence really? And then, who knows how many times this earth has been settled and destroyed over the course of time, or how many times God has created it, and how many times destroyed it? How many golden ages have come and how many iron ages? And then, the pride of individuals, castes and nations—how false it all is! Why doesn't man attempt to attain truth instead of running after that fallacy, and having attained it, why not maintain an ambition for moksha?'

'Remarkable! How beautifully you've made clear the fallacy of man's ego!' praised Hunar Sahib.

Yogi ji continued, warming to his subject:

'Truth, or the soul, or Brahma, or mankind—these things are referred to in the Upanishads by several names—are all different names for the same power, the same shakti, from which creation grew, and into which it will again be subsumed. Gaining this power, which spreads to every particle of creation even if it is not visible, and attaining it, is the greatest pleasure. That Brahma is not only the creator of every particle of this creation, that he is not only the source of all consciousness, but he is also the source of the highest bliss. These perceivable objects of the world are finite forms of that power with no beginning—unseen and unending; so too, the joys of the world form an unbroken link with the true highest bliss. That wise man who plunges into the depths of his soul and finds it, attains not only Brahma, but also the highest bliss, which should be the goal of every wise man!'

'Wah wah! Wonderful!' praised Hunar Sahib. 'You've expressed something so deep in such simple language!'

Yogi ji began to speak even more zealously, 'Rishi Yagyavalkya had explained to his wife, Maitreyi, that the soul is the source of all joys, and that the result is that the thing most dear to man is self-respect. Man loves another man or a thing because he sees self-respect in it. The wife is not beloved because she is the wife; nor is the husband beloved because he's the husband; nor is the son beloved because he is the son; nor wealth, because wealth is wealth: these are all beloved because they are "mine"! "I"—the soul—is bound to all of these. So then, instead of grabbing at these manifold forms of the soul, these manifold parts of joy, why doesn't man know that source of joy without beginning, without end, that imperishable source; why doesn't he grab hold of it and why doesn't he find the highest joy on attaining it?

293

'In order to understand the state of supreme peace,' said Jalandhari Mull with even greater zeal, 'imagine the sort of sleep that is devoid of dreams, in which man has no knowledge of the body, the senses, the mind, nor of external objects—of nothing—and he departs in this form, which is the wellspring of his consciousness. He attains supreme peace. He exists beyond joy and sorrow.'

Yogi ji was delivering his sermon with full force, when the stark naked child came running in, perhaps in an attempt to escape his older brother, and plopped down in Yogi ji's lap. Yogi ji finished his sermon, lifted the child from his lap and pushed him towards the door. The child turned back once, but there was something about Yogi ji's look that made him go away.

Then Hunar Sahib piped up, 'But you have attained the highest knowledge, Yogi ji, you must surely have attained this state in your soul!'

'No, no, my friend.' Yogi ji smiled politely in a way that made it apparent that he had in fact attained that state in his soul but he didn't want to come out and say so. 'What is achievable in the world of consciousness? In the world of consciousness man strays so far from the soul that rediscovering that condition—that supreme joy, that supreme peace—becomes difficult. It is not so simple to stray far from the soul, then return and dissolve into it. One requires deep knowledge, perseverance and yogic practice.'

Yogi Jalandhari Mull stopped for a moment, then spoke again. 'Hunar Sahib, why does this world seem lovely after all? Why does life seem so enchanting to us?'

He stopped for a moment to hear Hunar Sahib's response, but Hunar Sahib looked up at him like an idiot, as if to say, 'Sire, please tell us!'

Then Yogi ji continued joyfully, 'It's because our soul gets some bliss or other from this world, from this life. But sorrow plays no small part in this life, so sometimes we are badly wounded by the hardships of the world. Now, imagine a situation in which there is no sorrow alongside joy, a condition that is beyond joy and sorrow—one that is filled with the highest peace: a dreamless sleep. In order to attain this, we must surrender the false pleasures of this world, we must control our senses and we must dissolve ourselves in the soul. That soul, which is part of Brahma himself, which is dispersed throughout the world. To become one with the soul, to attain moksha by cutting the bonds of life and death, that is to attain the feeling of supreme bliss . . . and this isn't possible for everyone, only a specialist in yoga can attain that supreme bliss by rising above desires, sorrows and joy through yogic practice.'

'But Yogi ji,' laughed Chetan, 'in the old days, when knowledge had not made so much progress, man needed to suppress the senses and engage in difficult yogic practice in order to attain such a state, but nowadays, man can attain that supreme peace with an injection of morphine—to attain that supreme peace of deep sleep, in which there are no dreams.'

Yogi ji was stunned for a moment, then he smiled contemptuously. 'Whether or not that state can be achieved via morphine, I cannot say, but those taking morphine cannot just enter the conscious world whenever they wish. As long as the effect of morphine holds, man will not attain peace, whereas with Gyana Yoga, man, despite engaging in worldly tasks, rises above his worries regarding joy and sorrow. The greatest wise man and the greatest yogi will remain in the state of peace with or without meditation. He performs all tasks free of desires and with no expectations of good and ill consequences, and thus he is released from the cycle of death and rebirth.'

If Yogi ji were giving this speech from a stage, then Hunar Sahib would have risen and burst into spontaneous applause; but instead, adopting the pose of a supremely satisfied devotee, he pleased Yogi ji by crying out, 'Wah wah! Wonderful!' And this time, Ranvir and Nishtar praised him as well. But the moment he fell silent, Chetan laughed out loud.

'None of this seems accurate to me, Yogi ji,' he said. 'I haven't read as many religious texts as you have, but I have heard many, and to me, nothing is apparent besides self-deception. You say that there is only one soul that pervades all beings, and you also say that when we love other things, it's because we find self-respect in them, but then how is it that all of creation, whether beast or bird, will swallow one another down with the greatest impartiality? Can anyone consume their own body?'

Yogi ji laughed, 'That is the illusion of Brahma, my friend. To the unknowing one, it appears that one person is consuming another, or one beast another, or one bird another, but the wise man knows that the being that has emerged from Brahma is also contained in Brahma. This is the illusion of God. Didn't the god Krishna in the Gita ask who is the killer and who is being killed?'

'Then why has God done this?' asked Chetan. 'If no one kills anyone, then why are robbers and murderers hanged, and why are practitioners of yoga commanded to avoid "violence"? To me, God seems neither all-powerful, nor just, nor all-knowing. I see no truth in the cycle of rebirth nor in the fruits of karma. All these philosophies appear to me to be the marvels of man's limited intelligence and his fear of death. If God is all-powerful, then why did he create this topsy-turvy world full of violence, hatred, sorrow and pain? If he created it for his own enjoyment, then sin and merit mean nothing at all, man works according to his limited intelligence, customs and environment. Since man doesn't wish to die, he likes to imagine the next life; when those doing good deeds meet with hardship, and then he understands that he must surely have committed bad deeds in his previous life, because in this life he's only doing good deeds, and he thinks that in the next birth, he will most certainly attain the rewards for his good deeds.'

Just then the naked child came sniffling and whining to the doorway, and cried out, 'Brother, brother!'

Forgetting all his self-control and peace, Yogi Jalandhari Mull ji screamed, 'Get out of here!' and, flinging a vulgar Punjabi curse at the child's mother, he called out to her to come and take him away. The next instant, a fat, coarse woman came and dragged the child off. Then, Yogi ji turned back and continued as though nothing had happened, ignoring his question, 'If there is no God then who is responsible for creation? If there is creation then there must be someone doing the creating as well.'

'Then why wouldn't there be someone creating the creator?' laughed Chetan.

'But God, who is the creator of creation, who is without beginning or end, who is all-powerful, all-pervasive—who will create him?'

'Who says he has all those qualities?' asked Chetan.

'Those rishis who came to know the secret of the cosmos through the power of their yoga discovered the movement of the stars; they were the ones who also discovered God,' said Yogi ji.

'But isn't it possible,' laughed Chetan mischievously, 'that by the end of the last age, man had made as much progress as he's making now? He used science to find out about the stars and he learned the secret of the cosmos and then, because of some natural disaster, or because of some evil deed of his own, the world was destroyed, water flooded the land, and where there had been water, dry land emerged, and a few men were saved

297

somewhere on earth, and they remembered that knowledge and that knowledge came to us orally. If there was a God who created this cosmic game, I could never call him just. I see justice nowhere in nature. It runs on blind impulse just as the earth spins. Justice and injustice, joy and sorrow, merit and sin, good and bad—it's man who weighs all these things, and I believe that man should stop worrying about previous births and coming births, and instead develop a new religion that makes this birth better, happier, more just and more peaceful, and that he can only do this with the help of his mind, having learned from his previous experiences, and observing the life around him; he can't accomplish that absorbed in meditation, believing this world to be an illusion.'

Yogi ji stared at him for a few minutes silently, then he said, 'You're an atheist!'

Chetan burst out laughing. Hunar Sahib put his hand on his shoulder and tried to stop him from speaking further, but his mind was racing after being bored for so long.

'It's not a question of whether I'm a believer or an atheist,' he said. 'I just see a lot of conflict in what I've heard and what I've read. On the one hand, you have a yogi who has attained the soul, who has attained Brahma; he's protected himself from untruth, from violence, from theft, from non-asceticism and the greed for wealth. He's suppressed his senses, and attained God by means of bodily purity, satisfaction, devotion, study, reflection and thought. On the other hand, in Karma Yoga there is no need for this restraint. What's necessary is to perform deeds free from desire. If you are free from desire in your actions, you can slaughter people by the thousands and millions, and you can do so by any means necessary—lies, tricks and deceit. This was the sermon Krishna gave Arjun when Arjun hesitated to take up arms after seeing his kinsmen before him on the field of battle. Do you think that in the battle of the Mahabharata there was no lust for wealth, or land, or fame on the Pandavas' side? And do you believe that when Jayadratha killed Abhimanyu, Arjun wasn't saddened, and that when Arjun slayed Jayadratha, he had no desire to slay? If desire is removed from action then more than half of the motivation for performing an action is finished, and perhaps the fun as well. You do business, don't you?' Chetan asked suddenly, interrupting himself.

Yogi ji nodded his head in agreement.

'Don't you have to lie? Don't you take six annas for something worth four?'

'But I'm a businessman. It's my duty to do business. I continue to try to do that work which I've been given by God, free of desire, without worrying about good or ill consequences . . . and then on turning fifty, I will be freed of all this.'

Chetan laughed out loud.

'You have some sorrow and remorse,' Yogi ji said suddenly. 'You have no faith in God or the Dharma Shastras, and without taking refuge in God, you won't find peace. Sorrow and suffering are written in the fate of the atheist and the un-knower.' A flash of anger came into Yogi ji's voice, 'You should meet my guru, Shri Swami Apurvanand; you will benefit both in terms of knowledge and of peace.'

'I will get knowledge from Swami Apurvanand but these millions of other people—what of them?' laughed Chetan. 'Not everyone can acquire knowledge; people seldom find God, but in the effort to do so, they are abandoning dependence on God considering this world a dream, an illusion and a falsehood. The result is that we've been slaves for centuries, our mortality rate is highest among all the nations—lack of education, poverty and hunger hold sway, and people are engrossed in contemplating the highest meaning—in their concern for the next world, they've forgotten about this one. Who knows if they'll find happiness or not in the next world, but they certainly will find sorrow in this one. And our wise men, instead of focusing their attention on those problems, are absorbed in contemplating Brahma.'

Yogi ji acted as though he hadn't heard him. Suppressing his anger with great effort, he said calmly, 'Do meet Swami Apurvanand, you will definitely find peace.'

'I'm definitely unpeaceful,' said Chetan. 'But neither can I turn my face away from the world nor can I give up desire. My attention is neither directed at my previous birth nor the next one. I want to make this birth successful and happy. My circumstances aren't favourable, the atmosphere is not good, but I'll make my way through this one. It may take me a while, but I'll find my way.'

'But your Mahatma Gandhi is a worshipper of the Gita. He has complete faith in Karma Yoga.'

'I've not met Mahatma Gandhi,' laughed Chetan. 'And then, when did I say that everything in our philosophy is nonsense? Gandhi may have extracted some kernels of truth, whereas other wise men are just gathering up straw . . . Okay, well, bye!'

Hunar Sahib told him to sit down once, but when Chetan said he'd been out since morning and had to go now, he didn't insist. It was his duty to smooth the wrinkles that had appeared on Yogi ji's forehead from his conversation with Chetan, because Chetan had come with him. And he had to make some arrangements for the evening's tea after bringing up the topic of translation of the Upanishads. Besides this, he'd brought the files from *Widows' Aid* to show him too . . . When Chetan stood, he stood as well, but he didn't go to the door. He took Chetan's hand in both of his and pressed it with great affection while smiling, and said they'd go by Lala Govindaram's in the evening; he was trying to put together a poetry reading . . . if possible, he'd see him later in the evening.

Chetan said neither 'yes' nor 'no', shook his hand and left.

Evening

Evening

28

As Chetan walked through Mandi Bazaar as far as the station, his mind was caught up in thoughts of the soul and the Supreme Soul, happiness and peace, joy and the Greatest Joy, Gyana Yoga and Karma Yoga. Stopping for a moment at the tonga stand, he glanced around to see if any were going to Panjpir or Adda Hoshiarpur, but a train must have been pulling in, as all the tonga drivers were lined up at the stand—they'd already seated a couple of passengers and were looking for others. Not one tonga was tricking the officers and straying from the stand. Chetan quietly turned down Station Road. Although there was quite a bit of mud in the middle of this street as well, pedestrians had created a relatively hard footpath along the side. He let the legs of his pants fall loose and set out slowly.

*

He'd stopped in the middle of the street and guffawed loudly after emerging from Lala Jalandhari Mull's shop. He felt a childish glee at purposefully needling him and destroying his effortful pose of peace . . . . 'Goddammmmn yogi!' he said to himself. 'A few days in jail beat all the patriotism out of him and he set himself up as a philosopher.' A line from a couplet he'd heard years ago at a baitbaazi match in the *pona* at the Harivallabh Festival flashed in his mind and he smiled. "'If this monkey got his hands on a knot of ginger, he'd set up a dry goods shop" . . . Jalandhari Mull ji, "Sarfarosh"—the brave one—*The longing for sacrifice is now in our hearts* . . . Jalandhari Mull ji "Yogi"—the man who fuses his soul with the Supreme Soul and rises above joy and sorrow, thus attaining Supreme Bliss; supremely patient; unperturbed; the fully detached renunciant; he who influences others' minds silently . . . hahaha . . . '

But despite chuckling, he wasn't able to shake the topic from his head. Lala Jalandhari Mull was more of a fraud and less of a yogi, but was there no truth at all to his philosophy? That philosophy had influenced not just Indians, but foreigners as well; why was he the only one who had no faith in it?

When Chetan thought about it, he realized that his extremely religious home environment was the reason for this, as well as his education at Arya Samaj institutions. His Dada was not only a devotee of Chandi, but also a worshipper of Shiva, and according to custom he worshipped all the other gods and goddesses as well. He would only touch food to his mouth after intoning the hymn to Chandi for two and a half hours. His mother read the Gita with the same reverence with which she read Lallu Lal's *Prem Sagar.* For her, that text was not some social or personal philosophy but a part of daily religious observance. She believed that reading these books was a virtuous activity and that one attained liberation from doing so daily. What did she understand of the Gita's shlokas and their deep philosophy, Gyana Yoga and Karma Yoga! She just read the stories that came with each chapter. It gave her great joy to learn from those chapters who crossed over the ocean of life, and since she'd seen nothing but hardship in this world, she liked those stories very much. But Chetan didn't see any difference between the story of Satya Narayan (which was recited at his home every night of the full moon) and the stories in her books. The kind of logical thinking he learned from studying at an Arya Samaj school taught him that all those stories were entirely untrue—the difference between Gyana Yoga and Bhakti Yoga that he could see in the sections of the Gita and the popular versions his mother read . . . although not everyone is capable of understanding the subtle differences between Gyana Yoga and Karma Yoga, those versions had been added in so that ordinary people would be influenced by the deep philosophy after reading those shlokas again and again. The ordinary man doesn't understand what the soul is, but from reading the Gita again and again, he learns that the soul is immortal, indivisible and unburnable; it cannot be made wet, nor can it be dried, and thus the fear of death is lessened somewhat in the minds of ordinary people. What is attachment and what is desire, and how can man become free of desires? Perhaps ordinary people aren't able to understand such things, but from reading the Gita again and again, they begin to understand that they should perform just actions without worrying about the fruits of their labour . . . But how can an ordinary person find peace? How can he produce desire from detachment? These are things he can't understand, but he can gain some sort of understanding of the idea that anger gives rise to a foolish feeling of bewilderment; that it destroys the powers of thinking and understanding . . . Chetan knew several shlokas by heart that he'd heard from Ma again and again . . . but where Ma found peace from reading them over and over, Chetan found confusion.

As a child, when he used to listen to the story of the Gita from Ma, he had understood it to be literally true and could imagine it all—the battlefield of Kurukshetra, the armies of the Kauravas and the Pandavas, Arjun's chariot, Arjun gripped by confusion on seeing his relations and teachers before him—the son of Kunti setting down the Gandiva bow and Krishna delivering his sermon.

307

But as he grew older, the incident began to sound completely untrue to him. The Kauravas and the Pandavas must have existed, and the Mahabharata war must certainly have occurred between them, but it seemed impossible that Krishna would have stopped his chariot in the middle of the two armies and provided Arjun with all that knowledge found in the Gita. In that situation there was a need for at least a second chapter: Krishna could reveal his splendid form, but the Raja Yoga, Gyana Yoga and Bhakti Yoga, was all that necessary there? Ma considered Krishna to be God, and every word he said seemed true to her, but Chetan didn't like Krishna becoming a god and giving Arjun a sermon about how he should follow the shastras and observe the caste system. Under the influence of the Arya Samaj, Chetan had begun to feel a deep sympathy for Shudras. If the caste system was correct, then all that knowledge was forbidden to the poor Shudras. They were born only to serve, and generation after generation were fated to pass their lives in the deep darkness of ignorance. How could God have given a sermon about all this . . . and within Vibhuti Yoga, there were several such things that he had heard or read which he absolutely didn't understand. At one point, Krishna said, 'Among deceitful practices, I am gambling.'

'How can God say this?' he'd asked Ma. Then Ma read him the commentary that said God is infused in all the beings and objects in the world: high, medium and low—all of them—and all move only by the power of God. There is not one thing that is devoid of the power of God. God's divinity and power develop in a special way in all types of sattvic, rajasic and tamasic beings and objects, thus giving them special qualities, special influences and wonders.

But this explanation seemed contradictory to Chetan. God is diffused in all beings and that special quality in them contains a particular expansion of his power. Why this favouritism from

God? But poor Ma, what response could she give? To her, even his making this argument felt like a sin.

Chetan had read that entire chapter and the whole thing seemed full of incongruities and contradictory statements . . . God was not just gambling among deceitful acts, he was also the lion among beasts and the crocodile among amphibious creatures. He was Krishna among the Yadavs and Arjun among the Pandavas (how Krishna himself could say this was beyond his comprehension); among horses, he was Ucchaishravas, Airavat among the elephants, and king among men (Chetan objected deeply to this last bit. A Brahmin with royal patronage could say such a thing, but not God) . . . and then among munis he was both Kapil and Ved Vyas (this last bit seemed quite laughable to him).

But when he grew older, he learned that the incident described in the Gita had never occurred anywhere; Maharshi Ved Vyas had used this incident to insert the essence of the Upanishads into the Gita, and in order to make that knowledge comprehensible, he had made use of that particular incident . . . and then, if the poet Ghalib could consider himself a saint, then why couldn't the poet Ved Vyas become God? Ghalib had praised Mir. Ved Vyas praised Kapil (through the mouth of God).

And that was said by the Maharshi who had given the sermon about rising above the ego. Chetan suddenly smiled as he walked along trying to avoid the mud in the street, his thoughts all tangled up in the chapters of the Gita. Actually, the education he'd received in the Arya Samaj school and college had shaken terribly the Sanatan Dharma beliefs he'd learned from Dada ji and Ma. It's impossible to grasp the entire teaching of the Gita without believing in Krishna as an incarnation of God, but he didn't believe Krishna was an incarnation of God. In his father's words, he could consider him a great man, but he didn't believe that he was God and that he'd taken that incarnation to improve dharma due to its degradation . . .

The Arya Samaj did not believe in gods and goddesses, nor in virtuous reverence, nor in Bhakti or Vibhuti Yoga, but they had the highest faith in Gyana Yoga and Karma Yoga and Raja Yoga (the essential forms of the Upanishads) . . . but by that logic, Chetan also didn't believe in the values he'd got from the Arya Samaj. The Arya Samaj had the highest faith in the soul, the Supreme Soul, the cycle of death and rebirth and moksha. But there was nothing about these that seemed true to Chetan, that could be completely unobjectionable. Krishna himself says in the Gita:

> *Atha cainaṃ nityajātaṃ nityaṃ vā manyase mṛtam*
> *Tathāpi tvaṃ mahābāho naivaṃ śocitumarhami*
> *Jātasya hi dhruvomṛtyurdhruvaṃ janma mṛtasya ca*[10]

If, however, you think that the soul is perpetually born
    and always dies,
still you have no reason to lament, O mighty-armed one,
For he who has taken birth, death is certain; and for he
    who is dead,
rebirth is certain

But if Chetan had been in Arjun's place, he'd have said, 'Not only do I not believe in the immortality of the soul, I don't even believe

---

[10] Ashk's quotation has some errors. The original reads:
Atha cainaṃ nityajātaṃ nityaṃ vā manyase mṛtam
Tathāpi tvaṃ mahābāho nainaṃ śocitumarhasi
Jātasya hi dhruvo mṛtyur dhruvaṃ janma mṛtasya ca.
—*trans.*

310

in the existence of the soul.' He'd read again and again in the Gita that only 'one unusual philosopher among thousands, among millions, attains that soul, that Brahma,' . . . but who knows if he will actually attain it? Perhaps he understands that he's got it. Jesus, Mohammad, the Buddha, all of them got it, but there's such a difference between all of their beliefs. And in his moments of agnosticism, Chetan could find no path at all.

*

As far as Karma Yoga was concerned, Chetan did not understand how man could act, free of desire, and still be successful. Chetan felt that anger, which is said in the Gita to destroy intelligence, had a huge amount of power. Instead of confusing the memory and destroying the intelligence, it sharpened the flow of memory and fine-tuned the intellect. If God was gambling among deceitful practices, a lion among beasts and a crocodile among amphibious creatures, then among passions, he was most definitely anger— Chetan believed this. The question was really which type of anger. The creator of the Gita had not created a classification for the types of anger. Anger could be in one's self-interest, but it could also be for the highest good; it could be both moral and immoral; it could be both wrong and right. It could be that wrong, immoral and self-interested anger might create a foolish mood and destroy intelligence, but that which is called 'righteous anger' in English doesn't destroy the intellect, it makes it keener; this is what Chetan understood. It was said of Mahatma Gandhi that he was the great Karma Yogi of the age, but if on witnessing the crushing of enslaved Indians at the hands of English power, he hadn't felt distress (which is another form of anger), if the fire of anger had not ignited silently inside him, Chetan was not prepared to accept that without that distress, he would have been able to apply all his powers of wisdom to the foreign government with such devotion.

In Chetan's opinion, it wasn't just a question of anger, but of unjust versus just anger. And these two types of anger, appropriate or inappropriate, just or unjust, were linked with right and wrong action. The creator of the Gita got away with saying that 'great philosophers have gotten all turned about in deciding which actions are appropriate and which are not'. But it seemed to Chetan that the correct form of yoga lay in making this decision, not in fleeing from it and remaining calm . . . One time a British traffic inspector had called his father a 'damn fool', and his father had slapped him hard across the face. The TI had suspended him right then and there. Chetan's father's overwhelming anger was given something to zero in on with all his intelligence. In those days, when it was an offence even to speak loudly in front of the British, he had fought for himself and won. That TI was transferred from his line. 'If you are in the right,' his father used to say, 'then have no fear, God has given you intelligence, use it, dig in your heels with all your might. You will surely win.' And Chetan preferred this lesson over the lesson given by Ma, and he had used it to form a philosophy for himself. It was not the philosophy of the Gita. Perhaps it was half-baked and riddled with errors, but it was the one Chetan liked best. He had given it the title, 'Neo-Karma Yoga'. According to this philosophy, it was necessary for the practitioner of Karma Yoga to first decide whether his side of any matter was true or false, just or unjust, moral or immoral. Self-criticism would give one the power to evaluate one's own side, and when one had come to a decision (if one found one's self on the side of truth), one should apply one's self to defending that side with all one's power, making use of strong resentment, and just, unstoppable anger, and not cease until one is successful . . . '*Hope for the best and be prepared for*

312

the worst' his father always used to say in English, and according to this precept, he had taken from the Gita the message that one should not worry about the cycle of rebirth, one should try one's very hardest to succeed, but at the same time, one should also be prepared for failure.

He was not attracted by serenity, self-knowledge, knowledge of the Almighty and moksha—he was only attracted by this modern, Neo-Karma Yoga of his, and whenever he thought about it, this seemed much more difficult that the Karma Yoga of the Gita. Seeing inaction in action and action in inaction, becoming free of attachment and desire and presenting all of one's karma to God seemed just as difficult to him as learning to distinguish between good and bad actions and anger appropriate to justice and injustice. To him, it didn't seem possible to attain the sort of wisdom that would enable one to distinguish between lawful and unlawful karma without falling prey to self-deception. He was of the opinion that the true nature of yoga lay in arriving at the conclusion important philosophers labour mightily to determine. This type of wisdom can only be attained by continually examining one's feelings, one's psychology, one's karma with impartial emotions and by creating the power of self-criticism. Once one has realized that the act one plans to undertake is right and just, it seemed best to him to approach it with a fire free of anger, completely cool, but continually blazing in order to accomplish it and find success in it. He didn't believe in the slightest that one could meet with failure if one had realized all this and exerted the full power of mind and body. But he wouldn't worry about that, that much he had borrowed quite liberally from the creator of the Gita . . . 'Some day, I'll create a new Gita with this modern karma and yoga,' he said to himself, 'but before this I should read the Gita commentaries of Mahatma Gandhi and

Mahatma Tilak. I should read the Upanishads too from some authoritative account and I should also learn the beliefs of the Western philosophers on this topic . . .'

*

'*The Bombay Cat* . . . an amazing film from the Imperial Film Company . . . the bewitching acting of the Queen of Beauty, Miss Madhuri . . .'

Chetan lifted his gaze—the poet Hardayal was walking by, wearing a high three-cornered hat and jokers' attire, bell in hand, handing out posters for a new film, followed by some boys shouting out slogans and holding up posters for *The Bombay Cat* stuck to a bamboo frame. They'd probably just been all around the city, and now that they'd reached the cinema hall, they'd started shouting with renewed enthusiasm. Hardayal was tall, with sharp features, and wore ankle-length pyjamas, a kameez, a coat, and a turban with a tail in front. The past eight years had not changed the poet Hardayal a bit, and Chetan recollected how he used to listen to Hardayal's baits during the baitbaazi in the pona at the Harivallabh Festival when he studied in Class Eight, and how these words would appear at the beginning of every final line of his poems:

Hardayal prepared this bait . . .

As Hardayal's group entered the cinema hall, Chetan followed them in.

29

Just beyond the ceiling-height metal doors operated by pulleys at the bazaar entrance of the cinema hall was a large room, which was also fitted with an identical set of metal doors, and beyond that there was a long gallery alongside the pavilion which housed the one-rupee, twelve-anna, eight-anna and four-anna ticket classes. When this cinema hall had only been a tin pavilion, and travelling theatre companies used to come here to put on plays, the entryway had been at the rear, at the gali side. On that side, there was a yard that opened out from the pavilion and the ticket booth; but the new owner of the cinema hall (actually, the owner was the same, but the lease-holder was new) had opened the gate on the bazaar side, as this made it easier to get the crowd in. The office was on the other side, but the proprietor placed an armchair in the passageway and sat there in the evenings. He was thin, with a gentlemanly smile and a complexion the colour of wheat, and he wore an elegant suit. Just a few years ago, Chetan and Hamid had got together and really made a fool of him, and Chetan had gone to the movies daily for almost an entire year for free. He had even found out about Chetan's prank, but wasn't able to do anything about it (and this was certainly due to his gentlemanliness). Chetan smiled when he thought of the incident, and decided he'd go up to the front for a bit—perhaps he'd find Lala Mohan Lal in the office or outside the pavilion and pay his respects.

*

The incident when Chetan had tricked Lala Mohan Lal was from those days when Chetan had first met Hamid, and written to Meenakshi Ramarao for her picture and presented it to an astonished Hamid, and articles by Chanda Devi 'Kumud' had started appearing in famous film magazines. For Chetan, the greatest difficulty in writing articles about films had been that his entire knowledge of the cinema was limited only to what he'd read in newspapers and magazines. He wasn't able to save up even a four-anna piece to watch a movie. He got only one anna per day as pocket money; because he ate breakfast early in the morning, then walked more than three miles to college, he'd get hungry in the afternoon, and after eating two paisas' worth of barfi out of that one anna, he'd drink two paisas' worth of sweet (but thin) lassi. Hamid had asked him to go to the movies a couple of times, but he had put him off. Then one day, when his father had come to Jalandhar, his pockets had been full and he was in a good mood, so he'd handed out four-anna pieces to all of his sons. The next evening, after his father left, Chetan had told Hamid that he had four annas—if Hamid could watch a movie with him sitting in the four-anna seats, they could go.

Hamid had said that only the world's nobodies and nothings sit in the four-anna seats, and one's eyes can be ruined watching a movie that close, but okay, let's go; for you, we'll go ahead and sit in the four-anna seats.

It was a Sulochna and D. Bilimoria[11] picture. The first scene was etched forever in Chetan's mind: D. Bilimoria is wearing

---

[11] A famous actor in the era of silent films.

a military uniform, and stands with his elbows resting on the railing of the deck of a ship, watching the ocean; the ship is about to dock in the harbour of Bombay; birds circle above the ship . . . suddenly a slip of paper comes flying towards him and lands in his hand. It is a letter. He looks up: Sulochna stands on the other side of the deck. She had been reading that letter, when the breeze swept it from her hand. She comes to retrieve her letter. Their eyes meet and they become lost in one another's gazes . . . after this, Chetan didn't remember what happened. There was some villain who starts pursuing Sulochna on board the ship and carries her off. D. Bilimoria chases them . . . there's a car chase . . . a fight . . . and in the end, the happy reunion of the hero and heroine. . . .

And Chetan had been infatuated with Sulochna from that day on. At first, he'd only seen her in film magazines, but watching her on the cinema screen made his heart beat faster. When they came outside after the movie, Hamid had said, 'Come on, let's go tell Mohan Lal ji to order some good films. What are all these fight movies he's ordering?'

Although Chetan had liked the film very much, and it had seemed to him that Hamid was just being a snob, he didn't argue. 'Who is Mohan Lal?' was all he asked.

'He's the owner.'

'You know him?'

'Yes! I always discuss the merits of the films with him when I come.'

Hamid spoke English fluently. He always stood first in college debates and he didn't feel the slightest hesitation in conversation. Mohan Lal had got up from his chair and started to stroll about when the film had ended. It was his habit to arrive just a bit before the film began. After it started, he'd go and sit inside on some empty first-class sofa, or he'd walk home, or to the bazaar. Then, after the first show was over, and the second was beginning, he'd return.

'By the way, why don't you get films like *Kanthahar*?' Hamid stopped him and asked in English.

'*Kanthahar*! I haven't even heard of that,' said Mohan Lal, smiling simply.

Actually, in the new issue of *Film Land* (which Chetan subscribed to), there was much praise for the film *Kanthahar*. The famous Bengali hero of silent pictures, Durga Das, acted in it. He looked so handsome to Chetan and Hamid that they were now quite eager to see him on the big screen. They didn't understand that the movies discussed in *Film Land* were Bengali films, and the title wasn't pronounced *Kanthāhār* but *Kanthahār*; but in the same way that they couldn't pronounce Kumud properly and wrote Kumad instead, they said *Kanthāhār* instead of *Kanthahar*. They didn't understand these things, but then Mohan Lal didn't either. He told Hamid he must certainly inform him about good movies so he could order them.

Then Hamid introduced Chetan to him saying he knew quite a bit about the movies, and his wife Mrs Chanda Devi 'Kumud', BA, wrote for film magazines.

'Really!' Shri Mohan Lal held out his hand to Chetan and asked, 'Where did she do her BA?' (Because in Jalandhar, even the boys' degree college had only opened that year.)

Chetan had no definite answer to give. He blanched. But Hamid didn't miss a beat. 'At Women's College, Lahore,' he said. And then in the same breath he added, 'Chetan is an Urdu poet, and his stories are printed in all the newspapers in Lahore. You should have him write your handbill.'

'Yes, yes. Certainly . . . certainly!' said Mohan Lal eagerly.

And the two friends shook hands with him and went on their way.

*

'Yaar, now you've put an end to my ever coming for four annas,' complained Chetan as they stepped out on to the street.

'Why?' asked Hamid.

'How could a guy whose wife is a BA and graduate of Women's College, Lahore, buy a four-anna seat to watch a picture!'

'Arré, you write an awesome advertisement for him. He'll let you in for free.' And he guffawed loudly.

At the end of Station Road, Chetan parted from Hamid, his mind racing with the thought that he could watch a few movies for free by just writing an advertisement. But what difference did that make? Even he could afford to see a picture now and then (albeit only from the four-anna seats). But if only he could cook up some scheme whereby he could watch movies whenever he wanted. After some thought, he hit upon a plan to befriend Shyam Babu before making friends with Lala Mohan Lal. Lala Shyam Kishore was the owner of the pavilion that Lala Mohan Lal had rented and turned into a cinema hall. He had a famous litho press on Station Road by the name of 'Shyam Press'. Shyam Kishore might no longer be living, but he had two sons: they were of medium height, fair and chubby, and both wore glasses. The elder of the two was called Big Shyam Babu and the younger was called Small Shyam Babu. Chetan had even met the younger brother. In his first year, he'd got together with Hunar Sahib and written a collection under the title *An Evening's Journey*. They'd gone to the press to ask the price for printing it. How could he expand upon

319

such a slight acquaintance? Chetan pondered this question all the way home.

*

And in just a month, Chetan had come up with an arrangement for watching films for free.

*

In those days, Chetan, under the name of Chanda Devi 'Kumud', was in regular correspondence with the editors of several film magazines. G.R. Oberoi, the editor of a Lahore magazine, not only sent him free magazines, but had also given him a book on film scenarios, and several times had expressed a desire to meet (which Chetan put off quite clearly). He'd also begun to receive a magazine by the name of *Movie Mirror*, and he was engaged in serious correspondence with a film writer who had got the scenario of a short story by Chanda Devi 'Kumud' published . . . Chetan continued to engage in all this letter writing, but his attention was focused on another problem twenty-four hours a day: how to find a way to watch movies without paying for a ticket. In those days, there was an inter-college poetry reading competition at Government College, Hoshiarpur. A professor from Chetan's college had gone, and he'd also had an invitation to participate sent to Chetan. Hunar Sahib was asked to chair the event. Although a Muslim student at Government College had come first, Chetan had come second and won a five-rupee prize. In a conversation at the event, Hunar Sahib had urged him to get his stories published in a collection and told him he would write the introduction in verse. When Chetan had asked where the money would come from, he had told him he'd

320

have to arrange for the paper, but the printing could be done at Shyam Press.

Although Hunar Sahib was a resident of a village near Hoshiarpur, his maternal uncle lived in Chetan's neighbourhood in Jalandhar. Hunar Sahib had come back home with Chetan. He promised to get the paper for Chetan and arrange for the printing with the owners of Shyam Press, and then he also told him how letter after letter was coming to him from Lahore asking him to submit short stories, but these days he was just writing poems on Gora and Badal and the history of Rajputana, as well as other 'golden tales' . . .

Chetan got what he was hinting at. He told him he'd write not one but two stories for him. Since Hunar Sahib was doing so much for him, why couldn't he do him this small favour in return?

When they arrived in Jalandhar, the first thing Chetan did was to use those five rupees to get a suit stitched for himself. Then he wrote a short story for Hunar Sahib. Hunar Sahib talked to the chairman of the City Congress Committee, Lala Govindaram, and got him to donate twenty-five rupees' worth of paper, which Chetan brought to Shyam Press himself. The two owners of Shyam Press had a great fondness for Urdu poetry because they were in the printing business, and Hunar Sahib spent hours reciting poetry to them. He introduced Chetan to them, and told them Chetan was an up-and-coming writer who would bring fame to Jalandhar. 'He's got a short book ready for printing,' he added. 'I'm writing the introduction in verse. You must print it.'

'What, you give a command and we not obey it?' asked Small Shyam Babu, and he invited them to see a movie with him that very evening. Chetan had expressed his interest in films and said that his wife was always writing articles about them (he'd told the whole story to Hunar Sahib), and he mentioned his friend Hamid, adding that he knew absolutely everything about films, and asked if he could bring him along as well. 'By all means!' Shyam Babu had cried. 'And you should bring Chanda Devi ji as well.'

'She's in Lahore these days,' Chetan said, putting him off. 'But this friend of mine has a great interest in films. He's the son of the Divan of Khairpur. He plans to go into films as soon as he passes his BA. One day he'll become a famous hero for sure.'

And that evening, he arrived at Shyam Press with Hamid and Hunar Sahib, wearing a new suit, and carrying a thin cane in his hand. From there, they proceeded to the cinema hall and went to watch the movie from the gallery in great style. Chetan saw that Lala Mohan Lal had observed him entering the gallery with the younger owner of Shyam Press.

After the movie, Hunar Sahib and Shyam Babu had both warmly praised Chetan's stories to Lala Mohan Lal. Hunar Sahib also said that Chetan and his wife knew a great deal about films (Chetan had told him to do this beforehand). 'Get him to help you design some handbills and advertisements for films,' he suggested to Lala Mohan Lal.

'I already asked him,' said Lala Mohan Lal. 'But I'm seeing him now for the first time after many months.'

'I'll come by here more often now. Now that my book is being printed, I'll have time to come by to see you as well,' Chetan had said nonchalantly.

And he showed up the very next evening, spinning his cane. In the midst of this, he'd collected several handbills he'd seen being distributed for Lala Mohan Lal. He'd marked up all the errors in grammar, language and idiom. Lala Mohan Lal asked him to watch the movie, but a stunt film was showing that day. Chetan remarked dismissively that it wasn't a very good film and he offered a critique of its strengths and weaknesses based on the reviews he'd read in the papers. Then, over the course of the conversation, he enumerated the errors in spelling and grammar in the handbills, and mentioned that he came this way every day. He'd show him a draft of a handbill and he could take a look.

And thus he began coming by every evening. But even though he wanted to, he didn't watch any movies. He corrected the handbills, said something favourable about some films and criticized others, then left. In the midst of this, he came once again to watch a film with Shyam Babu in the gallery. Then an Imperial Company film was released, about which he had read great praise in the Bombay magazine *Movie Mirror*. He made an excellent handbill for it, and that evening he sat in first class with Lala Mohan Lal.

After this, he got into an evening routine of coming home from college, eating dinner, putting on his suit, taking up his cane and strolling off to the cinema hall. The people at the gate had grown so accustomed to him that even if Lala Mohan Lal wasn't there, no one asked him for a ticket and he'd just go and sit inside. Sometimes, when the gatekeeper had to go somewhere, Chetan even stood at the gate himself as though he were the owner.

*

As soon as he entered the passageway, Chetan recollected that incident from fourth year when the first talkie had come to Jalandhar—*Alam Ara*! It was advertised for months beforehand and pictures of the heroine, Alam Ara (played by Zubeida), in the attire of a nomad reclining on a cliff, were pasted in every gali and bazaar of the city—her long hair floated in the breeze and her sleeveless dress exposed her pale thin arms and her legs up to the thighs.

There was the possibility of such a great rush for the film that three sections had been divided off by thick poles in the gallery, and Mohan Lal ji had told Chetan a few days beforehand that there would be absolutely no free passes that day.

But Chetan's desire to watch this film was so strong that he couldn't help himself, and he did get to see it the very first day . . . he smiled at the recollection.

*

What had happened was that Zubeida had taken her place in his heart alongside Sulochna after he'd seen her in a couple of movies. Zubeida might not have been as beautiful as Sulochna— Sulochna was Anglo-Indian: tall as a cypress, with a curvaceous figure, large, round eyes, a sharp nose and a pointed chin. Savita Devi, another heroine of the screen in those days, was also beautiful, but she could not compare to Sulochna. Next to Sulochna, Zubeida was a skinny young lady with a round face, delicate features, and a flirtatious manner. She danced so well that Chetan couldn't take his eyes off her. It was this Zubeida who would speak in *Alam Ara*; she would dance and sing . . . whatever happened, Chetan needed to see that film . . . and Mohan Lal ji had indicated that he wouldn't be able to see it on the first day.

Chetan knew that if he went in the evening he might not even be allowed in. So that day he went to the cinema hall in the afternoon. There was no one in the passageway. He went back into the office. Lala Mohan Lal was sitting there. When he saw Chetan, he frowned slightly and said, 'Let the picture run a few days, then you can see it.'

'Yes, yes,' replied Chetan, carelessly. 'I came because there'd be a rush today—in case you needed me if there was a fight or something.' And he helped the gatekeepers throughout the matinee show. He worked just as diligently at the five-thirty

show as well. At the nine-thirty show, though the four, eight-
and twelve-anna seats were packed, there were some empty
seats in the one-rupee section. When the gates closed, he went
quietly and sat in a first-class seat. When the lights came up
at the interval, he saw that Mohan Lal ji was seated in the
seat right next to him. He looked over at him and smiled
faintly.

*

Mohan Lal ji wasn't there. The gatekeeper was an old acquaintance
of Chetan's. Chetan shook his hand, asked how he was, told him
his own news, and turned to leave.

'Please come in; won't you see a movie?' asked the gate
man.

'No, I'm not in the mood!'

And truly, in that one year, he'd seen so many films it had
put a strain on his eyes. When his exams drew near, he completely
stopped watching movies. After that, he lost interest in films for
some reason. Although he had free passes from the newspapers,
he rarely went to the movies, and even then, only when his wife
insisted.

As he came outside, he turned to the left, lost in those same
memories. Just then someone came up behind him and placed
both their hands on his waist, lifted him up, and spun him round.
As soon as his feet touched the ground again, he turned to see who
it was, and cried out enthusiastically:

'Hey, Laloo!'

The two of them embraced.

'Listen, yaar, how are things?' asked Chetan. 'Last time I was
here, I heard you were wandering around Jammu somewhere with
a cigarette agency.'

'Not just Jammu-Kashmir, I've been all over India, and now I've come back and settled down. Look over there, right across the way—that's my store! The company gave me the Jalandhar, Hoshiarpur and Kapurthala agencies.'

He slung his arm around Chetan's neck, led him across the street and brought him into his shop.

30

Anyone looking at Laloo Baniya would never dream that this man had just toured all of India: he was of medium height with a dark complexion and plump features, and was untidily dressed. He had been a classmate of Chetan's. His parents' only son, he'd been raised with great affection and was thus a laggard in studies. But since his parents had sufficient funds, he brought all his comrades from the mohalla to his rooftop room in Patphera Bazaar (where his father worked as a broker) and entertained them handsomely. Although his clothing was expensive, his right eye was always a bit rheumy and his nose runny. The one he wiped with the hem of his kameez and the other with his sleeve.

Chetan looked up. There was still rheum collected in Laloo's right eye and, as he spoke, he wiped his nose with his right sleeve as was his custom. Chetan had heard that Laloo had taken a cigarette agency and made quite a bit of money—but from his appearance and behaviour, he was still the same old Blockhead.

His friends had stuck him with the nickname 'Blockhead' when he'd gone to bring his wife home for the first time after marriage, and lost not just her jewellery and clothing, but also his wife herself.

The mere sight of his face made it impossible to forget that incident. Chetan always thought of the entire story the moment he heard Laloo's name. What had happened was that Laloo had run away from home after failing Class Eight, and there had been quite an uproar, not just in Baniya Gali but as far off as Kallowani Mohalla, and he'd been scolded roundly by his father. His father, Harnarayan Gupta, had been gaining in prominence in those days. There were great feasts at his home on the days of Shraddha. He usually sent something or other for the Brahmins of the gali and mohalla on various festival days, such as those marking the eleventh and twelfth days of the lunar cycle, so the Brahmins of the mohalla all pitched in, each in their own manner, to help bring Laloo back. Pandit Daulat Ram looked at his horoscope and told Laloo's father that it was nothing to worry about; Ketu was just looking a bit off, Mars was in the fifth house, which is the house of mental activity, in an unfavourable sign, and this had thrown off his mental speed. But that Laloo would definitely return within three days, three weeks, or three years. When Lala ji said that Laloo had failed his exam, and he worried about him committing suicide, Pandit ji assured him there was nothing to fear. For suicide, one must have Ketu and the moon in the eighth house and that wasn't the case here. Thus, Laloo would definitely come home. He had gone astray and was in the company of some person of low repute. 'I'll start the recitation for Mars and Ketu today,' he promised.

Pandit Shivnarayan initiated a puja for the peace of the planets. In order to strengthen the strong planets, he organized a *lagnesh* puja. 'The lagnesh, or the lord of the ascendant, is in the eleventh house,' he'd said. 'There are two auspicious planets aspecting it, and the lagnesh is in transit. Thus there is no possibility of any harm. I shall strengthen the hand of the lagnesh which is sowing disunity between Mars and Ketu.'

Pandit Gurdayal Jhaman didn't know any of this astrology business. He had a paan shop in Chaurasti Atari. Instead, he offered the services of his pupils in finding Laloo and began coming by every day to ask after him.

The mohalla's Khatris did business with Laloo's father, so they alerted those they knew in business centres and markets. Finally, Laloo was found scrubbing pots at a sweet shop in Ludhiana. Then, on the auspicious advice of Pandit Daulat Ram, he was engaged to be married that very month; when his marriage took place he hadn't even taken the Matric exam yet.

By the time he got to the Matric, he had failed three times, and three times he had run away from home. After the third time, his father ordered him to bring home his bride. So what happened then was that on their return to Jalandhar from his in-laws, the train stopped at the Adda Hoshiarpur Gate outside the big signal. Then something got into Laloo's head: either he felt like getting out right there when he saw that familiar gate, or he thought they'd get home quicker from there, or he was bored of waiting for the signal to go down—whatever the case may be, he waited a few moments for the train to move, then suddenly told his bride to get off the train. He got her down, and handed her the box of jewellery. He was just going back to get the rest of the stuff when the engine whistled loudly and the train started to move.

Laloo's bride must have been fifteen or sixteen. She'd never been to Jalandhar before. She just stood right where she was, veil up, clutching her jewellery chest. The poor thing didn't even know the address of the gali or mohalla of her in-laws. A scoundrel was watching all this from the gate. It was evening, and the workers from Khem Chand Hansraj's tin factory were walking along the line. This guy was one of them. He came forward and asked, 'Bibi, which mohalla are you going to?'

She pulled her veil down further and shrank back, but he said, 'Come, I'll take you to the station.' He picked up the chest and walked along the line.

Jalandhar station was probably about a mile or so from the gate. Nowadays, there's not even a full yard of free space from there to the station, but in those days, the line passed through a complete wasteland between the two. There was a pool of standing water near the line that was thick with reeds. It was there that he threatened the bride with a knife, told her to remove her ornaments, ordered her to sit there quietly and not say a peep, then took the jewellery and chest and disappeared.

In the meantime, Laloo, who had suddenly begun to insist on being called Shri Lal Narayan Gupta, and always wrote out his entire name, got down at the station and instead of going back to the gate, calmly proceeded directly home. 'So did Chinto get here yet?' he asked on arriving home.

'Chinto? Your bride, you mean?' asked his mother with astonishment.

'Yes, has she arrived?'

'Was she coming with someone else?' his mother asked.

Then Laloo explained what he'd done. As soon as she heard, his mother beat her head and rushed out, and a ruckus broke out from Baniya Gali to Kallowani Mohalla. The people of Chowk Chaddhiyan, Khoslon ki Gali and Chowk Anandon went rushing pell-mell to Adda Hoshiarpur. There was no sign of the bride there whatsoever. Then they broke up into groups and fanned out. It was the group that went along the line that found her weeping near the rushes, head on her knees, right where that scoundrel had left her. Some people also claimed that the scoundrel had carried off her honour along with her jewels, but perhaps that story was spread by malicious neighbours. Despite all this, Laloo assured his friends that the thief (he didn't call him the scoundrel) had not touched his bride. The bride had removed all her ornaments and given them to him and, he told them in whispers, he'd got proof of this on the wedding night—the bloodstains couldn't be removed from the bedding despite repeated washings. But the neighbourhood boys had not only given him the nickname 'Blockhead' after this, they also teased him so much about his bride and the scoundrel that he ran away yet again.

When Chetan went to Lahore after passing the BA, he had seen Laloo one day on Railway Road—he rang a bell as he distributed handbills for Lal Badshah Cigarettes, followed by errand boys in top hats waving large posters for Lal Badshah Cigarettes, crying out the slogan:

Smoke Lal Badshah!
Enjoy life!

And since that day he'd got a third name along with Laloo and Blockhead—Lal Badshah!

31

When Chetan went inside the shop and sat down, Laloo ran off and ordered a glass of lemon sharbat for him even though he had repeatedly refused his offer of a drink.

Sipping on the sharbat, Chetan looked his old classmate over. Then his gaze travelled to the crates of cigarettes stacked up from floor to ceiling in the back room, and he remembered the Punjabi saying he'd heard from Ma, '"*kha*" *kheh uṛāve fer vī* "*kha*" *khaṭṭ ke liyāve!*'—that is, a Khatri always comes home with money even if he's just been wandering about. Although the Khatris considered the merchant Baniyas beneath them, the two were the same in the eyes of the Brahmins by virtue of being in business. 'This arrant fool, this totally unintelligent Laloo, who ran away from home six times, who wandered off God knows where, now sits here calmly, a successful businessman,' Chetan thought, and for a moment, he felt jealous of his indecisive, messy friend, with his runny nose and rheumy eyes; but the next moment, he shook off the feeling. He was an intellectual story-writer after all, a newspaper man; his wealth lay in his power. And this guy was a Baniya with a dense brain . . .

'So listen, I hear Amichand has become a deputy collector.'

This was another blow to Chetan. This was the third time since morning he'd heard about Amichand becoming a deputy collector. He pitied the narrow-mindedness of the people in his mohalla. He wanted to ask sarcastically, 'Oh, so has he become the Governor?' But he didn't, and instead replied in a preoccupied manner, 'Yes, I heard from Anant. Now he'll go for training and he'll become a small-time officer. But he's hardly becoming a deputy collector today!'

'Chacha Sohan Lal has already started calling him deputy,' said Laloo. 'And I've heard that Amirchand [Amichand's older brother] is walking around the mohalla all stuck up, as though he's the one who's been made deputy collector, not Amichand.'

Laloo laughed as he said this and wiped his nose with his sleeve, and then he added in a whisper, 'I ran into Amirchand this morning. He said if Telu brings Bhago back to the mohalla, he'll murder him . . . now that his brother has become the deputy, he can do whatever he pleases!'

'Who knows when he'll actually become a deputy; now he'll have at least six months' training,' repeated Chetan.

But Laloo was on a roll and didn't hear what he said. He added, 'And Telu is bent on bringing Bhago back to the mohalla.'

Chetan was still thinking about Amichand. He kept remembering the time when he'd greeted Amichand so warmly at Shimla's Scandal Point, but Amichand's brusque manner and distant tone had left him cold. He scarcely heard what Laloo said about Telu and Bhago, and said, following his own train of thought, 'It was good Amichand placed in the competition this time. This was his final chance. If he'd stayed back this time as well, what else would he do but become a better class of clerk in some office?'

'Everyone has his own fate,' said Laloo. 'Babu Maniram spent his entire life sitting at a desk at the post office, but his son—who knows—he might be Governor some day.'

'Not Governor, son-of-a- . . . Governor!' snapped Chetan. 'If he just makes it to revenue officer by the time he retires that'll be a big deal. He's a crammer. It was just a fluke he passed. He sat for the competitive examinations three times before and never passed. Oh, sure, he'll be Governor one day . . .'

'Amirchand said that if we got self-rule today, Amichand would be a member of the Governor's council in ten years, or he could even become the Governor himself.'

'Amichand may or may not, but Amirchand will definitely become Governor one day.'

And Chetan guffawed loudly; he'd pushed the topic from his mind, and also got Laloo off the subject.

But Laloo wouldn't let it drop.

'Amirchand has just assured Bada and Debu that as soon as Deputy Sahib assumes office, he'll hire those two as his orderlies. Debu was the one who gave me the news, when he saw Telu in Mandi, and he said Telu's thinking of bringing Bhago into the mohalla.'

For the first time, Chetan paid attention to what Laloo was saying.

'Bhago? Who's Bhago?'

'Arré, Dharam Chand with the TB's wife!'

'What does she have to do with Telu?'

'She was the one who ran off with him!'

'With Telu? When? Where? He's Brahmin; she's Khatri.'

'You didn't know?'

'I've just come to Jalandhar after almost a year,' said Chetan. 'After Dharam Chand died, I'd heard that Lala Mukandi Lal had taken her and her children under his protection.'

'Yes, yes, when he was done with his brother's last rites, Lala Mukandi Lal had new kurtas, dhotis and vests stitched for himself. He bought a beautiful muslin turban, had Chiragh the dyer colour it pearl-grey, and arrived in the bhuvara one day, looking a dandy, and went and paid his respects to his sister-in-law.'

Lal Badshah laughed and wiped his nose with his sleeve, and then the gist of what he told Chetan in an enthusiastic whisper was that Lala Mukandi Lal had told his widowed sister-in-law, Bhagavati, aka, Bhagavanti, aka Bhago, 'Please don't believe that you are alone in this world just because my brother Dharam Chand is no longer with us. There's still Lala Mukandi Lal in the Andon (Anandon) family, and for him, there's no difference between his own son Mangal and his brother's children.' And from that day on, Mukandi Lal got up early every morning, did some calisthenics first, then filled water from the well for his sister-in-law's home, and brought her vegetables and other groceries himself. Then one day, he informed the people of the mohalla that he was moving out of his room in the bazaar. His sister-in-law had said that the house was empty and she was scared—without a wife, a home is haunted—but it also feels haunted without a man.

'Bassstard!' muttered Chetan. 'First he ruined his middle brother's widow, then he started laying a snare for the older brother's widow.'

'But the middle one's widow wasn't about to put up with it,' laughed Laloo. 'After her son Mangal and his bride had fallen asleep, Shanno went that very night to his room and raised such a stink, my God . . . she was screaming at the top of her lungs: "You ruined my honour and now that I'm old, you want to throw me out after using up my body! You gave me this disease! Yes, I'm going to die but I won't let you go, etc., etc.!" And people gathered and sat and enjoyed themselves downstairs at Gurdayal the paan seller's in Chaurasti Atari. When she realized they were listening, she began to scream even louder. Finally, Lala Mukandi Lal placed his turban at her feet and said, "Dear God, don't ruin my reputation like this in the bazaar! I put on this act for you people's benefit. Otherwise I'm hardly the age for this sort of thing. I wanted to keep home goods in the home, but if you won't accept it, that's fine!'"

Chetan was starting to enjoy himself. He laughed loudly.

Laloo told him that Shanno had no objection to home goods coming into the home either (at this point, he wiped his eye with the hem of his kameez) but how could she tolerate having a co-wife forced on her. So, starting the next day, she took Lala Mukandi Lal's place. She'd get up early in the morning and wash the plinth of the well after singing a prayer to the Satguru, then she'd fill the pots of water for her sister-in-law's home. She'd send Mangal to get Bhago's vegetables and other groceries. She'd go to the bhuvara two or three times a day to keep her sister-in-law happy. She brought her and both her children to her place as well. But after a short while, Shanno saw that Mangal had started spending quite a bit of time at the home of his skinny-as-a-cucumber aunt, she of the long chin—casting aside his lovely-as-a-flower bride—and feeding his aunt's children. One day there was a fierce fight over this issue between Mangal's wife and Bhago, and such unmentionable things were said by both sides, that the people of the mohalla covered their ears; Shanno had no choice but to take the side of her daughter-in-law against her sister-in-law. The two sisters-in-law listed one another's ancestors and showered upon them brand new 'sweet words', and then, still not fully satisfied, they began clawing at one another's hair.

Telu's roof and Bhagavanti's roof were separated by a small curtain. Telu did his calisthenics on the roof every day, after massaging his dark hearty body with oil, and he slept there as well. Nobody knows for sure when the curtain that separated the two roofs was pulled aside. The mohalla people found out when Bhago took her trunk of clothing and jewels and ran off with him one night, taking her children with her, and the mohalla people heard that Telu had taken a house right in Mandi, and that he now lived there with Bhago.

This time, both Laloo and Chetan laughed, and Laloo slapped Chetan hard on the hand and told him that Shanno had continued to curse the mohalla's Brahmins all day long, and the Khatris had continued to grit their teeth. But when Aunty Purandei came out of the bhuvara gesticulating angrily and began to sing the virtues of the Khatris and told them to go and catch Telu, report him to the police—why are you cursing at all these people?—then the Khatris, Amirchand foremost among them, announced that if either Telu or Bhago set foot in the mohalla again, he'd give them a thrashing.

32

Chetan said goodbye to Laloo, and was walking along towards Adda Hoshiarpur above Panjpir. He wanted to think about Neela, about the pain of separation that had settled deep within him; he wanted to think about Kunti—his desire to pass beneath her window and catch just one glimpse of her was more powerful than ever today; he wanted to think about Chanda—he'd fled early this morning to avoid spending time with her and now he was wandering about aimlessly. But after seeing Laloo, thoughts about Bhago had pushed all those others aside and preoccupied him now . . .

He had been studying in Class Eight when she'd come as a bride, or more like a slave girl, into the Khatri family of the mohalla. Chetan imagined her childhood—a small village in a verdant valley in the Shivaliks. Just a few homes dotting a mountain slope. Sloping slate roofs that shone like mirrors in the sunlight. A river flowing through the valley below. In the river, a water mill. Green and yellow paddy fields spread out across the valley. Pine trees. When their dry needles covered the slopes, she and her sisters would slip and slide as they walked along. Near the village, a swimming hole at one spot in the river . . . there they'd bathe to their hearts' content, swim, wash and dry their clothes, throw a ball and sing:

Bravo my Challa!
Mix the grain and water
Challa is on the pulpit
He doesn't listen to me
He listens to my mother
If she wishes, we will leave

or dance a *kikli*:

Kikkali of the Kaleer
My little brother brought a turban
My elder brother brought a dupatta
Shame on the son-in-law
who did not bring a thing

But when she was still a child, her parents had passed away. That was when her playing and singing had suddenly come to a halt. Her uncle had taken her under his protection. And to pay the price of that protection, she had to perform back-breaking labour. She took her guardian's cattle to graze, hoed the fields, planted crops, cut grass for the cattle and, if there was time, cooked, washed the dishes and brought water from the river. She worked so hard she didn't even notice when her body changed, and she began to be talked of in the village not just for her labour, but also for her youthful beauty. Proposals began to come in from the surrounding villages; the villagers believed anyone's fate would be enhanced by her presence in their home. But her uncle wanted cash; after preparing such a hardworking girl he didn't want to just hand her over to someone. He believed he should get at least one thousand rupees in cash for such a young and industrious girl, but when no one was willing to give even five hundred, let alone a thousand, and Bhagavanti was going on twenty, it seemed to her uncle that if she didn't get hitched to some post soon, she'd break her tether and run away. So he took her off to Mukerian to look for someone needy there, or someone from Jalandhar, Hoshiarpur or Ludhiana, and so lighten his load. Chetan's father was assigned to Mukerian Station then. Mukerian was the terminus in those days. There was a large market there. Farmers and businessmen from all over knew him. He was friends with police sergeants, doctors and sub collectors. If even a needle were to drop in the market, he'd find out about it. If someone from the hills came to sell their daughter, how could he not learn of it? When he saw the girl, he thought of Dharam Chand. Mukandi Lal was his childhood friend, and he'd already said several times, 'Bau Bhai, get my brother settled somehow, I won't forget the favour all my life.'

'You'll forget the favour that same day, you bastard, but don't worry, I'll thread the needle somehow or other,' said Chetan's father laughing.

He had a message delivered to the marriage broker with whom Bhagavanti's guardian was staying, saying that he was calling for his friend from Jalandhar, who would be there in two days. And that he should not talk to anyone else until he heard from him. He wrote a letter and sent it via the water carrier to Jalandhar and said that he should bring Mukandi Lal back with him.

Mukandi Lal came by the next train to Mukerian. He saw the girl. She wasn't all that beautiful, but she was tall, strong and youthful, and there was a kind of half-slumbering longing in her eyes that pulled at Mukandi Lal's heartstrings. He didn't think she'd make a bad sister-in-law. Bhagavanti's uncle was asking for a thousand rupees, but Pandit Shadiram reasoned with him and put pressure on the broker by insinuating that he'd be sent to jail for selling women, thus forcing him to take four hundred rupees. It was decided that the marriage would be conducted according to tradition. Lala Mukandi Lal would shoulder the expenses for both sides and, having sealed the deal, he went back to take care of the wedding arrangements.

Chetan recalled what Bhagavanti's husband, Lala Dharam Chand, had looked like: a skinny man of forty or so; a bit darker than Mukandi Lal; cruel by nature, serious and silent. He had remained unmarried due to a stain on the family honour. Had he parted ways with his brother Mukandi Lal, perhaps he'd have had no difficulty getting married, but he wasn't prepared to do so.

And Chetan recalled the story he'd heard from Ma about the stain on the Andon (Anandon) family . . .

*

There were four brothers in their home—Jivan Lal, Harjas Rai, Dharam Chand and Mukandi Lal. They had a small ancestral home behind Chetan's house, which was still just one-storey at the time, when all around it two- and three-storey houses had been built, and it looked like a well from the roof of Chetan's three-storey house. Lala Mukandi Lal's great-grandfather or great-great-grandfather had been a high officer in the court of Rana Ranjit Singh, or so they said, but their father had run a grocer's shop and following the principle of the Persian saying *pidaram sultān bud*—'my father was surely a king!'—Lala Mukandi Lal's elder brother had taken the name of their ancestor and laid the glory of his family thickly upon the people of the mohalla. Their father had not yet reached forty when he passed away. Then Mukandi Lal's two elder brothers, Jivan Lal and Harjas Rai, began sitting at the shop. In those days, Dharam Chand was apprenticed at the cotton tape shop, and Mukandi went regularly to the akhara. Jivan Lal's wife, Dammo, was very quarrelsome, so when Harjas Rai married Shanno, their hearths had to be separated in just six months. Mukandi Lal's mother stayed with her eldest son in

342

the old house, and Harjas Rai took Shanno and his two younger brothers to a rented house in the chowk outside the gali, right across from Chetan's sitting room.

'Ma, Chacha Mukandi Lal must have been very handsome!' Chetan had said to his mother once. 'He still is.'

'Yes, son, he was the most handsome of all the brothers, and then, he also went to the akhara and enjoyed himself while living off his elder brothers.'

'Shanno Chachi must have been about the same age as him?' Chetan had asked.

'A year or two older,' Ma replied.

'Ma, people say that when Shanno came here as a bride she was very beautiful.'

'Yes, son, she was very fair; she was radiant then. Harjas Rai seemed like an old man next to her.'

In six months the hearths had been separated again and in six more months the shops were separated as well. But Harjas Rai did not live long after he married. After just two years he passed away. Then Dharam Chand left the tape shop and took over his brother's shop, and although Mukandi Lal still went to the akhara, he started to take on household duties as well. He took on the responsibility of filling the water pots for the house, doing the shopping and anything else his sister-in-law needed. Harjas Rai hadn't yet been dead a year when it was said that Shanno had fallen ill. After that, it was said she'd had a son. An uproar broke out in the mohalla. Jivan Lal and Dammo were in favour of grabbing this ill-omened woman who had cast a blot on the Andon family by the braid and throwing her out. But Dharam Chand was not prepared to do this. He reasoned with Mukandi. He acknowledged that the boy was his before the elders of the mohalla, and the elders threw a *chadar* over the two of them, and Shanno became the wife of her husband's younger brother.

People spread all sorts of nasty rumours. Some thought the inappropriate relationship between the brother and sister-in-law had begun during Harjas Rai's lifetime. Dammo announced publicly that the sin was Dharam Chand's and he'd pulled a fast one on innocent Mukandi. But that wasn't true. Dharam Chand stayed at the shop all day—even his meals were delivered there—whereas Mukandi hung around his sister-in-law all day long, and this much was true: Whether or not they had an inappropriate relationship, Shanno was devoted to Mukandi during Harjas Rai's lifetime. 'Now whenever those two quarrel, Shanno makes this accusation at Mukandi,' Ma had said. 'She says that he ruined her honour, but the truth of the matter is that she was the one who ruined his.'

'But Ma, Shanno is so ugly now.'

'She got a sickness from Mukandi. As soon as he married Shanno, he began hanging around with girlfriends—he himself was spared but Shanno was disgraced.'

Chetan was acquainted with this matter, because even in those days, Shanno walked about with a wound on her thigh, and just like Ma always said in Punjabi of the Kaliyug, 'Chor uchkkā chaudhrī, 'guṇḍī raṇaṇ pardhān'—the thieves rule the roost and their molls are in charge—she was the headwoman of the mohalla in those days. She got up bright and early every morning. She now handled the task of cleaning the plinth of the well, she was the one who organized prayer meetings for the holy men and, just as Laloo had said, she was the one who had complained to Amirchand that her sister-in-law had disgraced the Andon family by running away with Telu.

Chetan laughed to himself. He thought about the things that had been said about Shanno from time to time, since his childhood up until just a few years ago. He imagined how Shanno had lit up the dark room of that home with her splendid beauty:

344

she'd been fair, tall as a cypress, and shapely. And he imagined her younger brother-in-law: eighteen years old, thin, strong, narrow-waisted, broad-chested, fair as milk, with golden-red hair. The brother-in-law was still handsome, but when you saw the ruins of Shanno it was difficult to even guess how the building had once looked.

There was nothing wrong with Dharam Chand. Serious and hardworking, he wouldn't agree to abandon his younger brother, and the blemish had remained on his name, and he had stayed a bachelor until he married Bhago.

*

Chetan was perhaps studying in Class Eight or Nine in those days and during the holidays, he always went to Mukerian. He was included in the wedding party of Chacha Dharam Chand, and had come with the procession to Jalandhar. After Ma had seen the bride she had come home and said, 'There's something about her eyes. I doubt that girl will stay put with the Andons.'

But as long as Dharam Chand remained alive, Bhago stayed with him. Lala Dharam Chand was entirely under her control. That same Dharam Chand who, despite the urgings of the whole world, wouldn't abandon his brother and sister-in-law, couldn't even stay with them six months after marrying. And so their homes were separated again. Again the shops were divided. Dharam Chand moved to the second floor of a house in the bhuvara. He gave the shop to Mukandi and reopened the tape shop in Chaurasti Atari. He lived eight more years after he married. He was forty or forty-one and Bhago twenty or twenty-one when they'd married. During those eight years they even had two children, of whom the girl was seven and the boy five. Dharam Chand had suffered from asthma even before he married. He'd been starved for intimacy.

He overdid it a bit. The asthma got worse. The silence of the summer nights was often broken by his continuous coughing. The people sleeping on the roofs were woken from their slumber and sleepy children were roused and started to cry. His detractors said that he was suffering from tuberculosis rather than asthma and avoided going to his house as much as they could. Thus years went by and his asthma increased and one night he passed away from a fit of coughing.

*

Somehow Chetan's heart was filled with enormous sympathy when he thought about Bhago's past. Her childhood had been marked by want; want had marked her youth as well; when she got a husband, he had been middle-aged; and on top of that, he was an asthma patient; his relations were base and wretched; what was so bad about her running off with Telu? It's not like Dharam Chand had left her any valuable property. If she stayed, she'd have to put up with Shanno's abuses, suffer as the target of the lust of her middle-aged brother-in-law just so she could survive. If she ran off with the man she preferred, who was her age (even if he was a Brahmin), was that such a bad thing? If she'd ended up with a Khatri, perhaps the partner wouldn't have had so much trouble. But do women really have a caste? Do rivers or the earth have a caste? She was no different from Kunti and Chanda . . . so courageous and so brash . . . but was not the tragedy of her life basically even deeper—she had been like a bird, soaring about in the free atmosphere of the mountains, and now she was trapped in the cage of Kallowani Mohalla. Where could she fly off to? If she flew out of one cage, wouldn't she just get trapped in another? Was the atmosphere in the Jhamans any better than that of the Andons? Wasn't there the same damp, the same suffocation, the same meanness? But that Telu, that dusky, muscular young man—his was the cage she preferred—for her, it was paradise. With Telu, she'd drink up all the poison of that suffocating atmosphere as though it were nectar. She was not born into the slavery of lower-middle-class cities, she had a zest for living her life according to her own desires, so why shouldn't she be bold? Chetan shook his head with displeasure. Just then someone placed a hand very lightly on his shoulder from behind.

'Vande Mataram!' said the man, and laughed slightly.

Chetan turned . . . the man was tall, but looked of medium height due to the hunch between his slumped shoulders; he had a wheat-coloured complexion and a sharp face (the long nose and sunken cheeks made it look even more angular), and wore an open-buttoned achkan coat, homespun churidar pyjamas, and a Gandhi cap on his head.

'Oh hello, Govindaram ji, Vande Mataram . . . Vande Mataram,' said Chetan.

'I heard from Hunar Sahib you were in town,' he said, walking alongside Chetan. 'I thought you would come my way, but I've been waiting two days and haven't seen your face. Tell me, are you well? I heard you'd just returned from enjoying the delights of Shimla.'

'Forget delights, I've just been experiencing frights; but frights are a new experience as well, that's what I've just been learning about . . . What are you doing over here in Panjpir?'

'I'm owed money for a block by one party, and since I'm short of cash, I thought I'd just bring it myself. Hardly anyone comes of his own accord to pay me at the shop . . . where are you coming from and where are you headed?'

'I ran into Hunar Sahib at Rudra Sen Arya's shop. I've just come from walking all over—Khalsa Hotel, Company Bagh, the Widows' Aid Society, and Lala Jalandhari Mull ji Yogi's place with

Hunar Sahib. I may be going back to Lahore tomorrow or the next day, so I thought, "Why not take a look at my old haunts?"'

'But you didn't come my way?'

'I was thinking of going over there on my way back from Kot Kishanchand through Puriyan Mohalla and Qila Bazaar. How could I come to Jalandhar and not take a round of Bhairon Bazaar? How could I pass by your door without knocking?' And Chetan laughed.

'Hunar Sahib was supposed to come this evening. He's translated the Bhagavad Gita into ordinary Urdu. He thought there should be a meeting about it and he'd read it aloud.'

'He told me to give you the message that he'll come to your room this evening,' said Chetan. To himself, he added, 'That's why he's covering the length and breadth of Jalandhar—so that everyone will come to the meeting.'

'When I found out you were coming, I was very happy. I'll definitely arrange the meeting, but if you can say a few words about this new poem of his it would be great.'

'I might leave tomorrow.'

'Come on, let's talk while we walk.'

'I'll come by your room on my way back from Kot Kishanchand.'

'Then come on, let's walk as far as Khingra Gate.'

And he put his hand on Chetan's shoulder in the style of a politician.

33

Bansi the vegetable seller of Lal Bazaar and Lala Govindaram, the stamp maker and engraver, had something in common. After the self-rule movement, they'd been seen about the bazaar much less. When the movement was at its height, the two of them were involved in it night and day; when there was a lull, Bansi sold vegetables or participated in swadeshi poetry competitions with Rehmat at his shop, and Lala Govindaram sat all day at the open window of his room above Dina Nath the bookseller and engraved blocks. At that time the modern-style printing blocks weren't yet made in Jalandhar, and Lala Govindaram engraved prepared blocks—the only one who did this work in the entire city. His room, which was on the second storey of the house, jutted out slightly over the bazaar and bore a signboard reading 'Block Maker and Engraver' that could be seen from afar. But the bugle of a political movement would sound somewhere in Gujarat, Maharashtra, or in central India, and Lala Govindaram would stand, abandoning his tools, forgetting customers and blocks, and wander about from gali to gali, mohalla to mohalla organizing rallies and processions. Bansi would ring the bell and make the announcements and proclamations, and Lala Govindaram would go to the homes of speakers and volunteers and gather them all together. Although from '21 to '31 (as long as Chetan remained in Jalandhar) he had organized thousands of meetings, he, like

Bansi, was not able to give any speeches in the meetings. He'd choose chairmen for his meetings who would be able to make up for the weaknesses of some speakers with their brilliant speeches when there was extra time.

But they had something else in common, more than their aptitude for successfully organizing meetings. Their love for the self-rule movement was unstinting and they were enormously industrious and dutiful. If they were determined to do something, they wouldn't stop until they'd completed it. In the days of the movement, they joined scores of pickets and went to jail eleven times in ten years.

Chetan was studying in Class Six during the movement of '21 when he heard both their names from the tongue of every child. Mahatma Gandhi was about to lead a procession. There was an extremely cruel district administrator by the name of Buck, who tried to stop the procession in Civil Lines in front of the courthouse. But the procession continued by. It was an incredible mass of people. The authorities were not prepared for such a large procession. Mahatma ji's car had gone ahead, but Buck rained down blows on the rest. Lala Govindaram first staged a sit-in in front of the courthouse. They beat him mercilessly, dragged him off and threw him into the police car and took him away. That night, Mahatma Gandhi praised Govindaram's heroism and dutifulness to a full assembly. And he said that no one could keep enslaved a country whose soil had produced a beloved son like Lala Govindaram. Mahatma ji gave his speech and proceeded to Ludhiana. As soon as he left, Buck decreed all assemblies illegal. And when people refused to give in, he gave the command to use lathis against them, and the skies echoed with cries of 'Victory to Mahatma Gandhi!' and 'Victory to Lala Govindaram!' They'd been wounded by lathis but they didn't budge from the rally. Buck attempted to quash the movement mercilessly but his violence only added fuel to the fire. In galis and mohallas people named all the neighbourhood dogs 'Buck' to relieve the resentment in their hearts. Around that time, a scary black stray dog showed up from God knows where in Kallowani Mohalla. Immediately the people of the mohalla dubbed him Buck. (When that dog went mad after a year, people chased after it with sticks and the brutal beating it received was surely intended for Deputy Commissioner Buck as well. People were unwittingly beating the crazy deputy commissioner, not the mad dog.)

*

The side of Lala Govindaram that Chetan saw during the days of the boycott of foreign clothing would always be engraved in his mind. Foreign clothing was collected from gali to gali, mohalla to mohalla, for seven days, and on the eighth day, at Nadiram's Tank, a bonfire was lit and the protestors were clubbed with lathis by the police. A list was prepared of the homes in the city that had not yet donated foreign clothing. Government officers were left off the list; the volunteers made it their mission to gather clothing from the rest. But there were some souls who were not persuaded by all their explanations, entreaties, shouts of victory and curses. The volunteers even called for their deaths, but they remained unmoved, as though those curses were not for them but for someone else. Among them was a well-to-do but miserly goldsmith by the name of Bhavaniya Ram. He would not donate even an old-fashioned, locally made rag, and this irked the volunteers; they felt that if one of their own people could not be prevailed upon, they'd surely fail with the foreign government. For six days, the volunteers visited his home constantly; different groups went, but it had no impact on him. The worst part was that instead of giving them foreign clothing, he roundly cursed both them and the Congress party. If it had been an ordinary movement, people would have torn him to pieces, but it was a non-violence movement, and the goldsmith was also a miser, and an eccentric to boot. When the volunteers finally gave up, Lala Govindaram himself decided to go there with two comrades on the final day.

In those days, discipline had become fairly lax in schools. The whole thing was a huge spectacle for the children. They wandered about the galis and mohallas shouting 'Long live the revolution!' When Chetan came out of the house in the morning, sometimes he'd go out with one band of children, sometimes another. He was quite eager to learn whether the goldsmith had won or the volunteers. Chetan went to watch with every group that came to his house. Sometimes he felt angry: Why didn't they just grab the goldsmith's turban? And sometimes he even felt a certain amount of respect for the goldsmith who remained unmoved despite all the pressure. He was eager to learn who would finally win the tug of war! When Lala Govindaram decided to go himself, he went along too.

The goldsmith's shop was about ten or fifteen shops into Lal Bazaar. Lala Bhavaniya was forging a piece of jewellery, his head wrapped in a silk turban incredibly filthy from continuous use. Lala Govindaram went and stood before his shop and said, very politely, but in a commanding tone, 'Lala Bhavaniram, your sacrifice for national independence has not yet been made. Take off your silk turban and give it to us.'

'"Take off your turban and give it to us"—as if you've opened up a turban shop?' grumbled Bhavaniya without looking at him, continuing with his work.

'Fine,' said Lala ji. 'I made a vow coming here that we would not allow you to be a party to sin. We will give our lives right here, but we won't budge until we've got the turban.'

And Lala Govindaram stood on one leg and turned his face towards the sun. Chetan didn't remember how long he stood there, or what mantra he recited. All he remembered was that Lala Govindaram's face gradually became imbued with a peculiar brightness, his veins tightened, his eyes rolled back and Chetan felt that if he continued to stare at the sun like that, it would climb down its rays and Bhavaniya and his shop would burst into flames. Just then Bhavaniya laid down his tools: he took off his turban and placed it at Lala Govindaram's feet.

*

Chetan had had great respect for Lala Govindaram ji since his childhood; he'd seen him working doggedly for the Congress movement, and Chetan was the sort of child who likes to wander about with his favourite leader, but is too shy and awestruck to speak to him. The first time he had come into contact with him was when he was studying in college and his older brother had quit the headache of running a laundry and, under the influence of his friend, the expert dyer, dry cleaner and nationalist poet Shri Rajaram, had jumped into the nationalist movement. His brother had ended up becoming a dentist, and was now happily pulling and filling his patients' teeth at his clinic in Anarkali, Lahore, and Shri Rajaram had opened a laundry in Ferozepur, or, who knows, perhaps he'd abandoned that too and gone somewhere else, but anyway, Lala Govindaram had been there as well. Chetan's awe of him had only grown since then, and whenever he came to town, he made sure to go by his room for fifteen or twenty minutes of conversation.

Lala Govindaram was a lover of literature; he always made sure there were plenty of poets at his meetings, and encouraged new ones. Poets were crucial for setting up meetings. A few poets would make a meeting more entertaining with their brilliant poems, and then the principal speaker would start his speech. When Hunar Sahib came to Jalandhar he went to read poems at a few of the meetings. So impressed by the Congress movement was he, that he'd stopped wearing a suit and started dressing in a homespun dhoti, kurta and cap, and writing nationalist poems with panache. Chetan was still in awe of Lala Govindaram, but Hunar Sahib's true self had been revealed to him. His nationalist poetry was as thoroughly empty as the drum of his personality. He never wrote poems that would get him arrested for treason. He made little effort for great gains; one achieves union with the beloved and doesn't miss out on paradise either. That's what his nationalist poetry was like as well:

> In every leaf is seen the majesty of the nation
> In every particle is seen the visage of the nation
> No idol can ever be so appealing
> To those whose hearts are filled with the visage of the nation

On one occasion (when he'd taken Chetan to a reading of his poetry at a meeting) he'd recited his poem in a lustrous voice. But he'd used the same poem at a religious meeting in Lahore on the occasion of Ram Navami; when he stood up to recite his poem, he'd changed only one word—he'd replaced 'nation' with the name 'Ram'!

> In every leaf is seen the majesty of Ram
> In every particle is seen the visage of Ram

It seemed to Chetan that it was Hunar Sahib's one goal in life to receive cheap praise cheaply. True literature, which requires labour, was perhaps not his thing. He'd knock together a poem, then make the rounds of the whole city reciting it to friends and acquaintances; after that, he'd organize meetings to recite it, and have it published in as many papers as possible. Sometimes Chetan thought, 'If he just invested half the amount of time he spends throwing all this together into true literature, perhaps he wouldn't have to do all this running around'; but by now this system had become second nature to him. Chetan had spent many years with Hunar Sahib, helping him out with all the running around and studying him, but he'd left all that behind long ago, and Hunar Sahib was still stuck in that same swamp. Wandering with him since morning, Chetan had full well understood what he was up to. He no longer felt one iota of respect for him and now Lala Govindaram was asking him to introduce his poem . . . Sure, he could give such an introduction to his poem, he thought, that Hunar Sahib would never turn his face towards Jalandhar again! But for one thing, Hunar Sahib was his elder brother's friend, and for another, he had once called him 'Guru', and although Chetan was no longer his pupil, Hunar still considered himself his guru, and Chetan was embarrassed by that.

*

As they walked towards Khingra Gate, Chetan told Lala Govindaram again that he would try to come that evening, but he didn't promise. If he hadn't seen Lala Govindaram he would definitely have dropped by to see him, but now, by good fortune, he'd set eyes on him, so it was possible he wouldn't go, because his father was coming that day. If his father had come, he might have to go out somewhere . . . and he asked him about the political goings-on in Jalandhar.

Lala Govindaram told him that there might be an agreement between Mahatma Gandhi and the government, and then the Congress would run for Assemblies and Parliament. If the Congress were to decide to run for Parliament, then his friends said he should stand for Parliament from Jalandhar . . . 'Hunar Sahib is insisting,' he said, 'that since I've spent the better part of my life in jails, I should also stand for election. He says this is also a type of struggle. As long as the nation doesn't become fully independent, the struggle will go on, whether it's in jails or Assemblies.'

'But what would you speak about in the Assembly meetings?' Chetan asked suddenly.

'Right now, there's really no need to speak,' said Lala Govindaram ji. 'Right now it's only necessary to raise your hand for "yes" or "no" votes when the leader calls out. Tomorrow, if Mahatma Gandhi tells us to empty the Assemblies and fill the jails, we need such men who will abandon their Assembly seats without hesitation and go and settle in at the jails. After thinking about all this, I've decided to stand for Assembly. No other man from Jalandhar could beat me,' he said and laughed slightly. 'Hunar Sahib assured me that he'd come from his village during the election days and stay in Jalandhar, and he'd recite a brand new poem about the election at every meeting.'

*

They'd reached Khingra Gate and although Lala Govindaram insisted that Chetan go with him as far as Sain Das High School's primary branch, and head over to Kot Kishanchand via Qila Mohalla and Puriyan Mohalla, Chetan didn't want to take such a roundabout route coming back from Kot Kishanchand; he'd just go through Puriyan Mohalla, walk through Bohar Wala Bazaar and return home. He promised that if it didn't get too late, he'd come by his room, even if it was just for a few minutes. And he held out his hand.

Lala Govindaram shook his hand fondly, tapped him on the back, and then went by Khingra Gate, as Chetan set out straight for Adda Hoshiarpur.

34

Adda Hoshiarpur was not far from Khingra Gate, and the sloping road from Puriyan Mohalla came out a little ahead of it. As Chetan set out after shaking hands with Lala Govindaram, he thought of that sloping road—it brought back so many bittersweet memories. He'd walked up and down it so many times—he would walk all around for miles just to pass below Kunti's window, just to catch a glimpse of her . . . and the strange thing was that after so many years, the powerful desire of his college days which had brought him running from miles away was still just as real, and he loved passing beneath her window just as much today.

But Kunti was a widow now. Why did Chetan want to see her again? Perhaps he didn't want to see her so much as to gain contact with those joyful days that had passed by as if in a dream—yet, just as in a dream, his sweet memories had evaporated as well . . . Kunti . . . the immutable symbol of his bashful love, even after becoming a widow, she was engraved on his mental canvas with her innocent charm . . . Maybe his love had not matured, but Kunti's married life would continue—Chetan had thought—her life would be successful—he'd feel happy to see her happy. Then he recalled how, after Kunti's wedding, he'd gone with Anant to Puriyan Mohalla, and Kunti, laden with her jingling jewellery and newly-wed's attire, was filling water at the well with a friend.

Chetan had chased after Anant, calling out loudly, with Kunti in earshot, 'You've got the energy of a newly-wed, bhai, how can I catch you now?' And as soon as she'd seen him, she'd started; the well wheel fell from her hand and the bucket dropped smack in the water with a whirr . . .

The strange thing was that the moment he thought of Kunti, Chetan felt alone in the middle of the crowded bazaar. Suddenly he didn't notice any of the diverting sights and sounds. Every memory of those days spent on the wings of his first love floated before his eyes. He was walking along the side of the street just so he could spend time alone re-living those happy memories. Perhaps it had rained more on the Company Bagh and Mandi side of town, because over by Khingra Gate there wasn't any mud and the street was clean.

. . . The full bucket of water had fallen into the water so hard that the rope snapped, and when the bucket broke away, the empty rope snapped back and wrapped itself backwards on the wheel. As Kunti jumped down from the plinth to avoid getting hit by the broken end of the rope, she laughed hysterically. When her friend leapt down after her and tried to catch her and smack her for her mischief, Kunti gazed into Chetan's eyes. She laughed, sprang ahead of her friend like a doe, and ran off glancing backwards . . .

'What difference would it have made to the Creator if he'd let those buds blossom a few more days,' thought Chetan. 'No matter how much greenery there is in the garden, if there are no buds peeking between leaves, laughing cheekily, there is nothing . . .' But the Creator had completely dried up the stream of her laughter . . . and he let out a deep sigh as he recalled that scorching summer afternoon when the sindoor was wiped from the parting in Kunti's hair, when her bangles were smashed, and when her laughter and smiles were forever locked away . . . when she had walked out barefoot in the scorching heat, wearing a white sari, for her last glimpse of the body at the cremation ground (that had been, until the day before, her husband, the father of her tiny child), she was silent, wounded to the quick . . . How thin she'd grown. Her face was pale as snow; all one noticed was her long nose and her eyes wandering in the boundless void . . . He could remember how she'd looked then as though he'd just seen her—her empty eyes, her long, thin nose, her colourless face, the set of her narrow hips, and the shocked desolation of her gaze—all of it came back to him in the tiniest details, not one gesture was out of place. Having taken her final glimpse of the body, she moved back a few steps, bowed over her husband's feet, and then walked back, just as she'd come, still and lifeless . . . and Chetan wished he could lie down on the burning earth beneath those soft, flower-like feet and not allow even the smallest bit of heat to touch them . . . 'Can those feet still leap from the plinth of the well the way they used to?' wondered Chetan. 'Can those lips giggle in that same way and can that waist double over with laughter? Perhaps never again' . . . and he sighed deeply again . . . and just then the sound of soft laughter came to his ears; he started and lifted his head—his heart pounded—it was Kunti . . .

*

Lost in his bittersweet memories, Chetan had arrived at that same slope near the road from Puriyan Mohalla which passed by Kunti's husband's press, and where he and his friend Guccho had sat waiting for the funeral bier on the front steps. Kunti was standing outside, about to walk down the steps of the house across from the slope. She was talking and laughing with a woman . . . She was not looking in Chetan's direction, but he would recognize that voice and that laugh anywhere.

Before Chetan could reach her, Kunti had said goodbye to the woman and departed. Chetan had thought she'd cross the street and come back towards her house. After her husband's death she'd gone back to live with her parents. But she didn't turn; she stayed on the same side of the street and set out towards Adda Hoshiarpur.

Chetan walked on with a pounding heart. He hadn't seen her face. She wore a simple white sari. She'd grown a bit plumper than before. But she was definitely Kunti, Chetan was sure of that. He thought of walking ahead and then turning and looking back at her. In the old days, he would have done just that. But Kunti was a widow now. He didn't have the courage. He continued along his side of the street, following her at some distance. She walked across the crossroads at Adda Hoshiarpur and continued straight. They reached the Gurukul at the Arya Samaj Temple. Chetan felt like going inside and sitting in the library for a bit. How many times had he heard Swami Satyadev's stories in that yard, how many evenings had he spent sitting and reading newspapers in that library? But Kunti continued ahead. Chetan had thought perhaps she'd turn left and go towards Devi Talab on the other side of the gate. But she continued straight towards Kot Kishanchand. Chetan kept wanting to hurry up and get ahead so he could get a sidelong glance of her; it also occurred to him that he should walk on the other side of the street . . . but for some reason his legs felt locked in place; neither could he walk ahead a few steps, nor could he get ahead of her, nor could he cross over to her side of the street. He continued at the same distance behind her, and at the same pace. His brain had completely shut down. His gaze remained fixed upon her ordinary white sari, and his entire body felt taut with excitement at the thought that perhaps by accident she'd turn and catch a glimpse of him. But there was no crowd, the street was empty, and Kunti walked along wrapped up in her own thoughts.

In the chowk outside Kot Kishanchand, she suddenly stopped to greet a woman coming from the other direction, and again Chetan heard her laughing.

The two of them were chatting and joking when Chetan passed them and walked on ahead at the same pace. But how could he turn to look? He simply didn't have the nerve. He looped around and turned towards the yard of Kot Kishanchand, and then he looked up briefly. It was Kunti . . . her face had filled out a little, but she still had that same scar shaped like the new moon on her forehead, those same large, round eyes, and that same pointed chin—just like Sulochna's. She wore neither powder nor rouge on her face, but she was radiant with laughter. It was a simple straightforward laughter, completely spontaneous. Just then Kunti lifted her eyes and glanced towards him. But Chetan looked away quickly. He turned. He wanted to walk up the steps of Rajat's home but his door was locked, so he went on towards Seth Hardarshan's mansion.

35

Chetan looked back once more before entering Seth Hardarshan's bungalow—Kunti was gone. Perhaps she had come to Kot Kishanchand to visit a relative or a friend . . . 'She was happy, she was laughing . . . perhaps looking after her son has helped her forget her sorrows,' thought Chetan. That one image of Kunti was forever engraved in his mind, when he had seen her at the cremation ground . . . and because of his great sentimentalism and foolishness, he had thought that she'd remain sad and depressed forever after . . . but time heals all wounds. It can help man forget immense sorrow . . . so why wasn't Chetan able to forget his own? Why had his wounds not healed? Why did they reopen at the slightest provocation? Chetan had no answer to his questions.

Vir Sen was wandering in the yard of the bungalow; now he walked abruptly up to Chetan and stood silently. Chetan turned and greeted him, then began to stroll about the yard with him.

Vir Sen was Seth Hardarshan's younger brother. He was tall and skinny; God knows what his father must have been thinking when he gave him the name Vir Sen—'brave warrior'—when he was born. He looked as though a strong puff of wind would blow him away. He'd returned from abroad just a few years before, but he didn't work at all. Whenever Chetan was in Jalandhar and walked in the direction of Kot Kishanchand, he sometimes visited

Seth Hardarshan's bungalow as well. Vir Sen would be quietly strolling by the bungalow or seated on a round cane chair staring at the ceiling. Sometimes he'd also find him out in the street— walking along one side or the other—lost in deep thought. He always wore fine clothing—a shirt and trousers—but his shirt had no collar, and from a distance he looked like a Christian priest. His complexion was not dark like that of South Indians, but it was a shade darker than the usual Punjabi colouring. His features were sharp and he had thin lips. If his body were to fill out a bit, he'd be handsome, like Seth Hardarshan. Chetan used to think he must have spent less time studying in England, than he did enjoying himself, and that's why his health was so poor. One day, he'd asked him in conversation if, while in England he'd only studied or had seen other sides of life as well? He'd answered him with just one sentence in English: 'If you throw me in the ocean, how can I not grab a board?'

The people of Kot Kishanchand considered him crazy, and Chetan had never seen him talking to anyone in the Rajat family or the Sondhi family across the way. But when his middle brother Shashi or his elder brother Hardarshan were not at home, Chetan would come and sit by him. He didn't talk quickly, but when he did begin to speak, he did so with great enthusiasm. Chetan had once asked the middle brother why Vir Sen didn't do any work, and he'd responded that his health had always been poor. In England he'd always had a fever. The doctors worried about his weak lungs, so they'd brought him back home. He wasn't interested in business and he wasn't able to complete any degree. Seth Hardarshan's business was flourishing, so he'd told Vir Sen that he should just eat, drink, enjoy himself and get healthy. Vir Sen was married and even had a child. But from the looks of him you wouldn't think he was a man who could keep a wife or father a child.

Vir Sen was at that moment in a great temper—as soon as he saw Chetan, he started to speak in English—'Revolution . . . revolution . . . revolution, it's the only answer to all of India's ills. The Congress screams, "Long live the revolution!" But those people don't want a revolution. What revolution means is that "down" goes "up". May the power go to those who have been ground down by poverty, starvation, unemployment and illiteracy for centuries. Revolution is what happened in Russia, when the power truly came into the hands of the poor and the labourers. This won't be a revolution; it will be a compromise. Their people are forging a compromise with the government. They're thinking of running for Assemblies. Will this bring about revolution? Never! It will be a compromise between the businessmen of two different nations. Even if, for appearance's sake, the leaders of the people go into the Assemblies, the true power will remain in the hands of the capitalists. Just you watch . . .'

Vir Sen walked excitedly around the yard a few times, then began to speak again, 'People think I'm crazy; they've kept me ill, they don't let me do any work. In reality, they are frightened of me, they're afraid of my ideas. They think I didn't spend time with the right sort of people in England, that I hung around with communists, that I became a Russian agent; they fear that if I become independent, I'll start a revolution in India . . .'

Chetan stood off to one side, looked this 'revolutionary' over from head to toe and laughed to himself. But Vir Sen did not notice Chetan's critical gaze. He kept pacing excitedly. After another round of the yard, he continued, 'But I'm not a communist, are there even any communists here? What I'm saying is what any person with eyes can see . . . the Congress will go into the Assemblies, and they'll fight after they go there. Then they'll develop a taste for power! How will they bring revolution after that? Why would the English leave behind such a large empire of their own volition? Only violent revolution can rip them out and cast them into the sea. They'll only leave of their own accord if they see something in it for themselves. The Englishman is a businessman, he'll only leave after striking up a compromise with the businessmen of this nation . . . and do you think the Congress is an organization of the people? The people are a façade! At its core are businessmen. Where do those lakhs of rupees for the Congress come from? The businessmen of this country donate them— this struggle for independence is a fight between this country's business interests and that country's . . . these businessmen will start a revolution . . . long live the revolution . . .' He shook his head with displeasure and laughed.

'But you are also a Baniya, a businessman . . .' Chetan began.

'The Baniyas are seated inside!' he said, turning suddenly and pointing towards the drawing room. 'I am an independent thinker!'

And without looking at Chetan, Vir Sen began to walk in circles again. Chetan stayed there for a few moments, then smiled and walked into the drawing room. Shashi was sitting on the mat in front. A fan spun above, and to the left, next to the door, some people were seated on couches with teapoys placed before them, writing out lists of some kind.

Shashi was the second of the three brothers; he was a bit shorter than his elder and younger brothers, his lips were plump, and he was much fairer than the other two. He had a round chubby face. As a child, he must have genuinely looked like the moon, which was why his parents had called him Shashi. He was a businessman with a cheerful nature. He had no especial interest in social activities and had left independent thinking to his younger brother while he himself looked after all the business.

'When did you come from Lahore?' asked Shashi.

368

'Not from Lahore. I've just returned from Shimla.'

'From Shimla?'

And Chetan told him with embarrassment of his stay in Shimla, and added, 'I've come here after a long time and I'm leaving again soon. I thought I'd come by to see you.'

'You did a very good thing. My brother has mentioned you many times. He's a great fan of yours,' Shashi laughed.

'Is he at home, or has he gone out somewhere?' asked Chetan.

'He's at home; he's resting. He'll come down shortly.'

In the midst of this, Chetan kept staring at the lists that were being prepared by the three or four deeply engrossed men seated in the room, who kept interrupting Shashi with questions. After a little while, Chetan asked, 'Are you preparing for the municipal election?'

'No, Bhai Sahib is not standing for the municipality this time,' said Shashi.

'Then what are these voter lists you're preparing?'

'These are lists of Assembly voters! Mahatma Gandhi is talking to the viceroy—the elections will be in a year or two. That's why these lists are being prepared.'

'Seth Sahib must be standing for the Assembly?'

'People are putting pressure on him to go into the Assembly,' said Shashi. 'The committee field seems very small for his talents.'

'Then will he stand on behalf of the Unionist party or as an Independent?' asked Chetan.

'No, people are telling him to stand for the Congress.'

'But Seth ji has never been a member of the Congress, he's never even gone to jail.'

'Going into the Assembly and going to jail are two different things,' said Shashi in the manner of a politician. 'People who are skilled at going to jail don't necessarily have a talent for speaking in the Assembly as well. As for Congress membership, that's just a matter of four annas. If the possibility of getting a ticket comes, that will be taken care of as well.'

Chetan was silent. He thought of Lala Govindaram and his long service to the independence struggle.

'Bhai Sahib has been going to the Congress Working Committee meetings. That's where it will be decided. But on one side is the Hindu Mahasabha and on the other, the Unionist Party, which has the cooperation of the government. It's not easy to fight against them. Bhai Sahib is under pressure from several quarters, but if he gets the Congress ticket, then he'll stand on behalf of the Congress. He thinks that if the Congress goes into Assemblies, then they'll show they can do better work than the government. If they are forced to come outside again, then when there's another agreement, when we get self-rule, they'll go back in. If Bhai Sahib goes into the Congress right now, then no one can stop him from becoming a minister when the time comes.'

'But what's the need to prepare lists so far in advance?'

'This is Bhai Sahib's way of doing things,' said Shashi. 'If we start finding out about voters now, it will be easy to find out who's important in which mohalla, who has influence on how many people. If a voter's name should be on the lists according to law but isn't, then it will be included as well, and if Bhai Sahib stands from the Congress or from the Mahasabha or as an Independent, we'll need these lists for sure, and we'll need to meet important people right away.'

'Why doesn't he stand from the Unionist side?'

'What he's trying to do is get the Congress ticket, and some friends from the Punjab Congress Committee have even said that the competition will be stiff and it will cost thousands of rupees. If a Congress member wins, it will be good for the Congress as well. Bhai Sahib is thinking ahead. If he doesn't get the Congress ticket, then we'll see.'

'So this is why Vir Sen was calling the Congress a bunch of businessmen,' Chetan thought to himself. He was going to say something about Lala Govindaram when Seth Hardarshan pushed aside the curtain of the inner room and entered—he wore a fine milky-white homespun kurta, churidar pyjamas, a homespun achkan and a Gandhi cap. Whenever Chetan had seen him before, he'd always worn a silk kameez, cotton churidar pyjamas, a silk achkan and a cap. 'So Seth ji has definitely decided to become a Congress member,' he said to himself.

Seth Hardarshan looked handsome in his homespun attire—he had a thin, sharp nose, and thin lips. He certainly did not look like a businessman. There was an innocence to his manner of speech that was instantly appealing. His name was apt. His parents must surely have thought of Krishna when they'd first laid eyes on him.

*

And just then, as he gazed at Seth Hardarshan, Chetan recollected the former owner of that mansion, Pandit Radharaman, advocate. Pandit Radharaman's father had left him quite a bit of money and he had been a famous advocate himself. He was among the most eminent people in the city. Chetan had first seen him when he was in Class Five. He was standing for election for membership of the Municipal Committee at the time, and he had spent so much money on the election, and done so much publicity, and there were so many posters pasted up in every gali and bazaar, that even the city's children were familiar with his name. When he won the election, there was a procession so magnificent that Chetan did not see its like again until Mahatma Gandhi came to town. There was a band, schoolboys, volunteers from the service committee—Chetan had seen the procession near Company Bagh, which

371

was when he first laid eyes on Pandit Radharaman. He was forty or so at that time, quite fair, with slightly sunken cheeks, large, drooping moustaches, an achkan, churidar pyjamas, and a large turban on his head.

He was also elected chair of the committee and, after that election, he began to participate in social affairs regularly. But eight or so years ago, news had spread through the city like wildfire one morning that Pandit Radharaman had gone bankrupt and run away from home in the dead of the night. Upon inquiring, Chetan had found out that for some years he'd been investing in the stock market and that he'd bought shares of cotton and lost lakhs of rupees. There was also a widespread rumour that he'd committed suicide.

But a few days later, they found out that he'd gone to a friend's house in Lahore and had now returned. A short while after that, they heard he'd surrendered all his property to the lenders and gone back to Lahore, where he'd set up a practice . . . And one day, Chetan had been walking towards Kot Kishanchand, when he saw that his mansion was being painted red on the dome above the enclosing walls, and yellow on the middle square parts. There he'd learned from a friend that Seth Hardarshan had bought the mansion, that he was a Tata agent, and had bought up Tata Steel company agencies in Jalandhar, Hoshiarpur, Ludhiana and Kapurthala. And just as Seth Dalmia's name became famous all through the region a few years later when he purchased the shares and property of Punjab's premier capitalist, Lal Harkishanlal, after he'd gone bankrupt, so too did Seth Hardarshan become the talk of the town among Jalandharites when he purchased Pandit Radharaman's property.

Although Seth Hardarshan was Punjabi, his father had done business in UP. Upon his death, the burden of his business fell on Seth Hardarshan's shoulders. He was the one who'd taken the Tata agency and he was the one who'd bought all of Pandit Radharaman's property and named his mansion 'Hardarshan Villa'.

*

Seth Hardarshan had only studied up to his BA, but his conversation, manner and accent gave one the impression that he was highly educated and cultured. In the very beginning, when he'd first arrived, he used to wear a closed-neck coat, a dhoti and a black cap embroidered with a silk border, but since then he'd started wearing churidar pyjamas and an achkan.

In the first Municipal Committee election he'd run as an Independent and got elected. This year, there had been a fair amount of opposition against him in the city. People thought he no longer kept good company; he'd started to drink and stories were spreading about his character; one side was insisting that it wouldn't let him become a member of the Municipal Committee . . . but he wasn't standing for election for the committee at all. He had his sights set higher . . .

The moment he entered the room, he said to Shashi, 'I'm off to meet with Rayzada Hansraj; just now I talked with Lahore on the phone, if he proposes my name then my nomination is assured.'

Then his gaze fell upon Chetan. Chetan got up and greeted him. He walked over to him, patted him on the shoulder and asked how he was doing. Chetan gave an account of his doings with some embarrassment.

'You, my friend, went off to Lahore and left our gatherings barren,' Seth Hardarshan laughed—a sweet, charming laugh. 'If you were still around, we'd have something to listen to now and then. We haven't seen any writers around for years now.'

'How could you have the time for literature and all that nowadays, Seth ji?' Chetan laughed self-deprecatingly.

'No, not at all!' he replied with a faint smile. 'How long are you here? Let's have a get-together.'

'I'm leaving,' said Chetan. 'I'm on a three-month leave. I have to go and take care of some work. Hunar Sahib's in town these days. He may be here a while, because he's promised Lala Govindaram that if he stands for the Assembly, he'll recite a new poem for every meeting.'

Chetan had purposely said this to gauge his reaction. He thought Seth ji's brow would contract slightly and his face would become clouded, but instead of scowling, he continued to smile sweetly. 'Lala Govindaram has performed a great service,' he said. 'He should definitely run on behalf of the Congress.' Then he stopped for a moment and added carelessly, 'People are saying the same to me, but I haven't done any service for the Congress. Lala Govindaram is the only one worthy of the position.'

Chetan laughed to himself . . . 'Hunar Sahib has recently done a translation of the second chapter of the Shrimad Bhagavad Gita,' he said. 'He's also rendering the Upanishads into simple Urdu poetry. He wants to get them published as well, but you know the situation for writers, that's what he's working on these days . . .'

'Please tell him to come and see me. This is virtuous work. If you do stay in town, do bring him over one evening and he can recite it to us as well.'

'If I stay, I'll definitely bring him by.'

'All right then, you must excuse me now. I have to go out for work.'

'If you are going by car, could you please drop me by Adda Hoshiarpur?'

'Yes, yes, of course.'

And Chetan said goodbye to Shashi Seth.

'Where does this Hunar Sahib live?' asked Seth Hardarshan suddenly. Then, without waiting for Chetan's reply, he remarked to Shashi, 'Shashi, send someone to invite him here.'

'He has many haunts,' said Chetan. 'But rest assured, I'll send him over.'

*

Vir Sen was still wandering about outside. Chetan said goodbye to him in passing, but he did not respond.

36

Although he'd promised he'd go straight to Hunar Sahib and send him to Seth Hardarshan after he took his leave at Adda Hoshiarpur, when he arrived below Lala Govindaram's room after going through Puriyan Mohalla and Qila Mohalla, he didn't feel like going upstairs. After speaking with Seth Hardarshan, he was firmly convinced that the Congress ticket would go to Seth Hardarshan, and not to Lala Govindaram. But this didn't make Chetan as sad as when Seth Hardarshan confirmed in a way that this independence struggle, which the people considered their own struggle, and for the sake of which thousands of people in Jallianwallah Bagh had been slaughtered, taking bullets to their chests, and thousands and thousands had gone to jail and climbed smiling to the gallows, was actually considered by the country's capitalists to belong to them. 'This is the reason (this was how Seth Hardarshan explained it to him) why Birla welcomed Mahatma Gandhi when he came from Africa. He put his home, his lands and his purse at his service . . .'

'So are the people in this struggle something like soldiers, who come in handy in battles between ambitious politicians or emperors?' thought Chetan. 'Will the condition of ordinary people remain the same when the country becomes free? If the English haven't left the country yet, and already Seth Hardarshan can join the Congress without having given the slightest aid in the struggle for the country's freedom, when the country is free, his own friends and relations wouldn't have authority over it. What would happen to Bansi the vegetable seller then, and to Lala Govindaram, and the thousands of volunteers like them and to their children and grandchildren?' And Chetan felt extremely sad. In Puriyan Mohalla, he'd walked below Kunti's window; he even turned and glanced back, and saw the window was closed—but instead of thinking about Kunti, he walked along pondering this problem. He stopped for a moment below Lala Govindaram's window. At one point, the thought occurred to him that he should go up and warn Lala Govindaram that Seth Hardarshan was making every effort to snatch away his authority, but then he walked on. He thought he'd talk to Hunar Sahib that night and tell him about it.

*

He was walking quickly out of Bohar Wala Bazaar, when suddenly a man sitting at a shop jumped up, rushed over, and grabbed Chetan by the arm.

Chetan started and turned.

'Ah, *Sarchashma*!'[12] cried Chetan on seeing his old classmate.

'What's new, Mr Poet Laureate?'

And the two of them burst out laughing.

'Sarchashma' linked arms with him and walked him back to his shop.

'When did you get back from Lahore?'

'I went to Shimla for three months—I've been back three or four days.'

'You'll stay a while, won't you?'

---

[12] Wellspring; fountainhead.

'No, I'm leaving today or tomorrow. But you tell me, how's your shop doing—did you write anything more, or are you still just a *Sarchashma-e-Zindagi*?'[13]

'The shop is going great—take a look, I have a new signboard.'

Chetan looked up—the board was fixed above the shop, right in the middle of the bazaar.

BHATIJE DI HATTI, it said in Punjabi—'The Nephew's Shop'.

'How did this "Nephew's Shop" signboard replace "Lala Amarnath, Second-Hand Bookseller"?' asked Chetan, sitting down on the stoop right outside the shop. 'Has your nephew joined you?'

Lala Amarnath slapped Chetan's hands and guffawed loudly, and instead of walking around to sit on his cushion, he leapt over the one-and-a-half-foot-high counter and sat down.

'No, there's no nephew, I'm the one who's become the nephew, and even those boys whose uncle I actually am call me nephew, and I have great fun with it.'

'But why?'

'I'll tell you in a minute, but first tell me this: will you drink lassi or shikanji?'

'No, I won't drink anything.'

'Then have a lemon soda.'

'Arré, no, yaar, tell me your story!'

But Lala ji told the soda-water seller next door to open up a lemonade, and then said, 'You remember, don't you, when I opened a shop next to the Panjpir Primary School, five years ago today . . .'

'. . . and you strung copies of *Sarchashma-e-Zindagi* along ropes all around the shop,' finished Chetan, guffawing loudly. He

---

[13] A spring of life.

held out his hand and Lala Amarnath slapped it with his own wide palm, laughing just as loudly.

*

Amarnath had been a classmate of Chetan's. He was of medium height, with a wide forehead, face, hands and feet. He was neither particularly quick in his studies, nor a slowpoke. In Class Eight, Chetan had attempted to write a novel. In those days, after reading *Chandrakanta* and *Bhoot Nath* and a few books of Arsène Lupin and Sherlock Holmes (which the Urdu translator had transcribed as 'Holuhmz', and which they all read with that pronunciation), Chetan had begun to write a detective novel in imitation of them, and he'd read a couple of chapters aloud to Amarnath. Then the two of them got together and cooked up schemes for getting it calligraphed and printed. Urdu printing was done at Shyam Press on Station Road, and right near the press was the Calligraphy Centre, so the two friends wandered over there to inquire about rates for having it calligraphed and printed.

But by the time he reached Class Nine, Chetan had begun writing poetry, and his novel fell by the wayside, or rather, he completely forgot about it. One day, Amarnath brought him home on the way back from school. He lived in Mohalla Mendruan, and it was right on the way. Chetan was astonished when he entered the sitting room. A rope was tied from one wall of the sitting room to the other, and from it hung numerous copies of a book, its pages spread out on each side like bird feathers. To the right lay a pile of copies of the same book on a low desk. Lala Amarnath had picked up a copy from that pile and placed it in Chetan's hand. A paper-bound book of five formes, double demy size! The heavy cover paper was a deep pink, and on it was written in large round letters:

Sarchashma-e-Zindagi
Kalme-zarrī-rakam Lala Amarnath Mehndru[14]

Chetan flipped through a couple of pages. On them were written essays on living life, in fairly difficult Urdu (which Amarnath had Persianized). The first essay was on the power of desire—who knows where he'd come up with the ideas to prepare the book. Chetan didn't understand any of it. He didn't like the language, nor did he like the style. Although he felt extremely jealous of Amarnath, he dismissed his work, and said to himself, 'He's a stupid guy, he's going to write a stupid book.' He gave great praise for his writing and printing of the book. Then he asked, 'Did you sell some too?'

'I just got it printed today,' Amarnath had said. 'All these copies were prepared last night; this morning, before going to school, I got all of these cut by Taj Ram binders in Bhairon Bazaar. Now I'll worry about selling them.'

'So did you bind them yourself?'

'What else? This is a simple paper binding. I'll put on the cardboard covers myself.'

Chetan offered him much praise for the binding. He had thought Amarnath would give him a copy of *Sarchashma-e-Zindagi*. But when Amarnath took the book from his hand and placed it back on the pile, speaking enthusiastically all the while, Chetan felt offended and held out his hand to depart. Amarnath came with him as far as the door. After he had shaken hands with

---

[14] *The Spring of Life*: From the golden pen of Lala Amarnath Mehndru.

him and come outside, he was burning with envy—Amarnath, whom no one at school knew as a writer, had become a man of letters and he, who considered himself a poet, story writer, novelist and who knows what else, was just wandering about aimlessly.

'Chetan . . . Chetan!'

Chetan turned when he heard his name being called. Amarnath was running after him with a book in his hand.

'Yaar, I forgot to give you the book!' And he held out the book in both his hands and presented it to him as a gift.

Although Amarnath had corrected his mistake, and Chetan's ego had been somewhat appeased, he was still unable to read it, even when he tried. If it were poetry, a story or novel, he'd have finished it on the way home, but he didn't understand any of the titles in the table of contents: The Power of Desire; Self-Confidence; Ego; *Vahadete Vajood*.[15] Although, like some of the other youths in the Punjab, he also wrote Urdu poetry, he had not read Urdu regularly. In class, he studied Hindi and Sanskrit— 'Where on earth did the bastard lift all this stuff from?' he asked himself as he placed the book in the cupboard.

The next day, when Amarnath asked in school how he liked the book, Chetan said, 'Wow, what a book! You yourself truly are the "spring of life"!' Amarnath was pleased by this, but from that day on he came to be known as 'Sarchashma-e-Zindagi'.

*

Chetan recalled that incident from their school days as he sat on the stoop sipping lemonade, and he smiled.

*

---

[15] In the language of Sufis, considering every particle of creation a part of the creator.

382

After that, for an entire week, Amarnath had gone to all the booksellers in Bazaar Sheikhan and Bhairon Bazaar, but no one was prepared to take even one of his books. Finally, he left some copies at Mahantram's shop after promising him that Mahantram could take his own commission before giving him his money when they were sold. Mahantram asked for a fifty per cent commission. Amarnath didn't want to agree to more than twenty-five per cent, but his experiences from the past seven days gave him no choice and he left the books there at fifty per cent (and that too, on loan).

After this, he brought all his classmates to Mahantram's bookshop on some pretext or another, and showed them the copies of *Sarchashma-e-Zindagi*, but although everyone congratulated him, not one of them showed the good sense of purchasing the book.

Then one day, when Chetan was going to his father's in Mukerian during the holidays, he ran into Amarnath on the train holding a bundle of copies of *Sarchashma-e-Zindagi*, trying to sell the books. Along with that, he was also selling copies of some other cheap books. 'Bhai, the book doesn't sell on its own. If there are other books with it, it's easier to sell.' And he told him frankly that he'd been selling on the trains for a whole month, and he'd sold his own book too—twenty copies in one month . . . 'Instead of giving a loan of fifty per cent to Mahantram, it's so much better to sell them to travellers at twenty-five per cent off,' he laughed, and held out his hand for praise.

'You're amazing!' said Chetan, slapping his hand, but to himself he said, 'He may or may not become a poet or story writer, but he'll definitely be a businessman.' He admired Amarnath's drive and dedication too, and when, after passing the Matric, Amarnath opened a shop on Panjpir Road near a primary school, Chetan was not surprised. He was passing by once, when he stopped on seeing Amarnath sitting there. He'd hung stories from strings tied to nails, and the small glass penholder he'd always used had been washed and set up outside the shop on the platform. He had set out lead pencils, slate pencils, holders, nibs and two boxes of chalk, and inside he'd suspended copies of *Sarchashma-e-Zindagi* over a rope, just as he had at home. He told Chetan proudly that he'd started the shop with just five rupees. He'd got the stories on credit, and when he sold them, he kept a fifty per cent commission and gave the rest back, then bought new ones.

*

Chetan cast one glance at this new 'Nephew's Shop'—every nook and cranny, inside and out, was crammed with pictures and books. There were frames of all sizes, mirrors and pictures on the left and right of the counter, and in front of his cushion. Books were stacked to the ceiling inside. Amarnath told him he'd created all this with those same five rupees, and he'd moved from Panjpir to Bhairon Bazaar, the centre of the local book business. First he did book binding. During Diwali, he'd begun to frame pictures, and sell stories and second-hand books, and starting this year, he'd started stocking new books as well. Dina Nath the Bookseller had given his own shop to his sons, and had himself opened up a shop across the way and called it *Chacha di Hatti*, or 'Uncle's Shop', so Amarnath had put up his 'Nephew's Shop' sign. Uncle's Shop hadn't got famous, but Nephew's Shop had become as famous as the dickens. How? To explain this, Lala Amarnath, aka, Sarchashma-e-Zindagi, aka Nephew Sahib, took out some handbills and posters from the rack to his right and showed them to Chetan.

On the first was written 'Nephew's Shop' in thick letters and beneath it were printed the details: that Lala Amarnath, bookbinder and framer, had also started to sell second-hand books and that the shop's name was now 'Nephew's Shop', and that the nephew was ready and waiting to serve everyone at all times.

The title of the second poster was DON'T READ ME, since a man immediately stops walking and begins reading the advertisement on seeing such a title, and below was an announcement that Nephew's Shop has opened in Bhairon Bazaar, and that Nephew Sahib not only sells stationary supplies, but also binds books, makes frames, buys second-hand books at a higher rate than others, and sells them cheap!

On the third was written in thick red letters:

All our problems have disappeared!
Nephew's Shop is open
Nephew's Shop is open
Nephew's Shop is open

On the fourth was a verse written by Nephew Sahib himself in red letters:

Stop, Uncle, look, what is this?
It's a shop, a nephew's shop, and the nephew
    sells books, very cheaply!

All the posters and handbills basically said the same thing. Lala Amarnath had pasted up the posters with his own hands in every gali and mohalla of the city and he'd handed out all the handbills himself, and now he was the nephew of the entire city.

Seeing the posters and hearing the tale of Lala Amarnath's struggle, Chetan said, 'Your book may or may not be the fount of life, but you yourself surely are.' And when he held out his hand chuckling, Amarnath placed his own broad hand on his, laughing in the same way.

'But what did happen to those copies of that book of yours? Did they all sell?' asked Chetan suddenly.

'There are ten or twenty copies left. I haven't sold them directly, but I have indirectly,' he said, and he looked around inside and then handed Chetan a large poster. Across the top was written in thick red letters:

A book full of the valuable secrets of life
  Sarchashma-e-Zindagi
Free . . . free . . . free . . . free

And after that were written the conditions for attaining this valuable book: anyone who had ten books bound at once, or five pictures framed, or bought five rupees' worth of books, would receive this valuable book free of charge.

'You've really done it, bhai!' Chetan stood up and handed back the poster. 'Everyone should learn how to fight the good fight from you.'

He shook his hand warmly and, regarding his thick-skulled classmate with respect for the first time, Chetan took his leave.

37

Chetan was walking into Papadiyan Bazaar when he saw Shyama of the Jhamans running headlong towards him. His face was pale.

'What's wrong?' asked Chetan as he drew near.

'I'm going to get Hansa,' he replied without stopping.

'What happened?' Chetan turned and called out.

But all he could make out from what Shyama said as he ran on were two words, 'Bhago' and 'Amirchand'.

Chetan continued walking. Up ahead, Hakim Dina Nath was quickly shutting up his shop.

'What's wrong, Hakim Sahib?' asked Chetan, laughing. 'Where are you off to?'

'There was a fight in the mohalla,' he said, quickly fastening the lock and slipping the key into his pocket. He picked up his bag of essential medicines and turned his steps towards Chaurasti Atari.

'In which mohalla? Ours or yours?' Chetan meant to ask in which chowk of the mohalla, Andon ka Chowk or Chowk Chaddhiyan, because Hakim Dina Nath lived near Chowk Chaddhiyan in Gali Bathaiyan.

'Yours!' said Hakim ji without stopping. 'Amirchand beat up Bhago.'

'He beat her up!'

'Shyama just told me. I'm going to go see what happened.'

Chetan thought about what Laloo had said. 'But she was staying in Mandi; did she come over here?' he asked.

'They say she just got here.'

Hakim Sahib was walking so fast he was almost running. Racing to keep up with him, Chetan asked, 'So how badly did he beat her? Will she survive?'

'I can't say. Shyama told me just now. She's wounded, she could be dying . . . What an idiot that Amirchand is. Now that his brother's become a deputy, is he going to kill the whole mohalla?'

In Chaurasti Atari, Chetan ran into his younger brother Shankar running in the other direction.

'What happened?' asked Chetan.

'Go to the mohalla quickly. Amirchand beat Bhago. She was bleeding from the head.' And then he said to Dina Nath, 'Hakim Sahib, please run over there. I'm going to get Parasaram from the akhara.'

Everyone in Bajiyanwala Bazaar was running towards the mohalla.

When Chetan reached the chowk of the mohalla with Hakim Dina Nath, there was already a huge uproar. A large crowd had filled the square—spectators were gathering from Khoslon ki Gali, Barhaiyon ki Gali, Chowk Chaddhiyan and Gali Baniyan. There were more women than men. Aunty Purandei stood on the plinth of the well, listing seven generations of Khatris, and cursing them all. Shanno stood on her roof, grimacing. 'She blackened her face when she went to Mandi—why did she need to come back to the mohalla? This was a respectable mohalla of daughters and sisters, how could such a loose woman live here?'

And Aunty Purandei was asking why Shanno hadn't thought of the daughters and sisters of the mohalla when she was getting cosy with her brother-in-law, and giving birth to a bastard son?

And Pandit Daulat Ram, his braid tied up, a shawl printed with the name of Ram wrapped around his body, his wooden sandals flapping, was sometimes trying to get Aunty Purandei to quieten down and sometimes clasping his hands in entreaty before Shanno.

And Bhagavanti lay still in the chowk in front of the gate of the Sunars. The women had revived her by sprinkling water on her face. Blood oozed from her head. You could hear her screaming 'Oh, oh!' all the way through the bazaar and she writhed about as though she were about to die.

When Hakim Dina Nath came forward with his bag, Aunty Purandei stopped him at the plinth of the well. 'Let Hansa come,' she said. 'We have to get the police report written first.'

Chetan's mother and Chanda were standing in the sitting room with their veils down. Chetan went and stood with them. Ma asked where he'd gone off to; they'd been waiting for him to come home and eat. And she told him that his father had arrived; he'd been asking for him. He'd gone off with Chacha Fakir Chand and would be back that night.

Chetan made the excuse that he'd run into some friends from Lahore. 'How did all this happen?' he asked his mother.

Then his mother told him that she had been upstairs, and had heard that Bhagavanti had come half an hour before. Bhago had left her things at the family home and asked Aunty Purandei to watch her children; then she'd come into the chowk and sat down at the gate of the Sunars and was chatting, when someone, Shanno, or Rajo, or Pyaru's mother, who, being Brahmins like the Jhamans, went and told Amirchand that Bhago had come. He had rushed out of the bhuvara shouting, and grabbed her by the braid and dragged her from her seat. He removed his shoe and beat her nearly to death. Blood was streaming down her head. Oh, how he dashed her against the hard floor of the mohalla, that cruel man.

'Where's Telu?' asked Chetan. 'Hasn't he come?'

'I haven't heard if Telu has come,' said Ma.

Chetan stood silently for a moment, watching the spectacle unfolding in the mohalla below. People were pouring in from the bazaar. The crowd was growing larger. A huge commotion had broken out.

Chetan watched carefully: there were three or four clear streams in the crowd. Some Brahmin women were on Bhagavanti's side. They believed that since she had taken a husband, she should stay in her home. They surrounded Bhagavanti and spoke about this loud enough for the whole mohalla to hear.

Chachi Dayavanti was waving her arms in the air, surrounded by some women, saying that they were under the rule of the British, not the rule of Amirchand; when he comes to power, then tell him (this was intended for those Khatri women who were opposed to Bhagavanti coming into the mohalla) he can pass a law that Khatri girls can't marry into Brahmin homes.

'Oh, did that happen just today? Didn't the Kshatriya kings give their daughters to the rishis in the olden times?' another woman was saying.

'Kings' and 'rishis'—Chetan thought of Lala Mukandi Lal and Telu and smiled. Pandit Daulat Ram, hearing what she was saying from the plinth, quoted the saint Shri Ramanand: *jāt pāt pūche na ko, har ko bhaje so har kā ho*—Don't talk to me of caste, he who sings to Hari belongs to Him alone!'

And Aunty Purandei was saying, 'Sister, Mahatma Gandhi says it's because of this caste business that we're not getting self-rule.'

'Then give your daughter to a Bhangi or Chamar, we'll get self-rule right away!' shrieked Shanno, and Aunty Purandei let loose a shower of 'sweet words' . . .

There were a few Khatri women with these Brahmin women who were siding with Shanno. Among them, Rajo of the

Chowdhrys, her face lined with premature wrinkles, her weeping, dim eyes blinking, was saying:

'Oh, sister, if just a man did it, then filth wouldn't spread in the home (she was apparently referring to Shanno). She didn't take up with her brothers-in-law!'

Hearing this, Pandit Daulat Ram started crying out, 'Hari! Hari!' and 'Radhe Sham!' loudly.

*

The second group was of Khatri women near the doorway of the Chowdhrys; they were not in favour of Bhago entering the mohalla. Principal among them was Anant's mother, Aunty Lal Dei. Suppressing all other voices with her own, she was saying:

'Oho, if all she wanted was to take up with someone, she could have kept doing it in Mandi. No one was rushing over to find out . . . but it's not right to rub it in her brother-in-law's face in the mohalla.'

'Indeed, may your husband live long!' said Dhanno the Khatri. 'A man's honour counts for something too. Mangal's father (Lala Mukandi Lal) is not like that. If he were here, blood would flow!'

Two or three Brahmin women who were against the Jhamans were also present. Pyaru's mother was saying, 'Oh, this Telu has really gone too far. He goes up to the roof and oils his body and does push-ups . . . Neighbours' mothers and daughters are one's own mothers and daughters.'

Dhanno interrupted her, 'Oh, Aunty, how can you criticize the men? If a woman herself jumps from roof to roof, what's a man to do?'

'Oh, I've never heard of a widowed woman going and setting herself up in another's home instead of shaving her head. There are ten widows in the mohalla who have spent their widowhood spinning. She's gone too far.'

'Oho, who knows what caste she is? Khatri women don't do such evil things.'

At this, Pandit Daulat Ram placed his hands over his ears and cried out 'Shiv! Shiv!'

*

A group of men, among them Pandit Shivnarayan and Gurdayal, were expressing their disappointment at the fact that Amirchand, being a man, had raised his hand to a woman. If Mukandi Lal had hit her, that would be another matter, since he was the one who'd been injured, but what was this Amirchand thinking to start beating her?

'Why did he beat a woman? Beating a woman is like beating the earth. If he was a man, he should have fought Telu.'

'Oh, it's his pride over his brother becoming a collector, that's what it is. You know what they say, "The poor Jat got a dish of water and drank so much he got the bloat."'

'It's like they say in the shastras, isn't it? "Doom approaches and brainpower departs,"' said Pandit Shivnarayan.

There was all sorts of gossip being whispered at the fringes of this.

'Which bastard is Amirchand afraid of? Amichand himself has become a collector. Did he kill a police officer that someone's going to tell his brother? After all we have to live under his rule now.'

'Whether he's a collector or a commissioner, right now, it's the British Raj. Someone who's beaten up a woman from another

392

family can't just sit at home. Now that his brother has become collector, is he just going to go around beating up the whole mohalla?'

And thus, everyone was speaking their minds. Just then the Jhaman boys, Hansa, Shyama and Genda, entered from the bazaar side. They were all carrying lathis. Right from the bazaar, they started shouting out curses, 'Where is that son-of-a-collector? We're going to see to his collecting today.'

But when they learned that Amirchand had beaten Bhago and gone off somewhere, and that his wife had locked the door from inside and was terrified, and there was no one to listen to them right now, they all rushed towards Bhagavanti.

Aunty Purandei said they should first go and fill out a police report. A boy produced a charpoy from somewhere in the blink of an eye. Bhagavanti was laid upon it, crying 'Oh, woe!' and shivering. Then Chetan came up and said, 'Her head is bleeding; get a certificate from a doctor first, then go and do the police report.'

'Oh, what will we do with a "certificate"? Are the police blind? Won't they see she's bleeding?' asked Pandit Gurdayal.

'Well then, our certificate is Hakim Sahib—he's right here with us,' said someone tapping Hakim Dina Nath on the back.

Hakim Dina Nath seemed suddenly to remember how busy he was. 'Shyama told me that Bhago's head had burst open. I've brought a first-aid kit. If you need to fill out a report then go and do it. I'll be at my shop.'

And he turned to go. But Pandit Gurdayal practically grabbed his feet and said, 'Don't be afraid, please, just please come along; the police will see her busted head, then you can bandage it up right there.'

Chetan wanted to say there was no use in that. It was enough to have the report written out at the station, but he considered it useless to argue with those fools. Four men lifted up the charpoy and set off for Charbagh Police Station via Baniyon ki Gali. The entire crowd followed them like a procession.

Although Chetan was exhausted from walking around since morning, and Ma had told him not to go, he joined the crowd just to watch the spectacle.

38

This small, narrow gali that went via Chowk Andon (Ananda) to Baniyon ki Gali through Rasta Bazaar to Charbagh, became so narrow by Kot Pushka that an ikka or tonga could not pass through it. Nowadays, rickshaws go straight to Kallowani Mohalla, but in those days, no one had even heard of a rickshaw. The tongas always stopped in the chowk, and from there the passengers would have to carry their luggage on their heads or shoulders for great distances to their homes.

Chetan had experienced a minor incident with regard to these same galis, chowks and tongas, one that was etched deeply in his mind, and he always recalled it at some point or other when he passed along those narrow lanes. He'd gone to fetch his wife from her parents' home for the bridal departure. He'd told the tonga driver at the Basti stand that he had to go to Kallowani Mohalla, which is near Chowk Qadeshah. The driver was quite rude. He stopped the tonga right in the middle of the chowk. When Chetan pleaded with him to go just a bit farther to Chowk Kharadiyan, he refused, saying there was no room for a tonga to turn up ahead.

'There is room,' Chetan had retorted with some annoyance.

But the tonga driver wouldn't budge. He said he'd been engaged up to Chowk Qadeshah and he wouldn't go any farther.

'If you won't go any farther, I won't pay you.'

'You can keep your money!' cried the tonga driver, and he took down all their things—the basket of sweets and their bundle—and before Chetan could say anything, turned the tonga and departed, muttering sailor-grade curses back at them.

Chetan called out to him again and again but he didn't even look back.

Chetan had stood there helplessly in the screaming sunlight of Chowk Qadeshah with his newly-wedded bride. His wife didn't know the way to his home, so he couldn't send her ahead and remain standing by the luggage himself. And he couldn't leave her by the luggage in a Muslim mohalla—and that too, one inhabited by goondas and lowlifes—and go himself (well did he recall what had happened to Laloo's wife). For a long time, he stood and waited for someone from his mohalla to come by so he could ask him to send his brother. When Chanda grew fatigued from standing there in the heat, Chetan finally told her to pick up the bundle of sweets, and he somehow picked up the basket and all the other stuff himself, and they set out. It really bothered him to come home carrying luggage like this on the third day of his marriage, and he worried someone from the mohalla might see them. When they reached the entrance to the gali a bit ahead of Chowk Kharadiyan, he told Chanda to put the luggage down. Then he piled it all up at Harlal Pansari's shop and took his wife home.

Chetan suddenly recalled that incident again as he joined the crowd of spectators in the narrow galis tailing Bhagavanti's charpoy (which people carried on their shoulders like a bier as they rushed along), and he frowned with fresh anger and shame. But this time, he wasn't angry at the tonga driver, but at his own foolishness. If he'd just said to the tonga driver, 'Listen, just take us four more steps, I'll give you another anna,' or if he'd said, 'Pehlwan, just go a little farther, our house is right over there; I have my new bride with me, I'd be so grateful to you!' wouldn't the tonga driver have agreed? Of course he would have. But he had threatened not to pay him, and the driver had insulted him and driven off without the money.

*

'Arré bhai, what happened, where is this procession going?' asked Ved Vrat Kaliya, jumping up from a shop at Rasta Bazaar and throwing his arm around Chetan's neck as he walked alongside him.

Chetan didn't like Kaliya putting his arm around his neck in this manner, but he didn't say anything. Although Kaliya was two years younger than him, there had been a time when he'd thought of him as his guru, because it was from Kaliya that he'd learned how to play the mouth organ. Chetan told him about Bhagavanti being beaten by Amirchand. Suddenly Kaliya asked, 'Where's Chacha Maniram? How did he let all this happen?'

'Why don't you ask your uncle Juliyaram,' replied Chetan sarcastically. 'Chacha Maniram must be busy meditating with him somewhere.'

And he freed his neck from Kaliya's arm nonchalantly.

*

Kaliya's father Gandaram sold sour-moong-dal laddus and papads, and his uncle, Pandit Juliyaram, was the postmaster. The two of them lived in separate households. Pandit Juliyaram's wife had long ago departed for heaven, leaving behind her two boys, and since Gandaram brought nothing home and spent whatever he earned on liquor and gambling, Pandit Juliyaram helped his sister-in-law as much as he could. People had cast aspersions on him—they said he hadn't remarried because he lived with his sister-in-law. But the thing was that his elder son was crazy, and he was afraid that if he remarried, a stepmother wouldn't look after him properly. But how could the people of the mohalla allow anyone to live peacefully? Then they'd taunted Gandaram with the fact that his wife lived with his elder brother. Fights broke out many times, and finally, one day, people heard that Gandaram had left his wife and children and become a renunciant. Paying no heed to the gossip, Pandit Juliyaram brought his sister-in-law to his home and she began to look after his sons along with her own children.

Pandit ji's elder son was a hearty lad of nineteen or twenty, and he was not only crazy, but also mute. He ran away from home several times and each time Pandit ji found him and brought him back. But he finally ran away for good one day and no one could find him. For three years, Pandit ji kept looking for him but no one knew where he'd gone. His disappearance bothered him so much that the moment Pandit Juliyaram retired, he grew a beard and became a follower of Vedanta (the younger son and nephew had both finished their studies and started working). He found companions in this pursuit too—his own subordinate, the assistant postmaster, Lala Maniram, father of Amichand and Amirchand. Lala Maniram was a rather tall, skinny, fair-skinned man. He was always silent, though angry by nature. His son Amirchand took after him—he was just as tall and fair, and sturdier than him. Chetan remembered one time when Amirchand had been filling jugs of water at the well and made fun of a girl from the mohalla; his father had overheard his remark sitting somewhere upstairs in the house. He came downstairs and beat the stuffing out of Amirchand with his shoes. Chetan had seen him beat Amirchand unnecessarily in this way many times. But in the company of Pandit Juliyaram— who genuinely looked like a holy man, with his shaved head, fair complexion and beard down to his navel—an extraordinary change came over Lala Maniram. It was as though he'd risen above the ordinary world, while still living in it. He'd taken a loan against half his pension so that Amichand could sit for the competitive exams. Amirchand had found employment after completing the Matric. He'd got married and moved in with his uncle Sohan Lal in the bhuvara. Amirchand didn't make it beyond the Matric, but Amichand always came first, and he'd always won scholarships. He'd broken the record in the FA, and his father had somehow got him admitted to Government College, Lahore. The third son turned out useless. A loafer and a no-account. He didn't make it beyond the Matric. Who knows why Lala Maniram never ever snapped at him—maybe it was because his middle son had turned out a scholar or because of Pandit Juliyaram's sermons. When Amichand was admitted into the PCS, he didn't show any especial happiness. He politely accepted people's congratulations and, according to his habit, went off to Chuparana to meditate. Twice a day, the two retired postmasters went to the well at Chuparana, three or four miles outside of the city. They did pranayama for two hours, and focused their minds on the Almighty.

*

'I heard Hunar Sahib's in town,' Ved Vrat smiled widely, changing the topic. What he wanted to do was to put his arm around Chetan's neck again, but who knows what it was about Chetan that made him lose his nerve. All he said was, 'There should be a get-together, Bhapa ji.'

Kaliya had quit playing the mouth organ long ago and taken up poetry as a hobby. Chetan was studying in Class Nine when he'd first seen Kaliya passing through the gali with his mouth organ. For two or three years after that, the instrument was stuck to his mouth at all times. No sooner would some new tune (from the theatre, cinema, or the famous bards of Jalandhar) become popular, than Kaliya would start playing it on his mouth organ. Chetan bought one too and practised with him for two or three weeks, but he couldn't get the hang of it. He preferred the flute. But Kaliya carried on as before, the instrument always at his mouth. He could play it continuously for hours. He was even able to breathe while playing. When Chetan was at home, he knew Kaliya was walking by the gali as soon as he heard the harmonica. Sometimes he wondered why the mouth organ had never found its place in art—he'd never seen a harmonica player in any band or orchestra. Its status had not advanced beyond parties of picnicking boys, and maybe this was why, once Kaliya passed the Matric, he gave up playing. He got a job as a clerk in the post office where the other clerks found his harmonica playing completely juvenile and began to avoid him. After Kaliya quit, Chetan noticed he'd suddenly developed an interest in poetry. He would come to Chetan and listen to his couplets. Sometimes he recited the couplets of other poets himself. But he was quite thick. He always recited the wrong couplets for the wrong occasions, and he spoke in a strange overly enthusiastic manner, his face plastered with a permanent grin.

'Hunar Sahib must be at Lala Govindaram's right now. There's a gathering happening there,' said Chetan. 'Hunar Sahib's translated the second section of the Gita into Urdu.'

'Oh, really!' Kaliya's eyes widened and his mouth opened with excitement. Without saying another word, he rushed off.

*

The street grew wider as they neared Kot Pushka. The pace of the procession quickened. They rounded the corner and passed the mansion of Lala Accharu Ram, advocate, on Charbagh Street, and then turned left, towards the railway station, where there was a police station at the corner. Chetan had passed this street hundreds of times since childhood, but he'd never once glanced in the direction of the police station, and he hadn't even known that Kallowani Mohalla was under the jurisdiction of this particular station.

They walked through the station yard and stopped in the entry corridor where there were two tables and two chairs. To the left of this hallway was a room with a table and a chair; an officer in plainclothes stood in the corridor. The members of the procession placed the charpoy outside the hallway.

'What's the problem?' asked the officer.

'Amirchand has beaten her.'

'His brother's been made deputy collector, so he's making it harder for the people of the mohalla to live.'

'Is this the British Raj or the Raj of Amirchand and his brothers—they think they can dishonour anyone they want!'

'Please go immediately and catch him and arrest him. He'll soon learn the price of string!' (This was Pandit Banarsidas—'He was a thread seller, after all,' Chetan thought to himself.)

People were pushing to the front of the group and speaking all at once.

But the officer appeared not to be listening to anyone. 'The chief isn't here. He'll be back in an hour,' he said carelessly.

'But she'll be dead in an hour. Don't you see? See how she's bathed in blood!' appealed Pandit Shivnarayan Jhawan.

Chetan knew the man wouldn't write a report without a bribe or threats, and no one would be prepared to give a red cent for the sake of a bribe. All the same, he came forward and said in English, 'Come on, let's take her directly to the deputy commissioner's bungalow. I'll speak to him.'

The threat worked. When everyone started to lift the charpoy disconcertedly, the officer called to someone inside, and a Sikh officer came out. The officer said something to the second and he came and sat in the chair.

'The sergeant has come! Have him write out the report.'

Everyone started speaking at once, as before.

'One man tell the story. We'll write out the full incident report. What is the lady's name?'

'Bhagavanti,' said Hansa.

'Husband's name?'

'Pandit Telu Ram!'

'Let her husband come forward!'

'Sir, he's in Mandi.'

'How are you related to the lady?'

'Sir, I'm her nephew.'

'Now, tell me, what happened?'

And Hansa told him that an hour or two ago, his aunt had come from Mandi to her home, and that she had been sitting at the gate of the Sunars chatting, when Lala Maniram's eldest son, Amirchand, had come and dragged her by her hair and beaten her with a lathi and left her half dead.

'No, he beat her with shoes!' said Shyama.

'You keep quiet; how could she be bleeding then?' Hansa shut up his brother.

'What had she done to him?'

'Nothing, sir.'

'Is he crazy, then?'

'No, sir, what happened was that Chachi is Khatri and from his community. After her first husband died, she married my uncle and went to live over there in Mandi. The Khatris didn't like that. Today she came alone, so he suddenly beat her.'

'Is he her brother-in-law?'

'No, sir, nothing of the kind. Just from the same caste.'

'Sir, Sergeant Sahib, so what if his younger brother has become deputy, he's threatening to turn all the Brahmins out of the mohalla.'

'Sergeant Sahib, is this the British Raj or Amirchand's brother's Raj, or the Khatris' Raj, or Kallowani's—how can other people's daughters and daughters-in-law be humiliated in broad daylight?'

'No, no, don't worry. We'll fix him,' said the sergeant, and he turned towards Hansa.

'Were you present there?'

'No, sir, my younger brother came to get me. The whole mohalla was present.'

'Then who will be a witness to this incident? If it goes to court, someone must be a witness. If the defendant says his name was falsely entered by his enemies, and that the lady beat her own head on the ground, then . . . ?'

'Sir, there's no shortage of witnesses. You go ahead and ask.'

'So many men are standing here. Why doesn't one of them have his witness account written?'

But at the mention of the testimony, everyone stepped back. Hansa requested Pandit Gurdayal, Shivnarayan, Pandit Banarsidas—all of them—to testify, but no one was prepared to come forward.

Then Chetan came forward and told him in English to go and make Amirchand understand that such excesses are not permissible. 'There were no men in the mohalla at that time, only women. All of them will tell you. These people are all just spectators. If something gets messed up, and this woman dies, the matter will go right back to you. Have Hansa sign the report, and go and investigate yourself.'

'Who are you?' asked the sergeant.

'I am an assistant editor at *Bande Mataram* in Lahore.'

Then the sergeant had Hansa sign the report (which he hadn't entered into the register, but had written on a separate piece of paper) and said that when the chief came in, an officer would go from the station.

'Sir, you won't find Amirchand at home right now. Please catch him early in the morning.'

The sergeant assured them that he would come early in the morning.

Then Hakim Sahib dressed and bandaged Bhagavanti's wound, during which she screamed loudly and moaned, and although she wanted to walk, everyone loaded her on the charpoy as before, and the procession turned back towards Kallowani.

'Now we'll see what kind of fun that son-of-a-deputy has,' said Pandit Vishvambhar Dayal happily. 'If his son stays in jail for two days, he'll forget all about his deputy commissionery.'

And Chetan laughed at those idiots.

*

On their return from the station, Bhagavanti's procession went gali by gali to Rasta Bazaar instead of going by way of Kot Pushka. The thing was that from over there, the route was a bit shorter, and everyone was in a hurry to get to the mohalla and deliver the news that the police would come early the next morning and arrest Amirchand and throw him in jail. They'd only got as far as Khoslon ki Gali when Chetan could hear his father's powerful, grating voice. It sounded like he was lecturing Parasaram about his duty.

39

There'd been trouble between the Khatris and the Brahmins in Jalandhar's Kallowani Mohalla longer than anyone could remember. Who knows if the struggle began with a tug of war for power or if the Khatris, caught in the clutches of the shrewd Brahmins, had rebelled (they were forced to fill the Brahmins' homes with money and gifts for everything from the pregnancy rite on the first indications of pregnancy to the birth of the baby; then the sixth day after birth, the eleventh, the first shaving of the baby's head, the sacred thread ceremony, the engagement, wedding, death, the fourth day after death, the thirteenth day, and every year after that during the shraddha ceremonies). Whatever the reason, it was perhaps because of this same rivalry that the great sage Vishvamitra, despite being a Kshatriya, decided to call himself Brahmarshi, or why the great priest Pushyamitra started a kingly line of Brahmins. This rivalry in Jalandhar's Kallowani Mohalla had reached such a nadir that the Kshatriyas (who were now called Khatris and shot arrows in the field of business rather than in battle) called the Brahmins (who were now Bahmans and, instead of giving the gift of knowledge, only took gifts) dogs and the Brahmins called the Khatris lying thieves. Both had come up with coarse sayings for one another. Those Brahmins who had become educated had stopped taking alms, and instead of inviting Brahmin girls and boys for feasts on Janmashtami and other festivals, the Khatris had started inviting boys and girls from their own community.

The Khatris were in power in the mohalla—they owned most of the homes and were also more well-to-do. There were three Brahmin homes: all three had priests in them, whose job it still was to partake in ceremonial feasts and beg from their patrons. For this reason, the Brahmins remained oppressed and the Khatris kept them that way.

But Chetan's father, at a time when it was rare for anyone to make it to middle school, had studied all the way to the Matric, and been hired into service by the railway. And then, he was a famed brawler, not just in the railway but throughout the city, and no one among the Khatris could compare to him . . . But he'd become a signaller and gone off to the far-flung stations of the Northwestern Railway. His grandmother, Gangadei, had stayed behind with his newly-wedded wife, Lajwanti—Chetan's mother.

Ever since Chetan could remember, he'd been hearing the tale of the insult they endured at the hands of the Khatris, besotted by a lust for wealth. One story he'd heard so many times that it made his blood boil despite his weakness.

The story was from the time when Chetan's father was in Relieving and was working at Hisar Station as a substitute signaller, and Chetan's mother, with great-grandmother Gangadei, were living in their old ruin of a house. One afternoon an uproar had broken out in the mohalla. What had happened was that Pandit Shadiram's crazy uncle, Chunni, who wandered all about the city stark naked, had come into the mohalla from somewhere. Who knows what their neighbour Dammo, Lala Jivan Lal's wife (who had only been there a short while since their marriage), was thinking. As she wound thread into a skein, she poked Chunni in the buttocks with her empty bobbin. He turned and slapped her—he was crazy, after all. Then Dammo beat her head and breast, and called for her husband and three younger brothers-in-law, and they beat Uncle Chunni so badly that his whole body turned blue. He somehow made it into the house as he was being beaten, and Chetan's mother locked the door. But the Khatris didn't stop there. They tried to beat down the door, saying they'd slap Chetan's mother just as Dammo had been slapped. For three days (this is how Chetan's mother told it), the three of them stayed locked in the house, and the Khatris kept coming and shouting curses at them, and great-grandmother Gangadei kept applying hot compresses to her crazy son's wounds. On the third day, Chetan's mother called to a Brahmin boy through the latticed air vent and asked him to fetch Chetan's father's friends Chowdhry Gujjarmal and Chowdhry Tejpal. They came and reasoned with the Khatris (who were actually their buddies) and helped her reopen the door to the house.

Chetan's mother continued to burn from this insult. Chetan's father came to Jalandhar a few months later on his way from one station to another, and his friends Dharam Chand and Mukandi Lal (Lala Jivan Lal's two younger brothers) joined his party to drink a few sips. When Chetan's father came upstairs in the dead of the night, Chetan's mother told him with great anguish the tale of the insult to her and his grandmother. Drunk out of his mind, Pandit Shadiram swore at Jivan Lal and all his brothers, and the mohalla's other Khatris, with dozens of curses related to mothers and sisters, and said that those bastards Ramanand and Chetan were born mice, the son he would sire now would be called Parashuram, and it would be he who would totally annihilate those bastard Khatris.

Those Khatris whom Pandit Shadiram proclaimed he would annihilate were all his co-feasters and co-drinkers, of course. Pandit ji sat them by his side and poured them drinks; in times of need, he even helped them with money, and always brought gifts for their wives and children when he was in town.

Pandit Shadiram had made that announcement when he was drunk, then forgotten it, but the neighbours who had heard him didn't forget. And when Chetan's mother was pregnant, people began to ask great-grandmother Gangadei, 'So, Dadi, when is Parasaram due?'

Chetan's great-grandmother would immediately curse seven generations of their ancestors. She could no longer see and she was over eighty. She always sat in the doorway of the old ruined house then. But the children and youths of the mohalla (both the boys and the girls) had such fun hearing great-grandmother's curses that they'd ask again and again, 'So, Dadi, when is Parasaram coming?'

And Chetan's mother, seated in the courtyard, or the kitchen, or the hallway, would rue the inauspicious hour she'd told Pandit ji about the crimes of the Khatris; he'd drunkenly announced it to the entire mohalla and now she was stuck with it. What if she had a girl rather than a boy? And Ma would pray to God that he make her husband's words stick this time; after this, let there be seven girls, but this time, let it be a boy . . . and she'd tell herself, 'May he be Parashuram himself, and may he take revenge for the insult to his mother.'

And perhaps God did hear her. Parashuram was born at one o'clock in the afternoon, and the peace and happiness Chetan's mother felt on that day in her difficult life is beyond description. By good fortune, Pandit ji was in Jalandhar at the time (he came swinging home at night via Bazaar Sheikhan). When he learned that a boy had been born in his home just as he'd announced, and that the mother had, according to his wishes, named him Parashuram instead of Anand or whatever, then he made a new announcement: that the name of his next son would be

410

Meghnad, he who conquered Indra, king of the gods; Ravana's son, the eloquent reciter of all four Vedas; he who had wounded Lakshman with his powers and rendered him unconscious—and that his fifth son would be Shiv Shankar, he who could open his third eye in anger and turn all of creation to ash.

In his zeal he had named all his future sons (because it was Pandit ji's firm belief that a man should have at least a dozen sons), but at that moment, this third son of his, who was going to destroy the Khatris twenty-one times, burst out crying on hearing this terrifying pronouncement. As was his habit, Pandit Shadiram picked him up by one leg and swung him around. He wanted to test the strength of his head that very moment, like Hanuman (Son of the Wind), by dashing him against the earth, but the baby shrank back and fell silent, and feeling well pleased by this test, the father announced that he was powerful and promised that he'd make him a sharp axe with which he'd destroy all the Khatris.

Although Pandit ji forgot his drunken announcement and the next night sat with those same Khatris and drank heavily, Ma did not forget it. She not only named her fourth son Meghnad, but also named the fifth Shankar, and made her third son as powerful as Parashuram. Starting when he was very young, Ma began telling Parashuram—who was ordinarily called Parasaram—the story of that child rishi who, in order to take revenge on an insult to his father, cut off the eleven arms of King Sahasrabahu with his axe.

Whenever little Parasaram would cry, Ma would say, 'You're crying! But you are Parasaram. You're Parasaram, but you're crying! Aren't you ashamed?' and the child would fall silent.

One day, he broke out in sores all over his body. Chetan's father was at that time the assistant station master at Ujar station, 'Bugana', near Hisar. His entire body was covered in sores, including the soles of his feet. When he moaned with pain, Ma reminded him of his name and he fell silent. Chetan was only two and a half years older than him, but even then he was amazed at the endurance and self-control of his younger brother. Those days had left an indelible impression on Parasaram's mental canvas and had somehow given him boundless power. Chetan (he was then just five or six years old) thought that his younger brother would truly grow up to destroy those evil Khatris. As Parasaram lay there writhing in pain for days, Chetan saw that no sound came from his lips even when there were tears in his eyes. Their father managed to find medicine from somewhere. His mother washed butter in water a hundred times, mixed it with the medicines and spread it on his body. From this he found comfort.

It was in Bugana that a buffalo stepped on little Parasaram's foot and injured it. He came home limping and shaking, and began walking around the room. His bloody foot left marks on the floor and tears streamed from his eyes, but he kept saying, 'I am Parasaram—I don't cry!' . . . 'I am Parasaram—I don't cry!'

When Chetan remembered that sight, he felt a lump in his throat . . . but he remembered that his mother had come running from the kitchen and when she saw her child's wounded foot, she didn't cry or scream. She hastily tore off the border of her sari, dipped it in water and bound his foot with it. Then she slapped her son on the back and said, 'Yes, my son is Parasaram—he's brave! He never cries!' And she held him close to her breast.

*

'If you all had been here, that bastard would never have had the nerve to grab your Chachi and drag her and hit her with shoes. You asses, why do you go to the akhara, why do you do thousands of push-ups? These muscles—this youth—when the hell are they

412

going to come in handy? Why don't you just go and drown if you're going to let these impotent Khatris lay a hand on Brahmin daughters and daughters-in-law?'

Chetan's father's booming voice reached all the way to Khoslon ki Gali.

Arriving in the mohalla, Chetan saw that his father was seated on the plinth of the well, his legs dangling, while Parasaram and Debu stood before him like criminals. Lala Fakir Chand sat silently next to him on the plinth. The pulleys of the well (where there was an enormous crowd by now) were completely empty. There was silence in the mohalla. The Khatri men and women had shut their doors and climbed up to their roofs. Over at the gate of the Sunars, some women of course stood and watched the spectacle, and some women and children also stood in the bhuvara, as Pandit ji showered both sons (he called Debu, the son of his friend Pandit Daulat Ram the astrologer, his own son) with profanities. Parasaram had come running directly from the akhara, and earth still coated his body. He and Debu both said they had not been in the mohalla at the time. Debu said that when he'd returned from Kutchery, he'd heard the story from his mother. Parasaram said that Shankar had come to get him; if I'd been there, no one would have had the nerve to lay a hand on Chachi.

'If you'd been here, he wouldn't have done it, I agree,' said Pandit Shadiram. 'But how could they dare, even in the absence of you two? This means he's not a bit afraid of your muscles, or he considers himself very powerful.'

As soon as they saw Pandit ji, the people in the procession placed Bhagavanti's charpoy right next to the well and stood around him. Bhagavanti sat up, moaning, and pulled down her veil some more. On hearing this last bit, someone in the crowd called out, 'Amichand's become a deputy, that's what gave Amirchand the nerve!'

'He's a deputy's mother___,' said Pandit ji, casting an extremely obscene curse in the direction of the bhuvara. 'We'll see what his goddamn deputy brother does; if he doesn't come and fall at the feet of this mother of his and beg forgiveness (he motioned towards Bhagavanti's charpoy), then I won't let that bastard live in the mohalla. I won't let that damn Amichand become a deputy. I'll go myself and meet the officers and ask them if that bastard will do justice when he becomes an officer just because he passed in some competition, when he commits a crime like this against the mothers and sisters of his own mohalla.' And Pandit ji turned towards the crowd of Brahmins, 'You bastards, why'd you have to go to the police? Eunuchs go to the police. The goddamn police run on money. Tell me who you want arrested and I'll spend fifty to a hundred rupees and have them breathing jail air in two days. What kind of wimps go running to the police? What you do is beat up Amirchand, lay him out, and then he, or his deputy brother, or the father of his deputy brother, goes to the police.'

And Pandit ji got up and slapped Debu, Parasaram and Hansa hard on the neck one at a time, to test their Brahmin strength. Although even the hearty wavered at a slap from Pandit Shadiram, and Debu and Hansa nearly fell over, Parasaram didn't budge— he stayed standing, chest broad.

Pandit ji was pleased and slapped his son on the back, and Debu stood up straight and said he'd wavered because the slap was so sudden—otherwise, he was no less than Parasaram and 'Bau ji' should slap him now and see.

Pandit ji made a fist and raised it, and Debu stood up straight like Parasaram; the next moment, Pandit ji's taut forearm smacked Debu on his right shoulder. Debu's left leg wiggled a bit, but a second later, he stood tall.

Pandit ji was pleased and slapped him on the back.

'I wasn't paying attention before, that's why I stumbled,' said Debu, chest out, crowing. 'That's right, I've pinned this guy loads of times.'

He meant Parasaram, who slapped his arms in readiness for a fight when he heard what he said, and cried, 'Come, child, let's see who gets pinned!'

And the next moment, the two faced one another, arms outstretched, and locked hands as they began their show of strength.

Pandit ji took off his turban, put it under his arm and reclined on the plinth. He'd forgotten all about Bhagavanti and was totally engrossed in watching them wrestle.

*

Debu had been a goonda since childhood, and Ma had made Parasaram powerful but noble, so Parasaram often lacked Debu's arrogance, thuggishness and bravado, though he did try to help him fight enemies. Every limb of Parasaram's body was taut, and all his senses were focused on not allowing Debu to win. Debu knew that if he won, Pandit ji would not only treat him to half a seer of warm milk, but he'd also give him a rupee or two as a prize, and he was trying to pick Parasaram up and throw him down as he had before. But for one thing, Parasaram had learned all his moves by now, and for another, Debu had stopped going to the akhara and was ruining his strength loafing about as a goonda, whereas Parasaram went regularly to the akhara and did thousands of push-ups and sit-ups and had become much stronger than before.

Debu tried once to throw him; he placed both his hands on Parasaram's shoulders, shook his arms violently and tried to knock him over. He tried to lift him and throw him by grabbing hold of his waist, and once he even tried to move away a bit and execute his famous move by ducking slightly and grabbing his ankles to knock him flat on his back, but Parasaram was watching like a hawk and rendered his every blow useless; after that, Debu was in a bit of a quandary as to what to do next. Parasaram shook his hand hard, stepped behind him and held him, and then, with lightning speed, he lifted him up and threw him down.

Pandit ji could no longer stay seated. He stood up and went over, and began suggesting moves to Debu. When Debu managed to get back up using the moves Pandit ji suggested, Parasaram grabbed his neck from below and managed to push him to the bottom again. Pandit ji suggested more moves. Again, he managed to get on top. But Parasaram brought him down again, and this time, he stiffened his legs, moving them out of his grasp, and began to rub him into the ground in such a way that he couldn't get up again, even if Pandit ji told him a thousand moves.

Pandit ji waited a while for Parasaram to knock him out. But Debu didn't fall unconscious no matter how long Parasaram ground him down. Then Pandit ji pronounced the two of them equal in wrestling. He slapped them on the back, gave a sermon about not fighting amongst themselves but working together to confront common enemies, and started off to Ramditta the sweet-seller's to buy them some warm milk . . .

Just as he was going, his eyes fell upon the crowd of Brahmins standing behind him and on Bhagavanti on her charpoy, the very existence of whom he'd completely forgotten. Bhagavanti pulled down her veil a bit more when she saw him.

'Look, blessed one,' said Pandit ji in his booming voice, stopping by her charpoy on his way to the bazaar, 'when you were Dharam Chand's wife, you were my younger sister-in-law. I was the one who arranged your marriage to Dharam Chand.

'Now that you've gone and set up house with Telu, you're still my younger sister-in-law and, in our religion, a younger sister-in-law is like a daughter. You are like a daughter to me. As long as I live, no one can dishonour you. Go, sit in your home. If that bastard Amirchand and his fraud of a father don't fall at your feet and beg forgiveness, I'll shave off my moustaches.'

And he ordered Hansa and Shyama to help lift her up and take her to her house.

Bhagavanti stood up with their help and touched Pandit ji's feet, then set out for the bhuvara, moaning.

She hadn't even reached the bhuvara yet when Telu appeared from the direction of the bazaar, lurching along with his jet-black, fat but muscled body.

Pandit ji grabbed hold of him right under the Committee lamp and asked, cursing continuously, why he'd sent his wife alone into the mohalla, and why he himself was skulking about over there and when would those push-ups and sit-ups come in handy, and that body like a dumb-bell? 'Have you oiled up your body and done all those push-ups and sit-ups so your neighbour can beat your wife with shoes while you sit around having fun in Mandi?'

Telu stammered unclearly that his wife had come without telling him. If he'd known, he'd never have allowed it. Shyama had just told him of the incident in the mohalla and he'd come running.

'Bastard, instead of stopping her from coming into the mohalla, why didn't you come with her before? Does this mohalla belong to Amirchand's father, or do you live on his estate, or do you eat his bread? The day Amirchand said he'd slaughter Bhagavanti and Telu if they came into the mohalla, why didn't you say, show me what you've got, why don't you? Go on and try to murder us . . . Why did you keep sitting in Mandi like a eunuch?'

417

Telu tried to stammer out a response but Pandit ji shut down his murmuring with a roar.

'Fact is, you son of a bitch, you all are getting weak as priests! You earn your own money, you eat your own food, and the Khatris in this mohalla consider you no better than a Bhangi or a Chamar.' And, stepping forward, Pandit ji grasped Telu's thick neck and shoved him forward. 'Come with me,' he said, 'and let's find this Amirchand and ask him why he raised a hand against his mother and sister; since when has Kallowani Mohalla become his father's estate?'

40

Chetan's father thought (this is what the people of the mohalla had told him) that Amirchand would be at his uncle Sohan Lal's, who ran a bangle shop in the bazaar a little beyond Jaura Gate. Sohan Lal had moved to the shop when his wife had passed away, and given the house to Amirchand. Amirchand had got married, had a child, and there was no longer room in the Chowdhry home where Lala Maniram lived.

But when Pandit ji arrived at the shop, Brahmin youths in tow, hurling profanities at the mohalla's Khatris, Sohan Lal said that Amirchand had not come his way. Pandit ji showered him with some especially 'sweet words', accused him of hiding Amirchand in the room upstairs and, before Sohan Lal could stop him, grabbed the knotted rope hanging from the ceiling, placed a foot on the step leading up to the shop, and jumped over the glass cases full of bangles, landing just inside. He made for the staircase going up to the rooftop room which was inside the shop.

'Bau, where are you going? There's no one up there,' called Lala Sohan Lal, jumping after him.

He was a fair man of medium height. He must have been forty or so, but his face was already wrinkled and his hair had gone salt-and-pepper. There was always some beautiful boy at his shop.

The boy would help him in the shop for a while, then go away. The women of the mohalla shrank from sending their little boys over there. Sohan Lal even tried to grab the hem of Pandit ji's coat to pull him back, but he freed himself with a jerk and ran up the stairs two at a time.

Amirchand wasn't upstairs. But there was a twelve- or thirteen-year-old boy, wearing dirty knickers and a kameez, sleeping on Lala Sohan Lal's bed.

Pandit ji grabbed him by the ear and lifted him up. 'Did Amirchand come here?' he asked.

The boy had been in a deep sleep. Pandit ji sat him up, but even when seated he appeared to be sleeping. Pandit ji barked the same question to him once again.

Just then, Lala Sohan Lal appeared on the stairs grinning.

'How should he know where Amirchand is, Bau?'

'Who is this?

'He works in my shop . . .'

'And sleeps in your bed,' said Pandit ji contemptuously. 'Look how old you are now, you ass, your hair's gone grey—but you haven't given up this habit. Why don't you take a look at your shrivelled face in the mirror?' And he sang out loudly:

Hey, Nanak, the fruit of evil doings is always evil!

Pandit ji continued to sing this refrain as he climbed down the stairs and jumped over the wares in the same way, landing back in the bazaar.

'Did you find him, Bau ji?' asked Debu.

'No!'

'He's probably at his aunt's place, or maybe he's gone to his father in Chuparana,' suggested Debu.

420

Since his aunt's house was also in the direction of Chuparana, Pandit ji decided he'd go over there, grab Amirchand's yogi of a father and go looking for the son with him in tow.

Chetan was extremely exhausted, so when they all got back to Chaurasti Atari, he turned towards Bajiyanwala Bazaar. But his father thundered at him that he must come along. He remarked softly that he was tired, but when his father cried again, 'I'm telling you to come!' he set out silently with them. He knew that the slightest debate would unleash upon him a torrent of the anger saved up for Amirchand. Thankfully, they'd only just reached the next intersection when they saw Pandit Juliyaram and Lala Maniram coming towards them.

'Tell me, Shadiram, how're you doing?' asked Pandit Juliyaram, patting his long beard that reached to his navel.

'Let's not talk about us sinners,' said Pandit ji. 'You tell me, how's your yogic practice; has God come down from on high to take up residence in your soul—or not?'

Pandit Juliyaram didn't respond to him. He continued to pat his beard and began to laugh, 'Bau, you won't change 'til the day you die.'

'Why should I? I'm not two-faced like you people; I may be a sinner, but I'm no liar.'

Pandit Juliyaram didn't respond to that either. His big, round eyes began to gleam, he smiled more widely and smoothed his beard with each of his hands by turns. A moment later, he changed the subject and said, 'So where are you off to with this army?'

'We were going to look for you. These new pupils of yours have ceased to worry about home and family, and have fallen in pursuit of subsuming the soul in the great soul, and this guy's "son of Rana Pratap" Amirchand is ruining the life of the people in the mohalla.'

Now Lala Maniram started, but no sign of agitation or worry showed on his face. 'What has happened, Bau Shadiram?' he asked calmly.

'What happened,' said Pandit ji, motioning towards the long beard of Lala Maniram's friend Pandit Juliyaram, 'is that this useless character was himself drowned, and he took you along to drown as well. He is growing out his beard and wearing a sandalwood tilak on his forehead to wash away his sin. He has no wife, and after eating nine hundred mice, this cat has embarked on a pilgrimage; but what sins have you committed? He's grown a beard. Is it not possible to worship Brahma without a beard?'

Pandit Juliyaram thought he should say something—his lips even moved—but Pandit Shadiram was drunk, so he thought it better to keep quiet.

Chetan's father spoke again, 'I'm asking, what use is all this yoga of yours, if you can't keep your boy under control? The bastard who can't control his own flesh and blood, how will he master Brahma? If he can't handle this life, what's he going to make of the next one?'

Pandit ji was so drunk he could have said anything, but Lala Maniram, who was quite a bit taller than him, placed his hands on his shoulders and smiled sweetly.

'Bau, brother, what are you angry about, what happened?'

Pandit ji narrated the entire story and told them of his announcement that by beating Telu's wife with shoes, his son had insulted not only Telu, but also himself, and that Bhagavanti was his younger sister-in-law and like a daughter to him, and that if his son didn't fall at her feet and beg forgiveness for his evil deed, then someone would surely die, and then they'd see how anyone could continue to live in the mohalla if they insulted him.

'Your son has become deputy, but does that mean you people will destroy the mohalla?' thundered Pandit ji. 'I'm not afraid of any deputy; I've told all of these people that if he doesn't go this very day and beg forgiveness, and doesn't swear an oath for the future that he won't ever do such a thing again, then we'll beat him with shoes until he's bald. I know he's feeling smug about his own strength and his brother becoming deputy, but we'll take all his strength and his brother's deputy commissionery and shove it back where it came from.'

Lala Maniram was not offended by Pandit ji's words. He patted Pandit ji softly on the shoulders to calm him down. Then he walked back to the mohalla with him and went straight to Telu's home, where he entered and placed his cap at Bhagavanti's feet, and told her that she was like a daughter not only to Pandit ji but also to him. And he was deeply ashamed of the deed his unworthy son had committed. He would go and find him right away, and as long as his son did not beg forgiveness for his actions, he himself would not eat.

When he came out of the Jhamans' home, he told Pandit ji to relax, that he'd reason with his son, and if he didn't listen to him, Pandit ji could do with him whatever he wished.

Pandit ji said he would be waiting in his sitting room. He'd not rest until he'd fulfilled the vow he'd made, and if Lala Maniram's son had understood and regretted his actions and begged forgiveness, Lala Maniram should let him know.

Released now from his duties in the matter, Pandit Shadiram gave two rupees each to Parasaram, Hansraj and Debu so they could go and drink some milk, and ordered Chetan to open the sitting room and put out small bowls, water and pickle. Then he stood just outside the sitting room and called out to Mukandi using a variety of curses related to mothers and sisters.

423

Lala Mukandi Lal had just come back from his shop. He called out that he'd be right over. Chetan opened the door to the sitting room, set out the glasses and small bowls on the table and lit the big lamp. Just then, Lala Mukandi Lal arrived. Lala Fakir Chand took a bottle of liquor out from under his kameez, which had just a bit more than half left in it. Pandit ji poured the liquor into the small bowls as he cursed Lala Mukandi Lal with 'sweet words' and told him that even if Mukandi's sister-in-law had set up house over at Telu's place, she was still the wife of his elder brother—how had he tolerated Amirchand beating her with shoes?

Lala Mukandi Lal swallowed his cup of liquor in one gulp, made a face at the bitterness and told him as he gargled with water that he'd been at the shop, and that Mangal's mother had only just told him what had happened.

'It was good she went to live with Telu, goddammit,' said Pandit ji as he poured the peg down his throat and wiped his lips with the back of his hand. 'She's still in the mohalla; if she'd gone off with some Muslim or Christian, what would you do then? Telu is a Brahmin after all, and Brahmins are born from the mouth of Brahma, you bastard!'

Pandit ji then filled his mouth with water to gargle. Just then, Lala Maniram arrived, bringing Amirchand with him. He hadn't actually gone anywhere. He had been right at home all along. At first he wasn't prepared to beg forgiveness, but when his father reasoned with him high and low, he went unwillingly to ask Bhagavanti to forgive him. When he came into the sitting room, he bowed down and touched Pandit ji's feet, and said he'd got overexcited and done wrong; Pandit ji was his elder, would he please forgive him.

Pandit ji was buzzed. He slapped him on the back and forgave him with generosity and gave him a sermon, instructing him that instead of fighting within the mohalla, they should stick together and fight its enemies.

When they had left, Pandit ji threw back another peg and drunkenly began to sing:

Oh Radha, you're not made of gold
Nor of silver either

41

Chetan had rubbed Pandit ji's temples with oil and soothed him to sleep with great difficulty, and it was not until after midnight that he returned to the room on the roof. The lantern was placed in the lattice window near the door. The wick was set so low it might flicker out at any moment. Chetan wished he could extinguish it. He couldn't fall asleep with the lamp on. But Chanda was afraid of the dark. He raised the wick slightly and cast a glance at his wife. She lay flat on her back, sleeping soundly, exhausted from her day. He always envied his wife's sleep. Whenever he woke suddenly in the night, it was impossible for him to go back to sleep. But Chanda fell asleep as soon as she lay down, and after that, it was hard to wake her again. Chetan recalled the house of Sardar Jagdish Singh (landlord and house proprietor) in Changar Mohalla, where they'd lived before he'd gone to Shimla. When he came home around two in the morning from the newspaper office, Chanda often did not respond to his knocking on the door at the top of the stairs, so he'd go to the back of the house and call from the gali. The whole mohalla woke up, but not her.

Chetan crept quietly into bed and lay down. His back was stiff. His entire body—his calves, the soles of his feet, his toes, his toenails—was in pain from wandering about all day. His eyes ached. But when he closed them and tried to sleep, he couldn't—the happenings of the whole day, the conversations with friends and acquaintances, and the violent incident in the mohalla, all of these began to spin in his mind: those same sights, those same events, those same conversations. His mohalla, his city, his people, the limited field of their thinking and activity . . . Anant, Badda, Debu, Pyaru, Ramditta, Hakim Dina Nath, Nishtar, Tanvir, Hunar, the Mahatma and the Yogi, the activist and the businessman, Laloo and Amarnath, Pandit Juliyaram and Lala Maniram—and above all, his father . . . He couldn't bear to remain in this atmosphere any longer . . . he needed to get out of this limited environment immediately and rise above it . . . He focused his thoughts and tried to erase all those images from his mind and go to sleep, but then he thought of the haughty, disdainful look on Amichand's face, and of Hamid taking his arm from around his neck (he'd forgotten that he'd done the same thing with Kaliya) and an invisible flame flared in his mind . . . He felt a muted anguish at his low state. His friends were advancing ahead of him. What was his own financial situation? He could consider himself a big-shot writer all he wanted, but his monthly income was no more than fifty rupees (and he'd only got fifty when he'd gone to Shimla; otherwise, at the newspaper office, he got only forty), and Amichand was going to be a deputy collector, and Hamid had become an officer at the radio, and what was he? The junior editor at a newspaper, always running at a financial deficit! Two of the four editors of that paper were always ill and he had to do twelve to fourteen hours of work a day. Even if he became a senior editor or a main editor, how would that change things? The senior editor earned one hundred rupees and the main editor one hundred and twenty-five. First of all, there was no possibility of a promotion at the paper, and then, if he went to some other paper, he certainly wouldn't get more than sixty or seventy rupees . . . he must break out of this vicious cycle! The grindstone of newspaper work had crushed the artist in him. How could he ever write good poetry or stories when he was giving most of his day and night to the newspaper? He hadn't been able to read even one new book for an entire year. He might not become a deputy collector, he might never be made an officer, but he would become a high-quality author . . . of course, so far he hadn't managed to become anything. His stories had been published in the daily papers before and were now too—but when he himself wasn't satisfied with them, why should others be? The very first thing he'd do when he got back to Lahore was quit his job at the newspaper . . . He wouldn't bring Chanda with him. He'd bring her when he'd got a job somewhere. But what would he do? This wasn't at all clear to him. He would definitely rise above this situation. The disdain of his friends would turn to envy. He'd freeze the condescension on the faces of Amichand and Hamid and other such officers; he would dazzle them . . .

Chetan wished he could get up and wander around on the roof. But he was extremely tired. He turned over softly. Chanda was in a deep sleep. Totally motionless. He couldn't even hear the sound of her breathing . . . He thought of Amarnath . . . 'The Spring of Life'—what a name they'd given him! But Amarnath had proven it true. If a thick-headed man like Amarnath could become focused and successful by working diligently, why couldn't he? This powerful force of desire, this obstinate, almost blind, single-minded devotion to his goal—that was the source of his life's success. That was the fount of life. His day had not been useless . . . he'd discovered the fount of life . . . he would become totally devoted to his goals and learn to be industrious. He'd push towards his goal, bathing the rocks of his circumstances like a stormy river breaking against the cliffs.

Suddenly the words of Yogi Jalandhari Mull echoed in his ears . . . the existence of man is not equal to even the thousandth

429

part of a particle in this vast cosmos—how can man consider himself so important? Instead of chasing after false pleasures and prosperity, why doesn't man search for truth, thus cutting ties with birth and death and attaining supreme bliss, the highest power, and moksha? . . . Chetan tossed about restlessly . . . Was this vow of his simply the same thing as chasing after falseness? If Amichand were to become collector and commissioner, not just deputy collector, and if Hamid were to become station director or controller instead of just programme assistant, and he himself were to become the country's most important poet and story writer, what then? Death is inevitable . . . so then his ambition, his powerful desire for progress—if all that wasn't false, what was? *This world has been made countless times, countless times the golden age and iron age have come*—Yogi ji's voice echoed in Chetan's ears. He felt like he was drowning. The small room felt claustrophobic. Despite his extreme fatigue, he got up and went out on to the roof. At some point during the conflict between the Brahmins and the Khatris in the mohalla, clouds had gathered in the sky. Chetan went and lay down on the cool cement bench . . . He lay there quietly for some time . . . slowly his mind began to work again . . . Perhaps the day of one's death is decided at the moment of birth, but then why should man die before this, and if the world drowned or flew away in a flash, then all would be drowned with it, or turned to ashes. As the Farsi poet had said, '*murghe amboh jashne daasad*'—the death of an enormous crowd is like a festival—if everyone died, he would too . . . but why should he long for a death-like peace before that? That desire for highest peace that man feels in order to attain the soul—that state of mind is like a dreamless sleep; if that's not another form of death, then what is it? If it's not a living death, then what is it? Aristotle had in fact called death a dreamless sleep. And then, if man even attains such peace after years of yogic practice, then what? If there is a god, and he doesn't wish for man to live, to attain that death-like peace while living, then why does he give man all these senses, why does he give him such a mind? Chetan got up and began to wander about the roof . . . He understood Karma Yoga a bit more than Gyana Yoga. He wouldn't become free of desire; he would yoke himself to desire and work hard. He didn't want release from the cycle of birth and death . . . he wanted to live life . . . the inspiration for living life came from desire after all; how could he continue his struggle if he quit that? Where would he get that powerful resolve, that attachment, that devotion? But he wouldn't worry about consequences good or ill. He wouldn't worry about success, rather he would try with renewed vigour to become successful, and he wouldn't go crazy with happiness at success either . . . and he thought of Lala Maniram. Surely he must have acted on this philosophy. If the son of anyone else in the mohalla had been made deputy collector, the father would have distributed laddus to the whole neighbourhood. He'd have invited musicians to play in celebration. But the father had taken the news that had made his older son go insane very simply. After hearing about his son's extreme behaviour towards Bhagavanti, he hadn't been shaken . . . and Chetan knew that he used to get intensely angry. He'd seen him beat Amirchand horribly several times . . . It could be that Jalandhari Mull ji had indeed become a yogi, fleeing from the hardships of jail, abandoning the desire for sacrifice—he may have wanted to maintain his prestige in society, but at the same time didn't want to take the trouble to follow the path of a political movement. It could be that Pandit Juliyaram's yogic practices were just another way for him to escape his frustrations. Whether he had touched upon some aspect of the truth, or found something, he didn't know, but the peace and patience that shone from Lala Maniram's face, the compassion and sympathy in his eyes, that was surely an indication of his inner harmony. He had perhaps learned to partake of pleasure and pain equally. He didn't know whether he had subsumed his soul in the great soul but he'd certainly found some touches of truth . . . and Chetan thought perhaps he'd sit with him some time and learn something . . . He'd not gained faith in God, nor did this world seem illusory, nor did the highest joy from what he'd read or heard, nor did highest peace seem desirable, nor even release. To take action and not worry about the fruits of one's labour was the only philosophy he liked; he'd adopt that one. He'd think not about death but about life. He'd think about how to make life better, how to live better. He'd think about rising above all this sin, all this narrowness, so that when death came, he wouldn't be filled with regret that he'd wasted this life uselessly, that he'd just wandered about his narrow confines like a frog in the well . . . He was an artist, if he could just advance human knowledge through his art even just a little bit, that's what he'd try to do . . .

And now he felt all his suffocation disappear and his spirits lighten. He went and lay down on the bed. The wick had burned down again, so he raised it. He stared at it for a moment. He thought about how countless scientists had laid down their lives for just this light. If mankind were to be freed from this world, if men kept the attainment of release as their goal, considering the world to be an illusion, then perhaps they would still be living in jungles, wandering about naked! But those attempting to improve life, those desiring to attain victory over death in this short life had discovered enormous power in hate; they'd invented countless things: trains, running water, electricity, radio—so many things. Generations of scientists laboured over conveniences man doesn't even have to think about nowadays, things he easily consumed . . . those scientists had thought not of death but of life . . . and he too would think about life.

Chetan turned over. He should go to sleep . . . he hadn't slept well for several nights. He hadn't slept for three nights during Neela's wedding, and he'd been up all the night before, and he'd been walking around all day. He would get sick . . . he tried to concentrate again, he thought he'd made a very important decision. He should fall asleep now.

But sleep was miles away. His eyes had stopped aching long ago. He opened them . . . he felt as though he'd just woken from a deep sleep. His eyes weren't tired and his mind didn't feel heavy . . . there had been no point in coming to Jalandhar. Wouldn't it have been better if he hadn't come for Neela's wedding? He had been in Shimla, and Shimla is quite far from Jalandhar, and he had been there for work; Neela was not his wife's actual sister, just her cousin. And his wife was there anyway; there was no need for him to have come. If he hadn't come, Neela would have gone to Rangoon and the distance in time and space would have kept his sorrow suppressed deep inside him. It wouldn't have come bubbling up again like this. Chanda had started to study. He was content. What had he got out of coming here? Sorrow, pain, frustration—with himself and with his environment as well! He wouldn't think about Neela any more. She was married now. What could he do now? He recalled his final meeting with Neela and felt as though a sharp spear had pierced his chest—how could Neela end up with a middle-aged man? What had he done? Why had he told her father to get her married? How sad would she be? He couldn't do anything at all to alleviate her sadness. Chetan turned over. Suddenly Kunti's smiling face after marriage appeared before him . . . Would Neela never be able to laugh like her? But Kunti could laugh even as a widow . . . the gentle laughter he'd heard twice just that evening in Kot Kishanchand echoed in his ears . . . and he had believed that Kunti would still be mournful . . . What a fool he was . . . And then he felt he was

433

learning some great truth, even greater than what he'd learned from Amarnath. Life doesn't stop, it struggles on through immense sorrow . . . and he was left with his failure in his love for Neela. One forgets what is near at hand but trembles with sorrow in separation from what one cannot have. He hadn't married Neela. He couldn't marry Neela. This was inevitable. There was no going back. So why couldn't he accept this and go about improving his own life? Kunti must have learned to laugh by centring her life on her child. Why couldn't he centre his attention on his art; why couldn't he pour all his sadness into his art? . . . He was suddenly filled with an odd sensation of lightness. He sat up. He felt like going outside . . . but outside, the sheets of tin covering the steel network over the courtyard clattered—at some point drops of rain had begun to fall. The strange thing was that he hadn't even heard the rain before now . . . He lay down again. The sound of rain falling on the tin had put him to sleep before, so he would fall asleep again today . . . He felt a cool puff of a breeze. He let his body go limp and began to listen to the harmonic vibrations of the drops hitting the tin above the courtyard.

42

It had been the same month—a different, enchanting rainy night—puffs of breeze blew then too, just as cool and sweet, and the rain fell in tiny drops. He had brought Chanda from Basti Guzan to his home for the first time after their marriage. Ma had made the bed downstairs in the small corner room. The large Muradabadi water pot, the glass of almonds and milk with dried, sweet dates, and the lantern in the window . . . Chetan's memories of that lovely night had chased away his sleep again. At some point the murmuring of the rain had ceased and his mind had been captivated by those tender memories.

Chetan had been twenty-one years old then, but still a child. Nowadays, young girls and boys learn quite a bit—even if it's all wrong—by reading cheap books about sex, but Chetan didn't know anything at all. Thoughts of what had happened with Kesar kept entering his mind and filling his heart with fear. He had ended up leaving Chanda at home and going over to Anant's. Anant had taken him to the station restaurant where he had ordered chicken musallam for Chetan, which, he told him, was highly invigorating. After this he had told him everything he needed to know about the wedding night—how a man should show his virility—and he gave the example of Pyaru, who had given his wife evidence of his manliness eight times on the first night, and when Chetan had admitted that perhaps he didn't even know anything about a woman's body parts, Anant had gently cursed his stupidity and told him to keep a flashlight handy . . . But Chetan felt revolted by the whole business . . . 'Is it necessary for all this to be accomplished on the very first night?' he had asked. 'Can't this happen in two or three nights, after a husband and wife have opened up to one another?' Anant explained to him that he should absolutely never do anything so foolish. He noted the misfortune that Hunar Sahib's brother had brought upon himself with just such behaviour; he explained to Chetan that the wedding night was organized for this very purpose and fleeing from it was cowardice. And, after encouraging him in every way he could, he patted him on the back, laughed, told him there was no need to fear and, urging him not to tarnish the reputation of his fellow men, he left him at his door.

*

Chetan went into the room and closed the door, and when he turned, he saw that Chanda was not sitting on the bed but on the low seat near the wall. She wore a pink Banarsi suit with gold stars and a red dupatta over her head, with a twinkling border of golden stars.

'Why are you sitting over there?' asked Chetan carelessly as he held out a finger to lift her up.

Chanda did not pull her hand back, nor did she shrink away or act flirtatious. She simply stood up quietly and came to sit on the bed. Chetan slid her veil back slightly. 'Let this moon shine fully, my beloved!' he said laughing.

But as soon as he said this, he was taken aback by the strange sound of his own voice. It seemed to him that what he said

436

sounded artificial and there was a want of the usual feeling in his tone. But when Chanda laughed gently at his words instead of becoming bashful and pulling her veil back down, the small dimly lit room was suffused with the pearls of her mirth.

Chetan was wearing Peshawari sandals. When he sat down on the wooden bed rail to remove them, he saw that his feet were caked in mud. As he washed off the mud and started cleaning his toes, Chanda suddenly asked sweetly, 'Do your feet hurt?'

'I wander about all day with bare feet or wearing sandals,' Chetan had answered carelessly. 'In the rainy season, I get chilblains on my toes.'

Chanda got up. She kneeled on the floor and softly cleaned between the toes of both his feet with her silk dupatta and then rubbed them with Vaseline. Chetan liked all this very much. He kissed her hands and pulled her to his chest.

Outside, a light rain fell and the monsoon breeze blew in through both windows. Chanda lay next to him. Chetan couldn't think of anything to say. Suddenly, he asked, 'Chanda, do you know how to sing?'

'I've never been taught,' she replied softly.

'Do you know how? It's fine if you haven't been taught.'

'I just hum ordinary songs.'

'Hum some!'

'But Ma will hear . . .'

'Sing me something quietly,' Chetan insisted gently as he kissed her forehead.

Chanda began to sing:

Yellow-green my bangles are
    Yellow-green they are, they are
Slipped them on me my mum-in-law did
    Slipped them on she did, she did

At the door I break those bangles
  Yellow-green they are, they are
  Break them, yes I do

'Why would you break bangles your mother-in-law had given you at the door?' asked Chetan, and he laughed loudly. Then he became serious, 'Look, don't you go breaking the bangles my mother gave you.'

Chanda giggled. Then she began to hum the next verse and her entrancing voice was oddly melodic and sweet, despite her lack of training. Chetan listened mesmerized:

These are the bangles my mother did give
  My mother did give indeed-oh
I roam about and show them off
  Yellow-green they are, they are
These are the bangles my husband did give
  My husband did give indeed-oh
I roam about, no shame at all
  Yellow-green they are, they are

'Wow, my darling!' He took his wife's face in both his hands and kissed her. Chanda beamed in response. All of Chetan's shyness disappeared. Chanda seemed so innocent to him—boundless as the green fields and entrancing as a monsoon breeze. He didn't even remember Anant's instructions. Chanda was neither proud nor flirtatious. She wasn't crafty or clever; she wasn't obstinate or wilful. She was as still as a vast lake at whose shores you could lie down, drink the water, or take a plunge. The lake would not rise up and crash into you like a swift river, it would react to everything calmly . . . and Chetan felt blissfully happy.

438

A little while later, Chanda sang another song on Chetan's insistence. The wife is sulking. The husband pleads with her, saying, 'Darling, I will bring you earrings, don't be so proud. I'll put them in your ears myself.' But the flirtatious, coquettish wife shakes her head and says, 'I don't need any earrings, don't you be proud either, I won't accept any earrings.' The husband says, 'I'll bring home a second wife, and I'll put earrings in her ears.' The wife curses him and says she won't stay, then. The husband says, 'I'll keep a prostitute and I'll put earrings in her ears.' The wife snaps that 'The prostitute is the king's mistress too, he'll have you locked up!' Defeated, the husband says 'I'll put earrings in your ears only':

Bring you earrings I will, I will
Bring you earrings I will
    Just don't be proud, my darling
    Don't be oh-so-proud-oh
I'll put them in myself, myself
I'll put them in myself

Oh, I won't take them, no I won't
I won't take them ever
    It's you who mustn't be proud, my man
    Don't be oh-so-proud-oh

I'll take another wife, I will, I will
I'll take another wife-oh
    Just don't be proud, my darling-oh
    Don't be oh-so-proud-oh
I'll give the earrings to her instead
    Put them in, I will-oh

Then I'll not live here no more, no
I'll live here no more
    It's you who mustn't be proud, my man
    Don't be oh-so-proud-oh

I'll find a whore and keep her here
Oh, find a whore, I will-oh
    Just don't be proud, my darling
    Don't be oh-so-proud-oh
I'll give the earrings to her instead
    Give them, oh, I will-oh

Belongs to the king, that whore, that whore
Belongs to the king, she does-oh
    It's you who mustn't be proud, my man
    Don't be oh-so-proud-oh
The king will lock you up, he will,
Lock you up he will-oh

The song was straightforward, as were the emotions it expressed. But Chanda sang the refrain so sweetly, drawing out the syllables, that Chetan was entranced and felt giddy . . . and that very first night he decided that he would scrimp and save to buy a harmonium and make his wife a 'musical master' . . .

*

Chetan turned on his side. Chanda continued to lie motionless. She hadn't shifted even once. She wasn't moving at all. Suddenly he felt like taking a peek at her. He propped himself up on his elbow and raised the wick a little more, then picked up the lantern.

He rested there and gazed at his sleeping wife's face in the light of the upheld lamp. He was startled to see that Chanda wore light make-up—her wheatish complexion was lightly powdered to make her look fairer. She wore a large bindi on her wide forehead. Her hair was done up over the ears just the way Chetan liked it. (Chetan thought it coarse and unsophisticated when she did her hair up in a topknot and he always told her she should part it straight and tie back her medium-length, dense hair so it covered her ears.) Her large eyelids were closed and her lips were coloured with *dandaasa* powder. Chetan thought her round face looked beautiful and innocent. He felt a sharp pang of compassion in his heart—perhaps she'd fallen asleep as she waited for him. She didn't speak much, didn't quarrel, didn't taunt; she was artless and loving—did this make her a mere lump of clay? Did she have no feelings of her own? He thought only of his own feelings, his own self-interest, his own side of everything. He kicked away whatever he had—what he longed for was what he couldn't get. His heart filled with remorse. He wanted to kiss those large eyelids. He leaned over. Just then Chanda opened her eyes.

'Go to sleep. It's past two,' she said.

'You weren't sleeping?'

Chetan put the lantern back.

'I was asleep before.'

'Liar!'

Chanda wrapped her arm around his neck and rested her head on his chest.

'Why, aren't you feeling sleepy?'

And she began to smooth his hair gently.

'I've decided I'm going to quit my newspaper job. Bhai Sahib's practice has just started. This working night and day gives me no time to read and write.'

'Leave it,' said Chanda softly, patting his temples. 'I was going to tell you that myself.'

A huge weight lifted from Chetan's heart. He had thought Chanda might object to his leaving the job, but she paused for a moment, then said, 'It's that job that ruined your health. That's why you can't get any sleep.'

'I've wandered about like a vagabond all day. I'm so tired, but I can't stop thinking.'

'That's because it's too late. Stop thinking and go to sleep.' She pressed his head to her chest and lightly brushed his closed eyelids with her lips.

Chetan felt a lump form in his throat. As he lay against her bosom, he placed before her all his agony regarding Neela, and didn't even hide from her his final gift to her cousin.

Chanda said nothing sarcastic; she didn't get annoyed or angry. She just kept patting his temples affectionately. 'You're worrying for no reason; it wasn't just because of you that Neela got married to him. Even if you hadn't spoken to my uncle, Neela might still have married him. After all, her sister Meela wanted her to. And then, you don't know Neela. She's not one to stay depressed. She'll get on fine with Jija ji.'

'Neela would definitely get on fine,' Chetan thought . . . If Kunti could come to terms with her widowhood and laugh, why wouldn't Neela laugh again? He was worrying for no reason . . . he'd go to Lahore tomorrow and immerse himself in that life. He'd try to improve what he already had, and he wouldn't worry about what he lacked . . .

'Chanda, you're much smarter than me,' he said, still resting against her bosom.

Chanda didn't reply. She pressed her husband to her breast like a child. Chetan felt burned and parched by the heat, exhausted and defeated, and he'd arrived at the shores of that boundless lake—his fate rested at the shores of those deep, luminous, clear waters. If he fled, he'd find no salvation, no peace.